Outer Rim

O'Ceagan Saga Book 2

Lillian I. Wolfe

This eBook edition is published by:
Pynhavyn Press * Reno, Nevada
http://www.pynhavynpress.com

This novel is a work of fiction. Names, characters, businesses, places, events and incidents either are the products of the author's imagination or used in a fictitious manner. Any resemblance to actual persons, living or dead, or actual events is purely coincidental.

All rights reserved. Quotations and short excerpts may be used for review; otherwise, no part of this work may be reproduced in whole or in part, by any means, without written permission from the publisher or the author.

Copyright © 2023 Lillian I. Wolfe
All rights reserved.
Published June 2023
ISBN: 978-1-942622-26-0

Cover Design: SelfPubBookCovers.com/Fantasyart
Digital heart image custom design combining elements from Graphics Factory, used with permission, and hand drawn design by Rene Averett.

Dedication

In remembrance of Larry, my brother, who I lost last year. He first sparked my interest in space and science fiction, introducing me to a genre that would become a passion over the years. We played in our "spaceship" (an old trunk mounted on a wooden horse) in our backyard and explored the galaxy as space rangers. Later, he went to work for NASA, where he helped make the moon landing a success. It was so top secret that I never learned exactly what he did.

Wherever you are, my captain, this story is thanks to you.

Acknowledgments

Even though this is space fantasy, I do try to cling to some of the realities of space and the potential exploration of it. In my quest to write a somewhat believable story, I have many people to thank, including Isaac Asimov, who applied real science to his narratives and made it easy to understand; Jack Chalker, who showed me fantasy fiction has no limits; CJ Cherryh, who reminded me to center on humanity even if the story employs a lot of aliens. To Gene Roddenberry, who gave us the first visualization of alien worlds and the magnificence of space. Thank you to Robert Heinlein, Larry Niven, Anne McCaffery, and a score of other writers over the year who showed me the way.

Table of Contents

Part One 1
Chapter One 3
Chapter Two 11
Chapter Three 23
Chapter Four 32
Chapter Five 43
Chapter Six 52
Chapter Seven 67
Chapter Eight 67
Chapter Nine 78
Chapter Ten 96
Chapter Eleven 107
Chapter Twelve 120
Chapter Thirteen 135
Chapter Fourteen 142
Chapter Fifteen 164
Chapter Sixteen 178
Chapter Seventeen 189
Chapter Eighteen 199
Chapter Nineteen 199
Chapter Twenty 215
Chapter Twenty-One 229
Chapter Twenty-Two 241

OUTER RIM – Lillian I. Wofle

Chapter Twenty-Three 255
Chapter Twenty-Four 265
Chapter Twenty-Five 265
Chapter Twenty-Six 279
Chapter Twenty-Seven 297
Chapter Twenty-Eight 308
Chapter Twenty-Nine 316
Chapter Thirty 326
Chapter Thirty-One 336
Chapter Thirty-Two 347
Chapter Thirty-Three 347
Chapter Thirty-Four 370
Chapter Thirty-Five 373
Chapter Thirty-Six 382
Chapter Thirty-Seven 391
Chapter Thirty-Eight 401
Chapter Thirty-Nine 409
Chapter Forty 417
Chapter Forty-One 429
Chapter Forty-Two 440
Chapter Forty-Three 447
Chapter Forty-Four 455
Glossary 464
Other Books by Lillian I. Wolfe 466

Part One

An Errand to Earth

Chapter One

Grania stopped at a transparisteel window facing her ship, which was docked at Tara Station. She gazed at the blowfish-like shape of the long haul freighter and noted the new patches on the starboard side. Workmen had completed the repairs to it the day before, replacing panels on the exterior and remodeling part of the interior that had taken quite a bit of damage in the freebooter attack she and her crew had faced thirty-eight days earlier. She was itching to get back onboard and back into space.

She turned to go to the entry ramp, pausing a moment to observe a conveyor belt pushing several large crates along the loading dock to the ship's cargo hold. She knew her brothers, Liam and Rory, were already down there settling the containers.

Things are going to be all right. She repeated that a couple of times as she boarded the ship and took the circular stairs to the bridge level. Pulling a deep breath, she keyed the door open and stepped inside. Her eyes moved from the navigation console to the communications station, continuing to the captain's chair. Her place now. Captain Grania O'Ceagan of the Mo Chroidhe out of Erinnua.

Her granda had officially handed the ship over to her, putting her in charge of this aspect of the family business. Frankly, she questioned her own competence. She'd been badly shaken by the events, and her confidence had taken a hard blow. Yet, Granda thought she was ready to handle it. Then again, he'd also sent an old mate of his on this trip, ostensibly for a final jaunt before the man retired to his farm life on the planet. Teghan O'Toole would be acting as her first officer, replacing Nansi. Her friend and long-time ship's mate had decided to remain grounded for a while longer. She, too, had been badly shaken by the previous trip.

Grania's throat tightened as she swallowed her nerves and checked out the new captain's console. The upgrades would be significant, not that she'd found anything wrong with the old one. She sank into the cushioned seat and flipped on the cameras, lifting her eyes to the screens on the back and side walls where the activity in and around the ship was displayed. As she flipped through the cameras, the images looked clear and well-defined. Her computer came up at her command, so she started a confirmation run to ensure everything checked out.

"Permission to come aboard, Captain?"

Grania turned her head to the familiar voice and smiled. "Granted. Glad you're here, Brendan."

Her youngest brother grinned as he stepped onto the bridge and gazed around. "Ya wouldn't know it had been blasted so badly, would ya?"

"The workers did a good job. Check out your station."

He nodded, a dark lock of his hair falling onto his forehead, and settled in at navigation, pressing buttons and bringing the system online. Her brother began charting the course for their planned stops on this trading trip. They'd be heading to Cardyff first, then out to Valhalla before heading toward Earth.

Grania spotted a light flashing on the communications console and hurried over to answer. She hoped for news from Vilnius about his pending transfer, but the call came from Tara Station control. "You are cleared to depart in one-hundred-twenty mites," the crisp voice of the station computer informed her.

"Acknowledged," she replied. Not much longer before they'd be taking their shakedown run. She glanced at the camera feed from the entry ramp and saw O'Toole starting to board. His wiry frame made him look taller than he actually was, but his step bounced with energy as he took the steps up.

Granda had told her the man had gotten engaged to a Bantry woman, so he planned this voyage as his last. Within two more mites, O'Toole was at the bridge entry, asking to come aboard. His pack was slung over his back as he greeted her.

"Tis kind of ye to allow me this trip, Cap'n. It means a lot to me." Wrinkles around his eyes and mouth revealed his age as he smiled, but he looked fit.

"Ah, you're doing me a favor, Mister O'Toole. My granda said you're one of the best second officers he knew, and since I am short mine this trip, it's glad I am to have you aboard."

"And where might I stow me things?" He shifted his pack part-way off his back.

"I'll show you to the first officer's cabin. It's on this same deck, so you're close to the bridge." He followed her as she led him to her old cabin mid-way to the aft of the ship and just past the stairwell. She'd cleaned her things out of it a few days earlier, but it still felt odd to be handing it over to someone else.

She opened the sliding door and ushered him inside the small but comfortable space. As ship quarters went, it was a decent size and had a well-maintained jump pod that doubled as a bed.

O'Toole gazed around it and nodded. "'Tis nice enough. T'will do fine, thank ye. I'll just get settled then and meet you back on the bridge if that's all right."

"It is. Let me know if you need anything." Grania stepped out and headed back down the corridor toward the bridge. She'd relocated her own things into the captain's cabin at the nose of the ship, a much larger space.

By the time she got back, Rory had come in and was checking out the communication system, flipping switches and turning dials to pull in different messages across the ship.

"How's the cargo looking, Rory?" Grania took her place and turned her chair to face her middle brother.

"Good. We have almost a full load with only two big crates leaving at Cardyff, and I show four coming onboard there. I hear we have passengers on this trip."

"You heard right. We should have a young lady showing

up anytime now, and we're picking up two fellows on Cardyff. All are heading to Earth." She glanced at the entry monitor as she spoke, wondering where their passenger might be.

"I'm hoping they aren't like our last ones." Rory lifted his eyebrows as he peeked at her.

"I don't think they will be." Their last passengers had been a b'ean sidhe and a puca, along with a trader who turned out to be one of the freebooters, setting up the attack on them. For all that, the man had given them a targassium crystal for power, saving both the ship and their lives when they'd been thrown into the Dark Sea. That was an experience she hoped to never repeat.

"Ah, I think Dari is coming on this trip." Brendan looked up from his console.

"Dari? He didn't say anything to me about it."

"He's feeling lonely since Sheilan hasn't returned yet and thought he might want the chance to see other places."

Surprised, Grania strolled over to Brendan's console. "Is he on board?"

Brendan shrugged. "I don't know. He's a puca. How can you tell when an energy being is around?"

"When did he tell you this?" Grania's suspicions rose. Ever since the puca had acquired Brendan's genetic pattern, she wasn't sure if she actually spoke to Brendan or Dari.

"Yesterday," he answered. "I don't know for sure if he means it. But if he did, would it be a problem? I mean, he doesn't eat or need a cabin."

"Who said he doesn't eat?" Rory asked, a big grin on his

face. "I recall him finishing off a tray of cakes at the house."

"No matter," Grania stepped between them, heading back to her console. "If he wants to come along, he needs to talk to me. Although, he might provide an extra pair of hands if we need them. We can make him work for his passage."

"I'd like to see—" Rory cut off mid-sentence as he pressed his headset to his ear and listened intently. "Call coming in from Zabrowski Station for you, Nia."

Zabrowski? Vilnius. She nodded and went to her station to pick it up.

"Hello, love," the deep baritone voice said as soon as she answered. "I hear you're taking your ship out soon."

"Indeed, I am. And what about you? I was expecting some news before this." She held her breath, anxious for the reply.

"Well, that's what I'm calling about. My transfer request has been delayed, Nia. Master Hartman has suffered health problems and won't be able to return to work for a while, if at all."

"Oh, no. What happened?" Her heart sank. Hartman was a good friend of her granda. He'd been station master at Zabrowski even before she'd started working the space routes.

"Heart attack. A bad one. The surgeon on the station barely got to him in time, but he may require a replacement. Even then, it could be a long time before he can return."

"So, what does this mean for your transfer?"

"For now, I can't leave the station since I was next in line; the agency wants me to stay until they know for sure if they will retire Hartman. This has been a big shock for me. He's a good friend, and I'm just grateful he didn't die on the spot."

"Oh, Vilnius. I'm sorry. I wasn't thinking about how close you were to him. Of course, it's a shock to me, too. I'll have to tell Granda. I'm just…" Her voice died. What could she say? She was disappointed, but he'd nearly lost a friend. Besides, she was getting ready to pull out and would be heading to Earth's station within a few days anyway.

"I know it's a letdown for you, but I'll see you when you get to the station. Maybe I'll have news by then. I just want to say safe travels, and I love you."

"Love you as well." Her voice caught a little as she ended the call.

"Bad news?" Rory asked.

Her face must have shown her disappointment. Grania straightened her back. "Yeah, the station master had a heart attack. Vilnius isn't transferring here yet."

"Sorry, Nia," Brendan said quietly.

She shrugged. "It's okay. Meanwhile, we have a ship to get ready to pull out in about fifty-two mites. Where is our passenger?"

"I think I see her coming if that reluctant girl being escorted toward our ramp is the one." He pointed to the screen showing the entry where a young woman was practically dragged by a middle-aged man and a woman. Each held an arm, pulling the girl along, and she clearly didn't want to come.

"Oh, tarnation. We have a recalcitrant passenger for this trip. I'm going down to meet them." Grania sprang to her feet and hurried down the steps to the entry ramp, arriving just as the couple with their rebellious offspring reached the boarding ramp.

"I'm Captain O'Ceagan. Is this Ms. Hennessy? We've been expecting you."

Dark blue eyes shot up to meet Grania's, a glare radiating from them and a scowl on her lips. The girl jerked her arms in her parents, she presumed, grip.

"It is," the man answered. "Our daughter is less than pleased to be making this trip, but she is betrothed to a man in Ireland on Earth."

"I don't want to marry some farmer I never met," the girl wailed. "This is barbaric."

"Nonsense." The woman tried to smile at Grania while attempting to calm her daughter. "It's a good match, and Callum is not a farmer, Orla."

"Shall we just bring her on board?" Mr. Hennessy asked.

"Ah, yes. Follow me to her cabin so she can get settled in." Grania turned and started up the ramp as Hennessy caught up with her and, under his breath, asked, "Is there a lock on the door?"

Grania held her shock in, but she seethed inside. *What are they doing to this poor girl? Have they sold her to someone on Earth? And they expect me to deliver her? Holy Father, what am I to do now?*

Chapter Two

Once the girl was forced into her quarters, Grania entered the lock code as requested, and the Hennessey couple followed her back to the exit, where they stopped. She turned to face them, her mouth feeling like it had sawdust in it. "In your booking message, you mentioned that you would pay extra for an escort to the family in Galway. Is that correct?"

Mr. Hennessey nodded. "That is correct, Captain. As you've seen, my daughter isn't happy at all about this arrangement but 'tis a contracted marriage for the good of both families. The O'Connor family is footing most of the bill. They—we all—want to be sure she arrives there safely, and they're willing to pay extra for the escort. You said you could do it."

"I did, and we can. I simply wanted to verify that I had the right of it. The address is in Galway and…" She paused to pull up the details on her comm unit. "Is this the correct one?"

He peered at the screen for almost a minute before saying, "Yes. That would be right."

While he'd read, his wife looked anxiously back to the ship as if she expected her daughter to come charging back down the ramp. "Please forgive Orla's rudeness. This is difficult for her. She's known about this agreement for over two years, but she recently got smitten with a young fella in town. Now, she's acting out over having to leave him."

Grania put her comm away and met the woman's eyes. "Are you folks sure you want to go through with this? Orla is clearly not a willing participant in the plan."

The father's mouth set into a firm line. "It's a done deal. A promise made to a distant cousin who wants to bring the bloodline back into the family. Orla will come around."

"I hope so," Grania said. "We'll see that she gets there safely."

They offered a hand salute, raising their palms upward before they turned and walked away from the ship. Just that easy to say goodbye to their daughter. Grania sighed and started back to the bridge. *Well, this is a sticky situation.* She originally had thought to have either Brendan or Rory accompany the girl to Galway, but now she might have to do it if Orla was going to be trouble.

They had another twelve mites before launch, so she hurried back to the bridge for the final preparations.

* * * * *

The trip from Tara Station to Wyvern Station at Cardyff took less than eight hours, with a minor jump gate a mere two hours out on either side. While Grania had released the lock on Orla's cabin, she'd assigned Rory to keep a close eye on the girl if she came out of it.

A distraught teenager hadn't been what she'd expected, so

she remained leery of what the girl might do. So far, she hadn't done more than wander down the corridor to the galley to get some food, then scurry back to her cabin.

"Kind of a nasty thing to pull on that kid, don't ya think?" Rory asked. Grania had seen him watching Orla make another foray to the galley, where she'd grabbed a pre-made sandwich.

"I agree, Rory, but I guess these strange marriage arrangements are still made. I can't imagine what that girl must be feeling to be forced into it. Or why her parents would agree to such an arrangement." Grania looked back toward the main screen as Wyvern Station grew larger. "As soon as Orla's back in her cabin, lock the door again. I don't want her to have a chance to get off at Cardyff."

"We have docking information coming in," Rory informed her. "Sending it to you and navigation now."

"Got it," Brendan acknowledged. He began adjusting the course to take them directly to it.

"Lower the dorsal sail in ten mites," Grania ordered, judging the time by the position of the red sun to the station.

The bridge door swished open as O'Toole came inside. He'd been down in the cargo bay, checking that everything was secure for docking while Liam took a short rest. This part of their trip had gone smoothly with no threatening events. Routine. This was the way most of their trips went, not like the excitement of their last one.

"All set down below," O'Toole announced, taking the seat at the alternate bridge station, a backup unit in case of problems with any of their equipment.

That had been a new addition with the repairs and remodel. It had cost them, though. Grania's knees had gone weak when the insurance company agent told her they wouldn't pay the total amount of the repairs. She'd already approved the plan for the remodel. It had left her family with a large debt on the ship, so they had the loss of income for the past forty-odd days and these new bills to recoup.

As the sails dropped and the ship slid as easily as butter into the docking slot, Grania jumped to her feet, eager to find her passengers and get to the station master. She wanted to check for any anomalies in the space lanes ahead that they would need to avoid or adjust to handle. Likewise, she glimpsed Rory reviewing the reports coming in from the station for other information as well as requests for outbound cargo. Business as usual. It felt great to be back at it.

"We can get a departure slot in three Earth hours," Rory called out as she went out the door.

Stopping just outside the bridge, she asked, "Think you can load cargo by then?"

"Umm, I have four prospects lined up, so I think so."

"Take it then." She grinned as she went to the lower level and down the ramp to the station. At once, she saw a pair of young men with shaggy dark hair who sat on one of the few passenger benches near the port. These might be their other travelers for the trip.

"Hello," she said as she walked up to them. "I'm the captain of the Mo Chroidhe. Might you be looking for me?"

Both rose to their feet. One was a shade taller than the

other, but from their looks, they could be twins. "Ethan Jones," the shorter one said, offering a nod. "This is my brother, Conan. We're bound for Earth's station."

"Captain O'Ceagan. We'll be pleased to get you there." She eyed their luggage—backpacks and four cases of musical instruments. All of it could go in their cabin. Pulling out her comm, she signaled her second. "O'Toole, we have our passengers here and waiting. Would you escort them to their cabin?"

"On my way, Capt'n," O'Toole's voice replied.

"I'm just going to check in with the station master. But Mister O'Toole, my second officer, will be here shortly to show you to your quarters for the trip. Welcome aboard, gentlemen."

As they nodded their thanks, she left them to go about her business. She was not the only ship's captain checking in with the station master and had to wait for almost twenty mites. The master was a cranky woman who'd clearly crawled out on the wrong side of the bed that morning and hadn't improved as the day progressed. Her voice was deadpan and irritated as she spoke to the captain ahead of Grania. She braced herself for equal treatment of her questions, but she smiled and greeted the woman pleasantly. "I'm Captain O'Ceagan of the Mo Chroidhe. I'm just paying a courtesy visit and inquiring about anything happening on the space lanes I should avoid."

"How would I know?" the master mumbled. "All day, all I get are complaints, questions I can't answer, and reports of missing cargo." She squinted at Grania as if she might know her, then shook her head. "Mo Chroidhe. That's old Paddy's ship, isn't it?"

"My granda, yes."

The woman looked up again. "Oh. How is the old coot? Is he with you?"

Old coot? This woman isn't far behind. Grania gave her head a shake. "No, he retired and handed the ship over to me. But he's well and enjoying the land life back home."

"Ah, that's too bad. I liked him. Always had a kind word and maybe a bottle of something with a bit of kick."

"Leprechaun whiskey, I would guess. I might have a bit of it stored on the ship. I can bring you a pot."

That softened the woman up. "Now, that's kind of you. I wouldn't say no to it, but no need to go out of your way."

"It's no trouble." Grania could send Brendan over with it. Sure, this woman would enjoy the sight of her handsome young brother.

"Well, thank ye." Her face split into a smile. "Now, as far as I know, there's no hindrances along the space lanes, no tumblin' meteor fields or anythin' like that. Had a comet cross about a week ago, but nothin' new headin' this way."

"Wormhole?" Grania asked, her mind recalling the one from Pelanan Station. It had popped them out into dark space, apparently from a sun flare that caused the tunnel to fluctuate.

"Stable. No variations in two years now. It won't cause you any trouble." The station master dropped her eyes to the table behind the counter, and her forehead wrinkled. "Ah, wait a moment. You said you were Captain O'Ceagan, right?"

Grania nodded.

"I have a message here for you. I reckon whoever sent it expected you to stop in. She handed Grania a message tube, a confidential message sent by a secure transmission and written into the cylinder, so no one except the sender and recipient could see the contents.

"Odd," Grania said as she put the tube in her uniform pocket. She'd play it when she was back in her cabin. "Any idea who it's from?"

"None at all. It's rare that we get one of those. No indicator of when or where it was sent from, but I see it was logged in here at 0400 hours this morning." The station master pointed to the line on her log for Grania to note.

Thanking her, Grania left the office, then went to check the boards for any additional information posted there. She did see a couple of cargo requests, but they were heading in a different direction. On the way back to the ship, she stopped to pick up a bag of Welsh cakes from the bakery. They'd make a fine afternoon tea treat for the crew.

As she waited for her order, she tagged Brendan and asked him to take a small jug of Leprechaun Whiskey to the station master and to be polite to the woman. Brendan whooped, happy to be off the ship for a short time. "Don't be late getting back," she added.

Back on the ship, she stopped in the galley to store the cakes, climbed to the bridge level, and proceeded into her cabin. In addition to the jump pod, the room held a double-wide bed along with a desk, computer, and alternate bridge controls. The necessities room featured a slightly larger shower, but it wasn't much fancier or bigger than any others on the ship.

Grania inserted the message tube into the computer slot and put on her headset to listen. She leaned her elbows on the desk, head forward as the words played in her ear. "Captain O'Ceagan, this is an ears-only message from Enterprise's chancellor, Marshall Everson. Captain, I selected you and your ship to transport a unique and top-secret cargo to the town of Hope Springs on Desolation. We will expect you to pick it up within the next forty-eight hours. Please confirm this message by keying the following code." The message then gave her a ten alpha and numeric code for her response.

Stunned, she sat back in her chair. It sounded like a government contract to deliver something of great value. Typically, these jobs were worth four figures of credit. But to Desolation? That was at the edge of the galaxy, along the Outer Rim. Even going to Enterprise to pick it up was out of the way.

She sent the code, adding a digit at the end to decline the offer, and waited for a confirmation. A brief message displayed on her screen with a contact number she should call to speak to the sender. Activating the connection, she waited a few moments before a man's voice answered.

"Captain, do you have questions?" the man asked.

"Is this Chancellor Everson?" she asked, not sure if this was direct to him or to an aide.

"No, this is his personal secretary. I am authorized to speak for him. Your question, please, Captain." The voice was all business, sounding more like a government agent than an assistant.

"I have the chancellor's request, but I regret that I must decline. The pick-up and delivery are completely out of my planned route and time schedule. Thank—"

"You misunderstand, Captain. This is not a request. It is an order from the highest authority. Your ship is ideal for the transport of our item. You will be well compensated for your inconvenience. It is imperative that the delivery makes it to our agent on Desolation within twelve days."

"Twelve days? Even with using the gates, that's not a lot of time. Why don't you select a faster ship?" Her head was reeling from the request. They would be at least two days at Zabrowski to off-load, reload, and deliver Orla to Ireland. Transit between stations and the jump gates ate up the hours also. The Mo Chroidhe wasn't built for speed, her solar sails providing more power when sunlight was available, but even with the targassium crystal, it would be almost impossible to make it.

A more serious thought struck her. "Who are you to order me to do anything? I don't know you, and I'm not a citizen of your world."

A soft chuckle from the man surprised her. "I wondered if you'd ask or just quietly comply. True, you're not a citizen of Enterprise, but this has ramifications for more than one planet. Chancellor Everson has the backing of the Amalgamated Union of Planets. You can check that out on your way here. I'll send you the contact code."

"Wait. If I do come, and that's a huge if, where do I go? It's a big planet."

"True, but it's not that big a space station. We'll find you when you arrive." He signed off then, leaving her hanging.

What the hell? Can the AUP actually order me to do something like this? She would check out the coded number the "secretary" had sent. Right now, she needed to get back to the bridge.

As she entered, Brendan looked up from his station and grinned. "I took the whiskey over. Mz Lewis was very pleased to get it. She seems like a nice lady."

Grania raised an eyebrow. Send a handsome young lad over to see her, and the crankiness disappears. Perhaps she should send Brendan for information the next time they docked here. She waved a dismissive hand at him and then turned to Rory. "How are we doing on the cargo?"

"All set. Loaded and ready to go. Our two musicians are settled in their cabin. The girl is still locked in. Just waiting for the departure confirmation from the station." Rory spun his chair toward her as she settled into her seat. "Oh, a coded message came in for you. I sent it on to your station."

Her eyes widened as she turned her attention to the computer messages. She spotted the coded one at once, and it took her authority to open it. Putting on her headset, she keyed in the code. Her mouth dropped in astonishment when the president of the AUP appeared on the screen. "Hold, please, for a live connection," a computer voice informed her.

Grania choked down a swear word and frowned. *What now?*

"Captain O'Ceagan, I believe you know me by sight if not from a personal meeting. By now, you should have spoken with an agent at Planet Enterprise, and you will know that we need to commandeer your ship for a special delivery to a planet in the Outer Rim. We don't make this request lightly, but the Mo Chroide (he pronounced it Crohide, and Grania cringed) meets the requirements for what we need to transport."

"Excuse me, President Dubeque, but we are not prepared for that long a trip. Our ship was just repaired, and we planned a shorter excursion than crossing half the galaxy."

"I understand your concern, Captain. However, our need is urgent, and we are prepared to cover all costs for the trip as well as pay you a healthy six-figure fee for the safe transport of our cargo."

Grania noticed Rory and Brendan watching her as they heard just her end of the conversation. "What if I choose not to accept?"

"Not to be threatening," Dubeque answered quietly, "but we may choose to withdraw your trading license for violation of article 25.476A, which states that the AUP can make a request such as I'm making for the safety of any member planet."

That hit her in the gut. *They could do that?* Basically, it would be pulling them out of the guild, which meant no trading of any sort. Her mouth felt dry when she replied, "I see. I'll advise my crew, and we'll make the detour."

"I thought you might see a reason to cooperate. I will let

our agent know to expect you."

As he ended the communication, Grania pulled her headset off, more furious than she could say. She hated being manipulated. She had no choice if she wanted to pay the bills and continue to run the ship. What could be so urgent or essential that the AUP would order this?

She looked up and saw not only Brendan and Rory gazing at her but also O'Toole, whose brow wrinkled like a folded fan. She held up a hand and flipped on the com to let Liam hear it.

"We've had a request from the AUP." She took a deep breath, then explained the whole thing to them. "So, Brendan, get busy and plot the fastest course to Enterprise. I believe there's a gate within a few hours of here that goes that way."

"We don't have a choice, Grania?" Rory asked.

She shook her head. "No. Not if we want to stay in business."

"It will be pushing the engines," Liam said.

"We can have a family meeting once we're underway. Right now, we are ready to back out of this dock, so let's get to it."

Chapter Three

With the ship well underway to Merlin's Gate, the wormhole point from Cardyff to Enterprise, Grania summoned the crew to the galley to sort out what changes they would need to fulfill the unwanted assignment. O'Toole elected to cover the bridge while they met, saying he'd abide by whatever they chose.

"Given that we'll be at least two days at Earth and it's taking us two days here with this delay, can we make it to Desolation in ten days? That's assuming our twelve days start when we pick up the freight." Grania had broken out the cakes she'd bought at Cardyff Station and took a bite out of one as she gazed at her engineer.

Liam wore a troubled look, worry showing in his eyes and thinned lips as he tapped numbers and calculations into his mobi device. He shook his head. "It's going to be close if we do, Nia. We can boost the engine some with the crystal, but it's been patched, meaning it could blow out if we put too much pressure on it. I don't feel at all comfortable with doing this. We could use a few extra days to make it."

She swallowed down a sip of her tea. "Maybe I can negotiate the time."

"If anythin' goes wrong or causes problems, it's going to

make that a hard deadline to meet," Rory added. He fiddled with his earpiece, which linked remotely with the communications board.

"Too bad we can't all do dirt travel like Sheilan and Dari," Brendan muttered, referring to the sidhe's ability to use the Earth's soil as a travel magnet.

"Now, wouldn't that be grand?" Grania said. Of its own accord, her hand went to the sealed vial she wore on a chain around her neck and tucked under her tunic. It held about three ounces of the Irish dirt that the b'ean sidhe had brought to Erinnua with her. She'd given it to Grania, and the captain promised to keep it with her everywhere she went.

Through it, Sheilan could come to Grania if she was in mortal danger or if she needed to warn the family of a pending death. Grania considered it a blessing and a curse, much like the b'ean sidhe. The sidhe could use the dark loam for instant travel, dirt to dirt as it were, able to make jumps from one patch of the special soil to another. Even one as small…

The thought froze her for a moment as she thought about Brendan saying Dari wanted to come along. Had he? She twisted the cap on the vial and lifted it off. She barely saw the gold spark that flew out of it, but within a couple of breaths, a young lad with reddish hair and freckles stood next to the table and grinned at them.

"'Tis about time," the puca stated. "I was beginning to think you were never going to open the bleedin' bottle." He made a show of dusting off his sleeves, even though they actually hadn't been in the dirt.

"Well, Dari, if I'd known you were traveling in it, I would have done it sooner," Grania said, the hint of a frown wrinkling her forehead.

"Did Brendan not tell ya I was planning to come along?" He turned his glance toward the subject of his remark.

"Ho, of course I did," Brendan answered. "But you didn't tell me how you planned to get on board."

"You're technically a stowaway," Liam added.

"'Tis not the first time." Dari seemed unconcerned as he eyed the plate of cakes. "Might I trouble ya for a cup of tea and one of those delicious-looking cakes?" He batted his eyes at Grania.

"For a creature that doesn't need food, you certainly seem to enjoy it. Go ahead, you little scamp." Grania requested the drink as he sat, snatched a treat, and took a big bite.

Although Grania didn't resent having the prankster on board, she was curious. "Why did you use the soil, Dari, instead of just coming aboard?"

"Well... ya see..." he said around the cake filling his mouth. He paused to gulp it down. "I wasn't that sure you'd welcome me if I just strolled right in. Now, once you were moving along, then it would not be easy to remove me from the ship, would it?"

"And you were in my pendant all along?"

"Indeed, I was. I made the jump from the dirt patch near your family home to the pendant before ya headed for the station. Honestly, I didn't realize I wouldn't be able to exit the doodad until you opened the cap."

"Oh, I guess that is a drawback, isn't it?" Grania spun the vial's cap closed. "Does this mean you can't get back in it unless I let you?"

The lad's eyes widened as if the thought had surprised him. "I reckon it does. But ya won't make me walk the plank or whatever ya do on a spaceship, will ya?"

She laughed, pleased to see that Dari had repaired his youthful form. It had been damaged the last time she'd seen it. "No, I wouldn't go that far. But you will have to work for your trip this time."

"Work? What would I do?"

"We have many odd jobs on the ship, Dari," Rory cut in. The corridors need to be cleaned and the floor in here mopped. I'd gladly give you my share of those chores."

"Yea, and I have some tasks down in the hold that you might do also." Liam grinned, enjoying the teasing as Dari's face reflected his alarm at this.

"We'll work something out, Dari," Grania said. "In the meantime, make yourself sparse when our passengers are out and about. I don't want you to frighten them with any of your horse forms or even have them wondering who you are. Is that clear?"

He nodded. "That it is, Captain Grania. I shall be as quiet as a mouse."

"A what?" Brendan asked.

"A mouse, lad. A sneaky little beastie that slips around after dark, looking for scraps of food. Do you not have any mice on Erinnua or on the ship?"

"No. To both questions." Grania shook her head. She'd heard of mice, but she'd never seen one. "Now, back to the issues at hand, and not a word of this to our passengers or anyone else. Work on the formulas, Liam, and let me know if we think we can make the deadline or not. If they're determined to have our ship for their delivery, then I will have to negotiate something reasonable we can do. Does anyone else see any problems with taking this extra run?"

None of her brothers looked too happy about it, but neither did they voice any objections other than the one Liam had presented. "All right. Then we'll see what the deal is and present our case if it isn't feasible. On the plus side, if we do this, we stand to make enough credits to pay off all the upgrades and uncovered repairs on the ship and still have a little left over for ourselves."

"That would be novel," Liam drawled out as he looked up from his mobi.

"Back to work, then. Dari, you can go onto the bridge and see if Rory or Bren have any things they need you to do."

"Aye, aye, Captain," Dari said with a salute and turned on his barefoot heels to follow Brendan. Grania rolled her eyes skyward. This was going to be an interesting trip, yet Brendan was right that the puca could be useful.

She noticed Liam lingering behind, not moving from his seat and still entering code. He looked more concerned than he should over the potential forced job. "Something on your mind, Liam?"

He looked up, meeting her gaze. "There is. I need to tell

you something. This extra time on the run, especially when you add the return trip to Tara Station, may cause me problems."

She moved closer and sat across from him. "How so?"

"Uncle Colm offered me a position on *Mo Spiorad* when it comes back to Tara. That should be in fifteen days, give or take a couple."

Grania felt gut-punched, her breath catching at the news. She breathed in. "When did he tell you?"

"A day before we left."

"And you didn't want to tell me sooner?" Her voice cracked a little. Even though she knew that Liam wanted to move up and captain a ship of his own, she wasn't prepared for him to do it now. He was the best engineer in this sector of space, maybe in the whole galaxy. Or perhaps she was biased, but she hated like hell to lose him.

"I figured I'd tell you when we were on our way back to Tara. This changes everything." He dropped his eyes as he spoke.

"Ah, Liam. 'Tis bad timing, brother."

"You know I adore you, big sis, but I have to make a move of my own. The path is limited here, and Uncle is offering me second with the probability of taking over the ship in less than a year when he gets a new one."

"He's expanding?" He'd caught her by surprise with that news. She hadn't heard anything about Uncle Colm wanting to add a ship.

"That's what he said." Liam shifted position, dropping his crossed leg to the floor and leaning forward. "I don't want to abandon you on this run, Nia, but if I have to get back before we can get there, then I'll ask to leave the ship at Zabrowski."

"But I need you to make that run to Desolation. I can't do it without you."

"There are other engineers—"

"Not at your level. You're the best. Dammit, Liam. Can't you hold on for the rest of this trip?"

"I can't miss this opportunity, Nia. If Uncle says he needs me to be there on that date and can't delay departure to wait for me, then I have to be there. Right now, we don't know for sure we're going to the Outer Rim, so let's not discuss it until after you meet with the official on Enterprise."

She bit back the sharp words that perched on the tip of her tongue and counted to five slowly in her mind. "All right. You've got a point. We'll talk about it after my meeting."

"Thanks." Liam rose to his feet, laid his hand on her shoulder, and squeezed it. "I'll give you my best 'til I leave." Her eyes followed him as he left the galley, striding down the hall to the stairwell.

Grania knew he would do that, but Holy Mary, she didn't want to have to replace him. He couldn't be replaced. She could seek the next best option available, knowing he or she wouldn't be as good. More than that, he was her brother, and they'd been on this adventure together for a few years. Mo Chroidhe was a family-run ship, and he was breaking the family up.

First, Nansi wasn't on this trip, then Vilnius was stuck at Zabrowski, and now Liam leaving. She felt like everyone was deserting her. Rory and Brendan would be relying on her to run the ship and ensure they were all safe. Suddenly, it hit home harder than it had before that she—she alone—was responsible for the Mo Croidhe and her crew. Even though she'd accepted it when they were stranded in the Dark Sea, she knew the vessel was still Granda's, that she was only taking care of it for him. Now, it was hers. She would make the decisions, and *she* would need to replace crew members when they left.

Climbing to her feet, she felt the weight of the job on her shoulders as she ambled out the door.

When she came on the bridge, she saw Rory fiddling with the comm computer. He tapped the screen as his face screwed into a frown.

"What's wrong, Rory?" She stepped toward him.

"I'm getting interference, or there's a loose wire somewhere," he answered.

"Have you rebooted? Maybe that will clear it."

"Already tried that." He pulled the earpiece out and slid his chair back to pop the cover under the console. Dropping to the floor, he slid underneath. "I'll check all the wiring. Merlin's Gate is only forty-eight mites ahead, and it should be coming in crystal clear."

"Could be some space debris interfering," she suggested. She turned toward Brendan. "Are you having any problems, Bren?"

"Not that I can see," he answered. "Everything is tracking the way it should. We're dead-on for the gate."

"Wait," Rory said. "I think I'm seeing a loose wire here." He grunted once, then again. "Damn pixies. It wasn't secured well enough, so it came loose." He slid back out and climbed up with his elbows on the console. "That should take care of it." He put his earpiece back in his ear, listened for a few moments, then gave her a thumbs-up.

"Great. We'll begin preparing for the wormhole. Have our passengers come out of their quarters?" She hadn't seen Orla nor the musicians since they settled into their quarters. Of course, she'd unlocked Orla's cabin so she could move around the ship, but apart from one trip to the galley, the girl had stayed put.

Someone else was missing. "Where's Dari?" For that matter, where was O'Toole? He was supposed to have been on the bridge.

Chapter Four

Liam watched as Dari wandered down the aisles of cargo, pausing now and then to poke his head into a crate to see the contents. *Handy trick, that,* Liam thought, although it unnerved him some to see the puca doing it. He accepted the creature for what he was, but seeing him in human glamour, but not quite corporeal, reminded him that the otherworldly sidhe could be a serious foe if someone crossed him.

He'd actually set Dari off to check to be sure all the cargo was secure before they entered the wormhole, but the creature was too curious for his own good. He used the male descriptor even though he wasn't positive the sidhe used the designation. He'd only ever seen Dari as a male, whether it was a human, horse, or seahorse.

Liam's conversation with Grania replayed in his mind as he turned back to programming the engines to conserve power while in the jump. While it hadn't gone as well as he'd hoped, he'd expected his sister to be a little upset about him leaving. She didn't know how much it hurt him to abandon her in the middle of this trading trip, but the possibility of missing the opportunity was too great.

Grania had gotten the captaincy when Granda retired, even though he was equally qualified for it. Maybe even more than his sister, but she had trained for it longer. Likewise, Grania knew he wanted his own ship, and Uncle Colm was giving him that opportunity.

Liam couldn't let it pass. It might not come around again. Just the fact that his uncle was skipping Callum, his own son, to give him the opportunity was a miracle in itself. Maybe it helped that he was a top-rated engineer. But being second on Mo Spiorad was the next step for him.

With the engines set to reduce power, he keyed the program to active when they entered the vortex. After that, the wormhole controlled their speed and trajectory. The ship only had to maintain a low level of energy to keep the computers and jump pods active, lowering the life support to minimum while all the vulnerable humans were safely tucked in.

As Mo Chroidhe's crew had learned on their previous run, the sidhe weren't phased by the jumps, which was another plus in space travel. He turned again to see the screen where Dari made his way down the last aisle. An idea occurred to him, something he'd talk to Dari about when he'd finished. A buzz on the comm alerted him to the captain calling.

"Yes, Captain. Engines are ready for the jump."

"Grand, Liam. Is O'Toole down there?" Grania asked.

"No. Dari is with me, but I haven't seen O'Toole since before the meeting. Wasn't he on the bridge?"

"Not when we got back. Rory and Brendan say he wasn't there when they returned. He's not answering his mobi. I'll send Rory to check the mid-deck. Looks like we've got a thirty-mite wait at Merlin."

"Copy that. Let me know if I need to adjust." Liam checked the time and made a mental note to call her if she didn't get back to him.

Dari wandered back to find him. In his young lad guise, he looked like a country hick, although the genetic source for it had been a young peasant lad in Ireland's eighth or ninth century. Rust-colored hair and freckles on a cheery face made him somewhat attractive and harmless-looking.

"So, tell me, Dari," Liam began as he entered the engine room. "Did you and Sheilan just wander around the ship while we were in deep sleep?"

"Not always, boy-o," the sidhe answered. "Sometimes we had tea and cakes and chatted. We go back a long, long ways, Sheilan and me. Other times, we popped into the soil and recharged. Even our kind needs to have a rest period now and then."

"But you weren't bothered at all by the wormhole or the low level of life support on the ship?"

Dari leaned against an equipment cabinet, and Liam half-expected him to fall through it, but he appeared more solid now. "Not in the least. We don't require oxygen or any of those elements to survive. Being energy beings, we can exist in almost any environment."

"Are there some that you can't?"

Dari lifted his eyebrows as he considered Liam's question. "Well, now. To be truthful, I actually don't know. So far, I haven't encountered it. While I have an affinity to water, I don't absolutely have to have it to exist, although I might find myself slippin' into a bit of hibernation if it turns into a long dry spell."

"So, water is your element. Does Sheilan have one also?" Fascinating. Liam thought it might be useful to know a way to control the sidhe if they ever had need. But he didn't intend to spread it about.

Dari shrugged. "I cannot say, for I do not know. She is a different type of sidhe. As far as I can say, nothing phases her. Although we were both somewhat hindered by the raw crystals that trader brought onto the ship."

"The unrefined targassium," Liam clarified. "You're saying that affected you?"

"A little. It had a… draining… effect on us. Me more than Sheilan, but we both felt it."

"Bedam." Liam's eyes narrowed as he thought. "You and Sheilan are wonders. You could be like a witching rod to locate targassium on a planet."

"Ho, now, lad. Do not be thinkin' to get rich usin' us as forecasters."

Liam chuckled. "Don't ya worry. I'm not, but you have to admit, you could gain some wealth for yourself by doing it."

Dari made a spitting motion. "Bah, why would I want wealth? I have all I need within me and our home plot of dirt."

"I guess you do. But could you do Grania, my brothers, and me a favor?"

Dari straightened up and shifted his naked feet uneasily. "What kind?"

"Nothin' difficult. Let me show you what I want." He

motioned Dari forward, then turned to a screen that monitored the engines. "See this screen. You can read the percentage levels on this line." He pointed to a horizontal bar with the levels marked in five percent increments. It currently showed ninety-five percent. "This one shows the percent required."

The next bar across the screen showed eighty-five percent.

"When we enter the wormhole, these will drop to twenty percent. Since this is a rebuilt engine and I've had a few fluctuations, could you keep an eye on it while the rest of us are sleeping?"

"You're just wantin' me to watch it?" Dari's brow wrinkled a little in puzzlement.

"Exactly. If it drops lower than twenty percent... Liam pointed to the marker, "...or goes above thirty percent, then I want you to hit the emergency button on my jump pod." Liam stood and motioned for Dari to follow him to the pod.

As Dari came up and peered at the side panel on the unit, Liam showed him a red button, a two-inch raised rounded protrusion on the side next to an emergency reserve of oxygen and a mask.

Dari pointed to it. "That button there, Mister Liam?"

The tall engineer nodded. Dari wasn't stupid, so he felt confident asking him to do this. While he didn't expect the engine to give them any problems, the leap from Merlin's Gate to Emrys Gate was a long one. He'd feel better if someone could monitor the energy output rather than relying on the ship's emergency program to wake him.

Dari thrust his shoulders back, and a toothless grin spread

across his face as he nodded.

"Good man," Liam said, then added, "But please don't touch anything other than the red button here, okay?"

"I got it. Only press this button if the percentage changes. You can count on me. Can I sit in your chair?" His gaze tracked to the comfortable-looking desk chair with armrests.

"Yes, of course. We'll be going through in about forty mites, so if there's anything you want to do before then, you go and come back when the bridge announces the jump."

Dari acknowledged and disappeared in a blink. Liam squinted at the place he'd just been. *Not even a trace of residue from his transformation. Amazing.*

* * * * *

Grania started searching for O'Toole on the ship's mid-level. She'd thought to send Rory, but the com feed from the gate picked up, and he was suddenly busy. Likewise, Brendan had his own tasks with verifying the course and making any last-minute adjustments based on the information the station sent. Usually, the route was solid, but if anything caused the wormhole to fluctuate, they needed to alter the entry path.

So here she was, the captain doing a cabin-to-cabin search for her missing second officer. She tried O'Toole's cabin first, thinking he might have taken ill and gone down to rest. When she got no response to her knock, she opened the sliding door and looked around. Not in the room, and the access to the accommodation was open slightly, so he wasn't in there.

Next, she tried Rory's space with the same result. Then Brendan's, where she came up equally empty. Maybe he'd gone to the galley, so she backtracked to that end of the ship again. Unoccupied, lights on low, and nothing to indicate anyone had been there. So, where was he?

She gazed back down the corridor where the passenger cabins were located. *He didn't go to check on the passengers, did he? But if he didn't, then where did he go?* With a feeling of trepidation, Grania knocked on Orla Hennessey's door and waited. A few moments passed, then the girl opened the door part-way and peered out at her.

"What d'ya want?" Her expression was flat, no smile, no frown, just a straight line and unexpressive eyes. Clearly, she wasn't happy and would bear watching when they got to Zabrowski. Now Grania understood why the family requested an escort to Galway.

"I'm sorry to be disturbing you, but I'm looking for Mister O'Toole. Have you seen him in the past hour or so?"

She shook her head.

"I see. Thank you. Ms. Hennessey, are you doing all right?"

A flicker of annoyance darted through her eyes. "Well enough, given that I have been sold like chattel to a family I've never met. How would you feel?"

Her voice challenged Grania. "I'd be angry, just as you are. Still, I imagine your parents are doing what they think is best for you."

"*Iesu Mwar*! They made a deal, and there's money

involved. Nothin' to do with what I want or my well-being."

"That may be true. But my job is to make sure you get there safely."

Grania started to turn away when the girl muttered, "Then what? You'll take your money and leave me to whatever horrible fate awaits me. You're as bad as they are." Orla keyed the door, and it slid shut with a soft whoosh.

Grania hesitated, almost knocking again on the door, but what could she say? That she was sure that wasn't the case? She didn't know. Were the people Orla was bound to going to treat her well? While she knew that some people sold their children to a slave market, she would not be a party to that kind of trade. At that moment, she resolved she would meet the family and learn their intentions before turning Orla over to them. Then, she'd have to decide if the girl was in danger. *And if she is, what will you do? That* was a question to ponder.

Taking a breath, she moved on to the next door and knocked again. She heard music coming from the cabin and thumped harder. One of the young men opened the door; Conan, she believed it was. He held a fiddle in one hand as he leaned against the opening.

"Excuse my interruption—" She broke off when she heard O'Toole's voice singing along with the other lad's guitar in the background.

"Mister O'Toole!" Her voice was loud enough to be heard at the end of the corridor. The music stopped abruptly, and a few heartbeats later, O'Toole's face appeared next to Conan's. He looked annoyed, but so was she. "I'd like to speak to you in private, sir."

His eyes blinked, and he turned to the lad next to him. "It appears I need to be going now. Thank ye both for your courtesy and the music. It was truly a pleasure. I hope we might do it again."

O'Toole stepped into the corridor and walked a few paces from the door as Grania followed him. He turned, fury distorting his face and his eyes blazing. "How dare you shout to me like that in front of our guests?"

Rage reared its talons within her, but she kept it under control. She answered with a calm yet firm voice. "And how dare you abandon your post without permission or even leaving a message of why?"

"I was watching the screens on the corridors, and I saw the lads heading for the galley, so I hurried down to advise them it was shut down until we were underway. I escorted them back to their quarters, and they invited me in. Does my job not include being hospitable to our passengers, *Captain*?"

Grania heard the scornful way he said her title. "Hospitable, yes, but not by shirking your duty. You had the com while the meeting was going. You left your station to party with those young men."

"Your granda would not approve. He knew the passengers needed reassurance and to be kept happy. A simple drink or two with them was all I intended. You, young woman, have a lot to learn yet."

As Grania stared at him, trying to form words to repudiate his, O'Toole turned and marched away, saying, "I will be in my room awaiting the jump."

Flabbergasted, she only managed a muttered, "But you haven't been dismissed," as he walked away.

Still in disbelief that O'Toole had been so disrespectful, she climbed the stairs to the top level. Why had her granda saddled her with this arrogant man? Was this a test of some kind?

As she stepped on the bridge, she curbed her anger, unwilling to let it carry over to her brothers. Brendan looked up from his computer and asked, "Did ya' find him?"

"I did. He's gone to his quarters to prepare for the jump. Do we have clearance yet, Rory?" She turned toward her chair as she glanced at him.

"Not exactly. A message came in for you a few mites ago."

A dimple formed between her eyebrows as her eyes narrowed. "Did you see it?"

"Umm, part of it," he said. "Then I saw it was 'captain's eyes only.'"

That alarmed her more than just getting a missive from the station. What now? She dropped into her seat and called it up. She read it once, then read it again. What the heck? She let out a breath. "We have an emissary coming from the gate station to see me. No detail about the reason or if this will delay us more."

"He's coming now?" Rory asked.

"He should be on his way." She tagged Liam. "We might have another delay. A visitor is coming from Merlin's gate. Please meet him at the airlock and escort him to my quarters."

"When is he expected?"

"Any time now. The message came in fifteen mites ago. Enough time for him to be almost here." Grania leaned back, speculating what this man might want.

Chapter Five

A short time later, Grania sat behind the sturdy desk in her cabin to wait for her visitor. Embedded within its lower levels, the alternate bridge controls were concealed by two sliding panels, but the communications screen rose from the desk to her right.

Within a few mites of her arrival, Liam escorted a diminutive man through the door. Dressed in the Planetary Provisional Government's dark blue tunic, he wore the office badge prominently on his left breast.

Maintaining formality, Liam said, "Captain, this is Senator Gabke, representative of—"

"Batterforce." Grania finished the sentence for him as she recognized the man. With big ears protruding outward and his small stature, he was well-known in interplanetary politics. "Welcome aboard the Mo Chroidhe, Senator." She paid him the honor of standing and offering her hand. "I am Captain Grania O'Ceagan."

"My thanks to you for receiving me on short notice. I have urgent business to discuss with you."

His voice was higher pitched than expected, and she suppressed a giggle. Clearly, it passed through a modulator for broadcast. Giving a nod to Liam, she said, "Thank you for showing the Senator here. You may resume your preparations for the jump."

Liam's lip twitched to the left side in disapproval of the dismissal. Nonetheless, he turned on his heel and left her quarters. She turned her attention back to Gabke and offered him a seat in a chair facing the desk.

His pale amber eyes rested on her face as he cleared his throat conspicuously. "What I am about to say is for you to hear only. I represent my planetary government as well as the wishes of the Interplanetary organization I serve. We are aware that certain political interests on Enterprise have contacted you."

He paused. Grania said nothing, keeping her expression neutral. *How did he know? Was the eyes-only communication sent to the ship breached by someone?*

When she remained quiet, Gabke asked, "Have you any idea what they wish transported?"

"None."

"I see. Are you going to do it?"

Her mouth tightened as she thought about how much to say. Both factions were governmental agencies, and she would have preferred not to be involved in whatever shenanigans they were perpetrating. "Let's just say that the shippers on Enterprise have been persuasive, and I am considering it, else I would not be preparing to go through Merlin's Gate."

"Just so," he acknowledged. "The fact is, our government would like you to accept the offer. We know of a subversive element within the Amalgamated Union of Planets, and we believe they might be shipping a weapon of some kind to the Outer Rim."

"A weapon?" she repeated, her heart beating faster. "And you would like me to do what exactly?"

"Transport it," Gabke replied. "Also, attempt to determine what they are sending and report back to us. There is unrest at Desolation, Captain. Trouble with the native population, and it's possible the AUP is interfering in local matters. If the shipment is harmless, then there's no problem. If it is, as we suspect, a weapon or weapons, then we need to take action to prevent a war."

Grania turned her head away as she let her eyes rove across the displayed artwork on the left wall, a Celtic impression of the Morrigan, the goddess of war. With blood-red eyes and mouth, the painting invoked fear. The image was a favorite of her granda. She quite liked it, although it represented the strife that often plagued civilizations. Now, this man, this Senator, wished to pull her and her ship into a possibly explosive situation.

She turned back to him. "To be clear, you want me to accept the cargo and take it to Desolation. While in my possession, you also want me to attempt to discover what is in the cargo. Is that correct?"

A crooked smile quirked his lips up. "It is."

"You are not asking me to do anything else. Just to what you have told me. Once we deliver the cargo, we will be free to depart and leave whatever troubles might be within it behind. Do I have the right of that as well?"

"You do. Depending on what you learn, the PPG will take any additional action if needed."

"Forgive me for asking, but what's in this for my crew and me?"

"The gratitude of the planetary government, which represents all the member planets. Erinnua is one of them, as are Cardyff and Caledonia."

"So, we may be risking our lives for gratitude." She brushed at the left sleeve of her tunic as if whisking dust off.

"Of course, not just that. We offer a generous fee for your services, and we will have an agent boarding your ship at Zabrowski Station as a passenger. We'll pay his transportation fees, and he will help assure your safety."

Now a passenger. They had this all planned out already. She felt they were being set up for something but couldn't figure it out. "How will I contact this agent?"

"He will find you, but I will give you this to help you identify him. He reached into the case he'd brought and pulled out a sealed plastic envelope. "Keep it secure, Captain."

She accepted it, slid it into the center drawer of her desk, and coded the lock. "One more thing. My crew is my family, my brothers. They should know what is going on also. I need their support."

The skin over the bone ridges in Gabke's forehead rippled as he stood. "Not *all* your crew are related. Be cautious of who you feel compelled to tell. The more who know, the more dangerous it could be. Will you escort me back to my shuttle?"

Grania rose and took the lead to the door, ushering him

out, then walking with him down the stairs from the ship to the boarding ramp.

"This will do, Captain. Thank you for your cooperation. Our agent will know how to reach me if you have need." Gabke turned and strode across the boarding dock with a spring of confidence.

Now, she had more to think about. Should she tell her brothers? Certainly not O'Toole, and how could she keep Dari from learning about it? Was the puca a liability or an asset in this endeavor?

"We have clearance for the gate in fifteen mites," Rory informed Grania as she stepped onto the bridge. "I've notified Liam."

"Good. Let our passengers and O'Toole know it's time to use the pods. Get to your own in T-minus-five." She hurried to her station to double-check everything. Not that she didn't trust her brothers to do it right, but Granda had taught her a new set of eyes could see things others might miss.

It hadn't taken long for the gate to clear their jump once Gabke departed. Clearly, he'd been the sole reason for the delay. The deal bothered her, nagging at her mind. She wanted to tell Liam all of it but hesitated to do so. With the distinct possibility of him leaving the ship at Zabrowski, she didn't want him carrying that information in his brain where he might accidentally say something.

Rory sounded the bell-toned alarm advising all that the ship was going into jump mode in five mites.

"All clear down here," Liam replied over the com, letting

her know the engines were set.

She checked the wormhole status just before Rory locked his station, then bounded to his feet. "Going now, Nia. You, too." He hastened to the hall and sprinted from there.

Grania barely noticed him as she transferred her station to the backup in her cabin, then locked it down before heading for her jump pod. These events were usually routine, but after being stranded in the black space surrounding the wormhole on their last trip, she carried a bit of apprehension.

* * * * *

Liam heard the alarm going off in his coffin-like pod as the lid began to lift. The lights were still dim, and he could detect the sparseness in the air as soon as he drew the first two breaths. Automatically, his hand crawled over the edge to reach for the oxygen mask by the unit. Turning his head that way, he focused on the freckled face peering nervously at him.

"Are ya all right, Mister Liam? I did as you said and pressed the red button." Eyes like saucers, Dari wrung his hands as he spoke.

Liam held up his other hand, indicating *wait* while he pressed the mask to his face and took three deep breaths. He climbed out of the pod and crossed to the bridge computer. He pressed two buttons—more precisely, button images digitally imprinted on the screen—and leaned in. "Voice command, Liam O'Ceagan, engineer, code 86599_avenger. Return engine room to normal oxygen at once."

"Complying," the tinny computer voice replied. The lights brightened as the higher oxygen level began pumping into the room.

Liam avoided looking at the screen displaying the dizzying vortex images of the wormhole's motion. His concentration focused on the two lines he'd set Dari to watch. Yes, they'd both dropped almost five percent, which meant one of the engines wasn't working correctly.

Most likely the repaired one, he figured, but they hadn't had adequate time to make a shakedown trip before heading out. With the shuddering and speed of this longer wormhole, it probably shook something loose in the engine, or something was blocking either the intake or the exhaust. He had to identify which unit was acting up and adjust the good one to compensate.

He turned slightly and noticed Dari standing a pace or so away with a worried look wrinkling his brow. "You did fine, Dari. Exactly as I asked. One of the engines has a problem, and I'll shut it down after I boost the other one."

"Will you not be fixing it?"

"On the fly? No, we'll need to get to the station at Enterprise before I can get out to repair it. But now, I need to see which one it is." He turned to engine monitoring stats to track the unit that had dropped power.

"Would ya' like me to pop down and take a look?" Dari made it sound like he was stepping out to fetch a coffee.

"What?"

"I can flash down and look at the situation with both the

engines. See if one looks different from ta' other."

"You mean, take your energy form and actually go inside the engine?" Liam was beginning to grasp what Dari proposed. He hadn't considered that the puca could do that.

"Aye. T'won't take but a few seconds to do it."

"Dari, is your vision like Sheilan's when you're in your energy form?" Liam saw the question in Dari's scrunched face. "I mean, she sees things in fractals, doesn't she? Do you also?"

"I get what you're asking now. I do, indeed. If I look at it, I should be able to see what's broken and where."

"Handy," Liam answered, "but do you have any idea what you're looking at?"

"Umm, maybe. Maybe not." Dari shuffled his feet as he thought. "But I can still see where the pattern does not look right. Shall I have a peek then?"

"Go ahead. Start with the starboard one."

Blinking out, Dari vanished again, and Liam turned his attention back to the information on the screens. He suspected the problem might be in the repaired engine, namely the starboard one, which was why he pointed Dari that way first. He admitted he was curious how objects looked to the sidhe when they were in energy form. How did they interpret the fractals?

More and more, he was thinking that having a sidhe on a ship might be a bonus. They could go places where he could not and stay alert through the space jumps. Apparently, they weren't bothered by the distortions in the wormholes that had a tendency to either mesmerize most life forms or drive them to madness.

He'd just about narrowed the drain down to the engine in question when Dari popped back in. "The engine on the right – that's the starboard, innit? — seems to have a tear in the metal near the intake vent. At least, it looks like that's where the problem lies when I compared it to the other one."

"Shite! It sounds like the repair was faulty and might have pulled loose. All right, Dari. That saved me some time. I know where to begin when we get to the station to repair it. Good work." He turned to the computer, boosted the port engine, and shut down the damaged one. "Grania isn't going to be happy about this."

Chapter Six

"Are you saying the engine repair was shabbily done, Liam?" Grania could scarcely believe what her brother reported. *The blasted repair tore? After what Balrog Ship Repair charged me to fix it, they better be prepared to cover the expense of redoing it. They will hear about this when I get back to Erinnua.* "Can you mend it when we get to the station?"

"I believe I can, so long as the station has the metal piece we'll need. The key questions are how long it will take to get and weld it into place. I'll have to work in space unless the station has an airlock hanger where we can park the ship." He rubbed his hand against his sleeve.

"Is there something else on your mind?" Grania asked as she noticed the action. When he was uneasy about something, Liam tended to rub his arm.

"No. Not really. Although I am curious about the Senator's visit. You haven't said anything about it."

"He only wanted to hand me a diplomatic pouch to take to Zabrowski. Something he wants hand-delivered." There, she'd blatantly lied to her brother. She turned her eyes back to the forward screen where the space station grew steadily larger as it floated in front of the yellow-green world that was Enterprise.

A planet with a similar atmosphere to Earth, yellow was the predominant color of the sand, stone, and most vegetation. The water on it reflected the color of the sand below it, which was covered with sea creature shells, making it a variety of green shades laced with the yellow of the sand. Unlike Earth, most of the planet was land mass, with only about one-quarter liquid.

When the settlers began setting up businesses on the world, they decided to make it a commercial hub, renaming it from Zenoso to Enterprise, suggesting the business aspect of the world. While some did turn to farming, most focused on importing, exporting, and manufacturing goods to ship to other worlds. They'd done quite well, even though not many ships plied this particular route.

For a freighter like the Mo Chroidhe, it was a distant world to visit. Even with the wormhole, the travel time through it had taken nearly fifteen hours. On the other side, they still had another three hours to reach the station. Comparing that with the jump from Palanan to Einstein's Gate leading to Earth, it took nearly four times as long. Grania's ship was used to short runs.

Of course, if they took on the task to the Outer Rim, they were looking at three long jumps, taking about six total days to carry them close to Desolation. Without the wormholes, they would have to travel over 900,000 light years to reach the galaxy's edge. In fact, without the wormholes, travelers wouldn't be able to make it to many places in the Milky Way Galaxy in one lifetime.

"I'll go back to engineering and check on the cargo to ensure it came through the jump without any issues. I have Dari down there with me, so he can help out." Her brother's voice interrupted her thoughts.

"That sounds good. Thanks, Liam."

He nodded and strode off the bridge, his pace suggesting he was annoyed about something. Probably her lack of detail about the senator's visit. At least, she surmised as much. She turned to see Rory watching her, a look of question in his eyes.

"What?" she asked.

"Just wondering if everything was okay. You seem rather thoughtful, sis."

"Well, I am fuming about the ship's repair to be done now because some workman buggered the job." She blew off his concern with the obvious problem. She felt weird about not telling them any details, but it was for their safety as much as hers. "Keep an ear out for a message from the AUP. They're supposed to direct us once we're here. I assume we'll be assigned a docking port as usual. Ask the station if they have an airlock repair dock for the ship. Tell them we need to do engine repairs. This is going to cost us a bit."

One more thing to add to the growing list of expenses the repairs had cost. Much as Grania didn't want to have to go to the Outer Rim, it would be a well-paying run, especially with the additional fee the PPG had offered. They could sure use the credits.

* * * * *

They proceeded without any odd communication or delays to a vast, barn-like structure housing the airlock for their dry dock. Brendan plotted a perfect course into it, even with their listing ship. The functioning engine worked to maintain the ship's balance once it hit the incoming air, but the freighter soon settled into the dock as the vacuum was replaced with oxygen.

As soon as the engines quieted, a message came through for Grania. Brief, but clear who had sent it. The AUP agent said he would be waiting for her at the station master's office and to come there as soon as possible.

"You have the com while I check in with the station," Grania informed Rory. "I might have more information on the transport when I return."

"Got it. I have a request from the musician lads. They'd like to know if they can go explore the station."

She hesitated. She had no idea how long they'd be docked, but she didn't see any harm in the young men having a look around. "Sure. Tell them to check in with you in two hours since I'm not sure how long we'll be docked here."

Enterprise Station was built in a V design, with two long arms providing docking space with a pair of dry docks at the outstretched ends of each one. The central hub formed a cap at the base of the V. Moving walkways made the trip from the far ports to the business section faster.

As she strode on the walkway toward the station master's office, Grania brushed a hand down her uniform tunic, a dark green slim-cut fabric with a patch on the left shoulder bearing the Mo Chroidhe's symbol—the same one painted on the nose of the ship. She wouldn't deny that a knot of apprehension like the Celtic lacing in the design twisted in her stomach.

This whole business unsettled her; not something that she would willingly choose. To her knowledge, Granda had never been involved in anything like this. Then again, if it was a confidential situation, he might never have told anyone if he did. Right now, she wished she could talk to him about it.

People of all races moved around the various businesses on the station, more non-human ones than most of the stations she'd visited ever had. Being a key trade hub, the planet and the station attracted far more entrepreneurs than her usual route.

At the end of the moving walkway, she stepped off, heading for the map of the shopping hub to get her bearings. The station master wasn't far from there, just to the left and two storefronts down. She turned her head to confirm it and saw the sign ahead. A few people milled in the vicinity of the entrance, perhaps waiting to go in or just meeting someone there. Thrusting her shoulders back, she marched toward it.

She felt the eyes on her before she saw the source. A man of average height and build stepped away from the wall space next to the office. Not at all imposing. At first, she questioned if he looked for her, but then he nodded twice and pointed toward a central conversation deck in the middle of the gallery. She veered to follow him as he pivoted and ambled to one of the private cubbies.

The raised deck provided a dozen glass-enclosed conversation spaces where people could conduct private business in plain view without anyone around overhearing. It afforded a secure, safe setting for a two-or-three-person meeting. He held the door open as Grania came even with him.

"Captain." He motioned her inside, then followed. Two comfortable-looking padded benches sat on the back and right-side walls. She took the back one, sat, and turned to face the other bench. He flashed a smile, then said, "I'm Tomas Fallon, an agent for the AUP. I'm pleased to meet you."

"Likewise, I guess. This all seems a little strange to me. To be honest, I'm feeling like I'm not being given any options in this situation." Her voice carried a stronger lilt to it than usual.

As Fallon sat, he crossed his legs in front of him and leaned back, getting comfortable. "That is not our intent, Captain. But we do need your to do the job for us. It's not as complex as it sounds. Simply load our crate on your ship and take it to Desolation. That might be the tricky part. We have a man on the planet, and you will need to get it to him on the planet's surface, not just drop it off at the Outer Rim station."

"Well, that's a problem," Grania's mouth twitched at the hint of a smirk. "The Mo Chroidhe doesn't have a landing base. She was built in space and lives there. She doesn't do atmosphere. Now, if your cargo fits on our shuttle, I can take it down."

Fallon ran a hand over his chin as he considered her response. "I don't believe it will be a major issue, although I imagine the crate is larger than your shuttle can handle.

However, the station has transport shuttles that should accommodate. You'll need to hire one of those, transfer the cargo to it, and personally take it down."

"Why me, personally?"

"We want the verification that you delivered it to the correct person. We're willing to pay a generous fee to ensure the job is done. With such a sensitive shipment, we can't risk an unknown person with the job."

She raised her eyebrows. "If you don't mind my asking, why did you choose me for this job? There are others with more experience who actually travel that route."

"I can't tell you the process for who the committee picked to handle this, but I do know that they wanted someone who was reliable and didn't go to the Rim regularly. Plus, your ship meets the requirements for the job."

Grania laughed. "I think someone must be misinformed. My ship is an old blowfish, solar-powered freighter. She's just had repairs, and even as we came here, we've had an engine problem. In fact, it could delay us from getting away from here, which brings up another issue. The time frame for delivering the cargo is too tight. My engineer doesn't believe we can make it."

Fallon studied her face for a moment or two. "I believe our logistics person calculated adequate time for the journey. Getting the crate to Desolation is urgent and must be a priority."

"Then, we have another problem. It's urgent to you, but I also have a schedule to maintain. I have to stop at Earth station and make an in-person delivery there before embarking for the Rim. It will take two days before we are back underway, plus almost a full day from here to Pelanan Station, where—" She held up a hand as she saw him drawing a breath to speak. "— where I have cargo to drop off and pick up."

"As I said, Captain, this is urgent. You can deliver your goods on the way back."

"I don't think so. If you want a ship that behaves normally, you don't want one to divert from its usual activities and commitments. Not meeting our contracted obligations of delivery and pick-up at Pelanan and Earth would not only look suspicious but would also greatly damage the reputation of my ship and crew. Just how *substantial* a payment are you offering for me to figuratively cut my own throat in the transport business?" She widened her eyes and stared him down.

Lips tight, he pulled his legs back, leaned forward with both elbows on his knees, and stared at her for what seemed like a long time before he straightened. "Excuse me for a few minutes." He rose to his feet and stepped out of the cubie. Glancing around, he walked to another one nearby and entered it. She figured he was checking with someone with more authority than he had.

After a dozen mites crept past, Fallon returned to the cube and sat again. "First, I am authorized to offer you 870,000 credits for the job, payable fifty percent up front and the remainder when the transfer to our agent in Desolation is completed."

"Not enough to ruin my reputation," Grania said,

although her heart leaped at the high six-figure offer.

"I appreciate your concern for that," Fallon replied, his dark eyes showing a hint of sympathy. "For us, this situation and our response to it could be a matter of success or failure. Time is vital."

"Well, future work is vital to me, even though I appreciate your concerns as well. It seems to me that the AUP is setting up a covert operation, and you want to use an unassuming ship with a woman captain to divert suspicion; otherwise, you would use a military or large commercial transport."

He shook his head, a smirky smile on his face and looked away for a moment or two. "You know the AUP can cause quite a few headaches for you and go so far as to pull your operating license."

"Ah, that would be the threat again. Coercing me to go along with the plan. Well, work with me then because I can't make my ship go any faster."

He let out a long-suffering sigh. "Would a new engine improve the speed?"

She blinked. Did he just offer to replace the engine? "At what cost?"

"Consider it part of your fee. We'll replace it faster than your man can repair it, then you can be underway from here within three hours. So, a new engine plus the delivery fee and actual travel costs. Does it sound more feasible now?"

Grania did some fast calculations. It would be tight, but a new engine could move them more quickly between gates than the old one, and the targassium crystal could interact better with the new one. Would it cause any problems with the older port engine? She wanted to consult with Liam but couldn't go into the details. This was her decision to make.

"I believe we might be able to do it. What are the consequences if we miss the deadline?"

"No payment, for starters. The AUP may take other action for failing to comply with your agreement. Worse if war breaks out on Desolation."

"You've really got me over the proverbial barrel here. Cursed either way. I don't see any way to turn this down without ruining my business."

"I take that as a yes. We'll send a crew over with your new engine in about thirty mites. In the meantime, the crate will be brought to the dockside for loading in less than an hour."

He rose and offered his hand, a scarred one, she noticed as he held it out. She took it and stood.

"A pleasure, Captain O'Ceagan. Check your account in about twenty mites." Again, he turned to open the door to usher her out. He was an old-fashioned gentleman despite whatever else he might be.

*****

"Well, I'm not exactly happy with the deal," Grania told Liam as they stood on the dock alongside the Mo Chroidhe, waiting for the promised engine and crew to arrive. She'd filled him in on the pertinent details of the agreement. While he was happy about the new engine, especially with it being part of the deal and not another expense, he still was nervous about making the deadline.

"It would be nice to have at least one more day for a cushion. It's going to feel like a race all the way for you. Have you started lookin' for a new engineer yet?"

Her heart skipped a beat as he said that, reminding her that his time would run out shortly. She shook her head. "Have you talked to Uncle Colm yet? Can he give you any leeway?"

"No, I have not. I'm thinking I can stay with the ship as far as Andromeda Station, which would give you time to get a new man trained. Does O'Toole have any engineering experience?"

"I don't know. I'd rather trust Dari than him. He's on this trip for a lark, not to be of any real help."

"I'm sorry, Nia. I'll see if I can squeeze in more time before I need to join the Mo Spiorad's crew. Maybe Uncle's had some delays."

"It would mean a lot to me if you could make the whole trip. Have you told Bren and Rory yet?"

"Not yet. I'll tell 'em when we get to Zabrowski and have a pint there."

"A little alcohol always helps, does it not?" She spotted a crew of five coming their way. "I think this might be our workers."

At the same time, Liam tapped her arm to point to a repair tug entering the lock with a shiny metal tube hanging in a sling below it. "And that would be our engine."

"Looks lovely. I'm going back on board to fill in Rory and

Bren, so they can begin prepping for the jump to Pelanan. We'll try to speed up the time we spend there. You handle these guys and learn anything you can about this engine and how much power it can generate. Make sure it works with the sails and the crystal."

"Leave it to me. I know what I'm doin'." Liam's voice carried a rough edge.

"Of course you do. Just my worries showing. Tag me when they bring the cargo, all right?"

"Will do." Liam stepped away and started toward the install crew as Grania took her own path back to the entry ramp for the ship.

Back on the bridge, Grania took a few mites to verify the credit transfer made it to the ship's account, which it did. She brought her brothers up to speed on their next jump so Bren could calculate the course and Rory could begin checking messages relating to Pelanan and the wormhole. This would be their first time back through it, and they were not too eager. The chances of a repeat incident were ridiculously high, but the dread of being stuck in that dead space lingered like the odor of burnt cabbage in the kitchen.

She opened her personal log, ready to record the engine's change date, when Liam tagged her mobi. "What is it?" she asked.

"You'll want to get down her, Grania. The cargo is arriving now. You need to see this."

"On the way." She sprang to her feet and down the short ramp that raised her console three feet above the others, telling her brothers, "Going back to the cargo hold."

In less than four mites, she was down the stairs and out the front entry to the ship, her head turning to see up the long hall of gates where a huge crate moved down it. Her mouth dropped open. Holy Mary, the thing was monstrous! Four lev-dollies lifted and guided it toward their loading dock while three men walked alongside to ensure it didn't slip or tip over. What the hell was the AUP shipping?

She sprinted down the ramp and raced to the back of the vessel, where Liam leaned against the hold opening, arms crossed, watching the procession coming toward him. "Do we have enough room for that?" she called as she ran up.

"I may have to move a few things, but yeah, I think so. So long as it's not too high. Now, we know why they wanted a ship like ours."

He was right. Besides the military ships and big freighters, most ships couldn't accommodate anything as high as this one. She wasn't all that sure it wouldn't be taller than the ceiling in their hold.

"I'm also wondering how heavy it is," he added. "This could put a lot of pressure on the floor if it weighs as much as it looks like it might."

"More than a loaded cold box?"

"Could be. Let's ask for the specs before we bring it on board."

She nodded, turned, and marched down the hall toward the men bringing the crate. "Who's in charge here?"

One of them pointed to the man at the back. Continuing

past the slow-moving parade, she waved at the last man. "I'm the Mo Chroidhe's captain. Do you have the paperwork on this shipment?"

He stopped, reached inside his overalls, and pulled out a folded sheet of paper. "This is all I got, lady."

Grania bristled a little at that. "It's Captain, not 'lady.'" She snatched it, unfolded the paper, and studied it. If the details were correct, it was seven meters tall, three meters deep and six meters wide. Weight-wise, it cited two-hundred-sixty kilograms, so it wasn't too heavy.

She thanked him, telling him to bring it on. They needed to adjust their space. Dashing back to Liam, she said, "It's almost as tall as the ceiling, but it should clear it without any problems."

"What about the cameras and the sprinkler system?"

"Try to find a path clear of those to get it to a place also unhindered by those. Do you want me to send O'Toole down?"

"I'll call him," Liam answered. "Although Dari's help might be enough so long as we can get it off the levs."

"Dari? Really?" She found that amusing. "How is the engine swap going?"

"See for yourself," he answered as he pointed to the edge of the walkway where a ladder angled down to the lower portion of the ship.

The workmen climbed over the hull like overgrown rats clinging to a metal balloon. They'd pulled the dead engine out, shifting it to anchor on the underside of the walkway where it would be out of the way. The tug still hovered nearby with the new engine.

"It looks like that's going well. I still can't believe they *gave* this to us. There must be a catch."

As Grania turned back to him, Rory tagged her. "We might have a problem. I've located our musician passengers, but it appears the Hennessey girl is missing."

"What?! Wasn't she locked in her cabin?"

Chapter Seven

Shifting her view from one side to the other, Grania strode through the station's core with purpose. She'd taken the starboard side from the main junction of the twin arms while Rory had gone to the port side. Where in blazes had the girl gone? She had to be on the station. No shuttle would take a teenage girl without travel papers and no credits to the planet.

The lads from Cardyff said she'd left the ship when they did. Apparently, she'd heard them going and caught up with them before they'd gotten more than a hundred feet down the corridor. They'd gone to the hub, where they'd bought her a non-alcoholic Naked Fairy drink and a roll, then she'd separated from them. She told them she wanted to explore, and they'd told her she needed to return to the ship within sixty mites.

That had been over one-hundred-twenty mites earlier. Ethan and Conan had returned to the ship, which was preparing for departure in forty-eight mites. With the new engine installed and checked out, Liam had told her he'd gotten the oversized crate into position and almost locked down. He'd placed it on the wall nearest to the cargo door, which was the massive floor-to-ceiling platform-style that dropped to form a ramp. He would be done in less than fifteen mites while she was still prowling the station looking for Orla Hennessey. She knew that girl was going to be trouble.

She stepped into each accommodation facility she passed in case Orla had chosen to hide in one of those, but so far, she'd seen no one who even resembled her. Up ahead, she spotted a clothing shop. Maybe Orla decided to browse in there. Young girls were attracted to pretty dresses, weren't they?

The place wasn't large, and only a few travelers perused the overpriced garments and other accessories. Nothing in here that Orla could have afforded if she'd had any credits. But Grania paused to speak to the clerk. "Did you happen to notice a teenage girl—about this tall—" She paused to indicate her height at about the middle of her upper arm. "black hair pulled into a ponytail and blue eyes?"

The clerk nodded. "I did see her. She looked around for about five mites, then left."

"Do you recall which way she went?"

She shook her head. "I wasn't minding what she did, only that she didn't have anything when she left the shop."

"How long ago was that?" At least she hadn't stolen anything.

The clerk's brow lowered as her eyes partly closed while she thought. "' Bout forty mites ago. Not long after, I discovered a wig had gone missing, but we caught that person."

Thanking her, Grania went back to the promenade and resumed her search. Now she knew Orla was in the area or had been within the past hour, so she might catch up with her before long. She skipped any food places since Orla didn't have credits. About the most she could do was explore areas without buying.

Twenty mites later, she'd reached the end of the station market area and found beauty salons, five clothing shops, arcades, restaurants, bars, and more meeting cubes. She'd seen no sign of Orla. She turned to go back when Rory tagged her mobi.

"Any luck, brother?" she asked.

"Not exactly," he replied. "But Bren contacted me. You're not gonna like this."

"What?" She felt a knot of dread in her stomach. What had happened now?

"The station security contacted the ship. They have a girl who claims to have arrived on our ship in custody. Seems she helped herself to a couple of items."

"Feck! I'll go there to see what I can do. You get back to the ship. I'll be along as soon as I can. With some persuasion, I might clear this up before departure time. Thanks, Rory."

He wished her luck, then she closed her mobi and headed toward the security office, which was a short distance from the station master's door.

She stepped into security, where several officers milled around a desk within the Plexiglas-enclosed office. The front counter sat along half the length of the front wall with a book-sized opening to allow communication with the female officer, who sat stiffly on a tall chair. To the left, a clear glass door opened into the office. The telltale electronic eye in the center of the handle advised that only the front counter officer could open it.

Grania had a sinking feeling she'd find her missing passenger in the middle of that hubbub. Stepping to the window, she straightened her shoulders, schooled her face to business-like, and said, "I'm Captain O'Ceagan of the freighter Mo Chroidhe. You have one of my passengers in your custody, I understand."

The woman's steely eyes didn't so much as flicker, showing no hint of friendliness. A reddish-blue blotch of a forming bruise on her cheek indicated a recent encounter with someone who might have punched her. "Your identification, Captain."

Grania extended her hand through the window, where the officer used a scanner to read her identi-chip. The device had been updated only ten days earlier to show her as the ship's captain.

"Wait a few mites, please. An officer will be out shortly." The woman made some notes on the electronic tablet on the counter as she dismissed Grania.

She saw a bench seat against the side wall and sat down to wait. She hoped she'd be able to get the girl away from the officers quickly, but the situation looked serious. If the shop owner pressed charges, Orla could be arrested, which would create a world of headaches for her, the least of which would be informing her parents.

As she waited, a man came into the office and approached the officer. While Grania couldn't hear the conversation, she could see that the fellow–a Thealin, judging by the reddish skin tones and the pale, almost washed-out color of his eyes—was adamant about something. The woman called back to one of the officers as the man thumped his fingers on the edge of the glass opening.

A few moments later, a big, formidably-built officer came through the door and headed for the man. They exchanged a few words, and the officer requested the door be open.

Grania hesitated only a moment before she hurried to catch up with him. "Excuse me, but if this relates to my passenger, Orla Hennessey, I'd like to be included in the discussions. She's a sixteen-year-old girl under my custody until she is delivered to her relatives on Earth."

The officer shot an irritated glance her way, then turned his eyes to the Thealin. "Do you have any objections, Mister Ayeadib?"

In response, the man eyed her up and down, then shook his head. "No. If the captain allowed the girl to wander off on her own to steal, she is responsible."

"Come in, Captain," the officer said, holding the door to allow both civilians inside.

"I am Officer Dortman, the top man on this incident. The girl is here, and she is a handful, if you don't mind me saying, Captain." He motioned to the desk where the officer directly in front of it had stepped aside.

Orla sat with hunched shoulders, head lowered, and a scowl on her face. Her hands were cuffed and locked to the top of the desk. Clearly, she'd been a problem for them to lock her down. She glared at Grania as if this was her fault.

"May I hear the charges against Orla?" Grania asked, fighting to maintain her calm.

"Two counts of shoplifting–a woman's wig and a dress—resisting apprehension and assault on a security officer. She's been uncooperative and surly and isn't carrying much identification. We were lucky to get her name and pinpoint it to your passenger list." Dortman turned to the Thealin. "Do you wish to press charges, sir?"

"I do," he answered without hesitation.

Grania scrambled mentally to come up with a solution. "Would you consider dropping them if I pay you for the stolen goods? As I stated, she is a minor. I believed she was safely confined to her quarters on the ship, so I was unaware she'd gotten free."

The man considered her offer, thinking it through for any loopholes. He sighed, his eyes darting to the surly girl, who stuck her tongue out at him, then returned to Grania. "You pay full price for goods and cost of my time to pursue her. A total of five-hundred-eighty credits."

While it was higher than Grania expected, she agreed to the terms, making the transfer. Satisfied, the Thealin turned to leave, pausing to say, "You keep her off station. Take away and never bring back." Then he stomped out the door.

Grania addressed Dortman next. "And, what will it take to drop the charges against her? My ship is due to depart in about forty mites. Can we settle this quickly?"

Dortman chewed his lip, then yelled to the officer at the

counter. "Hey, Sillman. Are you willing to drop the assault charges against the girl? Her keeper wants to settle."

"Maybe. For compensation for my injury."

"It's only a fecking bruise," Orla yelled as she yanked at the chains around her wrist.

Grania sighed. This was going to cost her. "Cleary, the shop owner is satisfied, so he's dropped the shoplifting charge. Can you come up with a figure for the other charges?"

"Wait here a few mites," he said, then disappeared through a door to a backroom that was not on public display.

Grania figured he was discussing the case with higher-ups or a lawyer. They'd come out with a total that would buy Orla's freedom. Most of the station security operated that way. They didn't really want to hold visitors to the station unless it was a major criminal act like murder, blackmail, or grand theft. If they were crew or passengers, they'd work out an arrangement. Still, a warning would be posted on their record that could prevent a return to that particular station.

While waiting, she tagged Rory, asking him to meet her at the security office. She figured she might need his help getting Orla back to the ship.

Almost ten mites had passed before Dortman returned and motioned her to another desk behind Orla's. As she came up, he slid a paper across to her. It listed the charges, the details, Orla's name, hers, and the ship. Each offense was itemized with a five-digit figure beside it. Cursed bumbling fairies, it would cost her nearly twenty-five thousand credits to get her out. She wouldn't get that back from her family. She didn't have a lot of choices, so she agreed and handed over her credit card for them to take the fee.

Just as they finished up and Dortman was instructing an officer to release the cuffs, Rory breezed in the door. His cheeks were red as he took deep breaths. He must have run all the way.

Orla stood, rubbing her wrists, complaining in Irish with swear words that made Grania blush. She hoped none of the officers understood the language. "Enough, Orla. We need to go, and I expect cooperation from you."

She sauntered past Grania to the door and pushed it open to run right into Rory. He caught her arm before she could dart past him and held on tight. She swung a leg back, preparing to kick him, but he was faster and swept her legs out from under her. She fell on her butt, fury in her eyes, but she went to spring to her feet before Grania made it to her.

Again, Rory had anticipated a problem and caught her with both arms encircling her waist from behind. "Now, are you going to behave and walk back to the ship, or do I have to make you?" As he spoke, he shoved her out the office door onto the promenade, directing her toward the moving sidewalk.

"I don't want to go back. I don't want to become a slave on Earth. You're all in a conspiracy against me." Her voice grew louder as she complained.

She's hoping someone will intervene, Grania realized. She wished she had a tranq gun with her to shut the girl up.

Orla wriggled and squirmed, trying to break free of Rory's

grip. In one swift move, Grania watched her brother press his thumbs to the back of her neck, putting heavy pressure on her nerves. Orla gasped, went weak-kneed, and almost passed out. In another few moments, Rory swung her over his shoulder and picked up the pace back to their ship.

Grania went straight for the bridge while Rory took Orla to her cabin. "How much time do we have?" she asked as soon as she hit the deck.

"Five mites," Brendan replied. Liam has the engines hot."

"We have clearance from the station to take her out," O'Toole added from the com station.

"Excellent. Rory will be here shortly; let's begin backing our ship out of this dock." She wrapped her hand around the railing leading to her chair.

"On it," Bren answered. She felt the first lurch as the ship pulled back from the dock. She hoped Rory was hanging on to rungs or something. Behind them, the airlock doors had shut, blocking the dry dock from the rest of the station. The Mo Chroidhe wasn't built to fly in the atmosphere, and it took over fifty percent of both engines' power to hold her in position. Ahead, the bay doors opened to space, and the ship rocked some as she pushed out, back into her element.

Rory lurched through the door, hanging onto the frame. "That was cutting it close."

"It was," Grania agreed. "Thanks for your help." She glanced over to the com station. "Mister O'Toole, you're relieved for now. Please check on the jump pods to be sure they'll be ready when we reach the gate."

"That's hours—"

She shot a sharp look his way, her mouth pinched together.

"Aye, Captain. I'll see to it." O'Toole turned the station over to Rory and slipped by her without a word. She could see the muscle in his jaw tensing when he passed.

Once he left, she took her seat and checked their position while they moved away from the station. They didn't have a good line to the sun from Enterprise, so they'd be on engine power most of the way to the jump gate to Pelanan.

Once underway, with the engines comfortably pushing the ship, Grania turned to Rory and asked, "Is the girl secure?"

"She is. I rekeyed the lock on her door and changed the code. She won't get out again. Do you suspect the same thing I do?"

"If you mean that O'Toole opened the door for her, then I do. I don't know what that man's game is, but I'm liking him less and less each day." He may be Granda's friend, but he wasn't helpful or likable.

After they were well underway, Grania went down to the cargo bay to get another look at the shipment they'd taken on board. She crossed to the cargo doors, where the crate looked even bigger, sitting against the wall near them. It dwarfed any other containers down there, including the cold box filled with cartons of sheep's cheese, a specialty of Cardyff.

"Wonder what's in it?" Liam said as he came up beside her. "What are they sending that is as big as this?"

She shook her head in awe. "I don't know. They didn't

give me any clues, or maybe they did. It could be a weapon of some kind. Fallon said there might be unrest on Desolation as troubles were heating up."

"Doesn't look like a tank, and it doesn't weigh enough to be one or even an AT-unit. Their paperwork is suitably cryptic: mining supplies and equipment."

"Balderdash. It's some big secret. Something new, maybe."

"We might have a way to get a look." Liam dropped his eyes to hers.

"What? Open it. No thanks. They probably have it rigged to blow anyone up who tries. The locks on it are coded; I already know that."

Liam smiled, a smug look on his face. "We have a secret weapon of our own."

"Really. What's that?"

He smirked as he replied, "Dari."

She almost choked on her laugh. "You're kidding! What is the puca going to do?"

Chapter Eight

At that moment, Dari sat down in his corporeal form to enjoy a cup of tea and a biscuit or two in the galley. Without a cabin of his own, he grabbed his refreshments when and where he could. He and Liam had rushed to get the cargo situated after that monstrosity of a box came on board. Despite his millennia of age, he still looked like a fourteen-year-old youth in this form. He could have used a little more muscle, but between them, they'd rearranged everything, and the new crate settled.

While he had a couple of older and bigger human forms he could use, one was too old, and the other was… Well, the other was a duplicate of Brendan O'Ceagan, which he'd promised Captain Grania he wouldn't use without permission around them. He'd gained that one quite by accident, with no intent of injuring the young navigator. A simple little accident, really, but it had been enough for Dari to absorb some of the lad's DNA to gain the pattern. The difference was that Brendan would age as a human while he, the marvelous puca, would always retain the image of the youth.

He sipped the tea, heavily laced with sugar and cream, and savored the sweet drink. Over the centuries, he'd gained genuine pleasure in this simple ritual of the humans around him. Although he would admit that accompanying Sheilan for centuries has also led him to adopt the custom since she'd done it frequently among the people. He supposed that a b'ean sidhe had to do something when she wasn't busy predicting doom and gloom.

Generally speaking, Sheilan wasn't prone to any tricks or fooling around. Still, now and then, she could surprise him, as was the case with the prank on the pirates' ship when they'd teamed up to scare them enough to give Grania the opportunity to fire a cannon bolt that disabled their vessel. That had been great fun for the two of them but not at all in the b'ean sidhe's calling, so to speak. In fact, it could have been why Sheilan was summoned to face the High Council. Or it may have just been because she left Earth to pursue her family, the one she, as a b'ean sidhe, had been assigned to assist.

For whatever reason, he missed her companionship. When he learned the ship was going out again and heading to Earth, he figured it would be an excellent opportunity for more adventure and to see his acquaintances in Ireland again. While he could have used the soil to travel, he still wasn't confident it actually worked. Sheilan disappeared, presumably to Ireland, then to the Council, but she'd yet to return, so maybe she couldn't.

His ponderings were interrupted when Brendan breezed into the galley. "Hey, Dari. How is it goin' with Liam? Is he keepin' you busy?"

"That he is," Dari replied. "'Tis been exciting working down there. Have you seen that huge crate we brought on board?"

"No. Grania said it was pretty massive. Tell me about it."

He made tea while Dari told him the whole story of bringing it aboard.

"We nearly knocked out two cameras and bumped the emergency alarm while getting it into place. Mister Liam used some words I've never heard before. And I thought I knew them all." Dari chuckled and popped a biscuit in his mouth.

"He does know a wide range," Brendan agreed and sat across from him. "Tell me, Dari. Did you happen to notice Mister O'Toole hanging around the passenger cabins before we got to Enterprise?"

"Not hanging around, no. I did pop into the young girl's cabin for a couple of minutes to check on her, and... Well, that man was in there with her."

"Inside? Doin' what?" Brendan's eyes grew large as his lips thinned.

"Talkin' is all I saw. I just thought it curious that he'd be there, but he was telling her about Enterprise Station and how we'd be stopping there."

"Were you there when he left?" Brendan asked.

"No. Their chatter was borin' me, so I went on about me business."

They talked a little longer, then Dari put his dirty dishes in the cleaner and told Brendan his break was up, so he was going down to the hold. "Unless you need me to do somethin' for you," he added as he paused at the sliding door.

Brendan waved him on. "Not right now. Go on ahead. I think Nia's down there now."

As he passed the passenger cabins, Dari paused,

dematerialized to energy, and popped through the girl's door. Even seeing her in fractal form, he could tell she sat on the bed with her knees pulled up. Intermittent lines from an oblong object braced against them told him she was using her tablet. As she read, she muttered under her breath, but he couldn't make out the words. All he could deduce was that she was an angry young thing. Too bad. As he recalled, her face was quite attractive and would be much prettier if she smiled now and then. On a whim, he zipped into the lock mechanism to ensure it was secure and hadn't been tampered with like it had been earlier.

Leaving her, he checked in on the lads. A pair of fractal forms sat at the shape of a small table, moving objects around on it. It would seem they were playing some sort of game, but Dari couldn't distinguish which it might be. Nonetheless, they appeared settled and secured. Their instruments rested on the bed and in the far corner of the room. He'd hoped they might be practicing so he could hear a little music. Perhaps, they might do that later.

He left them, zapped to the cargo hold, then resumed his semi-corporeal state. He spotted Liam and Grania standing near the newly-arrived crate and headed that way.

"There you are," Liam said when he saw Dari approaching. "I was about to come looking for you, but I realized I might not be able to even see you."

"I was taking tea in the galley," Dari replied as he nodded at Grania. "Did ya' need somethin'?"

Liam glanced at the captain, and she dipped her head once

to confirm whatever it was he seemed to be asking. "We do need you to do a little task for us. Can you pop inside this crate to see what's in it?"

Surprised, Dari turned his gaze to the box marked *Confidential,* along with a *Do Not Unseal* notice. "You want me to look inside it? Is that not a secret?"

Grania cleared her throat. "It is, but it is on our ship. We have no idea if it is dangerous to us or not. While I want to respect the shipper's wishes, I believe it might be good to know if the object inside is safe to transport. If you take a peek, it wouldn't be like we're opening it."

Dari puzzled over that for a couple of moments. She had some fine points, and he could see the fractal forms in the box without disturbing it in any way. Would that be harmful to do? Not that he was concerned about right and wrong in any matter. It wasn't in his nature, but he had been trying not to disturb the humans or cause any trouble while on the ship. He trusted the captain, though, so he didn't feel she would ask him to do anything illegal.

"All right." He took a moment to shift back to his energy form and darted for the crate. Weirdly, he dove into something that felt like it was pushing against him, a heavy charge of energy surrounding him. If he'd had a physical form, he would have compared it to swimming in molasses, difficult to shove through. He persisted, and a few moments later, he burst into a hollow shell within the crate, or at least that was the look of the fractal energy within.

In the middle of the hollow, a big thing with thick lines of slow-moving energy rested with a layer of non-active substance surrounding it. Dari could make out the shape but not what the object was. The subtle movement within the form told him it was a living creature. The whole pattern resembled a giant insect. One he couldn't identify.

He returned to the cargo hold, delayed somewhat by the charged energy that drained him, and he floated to the metal floor. This wasn't an unrefined crystal draining his energy this time, but something that carried its own power source within the crate. He lay on the floor for about a minute as Grania and Liam kept their eyes on the container, not even noticing the little golden speck of dust that had fluttered to the floor.

Feeling his strength returning, Dari changed to the semi-corporal form again and startled the humans. Grania lurched backward a couple of steps, her hand gripping her chest as a little cry of surprise squeezed out. Less shocked by the shift, Liam stepped back and said, "Didn't see you exit. What did you see?"

"Not anything that looks like a weapon," he said. "Nor an explosive or anything like that. I don't actually know what it is that's in there, but 'tis a livin', breathin' thing in some kind of hibernation, I think. It's covered with a thick, gooey substance I didn't try to penetrate."

"Can you describe this life form?" Grania asked, recovered from her momentary surprise.

"I can tell you what the shape of it is, but as to any detail, no. As near as I can tell, there's an outer box of a hard substance with a protective layer under that, then the other layer directly over the being. It's almost the full size of the inside box, so maybe a half-hand smaller than the box. The being looked like half a bee shape, elongated body from the mid-waist down to the bottom, where the covering substance was so thick that I could discern a design. The top resembles a human female, and the head has some flickering protrusions off it."

"Well, that's never what I expected," Grania said, breaking the silence after Dari's description. While it lacked detail, he'd given a good idea of some sort of creature within the crate. No wonder they didn't want it opened. But how would it help the people in Desolation? "You did a fine job, Dari. Thank you. You're looking a little transparent. Do you need to refresh?"

Dari eyed the container of soil hanging on her neck. As he recalled, Liam and the other O'Ceagan lads wore them also. "T'would be nice if you'd put a drop or two of water in that vial of dirt you're carrying and allow me to nap for a while. I'm sure it would be enough to refresh my energy."

"Of course," she answered. She lifted it from her neck and twisted off the cap as Liam dribbled a few drops of water from a bottle on the desk into it.

Changing to the speck of gold light again, Dari darted into the vial. Grania held it briefly before she set it on Liam's control console. "I'll just leave this here until he's recovered. Seems to me it'd be wise for him to carry a bit of the dirt around with him also."

Nodding, Liam said, "If we have a break before we get to the jump gate, I'm going to check the engines one more time, then take a little nap."

"Sounds sensible. After dinner tonight, it'll be another three hours before we reach the gate. Hope this one goes without any problems." Grania put a reassuring hand on his shoulder, squeezing it before she started up the stairs to the bridge.

Chapter Nine

To celebrate the journey, Grania invited their guests to join them for dinner in the galley. Usually, it was a first-day tradition, but this trip hadn't followed the typical pattern. She asked Ethan and Conan if they might play a few songs for the occasion, and they'd agreed.

Now they were underway again, she'd allowed Orla a free run of the ship's second deck. The girl had made a trip to the galley earlier to get a snack and a drink, although she had a food unit in her cabin. But it provided the opportunity for her to meet with Conan and socialize for a bit. At least, that was how Rory described it, as he'd seen them in the galley when he went down to get coffee.

"Good," Grania said. "Maybe she'll calm down some."

"What exactly is her problem?" Brendan asked, turning his seat to face her.

Grania tried to explain why the girl was so distraught and watched her youngest brother's eyes widen.

"No wonder she's miffed," he said with indignation. "I'd be upset if Da did that to me. I don't imagine her betrothed is any happier about it."

A brief smile touched her mouth. "You're likely right about that, Brendan. 'Tis not a common custom anymore, but once there was a time when most marriages were arranged. The father's job was to find a good match for his daughter, sometimes to the benefit of the family. Often the man didn't have any choice either."

She felt a jiggle at her neck as the vial wiggled. She'd retrieved it from Liam's desk once they'd gotten underway. When she opened it, the spark that was Dari sped from it, shifting to his young lad form as he touched the floor.

"T'was worse for the lords and ladies, even the royalty of the land. Their fathers arranged marriages for political reasons and for wealth. I saw it happen numerous times." Dari brushed at his shirt.

"So you can hear us talking while you're in the vial," Grania said. She'd have to remember that.

"Only when I'm awake. When I'm recharging, it's like a light being turned off."

"I see. But back to the conversation, it's not common to see arranged marriages happen now, Bren. And to be shipped off to another planet has got to be frightening for the girl. Although it doesn't seem like fear is driving her anger. More like misplaced romantic emotions toward a lad back on Erinnua."

"She should meet Brendan then," Dari said, winking at him as he said it. "He's clearly the most handsome lad on this ship. All the girls flock when I use his... He gulped at the expression of shock on Brendan's face. "Not that I've done it often, just once or twice."

His gaze shifted to Grania, who looked just as appalled.

"But I do not pretend to be you, and it never leads to anything."

Abruptly, Brendan laughed. "That's famous, Dari!"

Grania smiled, then it vanished as a thought came to her. "Dari, we're having a little dinner social this evening, and I'm wondering if you might be persuaded to cover the bridge for Brendan."

"Cover? You mean watch? But I do not know anythin' about it."

"You don't need to. Mister O'Toole will be overseeing the bridge, but I'd like someone to watch him. If Brendan—in this case, you—stays on the bridge, he won't be likely to do anything he shouldn't and will properly man the bridge. I expect he'll be annoyed that he wasn't invited to the dinner."

"I can see that," Dari said, a slight frown on his face. "I'm a tad miffed meself."

"Did you want to come? You don't really eat, do you?"

"It's not that I cannot. In my human form, I can use food the same as you can."

"I see. In that case, would *you* like to come to the dinner?" Grania smiled.

"Tell you what," Brendan spoke up. "How about I stay on the bridge, and Dari takes my place there?"

Grania shot a look at him. "Problem is, he doesn't sound like you, Bren."

"Well, he has my voice."

"He has the tone, the deep resonance of it, but he doesn't speak like you. No, he wouldn't fool anyone at the table who knows you." Grania appraised Dari's farm boy appearance and innocence and thought he might be all right. However, explaining him as part of the crew would be tricky. Mind settled, she said, "But he could come as this young lad from the past. I have a hunch."

"Come as I am?" Dari asked, his eyes roving down his peasant clothes, and an uncomfortable look settled on his face. "Do you have any other clothes that might fit me?"

"He's about the same size as Nanci, don't you think?"

"You could be right," Rory spoke up. "Her uniforms are still in her quarters, I think."

"Check on it, Rory. Are you sure you don't mind missing the dinner, Brendan?" Grania asked.

"Well, I might regret the singin' if the lads do it, but I won't be missin' the drama at the dinner table, so long as you save me some of the food." He grinned, pushing a lock of dark brown hair back from his forehead.

"Of course," Grania agreed. "And you can listen in if there's music. Even O'Toole can hear it if you open the feed to the bridge."

"Why are you wantin' O'Toole watched?" Rory asked as he removed his earpieces and rose to fetch one of the uniforms.

"After he deserted the bridge while we had our meeting, do you think I should trust him?"

"I have my suspicions also," Brendan added. "He's snoopin' around the ship. And I think he's the one who opened the girl's cabin when we docked at Enterprise."

"Why do you think that?" Grania asked. She had the same

thoughts but no proof. Did Brendan know something?

"Well, who else would have?" He spun his chair around, glancing at the navigation board before circling back to face her. 'Only the crew has the code to the room. None of us—" He indicated the three O'Ceagans on the bridge, "—nor Liam would have done it. He's the only other person with the code."

"Why would he do it?" Rory asked, still standing at the door.

"That is the question, isn't it?" Grania answered, running her hand across her chin as she thought. "He's a friend of Granda's, but I wonder how well he knows him. The man has been acting like he's spying on us since he came on board. And he's a surly duke."

"That he is," Brendan agreed. "He snapped at me while you two were off looking for the girl. Told me to redo my calculations 'cause they were wrong. Like he would know."

Grania frowned, chewing on her lower lip. Something wasn't right about that man. She wanted him off her ship. Just great. One more reduction in her crew if she sent him packing. She'd have to try to fill the positions when they got to Earth or maybe even Pelanan.

* * * * *

All crew members, except Branden and O'Toole, assembled in the galley shortly before their guests arrived. Liam was last in as he'd lingered to doublecheck the new engine.

"How is it?" Grania asked when he hurried in.

"Holding steady so far. I still don't trust that it isn't reporting back information about us somehow." Liam took his seat at the table.

When reconfigured for a full meeting or dinner, the table could seat up to twelve people. Although it crowded the galley, leaving barely enough room to walk around the chairs, it made for a cozy get-together.

Rory showed Dari to his place at the table. The puca looked official in Nanci's tunic and trousers. They fit reasonably well, although a little bit loose on him.

"I'm going to introduce you as Liam's apprentice," Grania told him. "They won't have seen you before, so it won't sound suspicious. Just don't say anything about the engines or the job, Dari."

With his hair neatly combed back, Dari appeared older and pretty good-looking. On a whim, Grania seated him next to where Orla Hennessey would be placed. She turned to Rory. "Go bring our guests to the table. I think we're ready to begin this evening."

As he left, she checked the auto-chef to ensure the main course would be ready on time, then ordered eight servings of octopus cocktails, a dish that used native Cardyff fish to simulate the taste of octopus in a tomato sauce with a touch of chili. Along with it, she poured a non-alcoholic wine in deference to their underage passenger.

The musicians arrived, bearing their instruments, two each, and set them in the rear corner of the galley, which was pretty much the only place they fit.

"I hope you have enough room there," Grania said as they pulled them out of the cases. "This isn't the grandest room in the world, but it is about the biggest one you'll find on the ship unless you count the hold."

Ethan flashed a grin at her. "It'll be fine, Captain. We have played in smaller spaces, don't you know? Some of them pub stages aren't bigger than an outdoor privy."

His brother nodded in agreement and, pulling out his guitar, began to tune it.

With their dark hair and slightly darker complexion from their Welsh blood, the boys were both handsome lads. The rhythm of their speech varied from that of Erinnua natives, and they tended to roll the r sound out into a purr. Still, their speaking voices carried a rich warmness that would probably translate well with their singing.

While they set up, Grania looked around for Rory. Was there trouble with Orla? Perhaps she wouldn't come. Then Rory ushered her into the room, and Grania raised her eyebrows in surprise and smiled her approval. Orla had dressed up for the evening. Her green dress complimented her skin, and her trim figure lent an impression of maturity that the girl lacked. She'd pulled her hair into a bun at the base of her neck with two locks curled on each side of her face.

In a frozen moment, the two musicians stopped to gaze at her in approval before they resumed setting up. When Grania indicated that Orla should sit beside Dari, Rory escorted her to the seat. Dari looked a bit uneasy, but then he broke out a toothy smile, which led to Orla blushing. While Grania might not have the faintest idea what was in the girl's head, she did seem to fancy Dari's looks.

Once everyone was seated, Grania lifted her glass to her guests. "Welcome on board the Mo Chroidhe. We are pleased to share this journey with you. I apologize for both the late greeting and the detour to Enterprise. We had unexpected and urgent business there but are back on course for Pelanan. We will be approaching the wormhole at E2 Gate in about three hours. Once we enter it, you can expect a full night's sleep in your pod as we will travel for almost ten hours before emerging near Pelanan station. From there, we have a shorter jump to Einstein Gate, which is a few hours from Zabrowski Station in Earth's orbit. We will do our best to make this trip pleasant for you. Now, I wish an enjoyable and safe voyage to all." She sipped the drink and sat at the head where the auto-chef began kicking out cocktails for everybody. She passed them around the table, each family member passing them on to their guests first.

While they did that, Grania introduced each crew member, including Dari Capall as an apprentice with Liam. Dari looked up, startled at the last name she'd assigned him, but it fit the puca well.

While the cocktail was received with mixed reactions, the girl not eating even a bite, the next course proved a hit as potato leek soup was passed around next.

"If I might inquire, what is taking you two lads to Earth?" Grania addressed Ethan and Conan.

Ethan set his spoon down, wiped his mouth politely, and

spoke enthusiastically. "Well, we won a competition to represent all Cardyff at a great music festival in Wales. 'Twill be the first time our world be sending an entry, so it be truly an honor for us ta go. We're also going ta be doing a three-month tour of the country, playing at many pubs, fairs, and even a castle or two. We be very excited."

His brother piped in. "We was up against two hundred other groups, duos, and solo singers, so we think we might do well. It be very excitin'."

"I imagine it is," Grania replied, lifting her glass to them again. "We are honored that you will be playing a few tunes for us."

"Our pleasure," Ethan lifted his glass back to her. "I think or hope that we be taking this ship when we return home."

"Well, we will look forward to that," Grania agreed.

The next course of shepherd's pie also proved a popular choice, with all of them digging into it. After that, the music started with the boys singing a lively Welsh folk song that no one understood except the singers. Grania tagged Brendan, so he could key in the audio from the galley.

They sat and listened, appreciating the talent and quality of the music even if they didn't understand the words. Grania noticed that Dari and Orla had gotten into a conversation. The girl leaned her head close to him, her words coming fast and with intensity, then she would pause and wait for his response. It seemed the two of them had found some common ground, and she doubted that Bren would have done better chatting with her.

Following the music, Grania served a final round of drinks with a pastry dessert, then sent their guests back to their cabins to prepare for the coming jump. Orla seemed hesitant to part from Dari, so she suggested he might walk her back to her cabin. She hoped she hadn't created another problem by pairing Orla up with the puca.

As Brendan and O'Toole, who left grumbling about not being permitted to see the lads perform live, went down to the galley, Grania checked everything on the bridge station to be sure nothing had been changed. While nothing seemed amiss, she was sure her messages had been opened, although she'd left nothing important in the file to be found. She'd moved the secret and encoded messages to a separate hidden file.

O'Toole's actions perplexed her more and more. She didn't understand what he was after. If this was just a final trip to Earth and back, why was he snooping around, doing things he shouldn't, and generally being annoying? Once they got to the station at Pelanan, she would call her granda and ask him a few questions about his "old friend."

She tagged Liam to ask if Dari was in engineering. He said he hadn't seen him. "Well, if he shows up there, tell him I'd like to talk to him." She wanted to know what he and the Hennessey girl talked about and if he might have made some headway with her. While Orla had utterly ignored everyone else at the table, barely saying more than two words to Grania or her brothers, she'd seemed quite taken and chatty with Dari. Could the puca be so much of a charmer that he could tame the little tiger?

Chapter Ten

Grania woke from her jump pod, eyes and ears alert to anything amiss. *Thanks be,* she thought as she sat up in her cabin to a calm situation. No lights blinking or alarms sounding. She got up and checked her link to the bridge computer to see exactly where they were. They'd just cleared the E2 Exit Gate and had a few hours before Pelanan Station.

Instructing the computer to wake the crew, she dashed into the accommodation for a quick shower, then headed to the galley to grab a cup of coffee before going to the bridge. By the time she arrived, the ship had passed the gate's small station and was on its way to its destination. Messages came in at the communications console, but Rory would be on deck soon to deal with that. She wanted to check power readings, then she heard Liam's voice.

"Morning, Captain. We're looking good down here. The new engine is smooth as Irish whiskey, and the old one isn't so bad either. No strange readings during the trip."

"Great. Looking good on this end, also. The ship's autopilot just made the adjustment for Pelanan. It looks like calm space ahead, but Rory hasn't reviewed any updates from the station yet." The door slid open, and Rory hurried in with a cinnamon bun and a coffee in his hands. "He'll be starting on it shortly. We'll let you know if there's anything to be concerned about. Did Dari show up?"

"He did, right before the lockdown for the gate. There wasn't time for him to see you. He manned the station while we jumped. Do you want to see him now?"

"Not this second, but send him up in about an hour. Tell him to grab a tea and a biscuit if he'd like and to meet me at my cabin." Grania wanted a private conversation with Dari, not one where anyone could overhear.

When Brendan had first mentioned that Dari might be onboard, she'd had reservations about the sidhe hitching a ride. Yet he was proving useful, although she acknowledged he was a wild card. While he was playing nice now, he could turn on a dime. Sheilan had advised her of his chaotic nature. Still, she hoped they could keep him on their side.

"So, what do we have?" she asked as she turned to Rory. He'd been running through messages as quickly as possible. "Not anything to worry about. The usual advisories from the station. Wait, there's something. A magnetic storm's ahead, and Pelanan Station suggests an alternate route."

"Send the information to Brendan, so he can make adjustments. Where is he, anyway?"

Rory shrugged. "Overslept?"

"Who oversleeps when the ship wakes them?" Grania asked.

After another few minutes, she began to be worried about him not arriving yet. Typically, he was in about the same time she was. "You have the com, Rory. I'm going to look for Bren."

Within a few minutes, she stepped onto the mid-floor, where most cabins were located, and headed toward Brendan's quarters. The door was locked, and she could hear the computer voice repeating a wake-up call over and over.

Overriding the lock on the door, she shoved into the cabin and hesitated a moment as her eyes darted to the jump pod.

Brendan sat on the edge of the bed, still wearing his sleep suit, and his head dropped forward as he rubbed a hand across the back. As he pulled it away, Grania saw the blood on his hand.

"Brendan. What happened?" she hurried to him, her eyes squinting slightly as she got closer. The pod lid wasn't fully raised, and it appeared he might have hit his head on it.

He brought his eyes up, a look of confusion in them. "My fault. I tried gettin' up before the lid was fully raised and caught the edge on my head. Knocked me back for a bit." He focused on her. "Just give me a few more minutes, and I'll be okay."

In response, she sat beside him and turned his head to get a look. Pushing his thick hair aside, she could just make out a gash of about two inches, bleeding a fair amount. "Stay put. I'll get a washcloth and the med kit."

She hurried into the accommodation, wet a cloth with warm water, then grabbed the kit. She didn't think it was serious, but it could be a concussion if it knocked him out for even a few minutes.

She wiped the wound carefully, then pulled out the pinpoint laser and used it to seal the injury so it wouldn't continue to bleed. Brendan winced; she could feel him pulling away. "Just a minute now, Bren. This will stop the bleeding. How long were you out?"

"I don't know. A couple of minutes, maybe longer. I wasn't looking at the time." His words slurred a bit.

"Okay, I'm going to treat this as a possible concussion." She broke open a preloaded cartridge, stuck it in the med-gun, and injected it into his arm. The medicine would prevent any clotting caused by the damage and help reduce swelling.

Going to his auto-chef, she ordered ice and wrapped the washcloth around the dozen cubes the machine produced.

"Okay, boy-o, lie back down and put this against the wound. Don't worry about coming to the bridge. You could be concussed, so don't try to get to your feet yet."

As Brendan obeyed her orders, she tagged Liam again. "Bren's had a hard head bump. Send Dari to his cabin now."

"Dari?" Bren questioned, a frown on his face. "What's he gonna do?"

"Stay with you," she answered. "I need to get back to the bridge, but he'll be here if you need anything."

A few moments later, Dari knocked on the door, then came in. Grania explained what she wanted him to do. "Mostly, just keep an eye on him, talk to him a bit, and call me if he seems less coherent or is in any pain. Oh, and change the ice in that washcloth in about thirty mites." In a lower voice, she added, "Don't let him get up and about."

She looked again at the partially-raised lid of the jump pod and wondered why it hadn't completed the lift.

Back on the bridge, Grania took over navigation and began to make the recommended adjustments to their course as she told Rory what had happened.

"Do you think the unit malfunctioned?" he asked.

"I think it's possible. The lid should have risen completely. Half-asleep, Bren didn't notice it. When I get these changes in, I'm going to check the completed work order to see if anything was done to the jump pods other than the two that needed repairs." She double-checked her calculations, made another adjustment, and pressed enter, then watched as the navigation map displayed the altered route in blue. It took her twice as long as Brendan could have done it, but the changes looked good.

Satisfied with the result, she set the auto-pilot before returning to her station. "Where's O'Toole?"

"Taking his time, I reckon. He's not rushed to the bridge once since he's been on board. Guess he doesn't see a need for it." Rory flipped a switch and got to his feet. "I'm going for more coffee. Want some?"

"I'll go after you come back. Knock on O'Toole's door while you're there." Her mouth turned up in a partial smile as her brother waved a hand of acknowledgment and stepped through the door. Coffee, of all things. Typically, she'd be having tea. The Vilnius effect—he'd gotten them all hooked on the more potent beverage. Her smile faded as she thought about her man. Was there a future for them? Their careers weren't compatible; they had completely different lifestyles. It seemed foolish to even contemplate it.

Grania called up the work order and results, a lengthy list. As she ran through it, she noticed it was divided by sections, with the second deck cabins listed in a group. She noted that all the cabin door locks and jump pods were checked and certified. Still, nothing irregular was recorded except the repairs on the one in the mid-deck cabin and the one that had been her mother's.

O'Toole arrived with a grumble. "Me back is givin' me fits. That was a bloody long jump to be lyin' in one position. I was just doin' some stretches to get the kinks out when your fella told me to get to the bridge, so what's the emergency?"

Grania straightened her shoulders and peered at him. Younger than Granda, the man looked in good physical condition, although he carried a tire of beer fat around his middle. Ah, but he griped about everything. "No emergency. We're just shorthanded. Brendan had a small accident and is resting, so we could use another hand on the bridge. You can take the nav station. It's pre-programmed and on auto-pilot, so you only have to keep watch to ensure it doesn't flip off the app."

"It has an alarm, doesn't it?" he grumbled as he took over the station. Under his breath, Grania heard him mutter, "…leaves…alone…but can't…herself."

She didn't have to guess what he was complaining about. She sat up, leaning a bit forward. "Mister O'Toole, you may be a friend of my granda, and you are here at his request, but I can tell you Paddy O'Ceagan would not tolerate a freeloader, and neither do I. Your agreement was to work as the second officer.

When I assign you a job, I expect you to do it to the best of your ability without grumbling or backtalk."

O'Toole's head had whipped around when she started speaking, and now his eyes narrowed with a glare of anger. "Paddy said you were a smart girl, but I think he meant smart-arsed. You run this ship like 'tis an excursion boat with tea parties and cakes. You'd crumble under a real emergency."

That was it. The last fecking straw. She held her temper in check, but her voice was like ice as she responded. "Since this is such an inconvenience for you, it will be my pleasure to relieve you of the problem at Pelanan station. You will remove yourself and your things from my ship. You're dismissed."

"Wait a minute, missy. The agreement was a round-trip voyage to Earth."

"And the agreement was that you would work for the passage. If you want to go to Earth, book another ship at Pelanan. I said, 'You're dismissed.'" Her chest tightened with the anger growing in it as O'Toole rose to his feet and shot a hated-filled look at her.

"Paddy will hear about this." He stomped off the bridge like a disciplined child.

He was right. Granda would hear about it–from her.

Rory returned as O'Toole cleared the door and glanced back at the retreating form. "What's with him?"

"I fired him." Nerves carried her down the few steps to the lower bridge level. Shaking with pent-up emotion, she *needed* that coffee now.

* * * * *.

Several hours later, they'd settled into their course, and communications from the gate station had quieted. Hunger-driven, Rory went down to the galley for a sandwich. When he approached, he heard the lilting melody of an Irish tune growing. It sounded like the lads from Cardiff had started a practice session there, a prospect he approved. So, he wasn't surprised to see Ethan and Conan jamming in the corner but was taken aback to find Orla in the room as well. She sat near them, smiling and clapping along with the music.

When she saw Rory, her smile vanished, replaced with a scowl. Evidently, she reserved her animosity for the crew. Then again, he did haul her aboard like a sack of potatoes.

The musicians were more welcoming, pausing in their playing to greet him with cheery expressions. "Ho, Rory. Things must be good up top if you be down here. We be learning this Irish tune for the young girl," Conan said, which was the longest remark Rory had heard out of him.

"Everything is good." He crossed to the auto-chef to order a hot ham and cheese sandwich and an iced energy drink. "Just getting my lunch. Carry on with the music."

Ethan waved a hand, then dropped it to the strings of his guitar while Conan lifted his violin to his chin again. As the lively tune filled the galley, Rory watched, aware of Orla's lingering hostility. For a few beats, he considered taking his lunch back to the bridge but decided against it. He wasn't going to be intimidated away from a leisurely lunch by a disgruntled teenage girl.

After another steely glare, Orla turner her back to him to watch the duo play. He'd thought she was melting a little when she'd gotten along so well with Dari, but apparently not. Just to be ornery, he ate slower than usual, stretching his break out through five more tunes.

When he'd done, he put his waste in the recycler, then ordered another sandwich and drink to take to Grania. Orla turned to watch him, letting out an exaggerated sigh as she shrugged her shoulders.

When he left the galley, he saw O'Toole coming up the corridor. Upon spotting Rory, the man deliberately turned around to backtrack from him. Midway up the steps, Rory glanced down to see O'Toole turn back and resume his course to the galley.

Apparently, he was in the same doghouse as Grania, although he'd done nothing to the man. For what it was worth, he agreed with his sister. O'Toole hadn't been much help on this trip, not even when he'd covered the bridge. Dari would have done a better job, and the puca knew nothing about spaceships.

This extra business with the detour to pick up the special cargo and hauling it all the way to the Outer Rim had his sister keyed up, even though she handled it well. But she didn't need the added stress of a snarly old spacer. He'd seen the worry on her face and wondered if there was more causing it. Then this thing with Brendan just added to it. Putting on a smile, he strode onto the bridge, his face splitting into a huge grin to see

Bren back at his station.

"Hey, how are you feeling?" he asked, detouring to see his brother.

"A little off, but not bad. I'm tough, you know." He found a smile, but he still looked a little pale.

"Yeah. Don't overdo it, though." Rory squeezed his shoulder, then hurried up to the captain's station.

"You know I had to come down to bring this old girl into the dock. I couldn't risk Grania denting her or the station."

A snort came from his sister. "And it's grateful I am. I haven't had to dock a ship in a couple of years, and my *old* brain may not remember how to do it."

He delivered the sandwich to Grania, who looked surprised. "Thanks for this, Rory. I was getting a bit hungry. Everything okay below?"

"It is. The lads are practicin' in the galley, and Orla is in there listenin' and singin' along."

"Are you serious? The girl is actually having a good time." Grania's eyes widened, her disbelief evident.

"Oh, and O'Toole was going to the galley when I started upstairs."

"Turn on the feed from there, Rory. I want to know what's going on," Grania ordered. She didn't like the old man hanging around the young people.

Rory hurried to comply and switched on the camera and mic for the room, bringing the picture up on the main screen. Music poured onto the bridge, a flow of sound filling the hollow spaces as Rory quickly adjusted the level to something more reasonable. No need to deafen everyone.

Everything looked okay, he thought. Orla still sat with Ethan and Conan while in the back of the room, O'Toole sat eating a hornack steak with spuds piled around it on the plate.

A growl emanated from Grania as she watched. "I'm cutting him off."

When she turned to her console, Rory figured she was going to change any options the spacer held to the less expensive items in the supplies, like sandwiches and soup. Steak of any kind was a rarity, but a hornack even more so. No matter, though. The damage was done, and they'd be docking at Pelanan Station in less than three hours.

Chapter Eleven

After they'd docked at Pelanan, Grania contacted her granda to tell him what had happened with O'Toole, and she'd fired him. While Granda expressed surprise the man had been so ornery, he agreed that she didn't have to put up with his shenanigans. "Well, you're going to hear an earful from him," she concluded.

"That I will, I'm sure. But I know you, and he can't tell me anything that will change my opinion of you. Truth to tell, I was surprised when he contacted me about hitching a ride to Earth on the Mo Chroidhe. I told him that he'd have to work for it. He'd been a good man when he worked for me about twenty-five years ago, but people can change."

"Thanks for understandin', Granda. I need to get going. I have some things to do before we head out again. It turns out we're going on a much longer trip than we'd expected." Grania bit her lip, thinking she probably shouldn't have said that, but she didn't want her family to worry when they didn't return as scheduled.

"Why is that, girl?"

After a moment, while she contemplated the safest reply, she said, "I accepted a government shipment that will take several more days to deliver. I can't tell you much about it, except the job pays very well."

A few moments of silence followed, then he replied, "Ah, I guess if it's worth a lot of credits, then it's a good job. You be careful, though. Sometimes these well-paying deliveries can carry some risk."

Wasn't that the truth? She thought about the penalty if they didn't deliver it on time. But she only told her granda that she'd take care of herself, her brothers, and the ship.

She said nothing of Liam's plan to go to work for Uncle Colm. Maybe he'd said something to the rest of their family or not, but it was Liam's news to deliver.

When she ended the call, Rory indicated another one was waiting for her, and she switched to that message.

A warm-sounding male voice greeted her. "Welcome to Pelanan, Captain O'Ceagan. I believe you're expecting this call."

Expecting it? Could this be the agent that the Senator had referred to? Wasn't he supposed to board at Zabrowski? She hadn't thought he would call the ship. "I guess I am."

"You were told I would contact you here, weren't you?" The voice held a touch of amusement like he was enjoying her uncertainty. "I believe a certain high-ranking person informed you."

"Yes, of course. Now what?"

"We meet. Can you come to Buster's Coffee Bar in thirty mites?"

She hesitated. "Yes, I think I can. How do I find you?"

"I'll find you. See you in thirty." He ended the connection

before she could say any more. Talk about a cryptic conversation. She had no idea who he was or what he looked like. She would be easy to identify with her uniform on, though, so it was in his star sector.

The boys from Cardyff were already asking how much time they could have at the station. Grania told Rory to give them two hours, which was about the time it would take for Liam to unload the cargo for Pelanan and bring new crates onboard. Already, Rory had started looking for outbound shipments to Zabrowski, Andromeda, Galaxy, and Longhop stations. As she turned to leave the bridge, she turned back toward Rory and added, "Make sure the Hennessey girl doesn't get out of her cabin until we're undocked again. I'm not wantin' to chase her over Pelanan Station."

She hadn't had the opportunity to speak to Dari yet, but that would have to wait. Besides, he had his hands full helping Liam with the cargo. She stopped in her cabin to pick up a button recorder, looked up the location of Buster's Coffee Bar, then hurried out to get to the meeting in time.

Buster's was located eight stops down from the security station, a place Grania had been too familiar with after the ship's last visit here. The coffee place looked like a grab-and-go coffee stand, but at the back, a few tables encouraged customers to sit and sip. About a dozen people were in line to order or pick up their drinks and pastries, while another three tables were occupied.

She studied the men in the lines, picking out three who might be the agent, but none showed any interest in her.

Unsure if she should get in line to order or just wait, she stood a little to the side and gazed at the menu on display. From behind her, a warm, sexy voice spoke. "Captain O'Ceagan?"

She turned, and her brain froze for a few moments. The man addressing her was the classic tall, dark, and handsome variety, although handsome was an understatement. He smiled, perfect white teeth dazzling like pearls.

"Ye...yes. I'm Grania O'Ceagan."

Warm gray-green eyes twinkled at her unease, which annoyed her a little. On a scale of one to Vilnius, he ranked right up there alongside her man.

"Let's go to the table at the back," he nodded toward the leeward corner where no one sat near.

He caught her elbow with a light touch and urged her in that direction. The action made Grania nervous as uncertainty set in. So far, he'd not identified himself nor even mentioned the Senator's name. How did she know he was legit?

As she sat down, she leaned toward him and, in a low voice, said, "You have me at a disadvantage. You know who I am, but I don't know what to be callin' you."

That mouth of pearls flashed again. "Fair enough. My name is Theos Camber. I work for the PPG handling...delicate...situations."

Her eyebrows shot up at the phrasing. "Is that what you call it?"

"Obviously, the AUP has given you a sensitive item to ship, and it wouldn't do for them to know the PPG is interested in the contents, so yeah, that's what they consider it. You don't, by chance, happen to know what's in the crate, do you?"

Grania shook her head. She wasn't lying because Dari's description had been so vague she couldn't honestly say she knew what it was. "The description on the manifest said farming equipment with a total weight of 260 kilos. No other detail."

"Would you like a coffee?" he asked, rising to go to the counter where the line had diminished to two customers waiting.

"Tea, please. And a pastry if they have one with strawberries."

"Got it. I'll be right back."

As he left, she admired the retreating view. The man's physique resembled a marble statue she'd once seen, magnificent and hard. Given his profession, she guessed that a fit body would be required. Holy Mary, she'd thought Vilnius was fit until she'd seen Theos. She didn't think a stop-your-heart gorgeous man with a ripped body would be the ideal choice for an undercover agent. Wouldn't he attract too much attention? He certainly did as he stood in line. Grania noted several ladies slowing to gaze at him. On the other hand, only two men slowed to appreciate the view, so maybe it didn't matter.

He returned in a few mites with the coffee and a pair of pastries, one with chocolate and one with strawberries. He slid hers across the table and sat again.

She took a bite of the flaky treat, added a bit of sweetener to the tea, and had just taken a sip when he said, "Now, we talk a bit of business."

Swallowing hard, she almost choked, then croaked out, "You mean you want more than to buy me tea?"

His perfect lips curved into a smirk. "Oh, yes. I do."

She felt heat come to her cheeks and looked away. Somehow, the words sounded more suggestive than Camber could have intended. She drew in a deep breath, then turned her face, calm and serene, toward him. "Let's talk business. What exactly has the PPG assigned you to do that involves me and my ship?"

"I have a dual assignment, Captain. First, I want to come aboard your ship. Ideally, I could be part of your crew or a boarding passenger."

"Wait." She held up her hand with the cup in it. "You expect to travel with us all the way to the Outer Rim?"

"Absolutely. I can't do all of my job if I don't get to Desolation when the crate does."

"Then what when you get there?"

"That part is privileged information, and you are not on the list." He pursed his lips and shrugged a shoulder as if apologizing.

"Oh, so I just deliver the crate, and you take it from there. Is that it?" She wasn't sure if she felt relieved or insulted. He nodded. "And the second part?"

"That would be to protect you and your crew until the cargo is delivered. Which is why I need to be on your ship."

"Do I have any choice?" Grania hated being manipulated or coerced, but she had a distinct feeling she couldn't refuse.

"Mmm, not really. Would it be so terrible to have me on board?" That sexy voice purred, and a zing of desire danced up her spine.

"Ah, let me ask you a couple of questions, Mr. Camber." She felt proud of herself to even recall his last name.

"Call me Theos," he said quickly and took a provocative bite of the chocolate pastry.

"All right, Theos. Have you ever worked on a spaceship?"

"Uh, no."

Hell, she already had someone with no training on board. "Then, I guess—"

"But I do have some training in logistics, engineering, and hyperdrive mechanics. I was recruited for the PPG before I gained practical experience."

"I see." She paused as she considered her situation. She needed an engineer, but would a rookie be good enough to rely on for the long jumps to Desolation? But as a passenger, she would need a free cabin for him, and if she hired an engineer and a second officer, she wouldn't have one.

"I learn quickly," he added. "I won't be dead weight, Captain."

No, he probably wouldn't. But could she keep her decorum around him? She imagined him in the tight trousers and fitted crew tunics and wondered if she could keep her mind on business.

"All right, then. I happen to need an engineering trainee who can come up to speed by the time we reach Earth. My brother is a top-notch engineer; however, he plans to transfer to another ship. But you'd be learning the ropes from one of the best in the galaxy."

He nodded. "That would be Liam, then. I would be honored. Is it a deal?"

"One more question. Wasn't I supposed to meet you at Earth's station?"

A sly smile tweaked his lips. "Yes, that was the plan. But I was headed in the same direction as you, so I decided to introduce myself here instead."

"So, you could have come aboard at Enterprize?"

"Not really. I needed to depart on a different ship for security reasons."

Drawing a deep breath, she nodded, wondering how much he already knew about her and her crew. Enough to know her engineer's name. "I see. Okay, then. Report to the Mo Chroidhe within an hour. In the meantime, I'll log the crew change and let my communications officer know you're coming on board. If I'm not back to the ship by then, Rory will show you to your cabin."

"Excellent, my Captain. I will see you on board in an hour." He took another bite, then added through the pastry in his mouth, "Or maybe a couple of minutes longer while I eat this."

She laughed, finished her own refreshment, popped to her feet, and headed onto the main walkway. *What have I done? But I didn't have much choice. At least, this way, the man will be useful.* How convenient that she'd fired O'Toole. She paused to call Rory and fill him in on her new hire.

"Fated fairies, that was a quick hunt, Nia," he said.

"Yeah, it was. And I think Mr. Camber will work out well. Not a lot of experience, but he's smart and a fast learner."

"Well, he's got to be better than O'Toole." Rory laughed as he said it.

Somewhere in the depths of her mind, Grania began to wonder about O'Toole's sudden request to go on the ship and his actions that provoked her to fire him. Was there more to it than what met the eye?

Grania stopped at the Station Master's office to check for any anomalies ahead. Of course, he remembered her from the last trip. She and the ship had made enough news that anybody who'd been on the station knew who she was, even if she hadn't met them before.

"How's the wormhole?" she asked after their initial greetings.

"Stable as a rock," he answered.

"Rocks can move. In fact, they can create an avalanche, so that may not be the best analogy."

"Smart ass," he muttered. "Let's just say it's calm, no influences on it from the star, and no problems with any traffic through it. You should be fine."

His toothless smile looked a little shifty to Grania, but she couldn't help being nervous about this jump. Not that any of the others couldn't have a similar incident. Still, it was good to know that the way ahead was calm, with no indicators of anything that could affect them.

From there, she checked the boards for anyone looking for

work, like a replacement for O'Toole. While Theos Camber may manage to take over from Liam, he wasn't a good second. Truth was, Liam would be an excellent second, but he already had that offer, and with a chance of moving to captain, she couldn't fault him.

As she went by a café with storefront tables, she spotted Ethan and Conan standing at the side with their instruments out and performing for the folks who were eating. The guitar case lay open in front of them in the true busker style, and several people flipped credits in it. Enterprising lads. She hoped they didn't run afoul of the local security.

She made one more stop at a bakery to pick up a large almond cake, something she could set aside until they'd made it through the jump to celebrate their safe passage. On the way back to the ship, Rory contacted her. Vilnius was holding, and he could transfer the call to her mobi. She found a quiet corner and waited as Rory made the connection.

"Hello, my girl," he said as soon as she spoke. "I've been tracking your ship. I expected you in sooner. Anything wrong?"

"No, no, we're fine. We just had a detour to pick up some cargo. You've been tracking me?"

"I have. One of the perks of being station master."

"I'd call it misusing your position for personal gain."

"What?" He sounded surprised. "It's not a big deal. I'm just concerned you haven't arrived yet. I'm anxious to see you."

She softened. "Well, same here. I'm looking forward to

being with you, but you know we won't be long at Zabrowski."

"I thought you had a few days?" His voice rose a little.

She glanced down. "Well, that's been shortened. We'll be going on from there to deliver an urgent package on a deadline. I'll tell you about it when I see you."

"Okay. See you in about twelve hours then, right?"

"That's the plan. Vilnius? Would you happen to know anyone with experience on your station looking for work? I need a new second for this trip. Nanci bailed on us. She may or may not return, but I could use the help now."

"I'll check around for you and let you know when you get here. Can't wait to see you, my gorgeous girl. I miss you."

She returned the sentiments, then ended the call. Her heart fluttered with the thought of being with Vilnius for even a few hours. At the same time, she was feeling the hopelessness about it all. How long could they go on doing this "see you a couple of times a year" thing?

She saw the musicians go past, heading back to the ship, and she ran to catch up with them, her cake box tucked in a cloth bag hanging on her arm.

So her surprise would remain one, she left her package in her cabin's cooler before heading to the bridge. She found Rory on the com, talking to Liam. "That's it, Liam. Let me know when it's in and secured. We have about thirty mites to our scheduled departure." He grinned at Grania. "That's our last piece of cargo coming aboard, and we're mostly full for Zabrowski deliveries. I hope we'll be pickin' up a lot there, or we'll be headin' close to empty to the Rim. I've sent a board message ahead that we'll have space for the stations on the way."

"That's good thinking, Rory." She gave him credit, suddenly worried that Vilnius might see it and be on her about not telling him. But he wasn't her boss and had no say in what she did, so if he got out of sorts about it, tough. She'd deal with it when she got there. "Did our new man check in?"

"That he did." Rory swung to face her. "Quite a healthy-looking fellow and he seems nice. I showed him to his cabin and introduced him to Liam. He's down there now, helping to load."

"Is he? Nice to have someone new who wants to work." She took the steps to her station, then asked her other brother, "How are you doin', Bren?"

"Course is set for the gate, and all the equipment checks out." He glanced from his console and gave her a thumbs up.

"Good. I know you've got it all done, but I'm askin' how *you* are, little brother?"

"Oh. I'm fine. A bit sore and a slight headache, but nothin' to worry about." He smiled, eyes alert. He seemed normal, with no slurring in his words or anything else that might indicate he had a concussion. She would have preferred he'd gone to the station medic to get checked out, but he'd said no.

She ran through the information on her console—the course, speed, engine power, and the amount they could get if they raised the dorsal sail between here and the wormhole. All good. Her crew knew what they were doing. She tagged Liam. "Is Dari with ya?"

"Not at the moment. He was here until the new man arrived. Good choice, by the way. But Dari left for a break."

When she came up, she checked the galley and didn't see anyone there. So, where was the puca? She hoped he hadn't gone to the station. She didn't have time to find him before they departed.

"Page Dari to the bridge," she told Rory.

If he was still on the ship, he would hear it.

Chapter Twelve

Dari's corporeal form, looking chipper and attentive, sat in front of Grania's desk in her office. When the Mo Chroidhe had come out of the wormhole an hour earlier, she finally tracked the puca down. Since he'd not appeared before they made the jump, she feared they'd left him behind at Pelanan, but he'd simply gone into his energy form and found a resting place in a potted plant's dirt.

"Not as cozy as the soil we brought from our world," he told her as he explained his absence before the jump. "But once I realized we were underway, I hurried into the engine room to keep an eye on the readings as Mister Liam asked me to do."

She shook her head slowly. "I see, Dari, but you had me quite worried. When you do that, please let someone know so we're not thinking we lost you."

He looked contrite with his eyes lowered like a scolded child. "I did not mean to cause you to worry, Captain Grania. But I am a rather old spirit, and I can take care of meself. Even if you had left me on the station, I could have popped back into that bauble around your neck in a blink."

Grania rolled her eyes, her hand touching the vial of dirt. "I imagine you could have. But just do us the courtesy. But that wasn't why I wanted to speak with you. I noticed at dinner that you seemed to connect with Orla. She was talking to you quite a bit."

He nodded. "That she was."

"I'm hoping you can give me a little insight into the girl's thoughts and problems. I will have to take her to her new family in Galway, so I'm hoping I can make this easier for both of us." Grania shifted in her chair, leaning forward a little to form a sense of camaraderie with the puca. "Can you tell me anything?"

"Well, I dunno if anythin' I say will help, but let me think. She was tellin' me how unfair the whole arranged engagement thing was, that her parents never even asked her. Just told her it was what would be. Orla said she didn't know the fellow at all and was fearful of the whole prospect of going to another planet to live. I can see her point in that. I was nervous about comin' to Erinnua, and I am not even stuck there like she will be on Earth." Dari wrung his hands some as he talked.

"Why do you think she opened up to you? She's been nothing but rude and irritable with Rory and me. I suppose we represent her parents' authority."

"I think that is part of it. Orla sees you as her parents' agent. Now me, I look like a lad about her age, someone she can talk to. I think she believes I've been conscripted to work on the ship, and I said nothing to change that view. Do you not think that she had to open up to someone?" As his eyes opened wider, his eyebrows lifted into a questioning look. Somehow, he managed to look even younger than the age of that youthful lad.

"I agree," Grania said, trying to put herself into Orla's position. If that had happened to her, she would have been furious, acting out as much as the girl. Maybe even running away from home. That worried Grania. When she had the girl in tow from the ship to Earth, Orla would probably be looking for a way to escape her fate. Damn, this didn't make her feel good about the job she was contracted to do. While she had planned to have Rory take the girl, she decided she would have to do it. But now, she might need help.

"Dari, I know you want to get to Ireland while we're in Earth's orbit. Would you consider going down to the planet with us and helping me escort Orla to Galway? Once we hand her over, you have time for your visits."

"You want me to help? Of course, I will." He bounced forward in his chair, excitement evident on his face.

"Excellent. Thank you. Now you can go back to help Liam. I'll talk to you when we're ready to take the shuttle to Earth."

Grania's slight smile as he left faded once he was out of the room. She feared Orla Hennessey wasn't going to be very cooperative as they moved her to Ireland. She certainly couldn't put any restraints on her, so it would be a matter of hanging on to her arm and persuading her to go along.

Getting Dari onto Earth wasn't a problem since no one would be checking papers or traveling visas from the ship to Earth, only on the return trip. And for that... well, Dari had mentioned the easiest way.

* * * * *

Several hours later, the ship settled into her berth at Zabrowski Station. From the starboard window, a beautiful view of Earth filled their view. Grania stopped to gaze at it, appreciating the planet's beauty. While Erinnua was similar, it wasn't the same. For starters, it was a smaller world with fewer oceans but many unexplored and unsettled land masses. No native population had lived on her planet, but abundant wildlife wandered over the many hills, forests, and canyons. Earth teemed with humanity, maybe hundreds of thousands more than animals. And yet, from space, it looked so serene and inviting.

As they shut the ship down except for life support, a call came through from the station master. Rory transferred it to her.

"Welcome back to Zabrowski, Captain O'Ceagan," the deep, familiar voice said.

"Glad to be here, Station Master Majeck. I'll be stopping by your office in about forty mites." They kept the formalities.

"Excellent. I look forward to it. You have 68 hours scheduled for your berth. Is that correct?"

"It is. Thanks." Usually, the station would just ask Rory, but this was Vilnius wanting to hear her voice. She smiled, happy to listen to him again.

They signed off, and she made a brush-off wave of her hand toward Rory, who grinned broadly at her.

"That was so cute," he teased.

"Aw, stow it, Rory. He was simply checking in."

"Yeah, doing the job he has an assistant to do and wanting to talk to the captain." Rory turned back to his console. She knew he was sorting through the messages and already looking for cargo to bring on board.

Brendan chuckled at their banter. "He's anxious to see ya', Nia. I can tell."

"Oh, can you? And what makes you an expert on it, Bren?" She dismissed his remark and called Liam. "Status, Liam?"

He ran through the usual details, reporting no problems with the engines. The new one operated very well, and the old one kept up as best it could. He, Dari, and Theos were starting to pull the cargo to be unloaded, which would take them quite a while. But it was all looking good.

"Sounds fine," she said. "I'm going off the ship in about thirty mites. You have the com while I'm gone."

Silence at the other end for several long seconds, and then Liam replied, "Copy that."

She started to end it, then made up her mind. "When I come back, let's chat, Liam."

He acknowledged, ending the communication.

She turned to her bridge crew and said, "Okay, lads. A fine job gettin' here. Dinner and drinks on me at Murphy's Pub in two hours. Tell the others. Make sure—"

"The Hennessy girl is locked in her cabin," Rory finished.

She retreated to her cabin to record the docking notes, transfer some credits, and finish any other business attached to releasing the cargo at this stop. Then, she paused to freshen up before meeting Vilnius.

Following the spoke of the docking arm to the station's central hub, Grania turned to the left and made her way to the Station Master's office. She'd been here often enough in the nine years she'd been on the ship to find it in her sleep.

She'd barely gotten in the door before Vilnius swept her into his arms, swung her around, and kissed her in front of everyone in his office. Luckily, that turned out only to be a clerk who worked for him and two other ship captains, one of whom had been deserted so her man could execute the enthusiastic welcome.

"Better get back to your customers, Station Master," Grania said, her face burning a tad with embarrassment. While she appreciated his exuberance, she thought it unseemly for his position.

Not that it bothered Vilnius much. He grinned, offered an excuse to the other captains, and returned to his desk. Grania took a seat at the front to wait for him to be free. Like her, the others checked in to inquire about conditions that might affect their travel or ask about the shuttles to Earth. Most of the information was readily available from their ship's communications systems. Still, the personal visit was a courtesy and a chance to visit with each official. You never knew when you might need one's help with a problem or repair.

While Vilnius chatted with the man he'd dashed away from, Grania watched him, her heart melting at the sight. With broad shoulders and long legs, he was a towering presence on the station, easily spotted in a crowd. His blue eyes flashed with energy as he spoke. She thought he was the most handsome man she'd ever seen when she first met him. The fact that she was a teenager and hadn't seen many good-looking guys had nothing to do with that opinion. She felt the same way now.

After the second captain was dispatched, Vilnius led her into his private office, not the public one. Closing the door, he reached for her again and pulled her tight to his chest. He cupped her face in his hands and pressed his lips to hers, the kiss more demanding than the greeting one. Here, they were alone.

Their tongues met and danced with each other, teasing, tempting, and daring. Within Grania, a fire ignited, warming her body with overwhelming desire. It took all her will to pull away. This was not the place for such passion. "I've missed you," she said, her voice a hoarse whisper.

"Me, too." His hand caressed her cheek, pushing back a tendril of her russet hair. "It's been too long."

She pressed two fingers to his lips, rubbing the lower one as she gazed at him. "We've been apart much longer, love. But I've never wanted to be with you so much as these past few months."

"I think about you every day." He continued to hold her, caressing her head, fingers sliding through her hair. He took a deep breath, reluctantly released her, then urged her to the plush armchair across from his desk. "Now, let's talk about your trip here. You said you're going farther than originally planned. What's happening?"

How much should I tell him? Grania considered that several times on the trip inbound from the wormhole. The mission was secret, but her plan to make the trip wasn't. She probably shouldn't tell him this was a government shipment, but this was Vilnius. Her lover, the keeper of her heart. And right now, the most frustrating part of her life.

Deciding on a partial truth, she said, "I was contacted by a government agency as I left Cardyff. They have an urgent shipment to go to the Outer Rim, and they offered a lot of credits to take it there."

"You're not serious?" His brow scrunched as alarm flashed in his eyes. "Grania, that's a really long trip. It takes three extended wormhole jumps to get there. Where on the Rim? Just to the station?"

"Pretty much." She didn't want to give him any details. "I'll get more information when I get there. But I just hand the cargo off to someone, and he takes care of it from there."

He nodded, but his lips told her he was not pleased. "It's not the safest place in the galaxy. You've never been that far out. It's not like the trade stations you usually visit. If you could compare it to anything, it would be like the early settlers to the planets having to deal with thieves, shysters, and quite a bit of lawlessness."

"Well, I won't be there long. In, drop the cargo, reload anything heading back, then depart. I figure we'll be docked for about four hours."

"I don't like it, but it's not my call, is it?" His mouth

clamped in a tight line while his eyes pleaded with her.

"No, I've made the deal. I have to go through with it."

"So it pays a lot?"

"It does. I just spent a small fortune getting the Mo Chroidhe repaired and upgraded. It will pay off the bills and leave us with a decent amount for our troubles. They're even paying our expenses. I couldn't turn it down, Vilnius." That part was true, even though the reason wasn't the lucrative deal.

"Promise me you'll keep in touch between each jump."

"That's going to be expensive," she objected. "We'll be fine. I'll send you a packet message when we arrive at the last station."

He groaned as if he were mortally wounded. "I guess it will have to do."

"So, when is the morning shuttle to London going down?"

"There's one at seven Earth time. Have business on the planet or just visiting?" He reached for a sheet with the shuttle schedules on it. "The next one will go at nine."

"I'll take three seats on the seven, and it's business, but none of yours."

He winced. "You wound me, love. Everything you do is important to me."

"Let me get my fiddle out." She mimicked pulling one out and drawing a bow across it.

He laughed. "Yeah, all right. You're your own woman, Grania. When do you want the return tickets?"

"Leave it open for now. And there will be only me on the return. I'm escorting a passenger down."

"Okay. Anything else I can do for you?"

She pressed her lips together in a seductive pout. "Plenty, but not here. I'm meeting my crew at the pub in an hour. Come meet us there."

"I'll do that. I probably better see if I have more customers and check on all the station functions before we close for the night. See you soon."

She kissed him once more, then slid out of the office ahead of him. The clerk, a bespectacled young woman, gave her a curious and not necessarily friendly look. No doubt, Vilnius hadn't told her anything about his fire-haired girlfriend.

Back on the concourse, she spotted Ethan lined up at the shuttle window to get a ticket. The boys were probably eager to get to Earth and their big plans, but the last evening shuttle had already departed.

She sashayed up next to him. "The next one will be in the morning, Ethan. I assume you're going to London."

He nodded. "Yes, Captain. Then from there to Wales."

"After you get your ticket, you and your brother can find several places for food and entertainment at the station," Grania said by way of suggestion. "You have a good evening. I may see you in the morning, but if not, it's been a pleasure having you on my ship. Good luck with the music."

He thanked her, and she moved down the concourse to the D arm, where the ship was docked. She figured she had just enough time to meet with Liam and change clothes before they went to dinner. Instead of entering the ship's front, she went to the cargo hold, where the trio was shifting shipping crates off.

Liam stood inside the bay, directing the mag-levs down the ramp where Dari and Theos loaded them onto the bigger loading carts. From there, the 'bots took them the rest of the way to their destinations. Dozens of cartons were bound for other ships for transport to other destinations.

Grania admired Theos' physique as he lifted the boxes, his stomach pulling flat. In contrast, his chest pulled taut, revealing their hard planes under his uniform tunic. The man definitely had muscles on top of muscles. He waved at her, then grabbed another box to slide onto the big platform.

She continued up the ramp to where Liam worked. "How much more to unload?"

"Another ten crates," he said, pointing to the mag-levs lined up down one aisle. "Once that's done, we can look at the incoming cargo. I think Rory found about two dozen shipments going our way."

"Not that much, then." She hoped to be able to fill the cargo bay again, but that wouldn't be enough.

Liam saw her disappointed look. "He's got another two days to find more, Sis. Ships are still coming in, so he might fill us up yet. We've got a couple of crates destined for a ship that hasn't docked yet, so they're not leaving the bay yet."

"You're right. I guess I'm just worryin' that we won't have a full load headin' out. If there's cargo to be found, Rory will do it." She had a lot of confidence in her middle brother. "Do you have time to talk?"

Liam glanced around at the waiting mag-levs, then looked toward the puca. "Hoy, Dari. Can you watch these robots for about ten mites or so?"

Dari nodded and made his way back up the ramp. "Sure. Anythin' special I need to do?"

"Just keep 'em moving. As one is unloaded at the bottom, send another down. Theos is keepin' up pretty well."

He turned to Grania and pointed toward the engineering cube. She followed him into the glass-enclosed office that housed the computers and kept it a clean room amid the dust in the cargo bay.

He sat on the table's edge as Grania leaned against one of the cabinets. "What's this about?"

"A couple of things, but mostly all related to you. Are you leavin' us here or going on farther with us?"

"Honestly, I'm not positive yet, Nia. I have a call into Uncle Colm to see if there's enough leeway to allow me to go on to the Rim with you. If so, then I'll stay. If not, I might be able to make it to Andromeda Station, then get a ship headed back this way again. Everything depends on his answer."

"That leaves me in a difficult position." She shifted her weight from one foot to the other. "Do I look for a replacement now or hold off?"

Liam shot a look at her. "I thought you brought Theos on board for that."

"He's a novice. Do you really think he can take over for you?"

He crossed his arms and rocked back. "Well, he is pretty feckin' smart from what I've seen. He's got the skills from an education standpoint, just not any real experience. If he could get in a couple of training runs at one of the centers, he could be better prepared in case of an emergency. That would be my suggestion."

"Really? Well, maybe I'll recommend it to him. I'm still looking for a full-time replacement, though. Theos is only temporary."

"Maybe you can convince him to stay." He grinned at her. Clearly, he'd seen the way she'd looked at him.

"Don't get any ideas. He's a fine-looking man, for sure, but I am still with Vilnius."

"Are you? Even if you two are rarely together?" Sometimes Liam saw more than she thought he did.

"Enough. So, when do you think Uncle Colm will get back to you?"

He shrugged. "I hope by tomorrow at the latest."

"In that case, I guess you won't be saying anything to Bren and Rory about leavin'."

He responded with a shake of his head. "Not until I know for sure. No point in getting 'em worked up."

"I agree." She paused and looked around the computer room, aware of everything the bank of machines did to keep the engines running, but she was not nearly as adept at handling it as Liam. If everything went smoothly, she could manage it; however, if an emergency arose, she'd be scrambling to refresh on everything she'd learned. She imagined that Theos would be about as lost. More than anything, she hoped that Liam would stay through the trip to the Rim. She didn't want to admit how much the journey worried her. Even though the jump gates were good, it was still unknown territory, and Vilnius' words had set her to worrying more about it.

"What else is bothering you?" Liam's walnut-colored eyes flashed his concern. He could read her like an engine repair manual.

"This whole business with havin' been waylaid into going to the Rim. I don't like the circumstances. While it seems a simple, straightforward run, I can't see why the government would pay as much as they're giving us for a simple delivery job." She rubbed her hand against her opposite upper arm as if chilled.

"I've thought about that, too. If that's a weapon of some sort we've got, I can't for the life of me figure out what it is. Dari said it's organic, not quite human. Who knows what's in the box, but they definitely want to keep it under wraps."

"I don't know. But I think the fewer people who know, the better for us. I haven't said anything to Rory and Bren, and we've also asked Dari to remain silent. Whether he can do that or not is another matter."

Liam smiled. "He's more discrete than you might expect for a wild creature. I'm beginning to like him." He paused and glanced back toward the loading ramp. "I'd better get back to work. We'll probably be a bit late to the pub, but I'll see you there."

Nodding, she watched him leave, turning toward the ramp to resume his job. "Please let him stay," she whispered before heading to the spiral stairs leading up to the next level.

As she passed Orla's cabin, she heard music coming from it. Not the live music from the lads, but recorded music, some modern band popular on Erinnua. She felt bad that the girl had to be confined to the ship until they left for the shuttle, but she couldn't keep track of her at the station. Maybe Dari could talk to her later and give her a feeling of security before they headed to Earth.

Chapter Thirteen

By the time Grania reached the pub, Brendan and Rory were settled at the bar, even though Bren still wasn't old enough to have more than one alcoholic drink. They laughed with some of the other spacers, telling tall tales and joining in a rowdy song now and then. Murphy's Pub appealed to most spacers because of the fun and camaraderie they found there. It was as Irish as you could find anywhere except in Ireland.

Grania grinned, but instead of joining them, she headed for a pair of large tables in the quieter dining room adjacent to the bar. When a waitress came over, she explained she was expecting five or six others to join her, so they combined the tables.

As she sat facing the entrance to the pub area, she noticed a man enter and sit near the end of the bar. While she wasn't sure what about him had drawn her attention, she continued to glance his way as he got a drink and sipped at it. She noted his eyes shifted her way as frequently as hers went to him. Nothing about him was unusual in her mind. Average-looking, maybe a bit taller than she was, but his body appeared fit and able, in better shape than most of the space jocks at the bar. Perhaps he was similarly attracted to her, but something about him seemed off.

With a dawning sense of recognition, she realized she'd seen him earlier. Not once, but twice. The first time was when she'd come out of Vilnius's office; he'd been lingering near the storefront next door, a men's clothing store. She'd barely noticed him then. The next time, she was standing next to Ethan at the shuttle's ticket office. He wasn't in line, but he stood off to the side, pressed back against the wall, seeming to gaze out at the passing crowd.

And now, here he was again. Coincidence? Zabrowski wasn't that small a station. It seemed like too much of a fluke. Why would he be watching her? Little nervous bumps raised on her arms and the back of her neck. Suddenly, she didn't like being alone at the table.

Fortunately, her brothers picked that moment to leave the bar and join her. Relieved, she urged them to sit across from her, hoping Vilnius would be along soon. In the meantime, the waitress returned to take the orders for drinks. She ordered a plate of corned beef egg rolls, a novelty appetizer that had started in the food fusion phase of the twenty-first century and had hung around.

While she glanced at the man periodically, he appeared less interested in her now, but another drink appeared before him. Shortly after that, Dari and Theos arrived, the puca still in his corporeal peasant form and definitely not of drinking age, although he was older than anyone on the station unless another sidhe was there. Theos, on the other hand, garnered gazes everywhere he went. The man was too gorgeous to be ignored. Even men noticed him, and the few women in the pub sat staring in open admiration.

The Greek god rested his eyes on her, then grinned and came around the table to sit beside her. Thank heavens, she felt relieved. As he settled, she leaned toward him and said, in a low voice, "I think the man at the end of the bar is watching me."

He laughed, shifted his eyes toward the bar subtly, then squeezed her hand. "I don't know him, but I'll check on it." He lifted her hand, turning his so that the back of it faced the bar, and held it still for a moment.

Grania looked puzzled at the action, then he stroked the back of her hand as a gentle expression filled his face like a man in love. "Camera," he said softly.

In a moment, she got it. Theos' ring was a small camera, and he'd just gotten a photo of the possible stalker. Or maybe someone just tailing her. Whatever he was, they would find out if he was known to the PPG's intelligence. Not reassured by this, she found it creepy.

Liam and Vilnius came in together, which surprised her a little, but they probably ran into each other on the way. Vilnius' grin faltered as he saw Theos sitting so close to her, but he recovered quickly, coming around on her other side. He leaned down to kiss her, then sat and asked, "Who's your new friend, darling?" His arm slipped around her shoulder in a claiming move.

She introduced them, making it clear that Theos was the new apprentice engineer who'd joined them at Enterprise. Nonplussed, Vilnius held out a hand for a shake, saying, "Nice to meet you. I'm the station master here and Grania's boyfriend."

Politeness abounded in the exchange, but the hormones increased as the two men regarded each other. Grania caught her breath, overwhelmed by the testosterone in the encounter. While Theos was there for protection, Vilnius had no idea and was making his claim clear.

Grania cleared her throat. "Okay, fellas, settle down. Let's get another round of drinks for the newcomers and order dinner. There's nothing anywhere quite like pub food. I can highly recommend the shepherd's pie."

Theos backed off then, eyes calming as he let the challenge die. "That sounds perfect."

Vilnius took the cue and nodded. "A steak for me, medium rare, with a loaded baked potato." Then he paused to envelop her hand in his. Across from them, Rory and Bren watched the match with interest and smirks on their faces. Grania felt like sliding under the table. What had gotten into Vilnius? Jealousy, clearly.

Theos excused himself and left for a few minutes, presumably to use the accommodation. Grania took the time to cuddle closer to Vilnius and suggested he back off a little. "Theos is a crew member, so there's no need for you to get possessive, love."

"Sometimes it's hard not to. You're so beautiful, my darling, Nia, that any man would fall for you." His voice was as smooth as cream as he said it. She tried not to laugh.

* * * * *

After dinner, Vilnius urged Grania to come to his apartment with him. "You have an apartment?" she asked.

She'd never been to his place before, so she assumed he rented a room or something. When they'd gotten together romantically previously, it had been in a hotel room or in her cabin, even on the narrow bed that provided. Now that she'd moved up, she had the larger bed in the captain's cabin.

"Comes with the job. Where do you think I live?" He wrapped an arm around her waist and led her to a locked section in the hub, where he used a key card to open it. Beyond the door, a short corridor led to a hallway that followed the curve of the station. On the outward wall, metal doors were spaced about thirty feet apart all along it for as far as Grania could see. Each entry bore a number, and some had a colorful design applied to make it easier to identify.

Vilnius led her to a plain door numbered eighteen and used his key to open the apartment. Stepping inside, he triggered the automatic lights, and Grania came to a halt, surprised at the beautiful yet modern dwelling. She hadn't thought about housing on the stations before. Of course, it made sense for the people who worked in the shops and the company that owned it to have some places to live on-site.

Since it was on a curve, the back of the apartment grew wider, arcing to follow the lines of the exterior station wall. They stepped into the living room, a homey-looking place with its big, cushioned sofa and matching chairs. An entertainment center sat opposite it on the wall. Toward the right, a spiral staircase led to an upper level, while another archway dominated the partition on that side. Just peeking through it, she glimpsed a kitchen in the back, along with the dining table and chairs up front. The whole thing looked larger than the galley on her ship.

"I'm impressed," she said. "I had no idea. Have you had this all along?"

"No, I roomed with a couple of people who work on the station. But once I got the station master's job, even temporarily, I also got the apartment. You have to admit, it's a pretty nice perk." He motioned to the stairs. "Bedroom's up."

"What? No foreplay?" she teased. At this point, all she wanted to do was sleep. With the need to get up at five to get back to the ship and get Orla before catching the shuttle, she needed rest more than sex.

"We can do that upstairs." He started up, so she followed.

As lovely as the downstairs, the bedroom didn't disappoint., Grania eyed the big bed with envy and a strong desire to fall into it and drift off. Pointing to a side door on the left, Vilnius said, "Accommodation."

To the right, he told her, was a study with his desk and books. Or it could be a second bedroom, he added.

While he went into the bathroom, she stripped off her clothes, down to her undies and climbed into the bed. The foam mattress gave enough to accommodate her curves comfortably. With a deep yawn, she closed her eyes, refusing to open them when Vilnius slipped into the bed.

"Darling?" His tentative whisper didn't even tempt her.

"Too tired, and I have an early shuttle," she murmured.

"All right. Alarm's set. How about I just…" He shifted beside her and eased his arm around her middle, tucking close to her body.

She fell asleep as he nuzzled her neck.

Chapter Fourteen

Orla walked between Grania and Dari, her shoulders stiff and unsmiling face forward as they marched to the shuttle. While Grania had slept well at Vilnius' apartment, she hadn't slept enough, so the battle with Orla to get her off the ship was unpleasant. The girl had been uncooperative and rude, her anger taking on the aspects of a demon. Dari had managed to calm her, convincing her it wasn't Grania's fault and nothing would change the outcome.

Finally yielding to the logic that if she cooperated, they wouldn't have to resort to forcing her by dragging her all the way or knocking her out cold, which Dari assured her he could do. All the while, the puca had said it so kindly Grania wondered if he wasn't using some kind of magic on Orla. While the girl trudged along, muttering and literally growling, she made it clear she was far from happy with the plan.

"You will like Earth," Dari told her with enthusiasm. "Especially Ireland. 'Tis a green, lush land with gentle hills and majestic mountains. And the sea. Ah, the water there is magnificent. Wait until you see it, Ms. Orla. You will fall in love with it, I promise you."

"We have season Cardyff," she replied. "And all the other stuff as well. Nothing you say makes me any happier about the situation. I am being sold off to the highest bidder, and I have no say-so in the deal. I would think you understand, Dari."

"I do, darlin' girl, but sometimes, you cannot do anything about a situation except look for ways to make it better."

She turned a pouty face to him, lips tight and turned down. "Better would be not going at all."

The steward showed them to their seats, a row in the middle with three seats across. Grania and Dari put Orla between them, so they could block any escape attempts. As Grania glanced across to Dari, he frowned, clearly unhappy with this task. Neither was she, but she'd agreed to the job. Of course, she hadn't known all the details until her parents had delivered Orla to the ship. It might have made a difference in her accepting the task if she'd known the circumstances ahead of time.

A few rows ahead and to the right, Ethan and Conan pushed their carry-on bags into the overhead storage before they settled in. Conan spotted her and waved before taking the outer seat beside his brother. It seemed they'd gotten seats on the early flight, which surprised Grania a little. She thought it had been completely booked before Ethan got to the front of the line. No matter, she conceded, until she noticed Orla had also seen the boys. Her interest in them sparked the most pleasant expression she'd seen on the girl's face since they started this morning. In its own way, it was disconcerting.

Following an uneventful descent to London's spaceport, Grania kept a grip on Orla's arm as they shoved their way through the people—passengers, crew, and general workers—

who were all going the opposite direction from them, it seemed. They'd just cleared the worst of it when Orla balked.

"I need to use the bathroom," she whined, planting her feet firmly when she spotted the women's accommodation.

Grania cast her eyes to the schedule to check the shuttle departure time to Galway. They had forty minutes and half a terminal to cross. And she needed to get the tickets for it. Exasperated, she said, "Can't you wait until we're at the shuttle?"

She shook her head vigorously. "No, I have to go now."

Cursing silently, Grania nodded. "Dari, go with her. Wait outside the room to escort her back. I'll get our tickets."

Orla didn't hesitate to turn toward the bathroom, getting a head start on Dari that the puca quickly made up.

Grania watched until he came even with Orla, then turned to get to the ticketing booths. Fortunately, the lines weren't too long and moved quickly. Grania got in the shortest one, hoping there wasn't a problem child in front of her that would delay the movement.

As she waited, she saw the boys from Cardyff turn away after purchasing their tickets and head across the way to the departure area. They would be going to Cardiff City, she guessed. No matter where in Wales you were destined, you started there. As she turned back to her line, she noticed another familiar face. Not a welcome one, though.

The man from the pub stood a few yards away from her, holding a coffee and sipping it as he leaned against a pillar near the beverage bar. It could be a coincidence, she told herself. Self wasn't convinced. It seemed too obvious. She looked away so he wouldn't notice her, but as she worked up the line, she kept glancing that way. He moved a little but remained in the area, finally taking a seat in the waiting area for the Dublin shuttle. She breathed a sigh of relief. He wasn't going to the same place. She hadn't even noticed him on the station shuttle down, but he had to have come on the same flight.

She wished Theos had come with her. Just knowing he might be tailing her left Grania uneasy. Then, she reached the desk and turned her attention to getting three tickets. If he hadn't needed to stay visible for Orla, she could have saved a ticket with Dari changing to his energy form.

As she stepped away from the counter, she looked around for Orla and Dari and didn't spot them. They should have been in the boarding area by now. She started to backtrack toward the accommodation when she saw Dari running toward her, thankfully not in a horse form, but from the alarmed look on his face, shifting might have been a possibility.

"She gave me the slip, the little hooligan," he said in a strong Irish accent.

"What? How?" Grania couldn't' see how she could have done it. The only way out of the bathrooms was through the door. "Weren't you watching?"

"I was. Alas, though, it was me own fault. The musician lads were nearby, and she asked to go say goodbye to them. It seemed harmless enough, so I stayed a wee bit back from them and watched. But I got distracted for a minute or so by a fellow asking directions. When I looked again, they were all gone. I looked all around for her, Captain Grania. I didn't see any of them in the area." Dari looked downcast; shoulders slumped as he hung his head.

"She ran off with them," Grania growled under her breath. "I bet they planned this all along. I figure the boys are going to Cardiff, so let's check that gate."

Almost as soon as she said it, she heard the announcement for the shuttle departure to Cardiff, Wales, stating it would be leaving in ten mites. She ran, dodging through people to get to the gate, reaching it just as people were boarding. She didn't see Orla or either of the boys, but they could have boarded already. She hurried to the check-in counter. "Excuse me, I am looking for a young girl with two young men. She's about four inches shorter than me, with black hair and piercing blue eyes. Do you know if they've boarded?"

The steward shook his head. "I don't know. I don't see everyone, so it's possible."

"Can I go aboard and look, please?"

He hesitated, clearly not sure of the protocol.

"Look, she is my charge until I get her to her family in Ireland. She just snuck away from us. You wouldn't want to have a runaway reported on your shuttle, would you?"

He looked shocked for a moment, then decision made, he stepped from behind the counter. "I'll go with you."

She told Dari to keep looking in the area and followed the man onto the shuttle. Grania gazed over the passengers, looking for any of the three people. She almost didn't catch them. Orla sat in the middle seat with a scarf over her head, and she wouldn't have noticed her if Conor hadn't been sitting on the aisle seat.

"There," she said to the man. "She's in the next to the last row."+

With a nod, he led the way to the back of the shuttle, urging a few passengers out of the way as they went. Grania hung back a bit, slowed by a man shifting his carry-on around. But she saw the steward lean across in front of Conor to tell Orla to exit the row. As she got closer, she saw that Orla argued with him, but he was insistent.

The girl broke into tears as she got to her feet, and the steward grasped her arm while Conor stepped out of the way to allow her to exit. Holding on to Orla, Grania heard him tell the two boys that he could call the authorities and have them arrested for abducting an underage girl.

As they left the shuttle, Grania pulled up her papers on her mobi, ready to prove that what she'd told him was true. As Dari came back toward them, he stepped up on Orla's other side while Grania sorted the incident out. After she'd explained and proved her story, the steward turned the girl over to them. Orla still sobbed as they hauled her back to the Galway shuttle. They were over halfway there when the boarding call for it went out. Dari and Grania broke into a run, hauling Orla along with the girl sometimes on her feet and other times not.

They barely made the shuttle, got Orla's bag in the overhead, and got belted in before the doors locked, and they began take-off procedures.

Orla glared at Grania. "You ruined everything. I was going to go to Wales and disappear there."

"How did you think you could do that?" Grania asked. "Do you have any credits? Think you could get a job? Were the boys going to take you with them while they toured?"

"I would have managed," Orla insisted. "Anything would be better than marrying someone you don't know." Tears began again, and Grania dug into her pocket for a wipe to give the girl.

They traveled in silence for the rest of the ride across the Celtic Sea and the green fields of Ireland until they landed in a rainstorm in Galway. *Talk about a dismal arrival,* Grania thought as she still gripped Orla's arm while they waited under an awning for her rental vehicle. The breeze off the bay carried more moisture and a chill that left both her and the girl shivering. By now, Orla was more disturbed by the storm than meeting her future husband.

Dari, on the other hand, was out splashing in the water, dancing like a child in the puddles forming on the sidewalk. She'd never seen him look so happy. Of course, he thrived in water. If she was lucky, he wouldn't turn into his water horse form, which would be hard to explain to anyone, let alone Orla.

She breathed a sigh of relief when her automobile pulled up to the curb. "Dari, our transportation is here," she called to the frolicking puca. Disappointment flashed across his face, and the grin disappeared. She ushered Orla into the back seat and indicated Dari should sit there also, although his clothes were dripping wet.

They would go to the hotel to clean up, then she'd contact the O'Connor family before she took Orla to meet them. She'd given a lot of thought to handling the first meet and decided that unless it went swimmingly well, no thanks to the current weather, she would bring Orla back to the hotel with them. That way, they could discuss Orla's problems and maybe ease her into the situation. No matter how she looked at it, Grania knew she only had two days to resolve the situation. Time was not on her side.

The hotel was in a suburb of Galway rather than the old part of town, and luckily, the shuttle port was built out in a less-populated area as well. Just not the same one. She relied on the navigation unit to get them to the correct location without any incidents, but in the storm, the device kept losing the signal, leading them to make more than one wrong turn.

"Do you have any idea where we are, Dari?" Grania turned to look back at the puca as she pulled the auto over to the roadside.

He rolled the window down partially to look out. Although it wasn't dark yet, the rain was heavy enough to make visibility poor. "I think we're about to Castlegar. That building looks familiar."

"Where is that in relation to Briarhill?"

He thought a moment, his face scrunching up like a deflated balloon. "We need to go back a-ways until we find a highway south."

"Any particular highway?"

"Umm, it has a number, but I don't remember what."

"Dari, I need a little more than that." Grania turned to look at the built-in navigation unit and punched in the hotel address again.

"I don't know why you're askin' him," Orla said. "He's not been here before, ya know."

Grania ignored her but perked up a little as the unit showed a major road. "Could it be the N6, Dari?"

"Does it run south?"

"Yes."

"Then take it." He rolled the window back up as Grania turned the auto around.

Once they reached the highway, they saw signs for their destination, and Grania relaxed. The hotel was near the road, and she considered it fortunate that the nav unit worked well enough to take them to it. Just as they pulled into the parking, the rain stopped.

"Thanks be," she said as she climbed out of the auto, told Dari to watch Orla, and then entered the hotel. It was not a big one, but it looked clean and well-tended. Breakfast was included, the young woman who tended the registration told her and pointed to a large room, a restaurant, presumably, to the left side. With the room key in hand, she returned to the car and told the other two to come along.

The room was cozy-looking with two single beds and a rollaway folded in the corner. The bathroom was spacious, with a shower and a tub. Nothing fancy, but it would do for the two nights they would be there.

Orla looked at the beds, then her eyes tracked to the roll

away. Turning her gaze to Grania, she asked, "So, what are the sleeping arrangements, or are you leaving me with the O'Connors tonight?"

"You and I will take the beds. Dari will either sleep on the rollaway or in the auto. It will be up to him." Grania pulled off her damp sweater and dug in her duffle bag for a clean shirt. She'd dressed in civilian clothes for this jaunt rather than her ship's uniform.

"Seems a little unfair." Orla crossed to the bed closest to the window and bounced on it several times. "Do you really have to leave me with these people?"

"You haven't even met them yet, Orla. Give them a chance."

"That's easy for you to say. You're not the one being abandoned here." She turned her gaze to the window.

Guilt hit Grania with a jolt to her stomach. Abandoned. That's what the girl felt, and she couldn't blame her. Her parents sent her off with little thought about how she would take it. She hated this job more and more. She made a mental note to never accept another one like it. "I'm sorry, really I am. But I was hired to bring you here. It's in my contract. Do you want to get cleaned up a bit before we go to meet them?"

Orla gazed down at her clothes, a simple shirt and sweater with a long skirt. "A little, I guess. Won't take more than a few minutes, then we might as well get this over with." She rose and shuffled to the bathroom, looking every bit as dejected as she professed to feel.

Dari still looked wet, and he didn't have anything with

him to change that. "Do you have a way to get your clothes dried quickly?" she asked.

He ran a hand down the front of his thin shirt and nodded. "Sure. Just look the other way if you do not mind."

A little smile twisting her lips, Grania turned her head away, wondering what he might do.

"All right. You can be lookin' now."

When she turned back, her mouth fell open in surprise as he was now in a dry suit. In fact, it was the one she'd gotten him when they talked to the governor in Abhainn Mhór. Even his hair was dry, although a bit longer now than when they'd had the meeting.

"How did you do that?" she said in a low voice.

"I have me talents, you know." He brushed a hand lightly at the suit's left sleeve.

"Whoa! Look at you," Orla said as she exited the bathroom. She had cleaned her face, applied a little makeup, and brushed her hair. "I didn't know you brought somethin' so fancy with you."

Grania used her mobi to call the O'Conner's comm unit and waited for a few buzzes until someone picked up. The voice sounded feminine. "Is this Mrs. O'Conner?" she asked. At the affirmative reply, she told her who she was and that she'd escorted Orla to town. Then she asked if they could come by so they could meet her. She'd been careful with the phrasing, not asking if they could drop her off and run.

As it turned out, the house wasn't far from the hotel, just a few blocks. By now, night had arrived, so the only light came from the dwelling and a street lamp. From what she could see, the place looked like it might be several decades, if not a century, old but reasonably maintained. Most of the buildings in the country that Grania had seen kept the style of the earlier centuries, so it could be older or newer.

Orla fidgeted, repeatedly stepping from one foot to the other and rubbing at her arms. Dari stood behind her, talking to her in a low voice, presumably trying to keep her calm. Grateful for the sidhe's presence and amazed that he'd kept his prankster nature in check for this whole excursion and, indeed, for their entire trip so far.

The woman who opened the door looked middle-aged, tending toward the plump side. But the smile on her face seemed warm and genuine.

"Ms. O'Conner?" Grania asked, not wanting to assume anything.

"I am," she replied, her eyes bright with excitement. "And you are the ship's captain, I presume?"

After confirming that, Grania stepped aside and urged Orla forward. "This is Orla Hennessey, whom you have been expecting. She pointed to Dari. "And this fellow is Dari, an apprentice on my ship."

The woman looked Orla over, her smile growing wider, showing an apparent approval of the girl. "Come in, come in. All of you, please come in." Upon stepping back from the door, she looked over her shoulder and called, "James, they're here!" She turned back. "My husband. We've been quite anxious to meet you, Orla."

More reluctantly, Orla padded into the house, her eyes going wide as if she couldn't quite believe it. Grania thought it looked quite big, probably more than Orla's home on Erinnua, and it was what her granda called homey-looking with paintings on the walls, knick-knacks on the end tables and charming lamps casting warm lights throughout the room.

Polished wooden stairs led to an upper story where James, presumably, started down the steps to greet them. Age lines creased his tan face, but he seemed fit as he bounded down. Still a good-looking fellow, Grania could see where he might have been quite handsome as a young man.

The introductions started again, and he gave them each a nod, then offered his hand to Orla, closing his other over the top of hers and holding it. "We are delighted you're here, young lady. You've had a long journey, and this must feel strange to you. But do come sit and talk for a bit." He released her hand and led her to a chair in the living room.

"I'm Margaret," Mrs. O'Connor said. "We are so grateful that you brought Orla here. Please come have some refreshments with me in the kitchen while James talks with her."

Grania hesitated, not sure she should abandon Orla at this moment. As she gazed to where the girl sat across from James O'Connor, she seemed okay and relatively at ease, although her eyes darted toward Grania a couple of times. The Captain noticed she sat with her hands in her lap and rubbed at her fingernails, the only indication of her nerves.

Dari stepped up close enough to whisper in her ear. "Go

ahead with the lady. I'll be keepin' an eye on her. Nothin' improper will happen."

Assured of that, Grania followed Margaret into the kitchen, where she poured tea and put out a plate of sweet biscuits while her guest sat.

"You needn't worry about her," Margaret said. "James is just getting acquainted and telling her about the family history. He thinks it might make it easier for her to understand why we wanted our son to marry someone from her family." She sat down opposite Grania.

"I have to admit, I am a bit curious about that as well. Did Orla's family tell you she didn't take this arrangement well?" Grania added a bit of sugar to her tea along with a splash of cream.

"Yes, they did indicate the girl wasn't happy. But, once she gets to know us and Sean, our son, we think she will be fine with it."

"I have to ask how your son feels about this? Surely, he has had his eye on someone local."

"True enough. Sean has dated a few girls from the University. It is a complicated situation, but the gist is that my husband's grandfather was a close friend of William Hennessey, Orla's father's father, before they decided to move to the stars. They made a pact to unite the families – there was something about the fortunes of both lines being tied into it. But he made James swear he would marry our first son to a girl from William Hennessey's family."

"That seems an odd thing to do given that bringing Orla

here has been expensive, and now, the girl is completely adrift from her own family." Grania picked up a biscuit and bit into it, savoring the rich taste of shortbread.

Margaret took one herself, dipped it in her tea, then nibbled at it. "I might agree with you. You have Irish blood, do you not?"

Grania nodded.

"With a name like yours, I would expect as much. Are things so different on that planet of yours with the Irish people?"

Grania thought about it. "I really don't know. We keep many Irish traditions as almost all the settlers were from here. But are we the same? I have only been here a few times for short trips. I think more superstitions and traditions might govern life here."

"Not as much as it once did," Margaret said. "I teach Irish mythology at University, so I can tell you our people were once very connected with the natural world. Our legends tell of otherworldly creatures and curses that would send shivers down your spine. Not many people believe in it anymore. Yet, every now and then, something might happen to remind us they exist."

Something like a b'ean sidhe, Grania thought, recalling her own experience with the supernatural world, although she now knew they were real and entities from another dimension. But Nanci feared the sidhe, and her granda knew about them. For that matter, one sat in their entry, not that anyone would know the nature of the young lad unless he changed his form.

"The point is, I suppose, that when these two young fools made their pact, they did it in a place of power... a so-called stone dance and used an ancient ritual that involved calling on gods and spilling blood."

Grania sat up stiffly at that, alarm in her mind. *Feckin' fairies, did they sacrifice someone or an animal?* Her face must have reflected her shock as Margaret's eyes widened, and she hastened to reassure her.

"Don't misunderstand me, Captain O'Ceagan. By blood spilling, I meant that the two young men cut their own fingers with a blade to get enough blood to put in a vessel for the goddess of fortune. Anyway, they sealed the pact and now..." She waved her hand around the room. "Well, we have had good fortune all our lives for three generations. James is superstitious enough to fear that breaking the pact might end it."

Grania wasn't sure what to think. More to the point, she didn't know what Orla was thinking either. Here the poor girl had been dragged across the galaxy to a place where she had no connections and was now expected to play a pawn in some ancient ritual. Was James O'Conner explaining the very same thing to her now? And did her Intended husband go along with this as well?

"Will your son be meetin' her this evening also?" Grania asked, curious to see the young man and ascertain if he would be a good husband.

"He's working late tonight. A project that needs to be completed. But he will be here tomorrow. It's a holiday, you know."

"No, I didn't realize that. We spacefarers tend to lose track of actual days. A lot of Earth-based holidays aren't celebrated. What is tomorrow?"

"It's Saint Barthol the Liberator's Day. Are you familiar with the saint?" Margaret refilled her teacup, offering Grania more.

She declined the tea with a wave of her hand. "I'm afraid not. We don't celebrate any saints' days on Erinnua."

Margaret's forehead wrinkled as her eyes clouded a bit. "Is the girl a Christian?"

"I don't know. I didn't ask her, but since so many of the people of Erinnua do believe in God, I imagine that she is. It's a question you'll need to discuss with Orla."

"Oh, it just seems odd that you don't celebrate any of those days."

"We celebrate Christmas and Easter," Grania said. "Even on the ship if we're not at home." She wanted to reassure the woman since it seemed important to her.

With a nod, Margaret accepted the information and appeared to relax a little more. "That's good." She drew a breath to say something more when James called her name from the living room. She hopped to her feet and grabbed a tray with another teapot and plate of biscuits set on it. "My husband is ready for the tea now, so I'll just take it out. Come along."

Did that mean they were done with the private conversation? Grania held the door and followed behind the woman. Orla sat just as they'd left her, prim with her hands in her lap and her back straight. She didn't look any more relaxed than she had before. The Captain glanced toward Dari, who watched but hadn't moved any closer. He shrugged.

"Here we go," Margaret said as she set the tray down. As long as they'd talked in the kitchen, Grania figured the tea would be strong enough to walk over to the cups on its own. Nonetheless, Margaret poured them each a cup, then stepped back. James gestured for her to sit and swept an arm of invitation toward Grania, ignoring Dari entirely.

As Grania sat in a hardback chair facing Orla, she noticed the anxiety in the girl's eyes. Whatever had been said hadn't reassured her, it seemed.

"We've had a very nice chat," James said, lifting the teacup to his mouth. "I believe she will fit into our family nicely, so we will proceed with the deal, Captain O'Ceagan. I will pay you the fee agreed upon tomorrow after Sean meets her. We are most grateful for your diligence in bringing her safely here."

"Indeed," Margaret piped in, then turned her eyes to Orla. "I have a lovely room upstairs for you, my dear. Did you bring your things?"

A look of panic shot across Orla's face as she turned her countenance to Grania. Her mouth fell open as if she wanted to object, but words wouldn't come out.

"Ah... We hadn't expected Orla to remain here tonight, so her belongings are back at our hotel. I think it might be better if she comes back with us. We can bring them all over in the morning when we come to meet your son." She hoped that sounded diplomatic enough.

James frowned, and Margaret looked crestfallen. "Is there a problem?" he asked.

"No, of course not. It's just that Orla would like a little time to adjust to the idea. Perhaps you can show her the room tonight? Then she'll have a better idea of where she can put her items tomorrow." They stared at her, saying nothing.

She smiled at Orla, hoping the girl would say something on her own behalf. "Is that what you still want, Orla?"

More silence as Orla's lip trembled, and she looked ready to dash out of the house.

"Please understand. Orla has just been separated from her family and traveled a long distance, so this is a little overwhelming for her. Give her a little time to come to terms with the reality."

Margaret unfroze first, putting on a kindly smile for Orla. "Of course. Would you like to see the room, dear?"

Grania nodded at the girl to encourage her, so Orla rose slowly to her feet. With her head lowered, she followed Margaret O'Conner up the stairs. James continued to gaze at Grania, finally clearing his throat and pouring a finger of brandy into his tea, then taking a sip.

"Did Margaret explain the situation to your satisfaction?"

"Not entirely," Grania answered. "What I would like to know is how your son feels about this arrangement? It's one thing to tell young people they will marry, but if there is no respect and affection, it will not be a happy situation."

"Sean will do as he's asked. He's a fine young man with

honor and decency. He has an excellent job in the science labs and the potential for a very successful future. He'll do right by Orla." He said it as if it answered the question.

"I see. But what if your son doesn't love Orla? Or she, him?"

"They will learn to love each other. It's not a new concept, you understand. Arranged marriages were common once. I've often thought it might be better than relying on one's hormones to dictate a match."

"I think you'll find that Orla is not as convinced by the idea. She'll want to meet your son and see if there is any spark between them. She wants to return to the hotel with me tonight, so we can discuss it."

"Very well. I think it would be better if the girl were to stay here, but perhaps you are right."

Grania felt the tension in her chest release. But she still had to deal with Orla. A pretty bedroom wouldn't win her over. She turned her gaze to the photos on the end tables, her eyes resting on a graduation photo of a handsome young man. Presumably Sean. He looked pleasing enough with a kind smile. She looked forward to meeting him. Another photo showed a young girl, not quite as mature as Orla, and she guessed it to be their daughter.

*****

Back at the hotel, the trio had dinner in the hotel's restaurant before heading to their room. Orla didn't say much, but she looked relieved to have the first meeting done.

"How are you feelin' about this?" Grania asked her as she removed her shoes and wiggled her toes. It seemed like she'd been in them a long time. She was used to her comfortable uniform shoes, not these heels—low though they were—that women wore.

Orla sat on her bed, playing a game with her mobi. She looked up. "About the same. I still don't like it and want to go home."

"That's not happening, I'm afraid. Even if these folks let you out of the deal, your parents can't pay for your trip back to Erinnua." They'd only paid a portion of the passage to Earth, while the O'Connors had picked up the rest.

"Then I guess I'll have to find a job here and try to get my own place." Her jaw tightened with determination.

"Look. Why don't you wait until after you've met Sean O'Conner? He doesn't look like a bad sort, and he's got a good job. He could take care of you well."

"He's also nine years older than me and probably more experienced. Why would he even go along with this plan?"

"Some sort of pact made decades ago, apparently. Just meet him tomorrow and find some time to have an honest talk with him. Tell him how you feel about it, but don't get nasty. He may be just as concerned as you are."

"I don't have much of a choice, do I? Maybe he'll reject me." She brightened at the thought, leaving Grania wondering what was running through the girl's mind.

While Orla went into the bathroom to get ready for bed,

Grania spoke quietly with Dari. "You have been amazing, puca. More help than I could have imagined. You can use the rollaway in here or spend the night wherever you wish."

"Anywhere?" His eyes sparkled a bit as he smiled. "You know I do not require sleep the way you humans do, don't ya'?"

"I remember. So, go do whatever you want. Visit your friends even. Just be back here at seven in the morning. We're having breakfast with the O'Connors."

"That I will then. Until the morning, good night." Without hesitating, he shifted into his energy form, and a miniscule golden ball darted through the walls.

Grania glanced behind her to be sure Orla hadn't seen that. He'd gone just in time as the girl came out dressed in her pajamas. She looked around. "Where's Dari?"

"He decided to go out for a bit. He'll probably be sleeping in the car rather than disturbing us. Now, here's the plan for tomorrow. We'll all have breakfast, and meet Sean, then Dari and I will leave you to get acquainted. I'll be back around mid-afternoon to see how things are going."

"Then what?" Orla asked dryly.

"Then we'll decide the next step, I guess." Grania wasn't sure what it might be if Orla rebelled at staying there.

Chapter Fifteen

Sean O'Connor turned out to be better than Grania had hoped for as he greeted them warmly, reserving a special smile for Orla. He was quite good-looking but mature, and the age difference between him and Orla was pronounced. She seemed shy, something entirely out of character for the outspoken girl. As it was, she'd pulled her hair back into a tight bun, eschewed any makeup, and worn drab brown and black clothing, all of which made her look even younger and immature.

Grania figured that was part of her plan to get Sean to reject her. Given the restraint he showed with her, it could be working. While she'd brought her bundle of clothing and other remembrances from her life on Erinnua, she showed her plainest side as she trundled upstairs to put it in her room.

In a way, the situation recalled Grania's first meeting with Vilnius. She was sixteen, and he was twenty-five, a good age difference just as with Sean and Orla. But she'd flirted with him, and they'd fallen for each other over time. Had she been forced to be with Vilnius, would she have been more reticent?

After exchanging a few words in greeting, they took their seats in the dining room for a good Irish breakfast. Mrs. O'Connor had hired help this morning so that she, too, could sit at the table. Sean told them about his job at the research center while Orla yawned two or three times, looking utterly bored. The O'Connors tried to engage her in the conversation, but she'd resorted to one-word replies.

By the time Grania and Dari could escape to leave the family to try to win the girl over, they were more than anxious to go. Once in the car, Grania turned to the puca and asked, "What would you like to do today? Visit with your fellow pucas or what?"

"If I could, I would like to see Sheilan."

"Didn't you tell me she was in the other dimension with the High Council?"

"Presumably. Still, it would be good to see her."

"Do you know the way there?" Grania realized she couldn't take him since it was through a gateway that humans didn't cross. But he could go if he wanted.

"Of course, although it has been a long time since I visited my home world."

"Do you not miss it?" Grania wondered if his situation was similar to Orla's. Stuck far from home with no recourse. But that wasn't true. He could go back, but he hadn't.

"Not so much. 'Tis pretty there, I admit. Clear air, lots of flowers, and flying things, but for me, Earth's become my home. I enjoyed my life here. Still, it might surprise you to know I am developing a liking for Erinnua as well."

"Are you? Well, with luck, Orla will find things to like about Ireland."

"What would you like to do today?" he asked her.

"If I remember the stories correctly, we're not far from

where my ancestor lived all those centuries ago. I'd like to see Grania O'Malley territory."

"Then you have the right guide along with you today. We need to head north from here to County Mayo."

As she took the car back on the highway, she drank in the colors of the land, the green shades of the grass and trees, while bright yellow flowers blossomed in the middle of the fields along the way. Outside Galway, the land was open, with only an occasional farmhouse. To her left, the Atlantic Ocean roiled toward the shore, crashing against the lower cliffs and sending up water sprays.

"Were you out in it last night?" Grania asked.

"In what?" he replied.

"The ocean. Your element, I believe." Her smirk showed her amusement. The water horse side of the puca was his dominant nature.

"Well, it is possible that a few companions and I made our way out to the bay and went for a moonlight swim."

"Good for you. And did you run along the beach in your horse form?"

"I might have done that, also," he confessed, a grin splitting his face.

* * * * *

Eventually, they came to a turnoff for Rockfleet Castle and meandered through a village before turning onto a dirt road leading along an inlet to a tower at the water's edge. "This is the place," Dari informed her.

She parked the car and climbed out. "It doesn't look like much." The square tower stood about four stories high and maybe thirty feet on each side of the base.

"Not as castles go. But for a tower house, which is what it was, it was quite fine. This is where the pirate queen Grania lived with her husband. Come take a better look." He started toward the ancient building.

As they drew closer, Grania began to appreciate the massive size of the stone construct. For its time, the building was impressive. It was also locked up as tight as a prison. "Guess we can't go inside."

She continued walking down to the shores of the Clew Bay. As she gazed out down the long arms of land to the open water, she appreciated the positioning of the castle. From here, the residents could see anything that approached long before they arrived. It seemed lonely. Perhaps in Grania O'Malley's time, the keep had been surrounded by small homes and animals roaming all about. Time had beaten everything down except the castle. That it was still standing could be attributed to the country maintaining its walls. Whatever had been inside was long gone.

Nonetheless, this century's Grania closed her eyes and tried to imagine what her ancestor was like. Strong, brave, and cunning were words she'd heard describing her. She hoped she was worthy of the name.

"Can you look inside, Dari? I'd like to know what the

rooms are like in it and if anything remains from her time."

Dari nodded. "I do not think anything would be left since the castle was used for centuries after by her family and other people who bought it. But I will take a look."

In a blink, he switched forms, and golden sparkles zipped away from her. Even though she was getting used to the puca, seeing him disappear so easily still amazed her. She walked back by the side of the castle, stepping around the corner, intending to wait near the automobile. Abruptly, she froze, her jaw dropping in surprise when she saw she was no longer alone.

A green sedan was parked near her rental, and her stalker climbed out. Her heart thudded against her ribs as a sense of foreboding settled on her shoulders. He was definitely following her. But he'd taken the shuttle to Cardyff, hadn't he? And he hadn't been on the shuttle with her when they'd come to Galway. So, how had he known where she was?

He started across the marshy grass toward her, not in a rush, just at a steady pace. She turned and went back around the castle, looking for an entry she might use to get away from him. Padlocks and chains sealed every entrance, and the windows were barred.

She stopped and turned at the side's end as the man rounded the corner. Although she had some hand-to-hand fighting training, she bore no other weapons. She pulled out her mobi, signaled the ship, and thanked her guardian deity when Liam answered quickly. "I'm at Rockfleet Castle in County Mayo, Liam. A man is following me. I saw him at the pub last night and again at the shuttle port in London. Tell Theos."

"What? Why? What can he do?"

"I don't know, but he needs to know. Just do it." She cut off the communication and straightened her shoulders, ready to meet this threat.

His pace didn't falter as he kept coming toward her. When he was about ten feet away, she yelled, "Who are you? Why are you following me?"

"Captain O'Ceagan, I presume. Did you think you would be handed an oversized parcel from a suspect government agency, and no one would be interested in it?" He walked a few more feet, then stopped a mere arm's length from her.

His intense eyes seemed to drill into her, making Grania cringe and look away from him. "I'm just doing the job they hired me to do."

"Really? And what does the box contain?"

"I'm sure that's on the record with the Enterprise station's transport records. All cargo loaded on a station has to be declared." She cited the standard rules regarding transport, which coincided with what her manifest declared. As far as the world was concerned, the crate contained farming equipment.

The man laughed, a rough bark that sounded false. "Too vague. Can't you be more specific?"

"No, I only know what the declared contents are." She stepped back, bracing herself in case he made a grab for her. She wasn't a small woman by any means. Tall, sturdy, and fit, she was a match for any man her size, and this one was only a little taller. So long as he wasn't carrying a weapon, that was.

"Not good enough. Maybe we should go back to your ship together and open that crate." He moved two steps closer.

She backed up more. "I repeat, who are you? What makes you think I would violate the terms of my shipping agreement?"

"I represent the Alliance of Anti-Political Involvement in Colonial Affairs. We suspect the box's contents violate what we stand for, and we intend to stop it. Now, the easiest way would be with your cooperation, Captain."

"Get a legal request authorized by a planetary court judge, and I'll cooperate. Otherwise, you're overstepping your authority if you have any."

"I see; you want to do this another way. Let's see if your brother will be more cooperative if his sister is in danger." He lunged then, literally leaping the short distance to her.

Ready for it, Grania evaded and ducked low, bringing her left shoulder into his midriff to knock him aside. He stumbled almost into the castle wall, not going all the way down but clambering back to his feet quickly. He brought his arm back to slug her as she dropped to her heels and swung a leg out to catch his legs.

This time he crashed to the ground, and she started to follow up with a kick to his gut. As her foot came in, he grabbed it with both hands and knocked her off balance. Grania fell to the ground on her back, struggling to roll away so she could spring back up before he was on her.

His fist connected with her jaw, jarring her head and neck

and causing a shooting pain that raced down her spine. The bastard wasn't playing gently with her, for sure. She flung an arm over her face to protect against the next blow coming while she pulled her knee up, aiming for his crotch. As his fist hit her arm, her knee plunged into his legs, just missing her target but still close enough to throw him off balance.

Flipping over, she scrambled away on her knees. The taste of blood in her mouth informed her she had a cut lip or worse. Catching her breath, she screamed, "Dari!" She hoped the puca would hear and could help, but what could he do?

She vaulted to her feet at about the same time her attacker did. She lifted her hands into a boxing stance, ready to punch it out with him. His hair mussed and blowing in his eyes from the light breeze from the bay, he wiped at the corner of his mouth where she'd managed to bloody him as well. Then he lunged for her again. Grania backpedaled, putting space between them as her mind scrambled to devise another defensive move while she kept her fists ready.

In an instant, a rearing white horse appeared between them. Just as suddenly, the man was backpedaling to escape the dangerous hooves coming his way. Dari hopped forward on his rear legs, attacking with the forelegs. The deadly feet barely missed their target as the man turned and ran for his car.

Grania chased after him, with Dari well ahead of her, then the puca disappeared again. When she swung around the corner, she saw the Percheron-sized horse in front of the fleeing man. This time, the hooves connected, coming down on his head and shoulders and knocking him flat.

When the man tried to roll away from the danger, the puca raced to intercept the movement. Dari rose on his hind legs again, his hooves targeting the man's torso, red blazing in his eyes and looking like the demon horse he was.

"Wait, Dari!" Grania ran across the open field in a half-lope. Her side ached, and she felt dizzy and off balance, but she didn't want the puca to kill the man. She needed more answers from him.

The thunderous hooves drove toward the ground. The man screamed, and she caught her breath. Barely missing the man's torso, the forelegs thudded into the moist dirt, tossing mud everywhere. The puca stepped back, tail swishing wildly as he lowered his neck, showing his teeth.

At that moment, Grania realized how dangerously fierce a riled puca could be. No illusion, solid flesh manifested in a moment, a complete contradiction to the gentle, fun-loving lad he'd been over the past few days. She shuddered as she came to a halt several paces away.

Her eyes tracked to the man lying in the dirt, barely able to move. Blood oozed from his head while his shoulders looked askew. Possibly a concussion and broken collar bones.

"Will more from your agency be coming?" Grania asked, shouting from where she'd stopped.

"Maybe," he gasped, his eyes still locked on the fierce animal hovering by him.

Grania saw his right hand move, reaching for something. "Don't try anything. If you're going for a weapon, you'd best stop now."

He whipped out a laser weapon and fired it at Dari. The beam went through the puca's left shoulder as she screamed, "No!"

The horse's shriek sounded more like a screaming banshee, but it didn't deter him as Dari reared up again, and this time the hooves crashed down on their target, crushing the man's chest. When he raised up a second time, Grania looked away. She heard the man cry out, then a scream and the thuds of hooves against flesh as they struck the body.

She couldn't look, her imagination filling in the gory details. She hadn't wanted the man dead. Nickering from the horse seemed to demand her to see. Turning her head, she caught her breath at the blood that covered the horse's forelegs with splashes painting his chest. Of the wound to his shoulder, not a hint remained.

Her stalker was a mess; his chest caved in, blood covering it and the ground around him. Nauseated, she turned her head away again. A brutal death and she couldn't have stopped it. Telling herself he'd threatened her and might have done as much to her or any of her brothers to get the information he wanted didn't ease her guilt. Worse, more might come from his organization. What the hell was in the crate that was drawing so much attention?

Her mobi buzzed, insistent she pick up the incoming message. She saw the caller's name and pressed the receive button. "Liam?"

"Are you all right?" he asked.

"Yes. I am now. Did you—"

Before she could complete the question, Theos was on the line. "What happened? Did you learn anything?"

"Only that he's working for the anti-political involvement league, and they're very interested in the shipment we picked up in Enterprise. The man is dead." Her voice was flat, unemotional.

"You killed him?" Theos sounded surprised.

"I had a little help."

"Does he have any id on him?" Theos pressed.

She stared at the body. "I haven't looked for any." And she didn't want to touch him to find out. Even being so near, the iron smell of his blood nauseated her.

"Then check now." Theos' voice was gentle but demanding. "I need to know more."

Getting to her feet, she forced herself to walk to the body and begin searching his pockets for a wallet or anything that might hold information. She tried not to look at the damaged body where blood pooled, no longer pouring out or trickling off him. The moisture extended to his pants pockets, but she dug into them, one by one, reporting back to Theos on each as she checked them. Finally, coming to a sealed pouch just above his right knee, she felt something within that could be what they wanted.

"It's secure. I can't get it to unseal."

"Can you cut it?"

"Wait." She told him, then went to her automobile to get a utility knife from her bag. Returning, she cut the pocket open and withdrew the folded wallet. She opened it, seeing the identification card and a photo of the man.

"His name was Alden Sternbach, thirty-five. The id was issued on Batterforce, at Linghall."

"Got it. I'll check it out. What are you doing about the body?"

"What the hell--?" She heard Liam's voice challenging Theos, who cut him off.

"She can't leave it lying in a field. Or she'll have to call the local police, which will be a delay we can't afford."

"I'll deal with it." She closed her eyes, swallowing hard. "We're in a remote area, and Dari is with me. He'll be helpin' me, so we'll figure something out."

"When are you coming back to the ship?" Liam asked.

Grania forced her eyes away from the body and focused on Liam's question. "On tomorrow's shuttle. The girl is with her family, and I think it will be fine. I'll be checking back there as soon as I'm done here. Oh, tell Theos, we need to talk when I get back."

"Be careful, sister." Liam's voice had a worried sound.

All the while she did this, the white horse had retreated a few yards and paced back and forth, watching her.

She stepped away from the body and waved at Dari, hoping he would switch back to his human form. Instead, the horse trotted over, red eyes still blazing. Grania felt uneasy, reminding herself that this was Dari, a usually friendly puca to her and her crew. But was this the fundamental aspect of the sidhe?

"What do we do with the body, Dari?"

The animal gazed at her momentarily, then lowered his head, grabbed a mouthful of clothing, and began pulling Sternbach toward the water about two hundred yards away. Grania bent to help, but the horse proved much better at dragging than she did.

Once they reached the bay's edge, Dari hauled the body into the water up to his mid-chest, then Grania saw the fish-like tail flip out of the water as he switched to his water horse form to take the body the rest of the way. Within minutes, he pulled the body far from the shore, then dove under the water, dragging it with him.

Grania turned to look at the trail they'd left. A wide swath of crushed grass and mud marked the path along with the unshod hoof marks from the puca. Her footprints followed alongside, but those wouldn't remain long in the grass if it began to rain again.

No one else had come to the castle, and if they did come now, all they would see would be Sternbach's rental, maybe a red stain on the grass, and the indication that something had been dragged through the grass. Perhaps a tiny boat. Until Sternbach surfaced.

She walked back to her auto, eager to get back to their hotel and clean up before they went to check on Orla. What was taking Dari so long? She sat with the heater turned on, warming her chilled body and gazing out toward the storm rolling toward the shore, hoping to see the puca's head rising about the water.

Then suddenly, he was there, just a few feet away in his

young lad form. He wasn't smiling, but he gave her a thumbs up as he walked the remaining distance and got into the car.

"Are you okay?" she asked, eyes searching him to see if he bore any injuries.

"Of course I am." He looked at her, eyes bright and a hint of a smile on his lips. "It has been a while since I have had occasion to do that."

"So, you've killed with your hooves before?"

"Many times, Captain Grania. Many times, and always for a good reason."

"Well, it's good we're leaving here soon. Once the body washes ashore, there'll be an investigation."

"It will not be soon." Dari looked smug as he ran a hand through his hair. "I secured him under the water with a decent-sized boulder holding him down."

Startled, Grania raised an eyebrow and reached to put the vehicle in gear. Then the mobi buzzed again, and she answered it, expecting it might be Liam again.

"She's run away," a woman's voice cried. Margaret O'Connor, Grania realized.

Orla had bolted.

Chapter Sixteen

"Tell me what happened." Grania backed the automobile up to pull away from the small parking area. She wanted to be as far away from this place as possible now.

"She and Sean were talking, getting along fine, it seemed, then she said she needed to get something from her room. Next thing we know, she'd grabbed her things and left the house without a word."

"How long ago?" Grania shoved the vehicle into forward gear and started up the hard dirt road toward the town.

"About forty-five minutes. As soon as we realized she'd left, we went lookin' for her, but we couldn't find her anywhere. I don't know how she disappeared so fast."

"Did she give any indication to Sean that she was unhappy or not wantin' to stay there?"

Margaret muffled the phone as she asked her son something. "No, he doesn't think so. He said they were talking about things they liked and what she might want to study."

Grania frowned. What in that conversation triggered her flee instinct? A moment later, the voice on the phone changed to James O'Connor. "Listen here. You get that girl back here. If she doesn't return, then the whole deal is off. I won't pay you a cent." His voice sounded stern and angry.

"I'll see what I can do, Mister O'Connor. I'll be lookin' for her now, and I'll call you back when I have something."

She ended the call before he could say anything more. To Dari's quizzical face, she said, "Orla's taken off. Something must have frightened her, but I have no idea what. Now, I need to find her. Any ideas, Dari?"

"Well, if she was fleein' and had no money to speak of, she might have gone back to the hotel." His shoulders lifted halfway to his ears in an exaggerated shrug.

"I don't know about that. She would know I'm not there, and even if I were, I'd want her to go back and settle whatever issue set her off. So where else might she go? She'd need to find shelter and food. And she'd need some money or credits."

"Maybe she peddled somethin'," Dari suggested.

"What? She doesn't have anything worth sellin'."

They continued down the road in silence, each with their own thoughts, until they passed through the town and turned toward Galway.

"Does she have a pendant of some kind around her neck?" Dari asked, breaking the silence.

Grania thought for a few moments, recalling Orla's face and her throat. "I think you might be right, Dari. I remember a chain around her neck, but I never saw what was attached to it. Maybe she had something valuable enough to sell. So, if she had some currency, where might she decide to go?"

Oddly, she recalled the hotel sign saying they had a free bus to the shuttle port. Would Orla take that for a quick exit from the town? If so, might she be trying for a shuttle back to

London? But then what? Wales? To meet up with the musicians?

"Let's go straight to the shuttle port to see if she's gone there. If she gets out of the area, I don't have time to find her. And even if I do, I may not be able to convince her to go back to the O'Connor's house."

As it was, Orla had a pretty decent head start on them as Grania had her mobi check the departure times for London and Cardiff. "We just might make it before the shuttle to London. Cardiff is two hours later."

Dari thought for a bit. "I know where the shuttle port is, so I could go ahead and try to find her. If she is there, I might be able to delay her."

"You can do that?" she asked.

"I'm an energy form. I can travel wherever I want so long as I know the place." He'd said it so matter-of-factly that Grania wondered why he'd come along on their ship at all.

"Then go. I'll get there as soon as I can."

He nodded, dematerialized, and vanished within two seconds. "Feckin' amazin'," she murmured, accelerating the vehicle up another ten kilometers. Sure, it pushed the speed limit, but everyone was zooming past her as it was.

When she got to the shuttle port an hour later, Grania parked in the garage and hurried into the building. Not nearly as crowded as London, she still had to wade through people lining up for tickets or food. She looked for the London departure lounge and turned that way, her long strides eating up the distance.

About forty people waited for the next shuttle, which would depart in about thirty mites, but she didn't see Dari or Orla. Next, she moved on to the one for Cardyff. Fewer people waited here, only a dozen, with the departure still over two hours away. No sign of them here either. Where else might they be?

Turning back toward the central hub, she spotted Orla hunched over her knees with her elbows supporting her head in her hands. Next to her, Dari sat, mouth moving so he was still talking to her. Her travel bag rested between her feet. She let out a grateful breath to have found her. Now all she had to do was convince her to go back.

She moved up and sat in the seat on Orla's other side. She could see the girl was crying, her shoulders shaking with her tears. Grania laid a hand on her arm. "What is it, Orla? What happened?"

Orla didn't want to lift her head, shaking it back and forth.

"Did Sean do something? Did he try to hurt you?"

"No," Orla managed to spit out. "He didn't touch me."

"Then what?" Grania's confusion was reflected in her voice. What had happened? If Sean didn't try to take advantage, what was the problem? Surely not the older O'Connor? "Was it his father? Did he—"

"No, not him either." She raised her head, wiping a tissue over her eyes and nose. "It's the whole situation. Sean doesn't want me. Nobody wants me."

"What do you mean?" Grania knew they wanted her there. What had Sean said?

"He asked me if I wanted to go to school and get a degree. Then he said he thought I was too young to marry." Her voice hitched on the words.

"I thought you had said so as well," Grania said. "You weren't anxious to be married. It sounds like they were giving you some space. That isn't rejection, Orla."

She wiped her eyes again. "I don't understand. My parents told me we'd be wed as soon as I got here. I would be a rich man's wife, and we'd have a home and family. I would make them proud by doing this. And now, he doesn't want me."

"What were you planning to do here?" Grania asked.

"Go to Wales to see if I could find Conan. He liked me and asked me to come with them. I thought…"

"Oh, Orla. You've misread everything." Grania put her arms around her, pulling her close. *Teenage hormones. Everything is a drama.* She'd felt that way a few times herself. "Let's go back to the hotel, get cleaned up, and talk this out. Then we can decide what to do. Is that okay?"

Sniffling, Orla straightened up and reached for her bag. Dari grabbed it before she did as he jumped to his feet. "I told ya'. Captain Grania will fix everything."

She wished she had that much confidence in herself.

* * * * *

Back at the hotel, Grania contacted Margaret O'Connor to let them know she'd located Orla, and they were talking. She would be back in touch later. Orla headed for the shower as soon as they arrived, so Grania, with mud on her clothes, a bloody lip, and probably a few bruises, got to sit and wait for her turn.

"Watch her while I shower," she told Dari when it appeared Orla was almost done.

"I can do that. I don't think the girl will take off again, but I will stop her if she tries." He sat on Grania's bed, leaning back on his elbows. Not a scratch on him. Whatever damage that was done when he's been the horse was quickly repaired, it seemed.

When Orla came out, she looked refreshed, although she still rubbed a towel through her hair.

"Isn't the dryer working?" Grania asked.

"It's fine. I just like to towel-dry it for a bit. Besides, you look like you really need the shower. What happened?"

"Long story." Grania cut her off and headed into the shower. As she removed her clothes, she paused to look in the full-length mirror, assessing her injuries. Several bruises sported blue-purple coloring, including one on her right cheekbone. Her lip was swollen around the cut inside where a tooth had torn the flesh. Muscles ached from moving in directions they weren't used to going, but at least she hadn't sustained any severe damage.

More than she could say for Sternbach. She wished it hadn't ended the way it did. She wanted to learn more about what to expect but couldn't blame Dari for defending her. The man would have gotten a grip on her if the puca hadn't acted when he did.

She stepped into the shower and scrubbed the dirt and blood off, relishing the hot water washing down her head and shoulders. As she shampooed her hair, she began to piece together how she might salvage the situation with Orla and the O'Connor family. If she failed, she would be out the money, not just for the trip, but for the excursion to Earth to deliver her. It represented a four-figure credit to their account. Frankly, she felt she'd more than earned it.

Dressed in clean clothes, she tied the attached green silk scarf around her neck and put her dirty garments in the cleaning unit. By the time she returned this evening, they would be refreshed and ready to go. Then, she went back to the room to talk to Orla.

The girl told them everything that happened. All the words Sean said were so polite but not at all what Orla had expected. In short, he wasn't talking about marrying her but seemed more concerned with getting her into a trade school or even university if she qualified. She didn't understand the whole deal at all. Her father had said they would get married; that was what the agreement meant.

Grania nodded as she listened, trying to figure out what Sean O'Connor might be thinking. "Certainly, Sean's parents are expecting the marriage to happen," Grania said. "They want to abide by the request put upon them by Mister O'Connor's great-grandfather. While it seems strange, they take the vow quite seriously. Are they aware of what Sean said?"

Orla shook her head. "I don't think so. They were quite

happy when I came down to get a glass of juice and seemed to regard me as part of the family. I felt bad about sneaking out, but I couldn't explain it to them."

Grania took a minute or two to consider the situation. "I can't send you back to Erinnua unless your parents consent, Orla. So, what are your choices here?" She waited a few moments to see if the girl had any thoughts. She looked at her hands in her lap but didn't say anything.

"You can stay with the O'Connor family if they agree, whether it ends up in marriage to Sean or not, or you can try to find a room to let and get a job to support yourself here. I don't think going to meet Conan in Wales will work out. Frankly, I wouldn't agree to it. He and Ethan are traveling and performing. They won't be staying in Wales or on Earth permanently."

"What do you think I should do, Dari?" Orla asked the puca.

"Me? My opinion is not worth much. But if it were me, I think I would look for the best offer. What benefits you the most?"

Orla sighed. "The O'Connors seem like nice people, and it is a lovely bedroom. Better than I had at home. I guess if they'll have me, that would be okay."

She didn't look excited about the prospect, but she would accept it, Grania thought in relief. Now, if they could clarify what went on between her and Sean, they might be able to settle this tonight.

They went downstairs to grab dinner at the restaurant, a

simple but tasty meal, then headed to the O'Connor house. When they arrived, Grania asked if she might speak to Sean alone. Margaret and James were agreeable as they showed Orla and Dari into the living room, where they could talk. She hoped they wouldn't question the girl too much and wouldn't scold her for her actions earlier.

She and Sean went into the kitchen to chat over the ever-present tea. Grania went straight to the crux of the issue. "What exactly are your intentions toward Orla, Sean?"

He sat back in surprise, a hint of a smile on his face. "Whatever do you mean? My father intends for me to marry her, and I likely shall. Isn't that what the arrangement was?"

"It was. But Orla had a different impression after talking to you this afternoon. Did you encourage her to learn a vocation or return to school?"

"I did," he nodded twice. "I like Orla. She has spunk, and she's pretty, but... My God, she is so young. Not just in years but in attitude, interests, your name it. She is naive about so many things. That's why I think she should go to school or learn a trade so that she can be out in the world to learn more." He paused, his clear blue eyes seeming to look ahead. "When she matures a little more in a couple of years, then I will court her like any woman I would consider for my wife."

"I see." Grania leaned back and twisted a finger through her hair. "So, have you discussed this with your parents?"

He shook his head. "Not yet. Clearly, we need to talk it through, but these are my terms."

"And if they disagree?"

"Then, we will have a long engagement." He smiled, his face looking pleasant and sincere. Grania hoped he was right.

After that, they discussed the whole issue with Margaret and James. At first, James balked, his face turning stony, but as Sean explained his thoughts behind it, he began to yield.

Grania kept an eye on Orla, whose eyes grew wide as she was discussed so openly. Still, when they finally reached an agreement, relief washed through her eyes, and her body relaxed.

"So, we're in agreement. Orla lives here while she attends school, and Sean will be her mentor. If, when she is older and more experienced with the world, Sean agrees to court her, then the agreement will proceed. But if the two are not mutually compatible, then you, James O'Connor, will not call foul on the deal and will not force the wedding. Is that agreed?"

Put in those terms, James appeared a bit flustered but finally agreed. Grania breathed her relief, followed by gratitude that the man transferred the agreed-upon fees to the ship's account.

As she and Dari started to leave, Orla came to say goodbye, hugging each of them. "Thank you. I didn't believe this could come to such a good ending. Now I can get to know Sean better before we are wed, and I have a future here."

"You do. Make yourself a good life." Grania hugged her before she left, and Dari did likewise, whispering something in her ear.

"What did you tell her?" Grania asked as she started the

automobile.

"To trust in herself and stay open to the possibilities."

"That's good, Dari. You're more of a philosopher than I thought."

"Not really," he grinned. "I got it from a bard in the tenth century."

When they returned to the hotel, Grania parked and turned to Dari. "You're free to do as you wish tonight but be back here at eight in the morning. My shuttle is at ten, and you need to be in this little tube before I leave." Grania held up the pendant of fae dirt on the chain around her neck, his passport back to the ship.

Dari winked at her before he vanished. She sighed, knowing he didn't need to travel with her to pop into the soil whenever he wished.

Chapter Seventeen

Sitting in the chair facing her desk, Theos grilled Grania on everything that had happened with Sternbach. He still couldn't understand how she'd killed him, and Grania wasn't about to reveal the truth about Dari. How would he react if he knew she had a puca on board? Hellfire, would he believe it even if she had Dari prove it? Even Irish people were reluctant to acknowledge that the sidhe existed for all they told the myths and blamed everything on them.

"I told you. I found a board and bashed him," Grania repeated. Theos hadn't seen the body, so why wasn't her story plausible?

"So, you hit him hard enough to kill him with one blow?" Theos shifted in the chair as he raised a skeptical eyebrow.

"Not one blow," she replied. "The agent was still trying to grab me, so I hit him again. That was the one that killed him. I hadn't meant to do it. I still had questions for him." That was the truth, at least. She had wanted to learn more before Dari's horse form killed him.

"Yes, it would have been useful to learn more. As it is, we might encounter another agent from the anti-political group since they've gotten wind of this shipment. And you dumped the body somewhere?"

"I told you already. With Dari's help, we dragged him to the bay and dumped him."

"Where his body will eventually float to the surface." He tapped his mobi and held it up for her to see. "Have you seen this?"

She leaned forward to see the news item more closely. "I saw it this morning before I caught the shuttle." And she'd been looking over her shoulder until she was back at the station. The report stated a fisherman had seen an altercation on the shore at Rockfleet Castle. He'd gone out for a stroll on the hillside and only saw it from a distance. Still, he told the garda about a man attacking a red-haired woman. He swore a giant white horse appeared out of nowhere and saved her, killing the man.

"So, what's the story with the white horse?"

She shrugged. "An illusion? I don't know. How much had the fisherman had to drink before his hike? Do you think some imaginary animal suddenly showed up to help me?"

"Of course not. But the man called the local police, who investigated. They didn't find anything except an empty vehicle parked there and no sign of the man who rented it. They'll keep looking, you know."

"Well then, let's try to be far away before they discover anything." She shifted uneasily in her chair. Bad luck, for sure. But with the horse being the culprit, she was innocent, and the fisherman didn't see her close enough to identify her. The only link might be her rental, but she doubted the witness could give any detail on it.

Theos ran a hand through his gorgeous curly hair. She silently chided herself for noticing. "Did you leave anything behind that might give them a clue?"

"Maybe some drops of my blood co-mingled with Sternbach's, but I think most of it will be hard to gather in the muddy grass. A squall was comin' ashore as we left, so it likely washed most of it away." At least, she prayed that would be the case.

He stared at her for a few moments. She held her tongue, not wanting to inadvertently say something that would add to the fabrication that didn't fit. Finally, Theos asked, "How long before we undock?"

"Three hours. Rory found another cargo load for the Andromeda Station transfer that will arrive shortly. That will give us almost a full hold."

Her brother had busted his butt to line up that load, even though it slowed their departure. But if Theos would leave her, it would also give her time to talk to Vilnius. Going through the trauma with Orla had given her a new perspective on her relationship with the station master.

"Let's hope the Irish police don't find anything to link you to the death. If they do catch up, you might consider how to explain the fisherman's account and put the blame on an imaginary creature." With that pronouncement, Theos rose and left her cabin.

Breathing a sigh of relief, Grania contacted Rory to let him know she was going to the station master's office and would return in time for pre-launch.

* * * * *

Grania found Vilnius in his office, talking to a ship's captain who'd just docked. Seeing her come in, he nodded her way and held up a hand, palm out to signal he knew she was there and to wait. She settled into one of the chairs along the wall and watched him as he charmed the officer. He was good at the customer relations thing, which was why he was such an asset to the station. Not everyone could handle the clients' sometimes-whiny requests as if the station should accommodate their every whim. The truth was Vilnius was even better with the mechanical and technical aspects of the station. He rivaled Liam in engine expertise as not many realized the station was a stable, orbiting spaceship that needed to be maintained, and that had been his job. Probably still was, if she knew Vilnius.

Finished with the man, Vilnius came out to greet her. "Are you free for lunch?" she asked.

"For you? Always." He turned to tell his assistant that he would be out for an hour or so, then caught her arm and led her out of the office. "Where would you like to go?"

"Somewhere private," she answered.

"In that case, let's pick up some sandwiches and go to my place."

After a quick stop to get lunch, they went through the private door for residents to reach his apartment. He fetched cold drinks from the kitchen, and they ate at the dining table.

"Your first meal here," he quipped jokingly.

It was true, though. Grania had hurried to catch the shuttle the only other time she'd been here. Now she had a short time before she'd be leaving again.

"Any luck finding potential crew members for me?" she asked.

He chewed on his first bite until he could talk around it. "Not yet. We don't get many uncommitted crewmen here. Every now and then, we might get somebody who has just separated from his ship, but most want a break before heading out again. Did you check when you were planetside?"

"I didn't have time. Thanks for looking, though."

"So, how long before you leave?" he asked.

"About two hours."

"You're not staying tonight?" His head came up from his sandwich, surprise reflected on his face.

Before the altercation in Galway that could explode at any time, she had planned to stay the extra night here, but now, she didn't have the time. "Sorry. Hot cargo that needs urgent delivery, so a long trip to make within a set timeline."

"Then, we don't have time to waste." He set his sandwich down and started to rise.

"Wait, Vilnius. I want to talk to you." Grania didn't move to rise, settling herself into the chair.

He sank back down again, his face going to neutral with a straight lip and eyes on her.

"Are you going to accept the station master job here?" she asked bluntly.

"I admit I am considering it. It's a helluva offer and something I thought I might get within a few more years."

"So, Tara Station was a pipe dream, then?" She tried to contain the hurt in her voice.

He leaned forward, reaching a hand for hers. She pulled it back. "Love, when I put in for Tara Station, I had every intention of transferring. Then Hartman's heart attack happened, and suddenly I was needed here. Even then, I didn't think I would be offered the position. The authorities made the offer just as you were leaving Erinnua."

"And what of us?" Grania kept her voice steady and expression even, not wanting him to see the pain.

"You could marry me and live here…in this apartment on the station." He flipped his hand to palm up, fingers wagging for hers like he was calling a pet.

"To do what? There's nothing on a station for me to do. I am a ship's captain. Mo Chroidhe may not be a big, fancy vessel, but she's mine. I've worked hard for this, so leaving her isn't an option." She lost her calm as her voice rose while she talked.

"Then, we continue as we are. Seeing each other when you're scheduled here."

"For how long, Vilnius? Year after year, two or three visits a year if we're lucky. I think we both want more than that." Her voice held a bitter edge to it.

"Nia, darling, I want you."

"But you want this station more," she snapped back. "Just as I want my freedom on my ship more." Tears sprang to her eyes. She'd spoken the total truth. They each desired the physical symbol of their success and identity more than they wanted each other.

Then Vilnius made an illogical leap. "It's the new guy on your ship, isn't it? Have you fallen for him, Grania? Is he better than me?"

"No! He's a temporary hire to help Liam. I am losing Liam. Did I tell you that? He's going to our uncle's ship. But Theos is only on for this trip to Desolation. There is nothing between us."

"Then what—?" Vilnius stopped at her look.

"I've wanted you for years, and after our last time together on Pelanan, I thought you felt the same. When you offered to transfer to Tara Station, I believed we would have a future. But I don't see it now. Not if you stay here."

"Nia, I love you. I've never wanted any other woman who came through here the way I desire and love you. There has to be a way."

Grania wiped a tear away from her eye, then rose. "Well, if you figure out one, let me know. I need to get back to my ship."

She started for the door before he clambered to his feet. He hurried to try to intercept her. "Nia, wait. I haven't—"

"We're done," she said, turning her face to him again, then rushed out the door before she changed her mind. Her chest hurt as her heart pounded. She'd broken it off, and now it felt terrible, like a part of her heart had been ripped out.

She strode as fast as she could without running to return to her ship, her sanctuary.

* * * * *

Going through the pre-launch steps, mostly double-checking Brendan's work and reading the messages Rory relayed to her, calmed her anxiety. She'd just broken up with the man she loved. After six years of meeting once or twice a year, Grania realized it wasn't going anywhere and never could. She wanted more from a relationship, but she wouldn't get it with a stationer, just as he wouldn't be fulfilled with a spacer.

Her mother and grandmother before her both worked on the ships with their husbands until Grandmother elected to retire and raise the kids, including any of the family's children. Uncle Colm and Aunt Amalie often left their son and daughter with Grandma when they were growing up. Grania had lived with her until she was fourteen, when her mom brought her on the ship to learn the family business.

No, a stationer wouldn't work. Not even one on Tara, she admitted bitterly. She needed to find a man who would share the ship with her.

A message from the spaceport surprised her, and she feared it had to do with the altercation in Ireland. On reading it, they'd sent a thank you for using their shuttle service and a questionnaire regarding their service.

Her nerves felt a little raw, ready to overreact to everything. She hoped they had no problems on this run to the

Outer Rim, and she wouldn't encounter any more spies after whatever the cargo was. Bad enough that she had an agent on board. At least Theos was helpful and had enough knowledge to assist Liam with the engines.

Luckily, her brother had finagled another two weeks before he had to report to Uncle Colm's ship. While she suspected their uncle wasn't pleased, he admitted he could do without Liam until they made it to Galaxy Gate. After that, he'd need to leave her to return to Pelenan, where he'd meet his new ship. Then she'd be relying on Theos unless she could get a new engineer.

"Everything's on board and locked down," Liam reported. "We're ready when you are."

"Good job, Liam. We'll take her out in fifteen mites, on schedule." Grania grinned and gave Rory and Brendan the go-ahead signal.

As they started to pull away from the dock, a signal came through for Grania from the station master. She hesitated, not wanting to hear his voice. But professional courtesy won out. "Captain O'Ceagan here."

"I want to wish you a safe journey and good fortune. I will continue to look for a new engineer and or second officer. Bon voyage."

"Thank you, Station Master," she answered formally, only partly amused by his old Earth sailing term. She ended the call and turned back to timing the deployment of the dorsal sail.

At an angle from her, Rory gaped at her, mouth open and eyebrows lifting sky-high. "Wasn't that Vilnius?"

"It was."

"That was short and not-so-sweet." Rory's look said a lot more than that.

"We... I broke up with him."

Now Brendan swung around to peer at her.

"Watch your screens in case anything gets in our way," Grania instructed. She wasn't going to elaborate to any of her brothers. "Both of you, pay attention to the business of getting away from the station."

"Aye, Captain," Brendan replied, snapping his attention back to his navigation screens.

Rory said nothing but seemed more interested in what was coming across on the communications channel.

Chapter Eighteen

Down in the hold, Dari sat on a crate and watched Liam showing Theos some details about the engines, especially the new one they'd acquired. For the puca, it seemed pretty boring.

He felt something had changed between him and Captain Grania after he'd killed that man. Sometimes, he lost control of his baser nature and accidentally killed someone he had not intended. That was not the case this time. The fellow had threatened her and clearly planned to harm her. He would not let that happen, so he did what he always did to protect those he cared about, including himself.

But the Captain had seemed shocked by it. He had caught her often looking at him with more scrutiny as if she was discovering his true nature. Granted, he could be fearsome, but he would never harm her. She was a friend to him and Sheilan. And he trusted her and his other companions on this ship to keep his secrets.

Jumping off the crate, Dari interrupted Liam for a moment. "You're not needin' me at the moment, so I am going on break. Just so yous know, Mister Liam."

"Yes, that's fine, Dari. Take your time. We have a long trip ahead." Liam turned back to show an engine illustration to the other man.

As Dari ambled to the galley for tea with biscuits, he thought the second level felt empty with no passengers on board.

Over tea, he reflected on his visit to the land where he'd lived for millennia. He had visited a few pucas he knew in the western hills, and they'd told their latest stories. Of course, none could come close to the tale he could tell, but it had been fun.

After he'd left them, he went to find Sheilan. He still knew where the linking sod was to take him to Eterien, the sidhe realm. Once he was there, it was an easy matter to locate the b'ean sidhe. They were connected in a sense, and he could hone in on her with little effort.

While she wasn't locked in a cell, he found her in one of the visitor orbs, which you could call detainment rather than imply she might be free to leave. Even though the sidhe lived in their energy state in their world, they could identify each other by their fractal images within the energy. Sheilan had been delighted when he'd popped in, saying as much right off, then she'd asked, "How did you get here, Dari? Did you use the dirt?"

"No," he'd replied. "I did not have the bravado to do it, so I joined Captain Grania's crew when they traveled to Earth. In fact, she is in Ireland now, delivering an intended bride."

"Really?" Sheilan's eyes widened at this news. "Who would have expected a starship captain to have to deliver people? Tis a strange world, is it not?"

"That it is. So, when are you coming back to Erinnua?"

"That is an excellent question, Dari. And I have asked it many times meself. So far, the High Council is still deliberating my status."

"Ah, no harm, no foul in what you have done, so why is it such a concern?" He gave her his indignant look.

"'Tis just their way, I guess. They are slower than those damnable Ents that Tolkien fellow wrote about when it comes to debating an issue."

"But you must return to Erinnua," he'd objected, fearful all this delay meant they would not allow it.

"Have faith that I can convince them," Sheilan answered. "It will be well. You'll see, my dear puca."

"Dari?"

Captain Grania's voice interrupted his thoughts. He looked up at her, seeing the warm smile on her face.

"May I join you?" she asked.

"Of course, you may," he responded. "I will get more tea for you."

"Thank you," she acknowledged, then added, "It occurred to me I never said thank you for saving my life. I admit I was shocked by both your form and your actions. I've not seen you that way before. Even when we were trying to resolve the problem with Erinnua's waters, I never saw your horse form. It's very powerful."

Dari set the tea down. "Indeed, it is."

"I want you to know I don't hold it against you that you killed the man, even though I didn't want you to do it. Still, he would have hurt me if you hadn't. Do you feel any guilt about doing it?"

"I never feel guilt," Dari said. "I do what I must do, and sometimes I kill when I don't mean to do it. But my nature is chaotic, and it never bothers me when I make a mistake."

One thing did bother him, but it wasn't because he killed someone. It had to do with the female sea dragon on Erinnua, who had broken off all relations because her brother died in the actions he and Grania's brothers had taken to end the radiation in the water. It wasn't guilt, but he regretted it, nonetheless.

Grania sipped her tea, took a biscuit, then looked him in the eye. "Dari, you know we have three long jumps coming up, don't you?"

"I have heard Liam talkin' of it."

"The thing is, the first isn't too bad, just about twelve hours in the jump pods. Then we'll have close to twenty hours of space travel to reach the next gate. It's the longest one, and we'll be in the pods for about forty-six hours. After that, we have another four days to the next gate, followed by a forty-hour jump. Once we're through that, we have three days to reach Desolation's station."

Dari blinked, not very good with numbers. "That sounds like a long time."

"It is. Almost twelve days. So, I am wondering what you might do in all that time? I mean, I know that sidhe don't require sleep or food. But is there anything you need during the time most of us will be sleeping?"

"Oh, well, I did tell Liam I would keep me eye on the engines and alert him if anything seemed wrong. I can do the same thing for you, Captain Grania. Would you like me to check on the bridge from time to time?"

A small smile tweaked her lips. "That would be very helpful. I do admit the jumps worry me, especially if anything should go wrong."

"Do not fret about it. I will keep watch while you all sleep. I know how to wake Mister Liam."

"You do, do you? Well, then, you will be our watchman through the jumps. But if you need anything else, like tea or biscuits, help yourself. You might avoid your human form if you require oxygen since the life support will be set to minimal."

"That will not be a problem," he assured her.

"One more thing I should tell you. Someone spotted us when we were at the castle and saw what had happened from a distance. He reported a wild white horse attacking a man. He didn't say anything about us dragging him to the water."

"People around there are superstitious. Though he reported the kerfuffle, 't'would not be hard for him to conclude that a puca attacked. The only wonder might be that the horse didn't kill both people."

She nodded. "I wanted you to know about it, just in case."

He snorted. "Nothing will come of it, lass. Trust me on this."

After she left, Dari thought about the report, chuckling to himself. So, the country people of Eire still remember the sidhe and are willing enough to tell others. 'T'was good to know they were not forgotten yet.

Chapter Nineteen

While the next few days crawled by for the crew, Grania considered their imminent journey and the limitations of her ship. The jumps were long but only a fraction of the time it would take to make the trip without them. With the galaxy's edge being nearly forty-six billion light-years from Earth, no one could make the trip in their lifetime without the gates. With them, the time was whittled down to less than fourteen days. Stops at two connecting stations before they reached their destination would eat up additional hours with cargo exchange and possible maintenance to the ship. No matter how she looked at it, getting to Desolation within the specified time would be tight.

She hated that she had wasted time on Earth with escort service, something she hadn't worried about before being coerced into the outer rim delivery. Still, she took satisfaction in knowing she'd help work out the difficult situation for Orla. But now, if anything went wrong between here and Desolation, it might make her miss her deadline.

Deep in thought, she jerked when her mobi abruptly chittered. She grabbed it from her bridge console. "What is it?"

"We need to talk, Grania," Theos' cool voice answered.

What now? Like I don't have enough to worry about. "My cabin is the best place. I'll see you there in about twenty-five mites."

She glanced at her brothers, seeing the curiosity on their faces, and said, "Anyone need a break? Now is a good time."

Rory sprang to his feet. "Me. I could use ten or fifteen."

"Make it twelve. How about you, Bren?"

"I'm good for now. But if Rory could bring back a Rocket pick-me-up, that would be helpful."

Rory gave him a thumbs-up as he dashed out the door, heading for the stairs.

"Do those energy drinks really work?" Grania asked.

"Oh, yeah. They give you a nice boost for about two hours. You should try one when you feel like you're draggin'."

"Maybe I will." She leaned back in her seat and cross-checked the course, trying to will the ship to move faster. As it was, Liam was pushing the freighter as hard as he felt safe to do.

When Rory returned, she told them she'd be in her cabin if anything happened. She exited the bridge and strode down the hall to her quarters in the ship's nose. Amused, she thought the boys would notice Theos passing by the bridge if they were alert. No secrets when you have transparent walls.

She grabbed a fruit snack bar and a bottle of water while she waited, wondering what prompted this meeting. A few mites later, a knock at the door announced her visitor. "Come," she said, a voice cue to slide the door open rather than an invitation.

Theos strolled in like he owned the place, shoulders back, his eyes on the mobi in his left hand. He glanced up from it as a brief smile parted his lips. "Thank you for seeing me, Captain." He didn't wait for her acknowledgment or offer before he commandeered the chair across the desk from her.

A man who is used to being in charge. Grania suppressed her sardonic smile, not wanting to give him an edge. "You have something urgent to discuss?"

"Not so much urgent as interesting and needed planning." He held the mobi up so she could see and hear the page he'd called up. Another news report from Ireland regarding the curious incident at Rockfleet. Seemed the police were now calling it an unsolved mystery.

"They haven't found a body yet," he said after she listened to the broadcast. "They even used a sonar scan over the whole bay and didn't turn up anything."

She shrugged. "Perhaps it washed out to the ocean."

"Lucky for us." He set the mobi in his lap. "I located a little information on Sternbach. He was a mercenary, an agent for hire. He didn't work directly for AAPICA but was apparently charged with discovering what was in the shipment from Enterprise. So, when he said that maybe someone else would come after you, he probably meant they might hire another operative."

"You're telling me we now have three agencies interested in this cargo—the UPA shipper, the PPG, and AAPICA. We should be alert at any stop for anyone else who might show interest in me or the ship. Is that right?"

He canted his head to one side as a close-mouthed smile stretched his face. "This brings me to my next point. You need to be cautious of any cargo or potential passengers from now on. Your brother is diligent about keeping the bay filled as much as possible, but bringing anything new on board could be dangerous. A passenger could be the next agent. The best step now is to avoid the potential threats."

"Well, that is a teeny problem, Theos. We're a merchant freighter. If we unload cargo and don't replace it when some is waiting to be shipped, it's going to look suspicious to anyone watching my ship, not to mention costing us income." She leaned forward in her chair and folded her hands on the desktop.

"I understand. But the cargo can be a huge risk. Someone could plant an explosive device in a crate to destroy the ship."

"What? Blow up the cargo they're so concerned about?" Her eyes widened. *Would they do that?*

"If they believe it's a weapon, and they don't want it used, then yes, they could."

"Theos, what is going on at Desolation? Why this mysterious shipment and all the interest in it? The manifest says farm equipment."

"Do you believe that crate holds farming items?" He rolled his eyes.

She shook her head, shifting her hands nervously.

Theos edged forward, hunching his shoulders. "Desolation is at war. Two factions on the planet are battling it out. So far, the government-supported side is winning or at least holding its own. The rebellious side is financed and encouraged by the Free Merchants Guild."

"I've never heard of them. Why would they support a rebellion?"

"Most of the time, they support merchants on any AUP planet, but sometimes, when they feel the planetary government is failing to encourage the world by…" He paused, seeking the right words to explain. …suppressing the trade and monetary equality needed for the economic growth, they actively oppose them."

Grania blinked, not sure she understood what he meant, but it sounded like the guild was encouraging the merchants to fight the local government.

He paused and took a deep breath. "Aren't you, at least, curious about what's in that crate?"

"Of course I am. But when I'm told something is top secret and the box is secured in a who-know-what way, I am not inclined to break into it."

"I suppose it could be boobytrapped, rigged to blow up anyone who doesn't have the code." He shrugged.

A thought stuck Grania at that point. "If AAPICA knows we have the crate, would they consider placing a device in any boxes we brought onboard at Zabrowski?"

Theos sat up, his eyes growing wider. "You'd better check your manifest to see if there's anything suspicious in your cargo. Look for items that aren't too detailed, like farm equipment, and from shippers you are unfamiliar with. I'll check the crates we loaded to see if anything looks odd."

"I'll get on it now." Grania turned to her desk console screen and tapped in the code to bring up the shipping manifests. "These all should have cleared customs and security at an originating point, but if an explosive was added once it arrived at Zabrowski, it wouldn't have been checked."

Shoving to his feet, Theos leaned part-way over her desk. "Let me know if you see something that needs closer inspection, *Captain*."

Grania turned her head toward him, her face only inches away from his. His scent made its way to her nose, a sweet lemony-spice fragrance she found alluring. Words failing her, she bobbed her head once as he straightened and headed out the door. Her gaze lingered as it shut. As her grandmother always said, "When a man was that gorgeously built, it would be a sin not to admire him." Theos Camber could be a god.

With a sigh, she turned back to her console and began going through all the items picked up at Zabrowski. Since they were headed for the Outer Rim, Rory had scored about two dozen shipments from shippers she hadn't dealt with before. Of those, twenty were transferred from other ships that had brought them as far as the station. That meant only four originated from Earth and had cleared customs there.

She looked at each one, reading the description and destination. Andromeda Station, one read, planet-bound for Sistima, final destination, then the recipient's name and address at Palermo, which Grania presumed was the city. It stated the contents to be cooking utensils, including pots, pans, knives, measuring cups, and stirring spoons. Pretty detailed. In short, probably the household goods of a family who had moved to the city.

She moved on to the next, noting the ones with brief or generalized descriptions. She ended up with six fitting the criteria. Then she realized a smart person would write a good description on the manifest, but that didn't mean it couldn't include something that wasn't on the list. Hellfire, any crates could include an explosive, even those they picked up on Enterprise.

Her spirits fell as she thought about the possibility that someone might want to blow up her ship to destroy the strange object they had on board. She never imagined this scenario in her dreams of being the captain. How would her granda handle this? Had he ever had to? It did occur to her that she might have a solution, but not one she could tell Theos about.

Grania shut her console down, updating everything to the bridge version, then stopped by the bridge to check in with Rory and Brendan.

"Everything is going to plan," Brendan assured her. "It's clear space ahead, nothing to worry about."

"What he said." Rory pressed his fingers to his earpiece. "No chatter anywhere, let alone about any problems ahead."

"Well, just keep listening. We don't have as much traffic going this direction as we do between Earth and home, so something could sneak up on us, like a cluster of meteorites."

"I know," he complained. "I'm scanning for them."

"Just keepin' you on your toes, Rory. I'm going down to grab a sandwich. Either of you want anything."

"A packet of chips would be good," Brendan piped up. "And another drink." He held up the empty soda container to show her.

Frowning in disapproval, she said, "Those things can't be all that good for you. How about some water or a glass of milk?"

"Ugh. That stuff we got at the station is awful. I'll be stickin' with the cola."

"Your stomach." She pivoted to face Rory. "Anything for you?"

"No. I am fine, and I have my juice." He tapped his earpiece, a single frown line crossing his forehead.

"What?" Grania stepped closer to him.

He shook his head. "Nothin'. I thought I detected a whine, but it went away. There's nothin' out there."

A look of concern touched her eyes, then vanished. If Rory said nothing, she believed him. But she also expected him to keep checking if he even had a hint of something. What might whine in space?

In the galley, she ordered a ham and cheese sandwich. One of the things she loved about going to Zabrowski was that they could stock up on Earth-produced foods. Pigs weren't common on Erinnua, although she'd urged her granda to import a few to start raising them now that he had the time. "From starship captain to pig farmer," he'd scoffed. But maybe she'd put the bug in his mind.

While she sat to eat, Liam came in for a break, just as she'd hoped he would. After a quick greeting, he ordered a bowl of Caledonian stew from the auto-chef, got a cold drink, and sat across from her.

"How are things going down below?" Grania asked.

"Good. Theos is doing fine, learning how the system works and the quirks of our engines." He hesitated, then leaning his elbows on the table, said, "Nia, what is really happening here?"

"What do you mean?" She tried to sound surprised by the question, but she had a good idea.

"You were in trouble when you called from Ireland. Why did you want me to tell Theos Camber? What could you tell him that you couldn't tell me? What was all that stuff he told you about?"

"Liam, I... I had a problem that I hoped he could—"

"You were in serious trouble," he interrupted. "I thought you could tell me anything. That you trusted me."

"I do. It's just—"

"That you could tell someone you just met a few days ago and offered a job in the engine room? Nia, it makes no sense. Yes, he has some education, and he's pretty good, but he has no practical experience and no references. Why would you hire him?"

"I didn't exactly. He—"

"Don't tell me you did it because he's so bloody good-looking."

"Would you let me speak without interrupting?" Her voice went a level higher, not quite shouting yet, but getting close.

When he shut his mouth and glared at her, Grania tried to frame her words and speak softly. "I'm not supposed to tell anyone, not you or our brothers. That crate we're hauling is hotter than we thought. Not in a good way. Theos is an agent for the PPG, which is concerned about what the AUP is shipping to Desolation. He contacted me on Pelanan and suggested he could come on board to help protect the shipment and us."

Liam's mouth dropped, and he drew a breath, "Does he know what it is?"

She shook her head. "I don't think so. He suspects it's a weapon." Then she told him a short version of what had happened when she called and asked for Theos.

"Dari killed the man?" Liam repeated, his voice expressing disbelief. "And the two of you disposed of the body. Feck, Nia. This is a mess."

"It's not a mess. I think it's being handled."

"What do you mean?" Liam shifted his position, moving even closer.

"Theos showed me a report from Ireland where it looks like the police there are playing it down. No body, no evidence, only an old fisherman claiming to see a white horse trampling a man. He even allowed it could be a puca since it appeared out of nowhere. So now, the police are thinking he was seeing things."

"If the body washes ashore…"

"That's another thing. Dari said he took care of it. I think he might have buried the body under something in the water. Something that won't get moved anytime soon."

"Our little Dari did all that," he said with wonder in his

voice.

"Why so surprised, Liam? Look at what he did at home for the Spighalira. We can't underestimate him." She dropped the gentle reminder about the water dragons they'd all helped to save at Dari's insistence.

"Does Camber know about Dari?"

"He believes he's human. He doesn't need to know anything else about him."

Liam straightened and dipped his head once. He rose and retrieved his stew from the auto-chef, which had now cooled enough to eat.

As he sat back down again, Grania said, "I have another little job for Dari if you'll pass it on to him for me."

While Liam ate, Grania explained her plan and stressed that it needed to be done when Theos slept.

Chapter Twenty

While the crew slept in their pods during the first jump from Sagan gate to Chang gate, Dari began a systematic, at least by his reckoning, examination of the crates in the Mo Chroidhe's cargo hold.

Before they'd jumped, Dari had watched Theos check the exterior of the boxes, comparing the manifests to the listings on each one, then running a scanner over the box. As he did so, he checked it off his list.

He'd stood for a long while in front of the biggest crate down there, running the scanner over all sides and shaking his head. "Not a damn thing," he complained to Liam. "The scanner can't get past whatever this shipment is packed in."

"I know," Liam answered as he ran a final check on the engine before entering the wormhole. "My sister and I scanned it when we first brought it on board. All we know is it has a coded lock. We were warned not to tamper with it."

"Top secret stuff, huh?"

Liam shrugged. "Seems like it. We have about an hour until we approach the gate. Why don't you wrap up what you're doing? You need to check on your jump pod and prepare for it."

"What's to prepare? You climb in, press the sleep button,

and close the lid. The unit does everything else."

Liam rolled his eyes as he approached Theos. "That is true, but it wouldn't hurt to check the status to ensure it has adequate oxygen and systimamine for the length of the jump. All three of these are long wormholes, longer than the ones we usually take."

Theos screwed his face into a scowl, put the scanner away then left to go to his quarters. Dari could see he hadn't been happy about the whole situation.

As for himself, he wasn't disturbed by the jumps at all, so he wandered around the ship as he chose. But for now, Captain Grania and Mister Liam had given him this inspection task, so he would do a thorough job of it.

He took the fore part of the ship first. Nearest to the cargo ramp and the secret crate, he stood in front of a box about half his size and dematerialized into energy, then darted inside. His fractal vision gave him a 3-D schematic of the objects inside. Line colors indicated the object's heat, with red being the warmest and blue to white at the cool end. These objects, round and flat disks, showed yellow to light green lines, meaning they were about room temperature and safe.

He didn't read very well, so he couldn't say if the objects inside matched the information on the crate, but he didn't see a threat.

Without changing back, he darted into the next box, repeating the process, examining the objects, and judging them safe. From there, he worked his way to the end of the row, declared them safe, and began on the next one.

Time passed in silence, save for the occasional rattle of some loose object, as they passed through the wormhole at high speed. After finishing half the fore part of the hold, Dari paused to gaze at the screen in the engineer's office, where the distorted lines and swirling patterns of the hyperjump displayed. They looked like twisted fractals to his senses, spinning and intermingling in some kind of energy pattern that formed the fold in space.

Dari understood the words but not the concept so much. He just accepted it for what it was, just as he did the soil travel he and other sidhe used to move from place to place. If they could distribute their dirt on all the worlds, then his kind could travel anywhere within seconds. He made a mental note to discuss it with Sheilan when the b'ean sidhe returned.

Liam slept in stasis in his pod in the middle of the room. Unlike the others, he preferred to stay close to the engines when they jumped so he could react quicker in an emergency. Dari watched the gauges for him, ensuring they didn't wander out of their range. Sheilan had said that humans couldn't tolerate the distorted lines and the pressure of wormhole travel, so it was easier for them to sleep through it.

After numerous hours, several tea breaks, checking on the bridge rounds and watching the energy gauges, Dari had made it through most of the cargo hold. Nothing presented as dangerous or explosive in all that he'd examined. He supposed that was reassuring, even if it was boring for him.

The only crate he had not checked out was the one they'd loaded at Enterprise. He stood next to it, considering what he might do. Although he'd already been into it once, he thought he could learn more about the thing inside if he took a little more time.

Changing back to energy, he zipped into the crate, effortlessly passing through the exterior shipping container and worming his way past the metal inside box that surrounded the creature. His fractal vision picked up all kinds of colors inside, from cold to normal to hot. As he studied the patterns of the box, he began to convert them to a solid object form in his mind. It resembled the transporter decontamination unit he and Grania had used when they'd jumped to the freebooters' ship a few months earlier.

The layer over the creature showed mostly on the chartreuse side. Dari could make out the contact points that led to the being within. It looked less thick than before, leading him to suspect it might be nourishing the dormant thing beneath it.

As much as he moved around the crate, viewing the creature from all sides, he still couldn't get a clear picture of what she actually was. Pausing, his energy glittering like little flecks of gold, he considered one possibility. In his catalog of forms, he had one that he'd accidentally acquired when he swallowed it. A fae small enough that he could change to it within the cabinet and sufficiently see enough, albeit in four separate images, to get a closer look.

While he rarely used the form, it was easy enough to switch and a moment later, a small white ball of light with a bug-like center floated in the space within the metal case. The real deal, Dari's whisp moved easily with wings flickering so fast, they made the ball of white appear solid.

He buzzed close to the creature's face noting the golden eyes appeared to be open but not seeing or reacting to anything around her. Given the upper body, which carried the form of a human woman, he had to think of her as female. A halo of tendrils flowed from her head, waving slightly in the still container. Mixed in with them were tubes that led to the heart of the yellow-gold substance that covered her. Feeding tubes, Dari thought once he saw them. He didn't doubt that she was alive and in a dormant state. Whoever had managed this must have been a genius, in his opinion. This rivaled any of the early feats of the legendary Tuatha de Dannen in whatever this was. He didn't know what to call it, but he suspected it was an altered life form.

Pulling back, his wings almost brushing the walls of the containment box, the whisp form eyeballed the solid plate, contoured armor covering her body until it joined with the lower portion. Here, the human aspect shifted to that of a bumble bee, an oblong-shaped abdomen with shortened, thick legs that jutted out at the bottom. Folded against her back, Dari saw a pair of folded wings that didn't look big enough to lift the body.

Whatever her purpose, he thought she was not a friendly creature. Not with the armor nor the steely expression on her face, even in slumber, and the extra-rich nourishment the shippers were feeding her. She wasn't a piece of farm equipment; neither was she a queen bee to establish a colony to help plants produce.

Over the centuries, Dari had seen a fair number of war machines, but he'd never seen one like this. Changing back to energy, Dari darted out, switching back to human as he touched the hold's floor. He shivered, creeped out a little by the strange figure. Every sense he possessed told him she was a ruinous missive.

One more thing he'd seen on his departure was the wired switch connected to the digital keypad of the container. Failure to provide the correct password would result in an explosion. He'd seen enough explosive material attached to the door to blow a hole in the ship. With all his history in Ireland, he knew a vast array of explosive devices, and this one bore all the earmarks of a catastrophic one.

All he had to do was give Captain Grania a clear image of everything he saw. Still pondering how he could do it, Dari went to the galley to get tea and cakes; an apparent mimicry of human behavior, he realized. Only now did he wonder if it came from the form he'd chosen to take.

*****

Before Grania could check the status of everything on the ship, Dari wanted to see her and Liam in the engineering office. She didn't like the urgent sound of the request, but she had given him the task. They needed to know if he had found a problem in the cargo.

She paused long enough the glance through the readings

as they'd come out of the wormhole, noting all reports appeared normal. Rory would study them in more detail. "I'm going down to engineering."

Rory swiveled toward her, his mouth hanging open. "Is there a problem?"

"Not that I know of, but Dari wants to talk to me. Perhaps there was an anomaly during the jump. I don't see any indication in the reports, though."

Even Brendan wore a worried look as he listened, his eyes darting back to his console, probably to check for anything he might have missed.

She grabbed a cup of coffee on the way, sipping at it until she started down the stairs. Liam waited for her in his office while Theos spoke to Dari near one of the crates that had broken loose during transit. She gazed at it a moment or two, noting it hadn't split open, just lost the restraining straps that had held it in place. That couldn't be the big concern.

As she entered Liam's office, he looked up from his logs, a twitch of his lips almost making a smile. "Morning, Nia. Before you ask, I don't know exactly why Dari wanted to meet at once. I suspect it has to do with the cargo."

"I agree," she said, leaning her backside against the console table, waiting for the puca to pull himself free of Theos. She knew Dari had seen her and was doing his best to extricate himself from the agent.

After another minute, he stepped away and hurried to the office. Grania glimpsed the frown on Theos' forehead as he no doubt wondered about the gathering he hadn't been invited to attend. Not when her own secret agent was about to reveal something she didn't want him to hear.

"Thank the gods," Dari said. "I could not escape that man with him jabbering on about the broken restrainin' strap like I could do anythin'. It had been fine until we were exitin' the wormhole, then there had been a hard jolt. Did ya feel it?"

Grania shook her head, as did Liam. "We were still waking up, I imagine." But it worried her a little, and she made a mental note to ask the station master at Chang if anyone else had noticed it or if it might be common to this particular wormhole.

"Anyway, that was what broke the restrainin' straps on it," Dari said.

He seemed agitated to Grania, but maybe that was excitement. "Is that what you wanted to talk about—the cargo?" She hoped to lead him to why he'd called the meeting.

"In a way, yes, that would be it. Not that particular problem, though, no. I did as you asked during the jump, and almost all the cargo is clear. But one of them has some smuggled goods in it that are not on the manifest. I cannot rightly tell you what the items are, but I noted it on the manifest."

"Smuggled, but not dangerous?" Liam asked.

"Not dangerous. Not that one, anyway."

Grania felt her stomach twist. He had found a threat in one of them. "What did you find, Dari?"

"Well, it is not new if you are worried, but it has to do with the mystery crate. I checked it out again and managed to get a better view of the creature within it."

Grania shot Liam a startled look, and he returned it with his own wide-eyed look. "Did you learn something in particular?" he asked.

"I did. I am goin' to try to draw you what I saw." He took Liam's mobi pad and stylus and began sketching.

Grania leaned toward him, getting a sideways glimpse of what he was drawing. It looked like a normal sketch of a person until the body bulged into a bulbous bottom. "I thought you only saw in fractals while in your energy form. Have you extrapolated this from those?"

"Ahh, I have another form I used, a small little sidhe called a whisp. I changed once I was inside the crate." He added more detail to the drawing.

"A whisp?" Grania repeated. "As in will-o-the-wisp?"

"A little like it, but it's not swamp gas. No, this is the real one. A tiny fae with very fast wings and a white glow."

"That is fascinating, Dari." Grania made another mental note of this particular form. It might have other uses.

Drawing completed, Dari shoved it on the table where they could all see it. Then, he explained what he had observed, what he thought the tubes were, as well as the gold-colored semi-liquid covering the being.

"Amazing," Liam said when he'd finished. "And scary. If this is some kind of weapon, what does it do?"

Grania continued to stare at the drawing, wondering the same thing. How would it work? It had wings. It had a hornet-shaped body and possibly a stinger. But what else might it have? Could it disburse any kind of poison? Or was it a giant pollinating insect?

"Now, we get to the other thing I must report about this crate. The inside chamber has a locking mechanism connected to an explosive." Dari explained everything he saw about that.

Liam's eyebrows shot to his hairline. "Well, that is something we definitely won't tamper with."

Grania nodded assent. "I would guess the only person with the password is the man to whom I will deliver it. Excellent job, Dari."

As Grania left Liam's office, Theos caught up with her. "What was that about?" he demanded.

"Nothing to worry about," Grania replied with a smile. "Dari felt a bump when the ship exited the wormhole and thought it might be something to worry about. I'll enquire once we're docked."

"That whole conversation was about a bump?" Theos looked skeptical.

"Pretty much. Did you feel it?"

"No, but I would have still been sleeping. How did Dari--?"

"He was awake early. No matter, it doesn't seem like the bump harmed the ship any except for breaking that one crate loose." She started up the steps before he could ask any more questions.

*****

Once settled in their berth, Grania and Rory stepped down the entry ramp on one of the two arms holding the Chang Station docks. Following a V-shape, the bottom was a rectangular metal building with no windows looking out to space. A twinge of disappointment struck as she'd looked forward to seeing the stars in this quadrant of the Milky Way. She and her crew had never traveled this way, but she figured she'd have ample time to gaze at them from her ship on the long trip to the next wormhole.

"Holy Moses," Rory said, his head turning from side to side. "This is a feckin' small station."

"It certainly is."

The arm where they'd docked showed ports for only six ships. If the other was the same size, it provided small capacity, so Grania concluded that few vessels came this way.

Once they turned into the main building and got a look at the football-field size, they also guessed that no one stayed very long either. The station master's office, a room scarcely bigger than one of the Mo Chroidhe's cabins, faced them as they entered. Grania touched Rory's arm, "I'm going to see the SM. Dari said we had a little hiccup when we exited. I'd like to see if he knows anything about it. You go ahead and look around."

Acknowledging, Rory set off to explore the station while she went in to find the master. He talked on a com unit, a headset over his graying black hair. He glanced at her, held up two fingers, and then returned to his call. She barely heard what he was saying, but it sounded like a language she didn't speak.

Chang Station was built by the Asian Coalition, so it didn't surprise her that the master was Asian and probably spoke a version of Chino-Japanese. She hoped he spoke English or French.

When he finally turned to her, his first words were in the garbled tongue he'd been speaking. She shook her head, her eyebrows edging toward each other. "Do you speak English?"

"Ah, so sorry. I do speak it. I should have realized. How may I help you?" He flashed a friendly smile, then stepped, coming closer to her.

She introduced herself, which drew a comment from him. "You are new to this route, Captain O'Ceagan. Welcome to Chang Station. I am afraid we don't have many amenities here. Not like Andromeda Station. We are a transfer center."

"I see. So not many visitors stop here?"

He laughed. "Oh, no. Just crates on their way from one section of space to another. How can I help you?"

"Actually, I have a question about the wormhole terminus." His eyes focused on her, eyebrows leveling out, and he crossed his arms over his chest, prepared to listen. As succinctly as possible, she described what Dari had told her about the jolt that was hard enough to dislodge one of their shipping boxes.

The master, his name tag read Ho Kawata, relaxed, his shoulders visibly releasing tension. "Oh, yes. Little bounces at the end are not unusual with this tunnel. It curves somewhat and, like a lip, ships go up and bounce off the end, depending on the position of the hole. Were there any damages?"

"No. I didn't see anything other than a restraining strap had snapped."

While she had thought about asking if Kawata knew any engineers looking for work, she decided against it. Her instincts warned her that anyone she might find here would be either a freebooter or another ship's reject.

She caught up with Rory, who'd found the only bar on the station, a six-foot box where a robotic tender served from behind the counter that crossed the front. Three round tables, each with a pair of chairs, sat in front of the free-standing facility. Her brother relaxed at one, drinking an Asian beer. "Made with rice and orange blossoms," he informed her. Raising the bottle, he added, "Try one of these, Nia. They're really delish." Popping a pretzel in his mouth, he took another swallow.

She ordered plum wine, served in a small bottle, and sat across from him. "Is there anything of interest on this station?"

"You're sitting at it." He adjusted his body in the seat and leaned back. "From what I've learned, a crew of twenty-five people covers the various jobs on the station, including the SM. They all live here and seldom go anywhere. They have a fast-food counter at the commissary but no other restaurants or food places. There is a little market and drug dispensary for emergencies. The clothing store only services locals, and most things must be ordered in."

"Sounds dull." Grania stole one of his pretzels. "No entertainment?"

"They do have a Video Vision theater that shows a new movie about every seven days, depending on how well the transmission signal comes in."

'Well, we aren't staying long, thank the gods. I hoped to buy some pastries for a crew treat, but no bake shop either."

"On the positive side, I did find some freight that's heading to Outer Rim Station." He looked positively pleased with himself, a sheepish grin on his face.

"Rory, we don't have room for more cargo," Grania answered, recalling Theos' words about not taking any on.

"Two came off, and these aren't all that big, Nia. We can fit them on. I've already talked to Liam about it."

"Are they coming over now?"

He dipped his head. "I know you're in a hurry, but one will be over in about twenty mites. So, we can be underway within an hour."

She jumped to her feet. "I need to get back. You can finish your drink and buy more snacks to bring on board." She gestured to the basketful of packaged chips and cookies at the end of the bar.

Hurrying down the short walkway to their docking bay, Grania called ahead to Liam and told him not to bring anything on board until they were inspected. "Have Dari meet me at the cargo ramp," she instructed. "Tell him to be in his energy form."

Chapter Twenty-One

When she got to the dock, Liam was talking with one of the loaders, a lean, wiry man with short bowl-shaped black hair who spoke poor English and mixed in Asian words. Liam had his mobi out, and using the translate function, it appeared.

He waved Grania over and explained, "They have these boxes to bring on board, and I'm trying to explain we need to inspect them. He keeps pointing to the manifest and saying it's done."

"Got it." Behind Liam, Theos loomed in the open hold, a glare on his face expressing his thoughts on Rory's action. Giving him a brief smirk, she turned to the loader and spoke slowly. "I am the captain of this ship. I must approve the cargo. Do you understand?"

He held up the paper and pointed to it. "It done."

She shook her head and turned her thumb toward herself. "Me. I must do it." She mimed her looking at the actual crates.

The man looked bewildered as if she had personally challenged his word. Liam played her statement translated to Chinese, then to Japanese. He listened closely, then pointed to her, "You approve?"

She nodded. "After I see." She stepped back a few steps and whispered, "Dari, where are you?"

A glint of golden dust sparkled in front of her face. "Good. Can you hear me?" The flakes dipped a little, and she took it for a yes. "Check out each of these boxes. Use your whisp if you have to, then let me know if there is anything dangerous in them."

The sparkles disappeared in an instant as Grania made a show of checking the manifests to the contents listed on the boxes. It proved more challenging than she expected since the contents were listed in Chinese characters and the manifest was in poorly written English. She knelt by one, noting the weight and pretending to read the contents. Theos leaned down until his mouth pressed almost against her ear and asked, "What are you doing?"

"Trying to verify the contents on the list."

"That won't do any good," he hissed. "Do you read Chinese?"

"No, I'm trying to get my mobi to translate."

"We talked about this. No new cargo coming on board, remember?" He squatted down to look at the label. "It says it's processed *rija* beans and *shu-dija*. Food crops from Yin Wa City on *Lánbǎnqiú*."

"You read Chinese?" Her mouth parted in surprise. How did anyone learn to read these symbols?

"Listen to me, Grania. It's not safe to bring any of these on board."

"And I told you we must maintain our image as a freighter. They have something to ship, and we have space in the hold. Rory made the deal before I knew about it. Besides,

I'm checking it out before we take it on board. Why don't you go get one of the scanners?"

Irritated, he straightened and went back into the hold, presumably in search of the requested item. Grania lifted her head and presented a half-hearted smile to the anxious loader as Liam came up beside her. "What's going on?"

"Theos is getting a scanner. We need to make sure the cargo is safe before we load it. Dari is checking inside the crates." She moved to the next box, Liam following her.

This one was marginally better, at least from the manifest side, and the contents on the crate were listed in words that matched. She tapped the wood and sniffed the contents, which were listed as spices. She couldn't detect anything, so at least they weren't loose.

By the time Theos returned and began scanning the first box, she was on to the fourth one. A glimmer of gold dust flitted across her vision before it zoomed into the hold. Dari was done. She finished, then told Liam to let the loader know she had to check available space to see if the crates would fit.

She hurried inside, went down an aisle to the port side and waited until Dari came strolling toward her. "Three of the boxes are fine," he told her. "One is filled with packages of beans and some kind of flour. Another has thousands of packets of spices, all nicely packaged and labeled. The third is trinkets, necklaces, bracelets, and such made from something like jade, but it isn't that exactly. But the fourth one looks like it's filled part way with some kind of dried plant lying loose, then a false bottom and some linens piled on top."

"Sounds like someone is smuggling illegal produce. Which container was that?"

"The taller one, still on the cart with the loader."

Grania knew which one he meant and recalled that the manifest had said tablecloths and napkins. She went back out, smiling at the loader. "We have room for only three." She held up three fingers and pointed to the approved boxes before pointing at the one on the mag-lev and waving it away as she shook her head. "I can't take that one."

The man started to argue with her, trying to say they had to take it. She kept repeating "no" until Theos stepped in and told the fellow in Chino-Japanese that they would not take that crate because they didn't have enough room for it. At least, that was what Theos told Grania he'd said.

As the man grumbled and turned the mag-lev away, Rory ran up. "What's happening? Why are you turning the cargo away?"

"Just the one," Grania said. "We don't have room for it."

"Yes, we do," he argued. "I mapped out the space, and we can—"

"Rory, we are not bringing it on board." Her expression and voice carried the stern authority of the captain. "Go to the bridge and let the station know we will be ready to depart in twenty mites."

Rory's mouth dropped, and he looked as if he wanted to argue, but he went through the loader, turning to the stairs. She sighed. She'd have to explain it to him later. She watched as Liam and Theos got the three agreed-upon crates on board.

As Theos went by with two boxes stacked on a dolly, he muttered. "I am not happy with this decision, Captain. I want to talk to you about it later."

"After we've left the station, I will be happy to discuss it." She left Theos and Liam to load the cargo, strode to the ship's main entrance, and sashayed up the walkway.

At least they wouldn't be a party to smuggling illegal goods to the Outer Rim. For all she knew, it could have been a trap set for her as well. Right now, anyone could be an enemy, even the agent on board her ship.

As she stepped on the bridge, she caught the surliness in Rory's face, the tight lips and narrowed eyes. He was annoyed or even angry with her. She didn't blame him for the cargo miscommunication. That had been her fault. She hadn't told him not to look for anything.

When she took her seat and began going through the departure pre-check, she noticed Rory had sent her the request to refund the rejected cargo shipment fees. As usual, the shipper had paid in advance, and she needed to authorize the transfer back to his account and state the reason for rejection. Insufficient space available, she noted as she sent it back.

She understood Rory's anger as he read the entry before transmitting it to the bank. Like all of them, the quality of their job built their reputation. In his eyes, returning a shipment was a negative to his efficiency. He knew they could have placed it, so it was a direct hit to his ego.

She called the departure countdown, feeling the slight bump as the Mo Chroidhe released from the dock and the engines began pushing her back into the sea of stars. They had several days of travel before they reached Andromeda Station, where they would dock for two hours to remove cargo. Despite its name, the station and wormhole weren't close to the Andromeda galaxy but were in the general direction of the Milky Way's neighbor. When they reached the Galaxy Gate at the other end, they would be much closer and get their first real look at it.

That part of this trip excited her. The rest of it wore on her nerves. In all the time she'd worked the Mo Chroidhe with her family, she'd never kept any secrets from them regarding the ship or their safety. So far, she was not telling Brendan and Rory anything and had barely confided in Liam. The boys knew they were transporting something dangerous, but how much of a hazard it was, remained her secret.

Once they cleared the station, they were close enough to *Hóng móguǐ*, the red demon star, to raise the solar sails and gain the extra energy while they could. Brendan's calculations to Andromeda Gate showed that they would be getting rays from it most of the way.

She opened the com to the ship. "We're underway. It looks like a smooth trip ahead and a lot of starlight feeding the sails. Keep a close watch on the radiation levels."

"Understood," Liam's voice answered. While the exterior was shielded, any small particle could hit the ship and damage it, effectively breaking the shield. If that happened, they would need to repair it quickly.

That done, they had nothing but time ahead of them.

Grania stood and crossed to Rory's station. "Come to my quarters with me."

She told Brendan they'd be back in a few mites and led the way. She took one of the two seats in front of her desk, wanting this to be less formal. Rory sat hard in the other, his arms tensed.

Taking a calming breath, she started. "I know you're upset, but we couldn't bring that cargo on board. Our scan showed it had a smuggler's bottom and some organic leaves not listed on the manifest. I suspect they were banned produce."

Rory swallowed hard, his throat constricting. "Why didn't you report it?"

"I couldn't risk getting delayed."

"So, instead, our reputation takes a hit. My ability." The bitterness in his voice came through, along with the scowl on his face.

"I'm sorry, brother. A lot is going on right now with this trip and the cargo we're carrying. I've been advised to be cautious about anything we bring on board."

He frowned. "What does that mean?"

"That we take as little as possible until after we deliver the package to Desolation."

He stared hard at her. "Grania, what are you not telling us? Who advised you?"

There. He'd called her on it. "I can't say. Just that it's someone from the government. That item we're transporting is hotter than a potato out of the roasting fire. Just trust me to handle this."

"Does Liam know?"

"Some of it, yes. But not the secrets I have to keep for now."

Her words wounded his pride. As brothers, they all considered themselves equally reliable. That she'd excluded him and Brendan came as a blow to Rory. She understood that but didn't have a way to undo it. "This is how it must be for now, for your safety as well as Brendan's."

He sat back, studying her face for a few moments before he said, "Liam's holding something back also."

"What do you mean?" She had a hunch, but she wanted to hear his thoughts.

"He's not talking to us much on this trip, not even at the pub. It's like he's distancin' himself from us. Haven't you noticed it? Then you brought that new guy on board to help him. When has Liam ever needed help?"

Hellfire. Liam needed to tell everyone he was leaving the ship. "He needs backup. Since I fired O'Toole, we were a person short, and Theos needed a temporary job to get him to the Outer Rim."

"So, he's only goin' that far?"

"Looks like. We haven't discussed him returning with us." She looked away, not wanting to reveal too much.

"More secrets," Rory said, his voice soft but laced with acid. "Is there anythin' else?"

Grania shook her head. He rose and left the room without another word. Had that little chat made things better or worse?

She took a few extra minutes to make personal notes in her

log before returning to the bridge. When she walked in, she noted that Rory was bent forward at his station, listening intently. She opened her mouth, but he held up a hand to halt her. He flipped on the broadcast switch, and a moment later, an uneven whine filled the bridge. The pitch was high, going down a couple of levels, then back up again.

"Is this what you've been detecting?" she asked, covering one ear with her hand. The sound cut off abruptly as he nodded.

"I recorded it this time."

"What in the Fires of Draco was that?" Liam bellowed over the com.

Grania hastened to explain. "Rory's been detecting this signal sporadically since we left Zabrowski. This is the third time. Are you thinkin' what I am?"

"If you're thinkin' we've got a tracking bug, then I am."

"It sounds like it to me, also," Theos butted in.

"You didn't notice it before Earth, Rory?" Liam asked.

"No. That is not to say it wasn't sending, but I didn't pick it up until after we'd left there."

Brendan swung around to face Grania, his face a portrait of concern. "Are you sayin' someone put a tracker on the ship?"

"Or brought it aboard," Grania replied, her thoughts racing to the possibilities. Any cargo loaded could have it or anything one of them bought... "Did anyone purchase anything at Zabrowski that could have a tracker in it?"

Negative answers all around. She hadn't brought anything

back from Earth except Dari, and he certainly wasn't carrying anything.

"I'm still suspicious of that engine we acquired on Enterprise. A gift like that begs inspection," Liam advised.

"Can you guys check it out?" With the engines located within the ship, they could access most of the area except where the thrusters exited through the ports. But it wasn't easy.

She heard Liam's deep inhalation. "Yeah, it will take a while, but I can look for it."

"Take care, Liam."

"We will," he answered. Grania hoped he'd figured out the easiest way would be to use Dari to get into the tight places. How did they ever get by without a puca on the ship?

From a different view, she hadn't had a visit from the b'ean sidhe, but would Sheilan be able to come to her if any of her clan was in danger?

Turning to Rory, she indicated to cut the ship-wide com, then asked, "Can you isolate a terminal signature in that signal?"

"I can try." He started tweaking knobs.

"Why would anyone be tracking us?" Brendan asked as he strolled toward them. "Have we done something wrong?"

Apart from accessory to murder? Grania shook that thought off. Only Liam and Theos knew she was involved... and possibly AAPICA or the FMG. She swallowed hard. "No, I don't think so, Bren. I believe it could be the PPG following our progress to Outer Rim Station. That suggests they thought we might deviate from their plan."

How the hell did we get sucked into this plan? she asked herself again. Damn politicians didn't give her a choice. Some people just held too much power.

"Can we do anything about it, Nia?" Bren asked.

"Not much. Just stay on course until we get the thing delivered, and hope that settles the whole account. If Liam finds the tracker, we can ensure it doesn't work anymore, but it wouldn't change much." She closed her eyes, wishing they didn't have so far to go. And she wished she could talk to Vilnius about it. Gods, she missed him. Even if they didn't speak often, she knew she could share anything with him.

End Part One

Part Two

Desolation

Chapter Twenty-Two

Suited up to avoid possible radiation or an accidental oxygen leak, Liam maneuvered his way through the narrow confines of the engine chambers. The new engine still gleamed with clean metal and no patches, while their older one looked dirty and blackened from burns. Metal patches in a few places marked damage points where the crew had repaired the unit over the many years it had served the ship.

His fingers traced over a newer-looking patch, lingering on the edges where it had been laser welded to the crystal ignition exhaust tube. He'd patched it on their last trip when they'd been ejected from the Pelanan wormhole. His patch had been rough and hasty, something to keep the bloody thing from leaking toxic fumes into the chamber. Not just a hazard to humans but volatile. Under the right conditions, it could have blown the ship up. This newer patch ensured it wouldn't break open if the Mo Chroidhe got tossed about.

He motioned to the suited figure following him to move to the starboard side. Like Liam, Theos Camber progressed carefully to avoid accidentally bumping any control buttons or switches in the area. Headlamps on their suits provided the only light as they moved along the side of the engine, checking the entire surface, from top to bottom. Liam even stretched out on the floor so he could shine the light underneath the apparatus to see if anything protruded from the metal.

Finding nothing, they moved to the port side and repeated the search. He wanted Theos to check as well in case he missed something. Unbeknownst to Theos, Dari flitted inside the engine, something neither of the humans could do. Liam knew nothing could kill the sidhe, although he did react to some elements, like the targassium in its unrefined form.

As they wrapped up the search, still without locating a tracking bug, they began checking the chamber walls. Theos took one side while Liam checked the other, each examining all the surfaces and the ceiling.

"Nothing here," Theos said through his helmet mic.

"I don't have anythin' either." Liam laid his hand against the metal hull and leaned against it. "I was sure we'd find a bug on it. What else would have caused that signal."

"Maybe it's inside the engine," Theos suggested, turning his head up to peer at the roof again.

"Well, we can't check that without shutting down the engine and disconnecting it from the hyperdrive, and we're not gonna do that." Liam gazed around the room. "Check all the connections in case whoever placed it put it on the lines or connectors." He edged his way to the nearest one that fed the power to the engine, crouching down to get a good look. On the other side of the unit, Theos did the same.

As Liam thought about it, he recalled the five workers who

came to install the gift. Four handled the installation, while the fifth appeared to be a supervisor. But Liam had seen him walking through the engine room, presumably checking the connections after the work was done. What if he had planted the bug?

While Liam had checked afterward, he hadn't been looking for anything as minuscule as a microscopic transmitter. "Hey, Camber, maybe this bug is smaller than we can see? Would one of the scanners be able to get a reading?"

"I doubt it. They're good at picking up larger objects, but they're not good with small items. A button could look like a blur on one. Now, a fractal scanner might do it."

"Fractal?" Liam repeated. "Is there such a thing?"

"There's a prototype, but it's not on the market yet." Theos shrugged.

"How do you know that?" Liam wondered what kind of connections Camber had. If it was being developed, it might be common knowledge in the scientific community, but not outside of it. Not until it was ready for production, at least.

"I know a few people," he answered breezily without elaborating.

I bet you do. Still, Liam had his own fractal scanner, and he hoped Dari would find something they'd missed.

They did another pass of the room, switching sides, but neither spotted anything that could be a tracker.

They'd barely gotten their suits off when Dari came down the stairs, bouncing off the next to the bottom step like a kid. His face wore that happy look it often did.

"Where have you been while we've been scouring the engines?" Theos asked. Sweat glistened on his bare torso as he reached for a towel to wipe it off.

Being in the hot engine room in the suit steamed them like a sauna. Liam already had his tunic half-over his head, pulling down on the bottom seam and smoothing it with his hand. "Yeah, I was thinkin' you were gonna join us." He winked his left eye to signal Dari, hoping he would get it and play along.

"I was. In fact, I was on me way down to join you when Captain Grania wanted to talk to me. So, of course, I could not say no to her." Dari shrugged his shoulders. "Did ya find anythin'?"

"Dust, a paper wrapper one of the workmen must have left there, but that was it." Theos pulled his shirt on. "You didn't miss anything except the heat."

"You found a paper wrapper?" Liam asked.

Theos glanced at him, reached into the suit's tool pocket, and pulled out a three-by-about-eight-centimeter piece of gray paper. One end had been cut with something that jagged the edges. He handed it to Liam. "Nothing exciting there. Just a usual wrap for electrical cords."

Taking it, Liam looked it over. Camber had it right. Nothing remarkable about it except for the watermark on it. It bore the insignia of the AUP, a circle of linked worlds. He looked closer, took it to his desk, pulled out a magnifying glass, and ran it over the watermark. A thin silvery line ran through the middle of it and followed down the length of the paper. Liam frowned. *Could it be?* "Where did you find this exactly?"

"Under the engine on the port side, kind of crammed back against the bottom mount. Why?"

He sat down, pulled out a thin pick from his tools, and prodded at the line, his lips twitching as it lifted out of the paper. "I think you found the antenna. Either the transmitter is embedded in this design, or it was near the mount."

"What design?" Theos questioned as he stepped over to look.

"The watermark. Did you notice it?"

"Not in the dark." He squinted to see the thin wire displaying a small loop where Liam had pulled it. "I'll be space-dusted. That's a smooth trick. And the emblem is—"

"Yaw, it is." Liam's smirk looked more grim than happy. He sat back. "I think I need to go back in again."

Camber drew a breath to speak before Liam interrupted. "I can do it alone. You go ahead and get a break. Bring me back a cold drink, will ya'?

Relieved, Camber nodded. "See you in about thirty with a drink and an energy bar. You look like you can use it."

As soon as he left, Liam turned to Dari. "Did you find anything?"

"I did," Dari answered and sat on the edge of the console table. "Down where you just mentioned under the engine, I detected a transmitter. It is about the size of that button there." He pointed to one of the electronic buttons on the console screen. "It is painted black, but that didn't alter the fractal pattern, and it has a tiny antenna on it."

"So that antenna relays the signal to the one on the paper,

which then boosts it out. Ingenious."

"That is not all," Dari said, his eyes narrowing as his lips tightened. "I also found a bundle of explosives inside the new engine. It is wired to the tracker box."

"You're sure about that?" Liam asked, his breath escaping in a long exhale. That... was not good news.

"I am. I may only be a dumb puca, but I have seen enough bombs and explosives in my many years to know one when I see it."

"Well, feckin' fairies. That puts another spin on this, doesn't it?" He set the paper down, debating whether to return it to where Camber had found it. He had questions, and he needed to talk to Grania before he took any more action.

To Dari, he added, "You did a great job. You're actually a pretty smart puca, Dari. I'm going to go talk to the Grania. Don't say anything about this to Camber."

"Do ya' not trust him?" Dari raised one eyebrow as he asked.

"No, I don't, to be honest." Liam rose, picked up the paper sleeve, and headed up the stairs.

Going part-way onto the bridge, he motioned to his sister and pointed to her quarters. She nodded, turning to talk to Rory while Liam headed up the corridor to the ship's nose to wait for her.

A couple of mites later, she hurried toward him, then keyed the sliding door, and they both went in.

"What have you found?" she asked, half-sitting on the edge of her desk.

"This," he showed her the paper, then laid it out on the flat surface next to her as he explained. She followed the lines he pointed out, her lips tightening as she understood what the AUP had done. Then he told her about Dari's discovery. Her eyes came up, widening with alarm, and her face a shade paler. Her mouth fell open a moment before she muttered, "Fecking hell! What kind of game are they playing?"

"Good question. But mine is, what do we do about it?"

"I'd like to rip it out, eject the freiling engine before they blow us up. But we need it. We don't stand a chance of getting to Desolation without it." She bit her lower lip as she thought. "Can we disable it?"

Liam sank into the chair facing her. "I don't know. And I think if we try to do it, they'll blow the ship, their cargo be damned. For some reason, they want to monitor our position, to know where we are and when."

She slipped to her feet and strode back and forth in front of her desk. "Why the explosives, then? Why didn't they just request updates from us? Why sneak around? Too many questions in my mind."

"All good ones, and I don't have the answers," Liam rubbed his jaw, wishing he could at least give her a theory. "The only thing I can think of is that they thought we might encounter some trouble along the way, and the explosive is to destroy their shipment before anyone else could get their hands on it."

"In that scenario, the tracking is to ensure we're staying on course and are not compromised to a different location. If for any reason, we deviate, they can and probably will assume someone is intercepting the shipment." She halted and clapped her hands together once. "Then we all die."

Liam lifted his eyebrows as he nodded. "That's about it."

"Does moving that paper with the antenna constitute attempting to disarm it?" She stared at the offending strip.

"I don't know. I hope not."

"Put it back." She shuddered. "As quickly as possible. We'll hope they don't have a clue we moved it." Pausing momentarily, she asked, "Have you said anything to Theos?"

"I showed him the antenna, but he knows nothing about the rest of it."

"Keep it that way. Tell Dari to keep silent also."

With a sly twist of his lips, he said, "Already have."

* * * * *

After Liam retrieved the paper and left, Grania dictated some notes into her log, outlining everything they'd learned about the shipment and the explosives. She wanted a record to go somewhere in case the worst scenario happened.

She made a copy and added an opening statement to it. "Granda, I don't want to alarm you, but we've gotten ourselves into a bit of a situation that could literally explode. Not my fault or the boys, but something we couldn't avoid. This log is to give you the details, but don't listen unless you hear we've been killed. I love you."

She keyed the family's confidential code on it and pressed

send. Her hand trembled slightly, nerves stretched, and fear pressed into her chest. She took solace in knowing that the b'ean sidhe would come if her death was a possibility. Unless she couldn't leave Eterian... But Grania preferred to believe nothing would keep Sheilan from coming, especially when all four of the family were threatened.

Her cabin had one of only three real windows on the ship. Triple-paned, space-worthy Transparisteel, it looked out on space's blackness from the starboard side. She turned a chair to face it and sat, staring at the vast blackness that met her eyes. While stars were plentiful in the galaxy, most of her view consisted of tiny pinpoints of light and large fields of blackness surrounding them.

But there, in the vastness, was a break in the vision as a spiral galaxy hovered at a near ninety-degree angle to the flat of the Milky Way. So distant that it appeared fully within its black box with millions of light years separating the two celestial bodies. But the colors in that spiral amazed her. Vivid and swirling slowly, it dazzled the eye.

She'd seen images and videos of it. In fact, she was sure Rory was recording it even now. Behind them, on the port side, the star, whose name meant Blue Cricket in Chinese, burned, a fiery orb three times bigger than Earth's sun, looking about the size of a tennis ball. But it blazed out toward the galaxy's end, a signpost for others to follow.

This was one of the joys of space travel, seeing other planets, other worlds, the end of the galaxy, and a glimpse at the edge of the universe. Scientists said it was endless and still growing, yet she couldn't imagine it. Unending was beyond what her mind could comprehend. Her life was finite, yet she couldn't imagine the end of it either.

Shaking those thoughts away, she went back to the bridge and asked Brendan for an update on their status,

"Steady as she goes, Cap'n," he said in a weird voice. "Isn't that what the sailors used to say?"

"Maybe," she answered. Crossing to peer over his shoulder at the navigation screen. "It looks good ahead. No space storms or squalls coming at us. Let's hope it stays that way."

"No reports about anything awry," Rory called from his station. "Anythin' on the tracker?"

"Liam found it, but we're leavin' it in place. Keep tracing it, and let me know if you hear anything different in the signal."

"Different like what?" he asked, his eyes pulling toward the crease down the middle of his forehead.

"Just different. Not the same, a bit higher or lower, longer or shorter."

"O-kay," he said. "I can have an auto-program handle that." He turned to take care of it. "Do you mind if I go for a jog after I do this?"

"Have fun." She grinned. Rory worked out more than any of the rest of the crew, running through the decks and up and down the stairs twice, sometimes three times a day.

* * * * *

The long stretch between gates wore on the crew as they looked for things to keep them entertained. Grania instituted movie nights in the galley where they could watch a vid of a recent movie if Rory could get one to download, or they tapped into their storage banks for a favorite. They would transfer the bridge stations to the consoles so they could all go at one time, but Liam rarely joined them, although Theos and Dari came in most times.

For Grania and her brothers, it turned into a more substantial bonding event. Until they'd come onto the ship, Grania hadn't spent much time with her younger siblings. Working together hadn't provided the camaraderie that doing fun things could. Sometimes, they even played digital board games, like a murder mystery one that they had fun guessing which one of them did it.

Theos had talked with Grania about taking on the cargo, warning her again about the danger. "Seems like we have that on board already," she'd argued. And she pointed out that the scans hadn't revealed anything other than what the manifest had listed, except for the one they rejected.

While she found Theos extremely attractive – with those amazing features and well-toned body, what woman wouldn't?—she kept him at a distance. In her mind, he represented as much danger as the explosives on board. She didn't know if he would protect them or was strictly on board to follow that strange cargo. When push came to shove, would he dump them? If the she-bee in the box turned out to be a weapon, would he set off the explosive to destroy them all?

In the meantime, Liam's departure loomed over her. He still hadn't told his brothers, but Grania knew he must leave the ship at Andromeda Station. He'd stayed with them as long as he could, but he needed to get to his new assignment. She'd been looking for possible crew replacements at Andromeda, but the pickings were scarce.

She sat at the console in her room, reviewing a list of spacers on the station who had indicated they were available to work. None of them sounded like a fit with her crew, and most didn't have experience with a solar sail vessel. Not many of them existed anymore. Her family had three of the thirteen registered ones.

An incoming message from Zabrowski Station beeped on her console. Puzzled, she opened it. Why would Vilnius contact her? It was brief and to the point, strictly business. He'd located a potential engineer for her, who would be waiting when she reached Andromeda Station. He included a unique mobi code for her to contact the candidate. The only thing remotely personal was the safe travels closing at the end.

She couldn't blame him. She'd broken it off, but how little he seemed to miss her stung. She hoped Vilnius had checked the person's credentials, but the decision was still hers. If she didn't like the guy—or gal—then she'd continue to look. But so far, none of the six jobseekers she'd seen on the station seemed very promising, not for the engineer or her second on the ship. Maybe she should promote Rory to that position and look for a new communications officer?

After some thought, she went down to the lowest level, finding Liam in his usual spot inside the engineering office. He had a panel on the left console open, checking the wiring within, or so it appeared.

"Trouble, Liam?" she asked as she stepped inside.

Surprised, he glanced toward her, then resumed his task. "No. Just replacing a connector. They wear down sometimes on the moving parts. What's up, Nia?"

"I've been thinking that it's time you let Rory and Brendan know you're leaving us. Unless…" Her voice trailed off, waiting to see if she had his attention.

"Unless what?" He finished his task and turned to face her.

"Well… Would it make any difference if I made you second on the Mo Chroidhe?"

He stared at her for what seemed like a long time in those two or three moments. "You know what I want. You can't give it to me. It isn't just a second officer position on the *Mo Spiorad*. It's almost a guarantee that I'll become her captain within a few months."

She shifted her eyes to the floor, vacantly seeing the welding that held the panels together. Beneath them, the rumble of the engines sent a vibration through the floor that carried up her legs. "I get it, Liam. But how can I replace you? You're not just the best engineer, but I rely on you so much. I talk to you about everything and trust your judgment. I can't get that with a new man, no matter how good he is."

Liam took a deep breath, then pulled her into a hug,

something he seldom did. "Do you think this is easy for me? It wasn't a simple decision, but it was the best opportunity. I'm steppin' into an unknown situation, working with Uncle Colm and learnin' the way they do things. I will miss you and the boys," He paused and leaned back from her. "And my engine room." He chuckled. "Bet you didn't think I'd say that."

She squeezed her arms around his waist again. "I'll be lost without you."

"You can mobi me anytime, you know. Granted, the gap in transmissions may take a while, but I'll always be available to talk."

"Thanks for that. Now, when are you goin' to announce it? Rory's noticin' the change in you."

"Soon. I promise."

She narrowed her eyes a little as a thought occurred to her. "How about dinner the night before we enter the wormhole? That way, no one has to think about it too long before we're takin' a long nap."

Laughing, he said, "Brilliant."

Even though she smiled and made light of it, the warm fuzzies disappeared as soon as Grania started back up the steps to the bridge. That was her last shot to keep Liam on the ship, but his ambitions were higher than she could offer.

How would she ever find a replacement as skilled as her brother?

Chapter Twenty-Three

Time passed without any incidents until they approached the next gate. Rory detected another whining signal and recorded it. "I'm still trying to locate the source," he told Grania as she listened to it.

"It sounds exactly the same," she said, leaning closer to the console's speaker as if it would provide some detail she might have missed.

"It does, but it isn't," Rory said. "The difference is minuscule. I can't detect it, but the computer can. Best guess, it's a coordinate showing our position."

"Have there been any ships near us on this leg?"

"Nope. Nothing at all. No patrols, no other shipping vessels that I've detected. We might as well be in the Dark Sea for all the chatter I've picked up since we left Chang. The only message to come in was the one from Zabrowski." He stretched his arms toward the ceiling, then stood and walked around his chair several times.

"Boggers, I'd hate to have a failure out here with no one likely to come along." Grania frowned and leaned back. "Have you detected anything in the path ahead of us, Bren?"

Like Rory, Brendan had gotten to his feet to walk around a

bit. Too much sitting at their stations wasn't doing any of them any good. "Nothing I've detected. I noted an ion storm off to the port side, but it was too far away to affect us."

"That's lucky, I guess, but the most it might have done was interfere with communications." She winked at Rory.

"A little static might have been welcome."

Her eyes rolled up to the overhead screens, seeing that the starboard one showed the nearby galaxy, barely changing from day to day. Although it moved, the change was so tiny you didn't notice it unless you compared it to an image from several days earlier. Beautiful though it was, the novelty was wearing off. Astronomers warned that it was moving closer to the Milky Way, but it had a long way to go from what she could see.

"We should be getting a signal from Andromeda Gate soon, shouldn't we, Rory?" she asked.

"In a few hours, I think," he answered.

"Grand. Okay, we'll have a last dinner before the jump tonight in the galley. Everyone there, no excuses." They could use the mobi units to monitor and transfer the bridge as usual.

"Is there cake?" Brendan asked, grinning.

"Maybe. Aren't you interested in the main course?" She tried not to laugh, but Bren had a voracious sweet tooth. A tall, skinny kid with a high metabolism, he could live on them.

He shrugged. "Sausages would be all right, so long as there's cake or pie."

Laughing, Grania left the bridge to retire to her cabin for a bit. She still needed to find help and was beginning to feel more desperate every day. She'd switched to seeking someone to handle the communications to free Rory up. Worst case, she still had Theos to take over in engineering once Liam left. At least until they got to the Outer Rim station.

The ship finally reached the station's transmission range, and Rory reported a few messages had come in. Among them were the posts from the positions and passengers board. *Some resemblance of civilization is coming up,* Grania thought, relieved to make contact.

By the time she headed for the galley, she had one possibility. A woman who'd separated recently from her ship. Or, more precisely, the ship had separated from the crew. It came into Andromeda damaged beyond repair, leaving the four-person team stranded there. According to the posted information, the engineer was injured and in sick bay.

Half the crew was already seated and chatting when she arrived and took her place at the seat nearest the auto-chef. Captain's dinner on the Mo Chroidhe meant she chose and served the meal. Liam and Theos were last to arrive, minus Dari.

"Is Dari not joining us?" she asked as they took their seats.

"He said he'd be along in a few minutes," Liam replied.

Curious about what delayed the puca, she went ahead with her welcome to the wormhole speech. "Gentlemen, we're about to embark on another first for the Mo Chroidhe. We're coming into Andromeda Station in about six hours, ship time. We won't be there for more than two before heading for the gate and a nice, long sleep. On the other side, we will be even closer to that spiral galaxy we keep staring at. First time ever that this ship has traveled this far, and there's more to come. Let us dine together tonight and toast our new adventure." She held up her glass of wine, then sipped as the rest repeated the gestures.

"Wouldn't it be more appropriate to give that speech when we reach Desolation?" Rory asked.

"There will be a different one when we get there." She shot the answer back as she pulled a tray from the fridge. She began passing around the appetizers, shrimp cocktails huddled in lettuce. Dari walked in mid-way, and Grania blinked in surprise.

The young lad aspect of the puca wore a familiar-looking dinner coat. "Where did you find that coat?" she asked the puca.

"'Tis a surprise," he stated proudly. "I wanted to be more presentable this evening, so I ran across this left on the hanger in the room the chief pirate used."

That was where she'd seen it. They'd missed cleaning out one of Harhiman's suits. While it looked a little big on Dari, she had to admit he looked suave.

Dinner proceeded from there, everyone chatting and laughing as Grania passed the roast pork around the table. They didn't often get pig meat, but they always stocked up with roast, ham, and bacon when they had a respectable refill of provisions from the Earth run. This was a special occasion, even though Liam hadn't made his announcement yet.

After they'd eaten, Liam rose and tapped his glass with the dessert knife. "I have somethin' to say."

Everyone's eyes turned to him except Grania's. She dropped her eyes to study the table. This was the moment she'd been dreading.

Liam cleared his throat, his voice reflecting his tension. "I will be leaving the Mo Chroidhe at Andromeda Station. I have been offered a post as the second officer on the *Mo Spiorad*, Uncle Colm's ship." He paused as Brendan hooted out a cheer. Next to him, Rory looked crestfallen, his shoulders slumping as his mouth fell open.

"You're leavin' us?" Rory asked. "I mean, it's great, but we're on this long trip, and you're not goin' on with us?"

"I have to, Rory," Liam explained. "I need to join my new ship, and I barely have time to get back to it. I was lucky to find a faster ship headed to Pelanan, where I'll meet it. But I wanted to come with you all as far as possible."

"I don't..." Words failed him before Rory blurted out, "You could be second on this ship, couldn't he, Grania?" He turned to her, eyes beseeching her to agree.

"She already offered," Liam spoke quickly. "The deal with Uncle is that I will be next in line to be captain, and he's planning to buy a new ship in a few months. So, I'll be moving up to head the Mo Spiorad."

"Congratulations!" Dari cried out, hopping from his chair like a kid. "That is truly fine news, Mister Liam."

Next to Liam, Theos raised his eyebrows amid a frown. Grania assumed that Liam hadn't said anything to him. *Time to make the toast*. She lifted her newly-filled glass again. "A toast to Liam O'Ceagan, the best engineer in the galaxy and about to become one hell of a captain-in-waiting! We're going to miss you, brother."

Liam nodded, drank a sip, then sat down like his knees wouldn't hold him any longer. Rory wasn't exactly cheering. Barely smiling, in fact. Although it had been a shock, he would come around. Like her, he probably felt blindsided by the announcement. Which made her feel guilty about keeping secrets from Rory and Brendan.

After a round of backslapping and congratulations, Liam excused himself to return to his engines and prepare to leave the ship when they docked. Grania watched him depart with sad eyes and a downturned mouth, fighting the sorrow she felt. She glanced at Rory, made a mental note to talk to him in the next hour, then finished her wine and began shooing everyone out so she could clean up.

As they all left, Dari lingered. "A hard blow, that, is it not? But do not be sad, Captain Grania. 'Twas bound to happen sooner or later, you know."

She bobbed her head. She'd known it from the time Granda had let them know his intentions to retire, so when Grania got the ship, the next step for Liam was to leave. "'Tis a bad time to go, Dari," she said, her words soft in the humming silence. She picked up the dishes to put in the cleaner, tossing any waste, not that there was much, in the recycler.

"I can help ya' here," Dari volunteered, picking up the utensils and glasses. "You go ahead to the bridge, and I will finish this."

"Thank you, Dari." She set down the napkins she had in her hands and left.

As she reached the stairs, Theos stepped out from behind them, clearly having waited for her. Startled, she jumped back a step. "You surprised me."

"Sorry. Did you know Liam was doing this?" He looked concerned.

"He told me when we went to Enterprise Station. He hadn't expected our trip to turn into a long excursion." She watched the expression in his eyes, seeing concern and a touch of anger.

"So, now you don't have an engineer?" His voice was tight.

"Well, I do have you. You have a degree and only a little experience, but I hope it's enough to get us through the next two wormholes to Outer Rim station. Then, I hope to get someone to replace Liam, not that it's possible. He's as familiar with this ship as any engineer could be."

"I didn't come on board expecting to be the engineer. Helping him was my cover." Theos stepped a little closer.

"Well, now, doing the job is your cover. Frankly, I don't know what else you have to do here, but that's where I need you. Otherwise, you're just getting a free ride."

"I wouldn't call it that." He objected, showing his teeth in an annoyed scowl.

"Not a handsome look there, boy-o. What would you call your purpose here?"

"Security."

She stared at him, almost laughing. "Really? We have a weird crate on board that may cause problems, explosives in the engine room, and you say—"

"Wait a minute! Explosives? What are you talking about?" He was in her face in a heartbeat.

"Oh, I guess Liam didn't tell you about that. Oh, wait, I told him not to." She stepped back, putting a foot on the first step to the top level. "Truth is, Theos Camber, I don't know exactly what your mission is here. And I don't really trust you. So, if you can't pretend to be the engineer I need, then you might as well get off the ship at Andromeda as well." She started up the stairs, ignoring him as he spoke.

"I need to stay on until this crate is delivered."

She continued upward.

"Fine. I'll be your damn engineer. But don't blame me if something goes wrong."

She reached the top and turned toward the bridge, feeling righteous about standing up to him. She didn't tell Theos she might have a possible replacement waiting at Andromeda Station. To be honest, she wasn't sure the candidate would be a good fit or recovered enough to work.

Three hours later, Grania sat back in her command chair and gazed at Rory, watching him field the messages from the station while tracking other chatter as they approached it. Pushing to her feet, she strolled to his station, leaning closer until her face was even with his. "Come to my cabin after you run your next check on the station messages. I want a chat with you."

His eyes opened wider with an unspoken question in his look, but he nodded.

They would be docking in about 120 mites, so communications still flowed in, but they came in bursts. Retreating to her cabin, Grania settled at her desk, switched the console to duplicate the command station, and looked for any incoming missives.

Rory came in about twenty mites later, his steps tentative. "You wanted to see me?"

She looked up, a fond expression altering her features from stern captain to gentle sister. "You were upset with Liam's announcement."

He nodded. "I hadn't expected it. He never said..."

"I know. He didn't want to hurt anyone, but there isn't a way to say goodbye to family."

"That it, isn't it? We are family, and he's going to– to..." He stopped at a loss for words.

"To another branch of the family?" she supplied. "It's not betrayal, Rory. It's ambition, and he accepted an opportunity. Were our positions reversed, I would have done the same thing."

"Won't ya miss him?"

"I will. More than anything. But that's not why I wanted to speak to you. I need a second officer. I'd like to offer the position to you, Rory. Will you be my second?"

He looked stunned, eyes going wide. "Me? Are you sure?"

"I am. I've started looking for a communications

replacement and hope to have someone soon. But I need someone who knows the ship well and can fill in anywhere; I believe that person is you."

He closed his eyes, took a deep breath, then opened them again. "Thank you. I will do a great job for ya."

She nodded, smiling. "I know. You can get back to the bridge. I'll announce it after we dock."

With a new spring in his step, Rory left her cabin. She felt good about giving him more responsibility. Turning to her console, Grania checked the timeline, noting that they'd made their target getting to Andromeda. Still, they'd have to hustle to get the cargo off, then get to the wormhole. She hoped everything would continue to go smoothly.

Feeling optimistic, she sent a message to two potential future crew members. She hoped they would be available for an interview once the Mo Chroidhe was settled at the station.

She'd no sooner let out a held breath before her comm beeped, and Rory's face appeared. "I have a message from the station, and we have a problem."

"What?" Grania frowned, her thoughts flipping through possible scenarios as she scurried toward the bridge.

Chapter Twenty-Four

For the third time, Grania said, "I don't understand why you can't authorize our docking."

The green-haired man who replied gave her the same response without more elaboration. "I am sorry, Captain. Your request is insufficient. We need additional details on your cargo before we can authorize docking.

"I sent the file a week ago when I accepted a delivery for Desolation. I have a confirmation that it was received. What else do you need?"

"You need to provide more information on a crate listed with farm equipment. My superiors say it is too vague."

"It's a government shipment," Grania answered, trying to keep her temper in check. "They didn't provide any more details. Look, I am on a tight delivery schedule, and my ship needs to dock right away."

"I am sorry to delay you, but my—"

"Let me talk to your superior." Her voice took on that tone of command that no one wanted to defy.

"I am sorry. I cannot interrupt him right now."

"Then get me the station master."

The man looked shocked at the request, but before he could reply, Theos strode onto the bridge and asked, "What's going on, Grania?"

She provided the short version, ending with, "They won't let us dock because of the *package*."

"Clear the bridge," Theos said, stepping forward to address the station assistant.

Rory shot a sharp look at Grania, and Brendan's jaw dropped as Theos' spoke. Grania hesitated a moment, a surge of anger building before she forced herself to calm down and said, "Rory and Bren, go for a break." Turning to face Theos, she crossed her arms over her chest and glared at him. "I'm staying."

His head dipped in a curt nod, then he reached into his inner pocket and pulled out his identification card. She could see the PPG logo on it as he held it up to the camera, and the man squinted to see it.

"I'm Theos Camber, a PPG agent assigned to protect and deliver the cargo in question. It is high security, and you do not have clearance. Now, please transmit the immediate docking instructions to our ship."

"Of course, Agent," a different voice said as a rotund man stepped in front of the assistant. "I'm the station master, and I will authorize your docking immediately. He turned his head toward the green-haired man and said, "See to it, Fernibot."

As the man darted out to follow instructions, the station master plastered on a smile. "Sorry for the inconvenience. I wasn't aware of the status. You should be able to dock in ten mites. Welcome to Andromeda station." He ended the transmission before they could reply.

'"Wasn't aware, like hell," Theos muttered.

"Impressive superpower you have there." Grania tipped her head toward his card. "You know I'm going to have to tell Rory and Brendan something about your usurping act."

He shrugged. "They've probably guessed. I'm more concerned about who's behind that request for details on the cargo."

"I agree with that. I've never been questioned about my cargo." Grania leaned against the lower deck railing. "Do you think someone on the station is interested in it?"

"Maybe. Or it could be someone who knows someone in the SM office, is fishing for information." Theos turned, started down the few steps, paused, and met her eyes. "I think we can expect some trouble, either at the station or when we move to the next gate."

She swiveled to face him, bobbing her head in agreement. "Thanks for your help, Agent."

He flashed a brief smile before he left the bridge, and Grania lifted her com to summon her brothers back to get the ship docked.

* * * * *

Grania strolled toward the young woman, who stood outside the Galaxy Café & Bakery waiting for her. She judged her to be about her age, slightly shorter, and a bit nervous. The potential new hire fidgeted with a bracelet on her wrist while her eyes darted around the station. When her eyes caught sight of the Captain, she straightened her shoulders, suggesting she had trained with the space patrol.

"Hello, Ms. Narasimi?" Grania asked tentatively, not wanting to assume she had the right person.

The recruit nodded and rubbed her lips together to wet them. "Yes. Captain O'Ceagan?" Her startlingly deep blue eyes turned to Grania as she extended her hand for a shake.

Taking the offered hand firmly, Grania clasped it for a brief shake, then motioned to a table in the front and to the side. "Let's get a coffee or tea and chat for a bit." Sitting with her back to the shop and facing the promenade, she gazed at the meager number of people on the main walk at Andromeda Station.

Easily as large as Zabrowski, the facility didn't have nearly as many travelers as the other one did, an indication of the sparse population of this sector. Few ships made this their regular route, and only settlers in the area would be likely to travel anywhere. So far as shops, the place was half-empty, with no tenets but living quarters and a hotel available.

After they ordered their drinks, Grania offered a friendly smile and said, "Now tell me about yourself, Ms. Narasimi. Where did you train? How long have you worked in communications?"

"I trained with the Star Academy on Batterforce for two seasons. Then I went into service with Star Patrol for two years, where I got practical experience. Once I left there, I worked for an independent freight line, serving on three different ships in the four years I was there. My last job was on the long-range freighter Starduster II. That was a really old ship. We encountered a particle storm and took some serious damage getting here. The ship barely made it."

As Narasimi paused, Grania commented. "I saw that. Where were you coming from?"

"Half-Moon Station just after the jump from Centauri Gate." She took a quick sip of her coffee. "I have worked both the Real-Tek and Sound Design boards and know how to repair them."

Grania noted it. The Real-Tek was almost like their Royal Crown communications board, so she wouldn't have too many adjustments to make. She then told Narasimi about the Mo Chroidhe, that she was an older ship but well-maintained, and the crew was mostly her family. "We're heading to Terminus Station on this trip, but we don't normally come this way. Most of our trade is in the Earth to Storm Hold sectors. Would that be acceptable to you?"

She thought for a moment, then said, "Yes, I believe that is fine."

"Are you looking for a long-term position?" Grania asked. If the woman worked out, she wanted to know if she was in for the long run or only a couple of years.

Narasimi's mouth twitched to a lopsided, almost smile. "That depends on how the job works out for me. If I like the crew and the ship, then I would be open to making it long-term."

"Fair enough," Grania replied. "We will be leaving in about ninety mites. Can you be aboard by then?"

"Yes, Captain O'Ceagan. Which dock?" Her smile blossomed, and her eyes lit up.

"We're at dock B, berth nine. My name is Grania, and most of my crew, being my brothers, call me that unless they get formal. My brother Rory is my second, and he is at the ship. I'll let him know you're coming."

"My thanks, Captain…Grania. My first name is Kachiri."

"Welcome to the crew," she said, finishing her coffee, then rising to go connect with her potential engineer. She had the code Vilnius had sent, went to a message pick-up kiosk on the station, and entered it. A computer-generated voice confirmed her entry and told her to go to Meeting Room four next to the Station Master's office in fifteen mites to meet her party.

Odd way to set up a meeting. Grania hadn't encountered it before, but it took all kinds. She had no idea who this person was or anything about him other than Vilnius had said he was an engineer.

Thinking about her ex-lover, even in his professional capacity, sent a pang of longing through her. Maybe she'd been too hasty in breaking up with him. When they'd started the relationship, neither wanted a permanent attachment that could interfere with their individual ambitions. Somewhere along the way, that had changed. If he had transferred to Tara Station, she would have seen him at the end of every trip she made. At Earth, she would only manage once or twice a year. Unless she changed to a more frequent schedule. Even at that, would it be the romance she wanted with him? Would it be enough for either of them?

She wandered down the promenade, stopping at a vid store to browse some of the latest movies. While they could download some to the ship, others weren't available, so she bought three new ones they hadn't seen. As she tucked the vid sticks into her pocket, she felt a hand on her shoulder. She turned, prepared to defend herself if someone was attacking her.

Then Theos Camber's voice said, "Find anything interesting?"

Grania let out a relieved sigh. "Don'ya be sneakin' up on me like that." When startled, her Erinnua accent came out in full force.

"Sorry. I spotted you as I went by. Is everything okay?"

"Yes, of course." She started walking out of the shop, and he fell into step beside her. "Why are you out here?"

"Checking in with my bosses. And Rory has two shipments lined up. He sent me to check on their status. You know what I said about it?" His lifted eyebrows made it an accusation.

"Appearances," she answered. "Check the crates with the scanner. If they're all clear, we're good to go. I'm meeting with a possible new engineer in a couple of mites. If he pans out, you're off the hook. Otherwise, I hope you're ready to take over."

She and her brothers had said goodbye to Liam shortly after they'd docked. She'd fought back the tears that threatened at seeing him go, but he'd promised to keep in touch with her, adding that she could contact him any time she needed to talk. Nonetheless, her heart cracked a little watching him walk away with his gear slung over his back and a lev-dolly following him with his two travel bags.

Theos grimaced, distorting his handsome face. "Then I hope you're interview yields a very positive result. And I'll check the cargo thoroughly."

He wasn't happy about the cargo, but too bad. Grania's business was moving freight, and Rory was absolutely right to fill the hold as much as possible. Theos couldn't seem to grasp the concept.

She stepped up to the assigned meeting room, entered the code, and then pushed the door open. At first, she thought she was alone, but then a short, dark man stepped into the light from a corner.

"You're the Cap'n, I reckon," he said. His voice was clipped and slurred a little. His shocking white-blonde hair contrasted with his dark skin like a skyrocket in the night sky.

She nodded. "I don't have your name, but I presume you're familiar with spaceship engines?"

"Y'am. I work on 'em many years. You need one. I need transpo to Desolation."

"Ah, I see." Grania let out a breath she didn't realize she'd taken. "So, just a short-term job for you, I take it."

"Yes, Cap'n. I have a job waitin' there."

"Do you have credentials?"

He nodded and handed her a data stick. She stuck it in her mobi and quickly scanned through it, seeing his name – Raj Sindhu – and the list of jobs he'd held, followed by four recommendations from previous captains. No red marks as far as she could see, so he checked out in that respect.

Something nagged at her, making her uncertain about hiring him. "How did you end up jobless here?"

"I take leave from last ship. It no go where I need." He didn't elaborate, but to her, it sounded like he was a man who took opportunities to travel around the galaxy. While she'd heard of vagrant spacers, she hadn't met one before.

"I need to check something out before I decide," she told him. "Can you wait here ten minutes?"

He pursed his lips, a hint of disapproval, but nodded. "I think about you as well."

Blinking, she exited the room and contacted Liam. "Already?" he said as he picked up.

"Yeah, I need your thoughts on something." She leaned against the wall and told him about the potential engineer.

"Vilnius recommended him?" Liam asked.

"Not really. Vilnius said the man checked out and might be a match. I don't know, Liam. With all that's happening, he worries me."

"Then decline, Nia. Camber is good enough to get you to the next station and on to Desolation. From there, you may be on the hunt for someone, but I'll keep a lookout for anyone who might work who is at either location."

"Right. Thanks. I miss you already."

She started to go back in the room, then tagged Theos. "I need your input." Then she told him to meet her in room four soon as he could. Liam's advice sounded good, but she worried about trusting the engines to Theos. She wanted him to vet Sindhu. The real worry was whether he was a competent engineer or a plant.

While she waited, a young girl, maybe the age Orla had been, approached her. "You're on a ship, aren't you?" she asked, her voice hitching.

Grania nodded. "Does your ship take passengers?"

"Not at this time. Sorry."

"Aw, dammit. I'm desperate. I need to get to Outer Rim Station, and the ship I was gonna take has been delayed by eighty hours." She looked like she was going to cry.

"Maybe another is coming in soon," Grania offered.

"Are you sure you can't squeeze me on? I promised my folks I'd be home by the weekend, you know? I don't take up much room, and I only have this pack." She pointed to her backpack, which was slung over her shoulder.

"Well, I ..." Grania felt sorry for the girl. She couldn't do any harm.

"I can pay," the waif added quickly, her head slightly tilted and eyes pleading. "I have the money in cash. My grandparents gave it to me before I left them. Can you at least check with your captain to see?"

"I don't need to," she answered. "What's your name?"

"Heidi Geers. I actually live on Outer Rim Station, so it's just the one stretch to home. My parents run a supply store there for the residents. You know, all the necessities one needs in one's home." She blinked her eyes innocently.

"Let me check something out. I have a meeting coming up now." She spotted Theos coming toward her. "Can you wait here about ten mites, Heidi?"

As she nodded, Grania stepped away to meet Theos. "In here," she said, opening the meeting room door.

"Who's the girl?" he asked, glancing back toward Heidi.

"Someone who's looking for a ride."

He shot a pointed glance her way. "Don't think about it. It's risky."

"She's just a kid." Grania led him to where Sindhu waited.

After a quick introduction, she explained that he would be working with Theos, so she wanted them to chat before she decided. Stepping away from them, she pulled out her mobi and entered Heidi Geers's name into the inquiry data. Quickly, it showed that the girl had debarked from the Brazen Lady almost two hours earlier that day. No indication she left the station and no negative marks on her record. She seemed on the up and up. Age listed as sixteen standard years, which meant in Earth years. Various planets had such a rotation variance that the standard, at least for humans, was to use Earth years.

She was still a kid. Grania couldn't leave her stranded on the station waiting almost four days for a ship out. She returned, found the girl still waiting, and smiled. "Okay, Heidi Geers. We can give you a ride to Outer Rim. I'm Grania, the

Captain of the Mo Chroidhe, which is docked at B, berth nine. I'll alert my second to look for you."

"Thank you! I promise I won't be a problem on board." Her grin filled half her face. "I'll just head down there now, if that's okay."

Grania waved her on, then turned back to the meeting room. She slipped back in, standing at the back of the room to listen as Theos asked a few engineering and scenario questions.

Sindhu responded readily with short, to-the-point answers. "Would I be reporting to you?" he asked Theos.

"Not really." He paused and turned to face Grania. "Isn't that the plan, Captain?"

"Right," she replied, striding forward. "You would be the engineer, Mister Sindhu. Mister Camber would assist you but is mostly in charge of the cargo. He's been working with my former engineer for the past nine days, so he is familiar with the equipment and can assist you as needed." She turned to Theos. "Any comments, Mister Camber?"

"No, I believe this man will do fine in the job."

"In that case, welcome to the crew, Mister Sindhu. Will you show him aboard and to his cabin, Theos?"

"Of course." He leaned closer and asked, "Is there a cabin for him?"

She almost laughed out loud but suppressed it to a smirk. "I forgot Liam mostly stayed in the control room. But yes, room six, starboard, is the engineer's cabin."

As they left, she tagged Rory to let him know the girl was coming and they had a new engineer. Things were looking up until she looked at the time. Fickle fairies, they were almost an hour late in departing. How had this taken so long?

She hurried to one last stop to pick up some sweet treats for the crew's prejump break. It had practically become a tradition. She fretted back to the ship with a box of assorted tarts in hand, knowing that their time schedule was tight, and if she missed it, it would mean the loss of their bonus fee for on-time delivery.

When Grania arrived on board, she found Rory running through the controls on the communications board with Kachiri. He crossed to Grania's station and spoke in a soft voice. "She's doing great, Nia. Her experience is varied, and she adapted to the changes easily. I'm ready to turn the com over to her."

"Already? That's great, Rory. So, how soon can we get out of here?"

"Another twenty mites. We're waiting for final clearance for the gate."

"Okay. Send our guest to her cabin in fifteen if we hear from them soon. If they haven't notified us by then, check with the station. Make sure Ms. Geers is settled properly in her jump pod."

Grania knew she wouldn't have Sindhu after the Outer Rim and figured Theos would leave the ship unless he needed a lift back to another station. So, while she waited for the okay, she began looking for an out-of-work engineer there.

Once they got the confirmation and the Mo Chroidhe began to move, Kachiri reported that tracking-device whine was back again. How did they know when the ship was moving?

Chapter Twenty-Five

Once they got underway, Brendan headed down to the galley for a quick break. He returned to the bridge a little later with coffee and a pastry in hand. "Sorry. I ran into our passenger there. She's quite the talker."

Grania raised an eyebrow. "I'm surprised she headed into the galley that fast. Maybe she didn't eat at the station. Did she say anything interesting?"

He shook his head, "Naw. She was just tellin' me about her visit with her grandparents and how she was anxious to get home. She lives on the Outer Rim station. Did ya' know?"

"She mentioned that. Anything else?"

"I think she kinda likes me." Brendan raised his eyes from his console to look at her, a smirk on his face.

"How so?" Grania checked her messages, noting she'd had no responses regarding two inquiries she'd made to Galaxy Station. She didn't have a lot of hope for finding an engineer there.

"She asked a lot of questions about me job and what things she might do for entertainment on the ship. When I mentioned we had a few games on board, she asked if I would play one of them with her. I told her I wouldn't be havin' much time between now and Outer Rim. She looked disappointed."

"Apparently, boredom's already set in," Grania commented. She could see where a young girl would be attracted to her youngest brother, so she suspected her interest amounted to flirtation.

Settling into their usual routine, they raised the sails as soon as they were within range of the star's light to gather as much power as possible. Grania urged Sindhu to push the engines, hoping to reduce the time to Galaxy Station. All the while, that giant galaxy with its myriad of stars muted through the dust clouds at the Milky Way's edge seemed to draw closer and closer. She found herself staring at the screen more often than usual.

Finally, she turned the bridge over to Rory and went to her cabin. She sat at her desk, turning her chair to face the window that looked out toward the space ahead, and gazed, mesmerized by the actual view of Andromeda. What was so fascinating about it? It wasn't colored like the images in books, but she could almost make out the spiral patterns of the stars within it. And dear God, it was bright. In the face of this astonishing view, she felt insignificant. A mere speck in the Universe.

Her thoughts wandered to Vilnius with second doubts about breaking off their relationship. Was she really meant to be a ship's captain? Would that give her all the satisfaction she expected if he wasn't there to share it? But she couldn't see herself living on a station. What would she do there that wouldn't drive her crazy? She'd been born into this nomadic life.

A knock on her door interrupted her meditation. She keyed it open, calling out, "Come in."

The door slid aside, and Theos stepped through, a severe look on his frowning face. "I thought I should tell you I just caught Miss Nosey in the cargo hold."

"Heidi wandered down there?" Grania asked, not overly concerned but curious why the girl would do that.

Standing directly in front of her, he crossed his arms. "I found her studying our very special crate, showing more than a passing interest in it. When I asked her what she was doing, she said she was bored and thought exploring the ship would be interesting."

"Well, I suppose that might be true. She'd talked to Brendan a little earlier, asking what she might do on the ship. We don't exactly have a rec room for passengers."

"She could watch programming in her cabin like most passengers do. Anyway, I sent her back to the upper decks, telling her the cargo area was off-limits to passengers." He relaxed his shoulders and dropped his arms. "Grania, I don't like that you brought her on board."

"She's a kid." Grania stood, dismissing the whole incident with a hand wave. "Not a spy. A giant box among the rest of the cargo probably stood out. Was she doing anything more than looking at it?"

"She touched it. When I spotted her, she had a hand on the seal, and I think she read the contents label. Why would she be interested?"

"Curiosity? I don't think it's anything to be concerned

about, Theos. But you've told her to stay out. That should be the end of it." She crossed to her desk and sat down.

Placing his hands on the edge of the desk, he leaned toward her. "I'm saying we need to keep an eye on her. I have pretty good instincts, so I find it more than a little concerning that she was interested in that particular item."

"All right. I hear you. Let me see what I might do to keep the girl entertained." She already hard an idea that might work.

When she returned to the bridge, she strolled to Brendan and leaned closer to talk to him without Kachiri or Rory hearing. "I need you to do something for me. Find Heidi and spend some time with her. Play a game or talk for a bit. Find out what you can about her."

He frowned, a puzzled look on his handsome face. "Why?"

"Because she may be okay, or she may be more interested in our ship than I first thought. Be discreet, and don't tell her anything about our over-sized cargo item."

He nodded. "I'll do what I can." He slid out of his chair, and Grania touched his arm.

"Bren, flirt if you have to."

He wrinkled his nose like that was a distasteful prospect. As he left the bridge, Grania asked Rory to cover the navigation station for a while.

As Rory settled in, he asked, "What's going on?"

"I have a little task that only he can do," she said vaguely. "It won't take too long."

Rory lifted an eyebrow but nodded and turned to his task.

Since the ship was on a programmed course, all he had to do was make sure it didn't deviate and look for anything unforeseen crossing their path.

Away from the station, the communication console activity dwindled to space static and not much else, so Grania also sent Kachiri on a long break, covering for her. Had she made a mistake in bringing Heidi Geers on board? She refused to believe that the teenager could be a threat.

*****

When Brendan returned a little over an hour later, he approached Grania, who still manned the communications console, and spoke quietly. "We chatted for a while, then played a video challenge game, and she seemed all right. After that, she began askin' a lot of questions about the ship. More than most people would ask."

"Like what?" Grania saw Rory had turned toward them and was trying to hear. She motioned him over.

"Well, where we'd started our trip, and I told her Erinnua, which she had never heard of. But then she wanted to know where we'd gone from there. Which stations. I skimmed over that, not mentioning Enterprise."

"Why does she care?" Rory asked.

Brendan shook his head. "She even asked if the Mo Chroidhe had weapons. I laughed at her and didn't answer. Then she remarked about the big crate in the hold, even admittin' that she'd sneaked down to see what we had. I told her I didn't know."

"That's good, Bren." Grania frowned as she listened. Heidi was showing too much interest in their cargo. She tagged Theos. "You may be right about the Geers girl. Secure the cargo bay. Let's not give her any opportunity to get in there."

"Anything else?" she asked Brendan.

"We got ice cream in the galley—the stardust delight is really good. And she flirted with me."

"Did she, now?" Rory grinned.

Brendan scowled at Rory. "Yeah. It made me uncomfortable. I'll go back to me nav board if ya don't mind."

"No hope for him, Nia." Rory laughed and moved to take over the communications station.

"Don't tease him. But this girl worries me. Let's stay alert to what she's doing."

Deciding to check in on her, Grania climbed down to the mid-deck and tapped on Heidi's door.

Blonde hair falling over her forehead, Heidi peered out the partial opening of the sliding door, and her face split into a smile. "Captain! What a surprise. Please come in." The door slid open the rest of the way to allow Grania admittance.

A quick scan showed Grania that the girl's clothing was mainly stuffed inside her backpack, with only a couple of shirts hanging in the small closet. A mobi device sat on the desk, and not much else disturbed the room other than a personal hygiene kit on the table near the accommodation. She traveled light, too light for a girl who'd been a long distance away visiting family.

"I stopped by to see how you're settling in. Do you have everything you need?"

"Oh, yes! The cabin is great, and even an auto-chef. Some big passenger ships don't even offer those in their rooms. Did you know that?"

"I didn't, actually. While this one isn't programmed to offer as much as the one in the galley, you can get beverages, sandwiches, and snacks. Although I heard you visited the galley, so I guess you've seen the big one in there."

She nodded. "Yes. It looks like it offers lots of choices. Bren got us some ice cream earlier. Great-tasting stuff. I'd never tried that flavor before. He's such a gorgeous boy, but he seems so shy."

"He can be that way," Grania admitted.

"But he's so handsome and sweet. The kind of guy I'd like to find back at the station."

"Uh-hmm," she agreed. "You say you were visiting your family. Grandparent, wasn't it?"

"Yes. My father's side of the family."

"What planet was that?"

"Tabor." Heidi didn't hesitate.

"Really? I've never been there. What's it like?" Grania leaned back against the desktop, trying to look casual.

"Oh, it's a rural place where they live. A fair distance from Jonasberg, the main spaceport city there. It's rough-looking, with lots of gray dirt and craggy hills. Then you come to lush, fertile valleys where rivers run through, coming from the central mountains.

"Sounds different. Maybe not too people-friendly. What about animals?"

"I'm not too familiar with them. They don't come around people. Lots of them are poisonous, so people try to avoid them as much as possible."

Grania asked her a few more questions, deciding she'd heard enough. When she left Heidi, she was reasonably sure the girl hadn't told her anything more than she would find in a brief search. She didn't talk about her family except for the little bit she'd told her earlier that her folks had a general store on Outer Rim. One thing Grania felt confident of was that she was lying to her. She also knew the girl liked Brendan, although that, too, could be an act.

Whatever Heidi Geers was up to, Grania felt the girl needed to be watched. She called Dari and Brendan to her cabin and outlined her plan.

"Clearly, Heidi is taken with you, Brendan, but I can't free you to spend a lot of time entertaining here. So, that's where you come in, Dari." She pointed her finger at the puca, who shifted to a ramrod-straight position in his chair.

"Me?"

"Yes. With Bren's permission, of course."

The slow-growing smirk on her brother's face told her that he understood what she wanted. "Do you mind, Bren, if Dari impersonates you for a while?"

"Not at all." Brendan's eyes twinkled with amusement.

"Wait a minute," Dari said. "I do not know anythin' about navigating a spaceship. Not even a rowboat, mind you." He shook his head vigorously.

"You won't be on the bridge." Grania clarified her thoughts. "You'll be the Brendan entertaining the girl."

His youthful mouth fell open, almost making her laugh at his shocked expression.

"No. No, Captain Grania. I have no way to get intimate with a girl."

Now, Grania did laugh. "I'm not asking you to do that. I simply want you to be your charming self as Brendan and spend time with her. In short, don't let her out of your sight."

"Oh, I see. I think." Dari sat forward. "I am to look like Brendan and keep her occupied with talk, games, and stories."

"That pretty much sums it up," Grania agreed. "But also, be alert to anything she says that might suggest she is interested in our cargo. We suspect she is, but we don't know how much information she might have about it."

Dari sat back, an impish grin lighting his face. "I think I can do that."

Chapter Twenty-Six

A short time later, Brendan–or at least someone who resembled him—went down to the mid-deck, looking for Heidi Geers. He found her in the galley, eating a bowl of spaceman's chowder, a mix of whatever vegetables were available, a bit of meat, and a creamy broth with lots of spices.

"I thought you might be in here," he said as he poked his head into the room. "I've got some time off, so I thought we might spend some of it together if ya' like."

She giggled like one of the coquettish Irish girls did, and he half expected her to blush. "I thought you had to be on duty."

"Well, I was, but the Captain said I could take the time before we get to the next gate. So, what would ya' like to do?"

"How about we play Crags and Craters?"

Dari, posing as Brendan, shrugged in agreement, but he didn't have a clue what she was talking about. It turned out to be a video skill game where they each had a controller, and they had to fly through craters and over crags while avoiding falling objects. And each other, he soon learned as she guided her ship icon into his, bumping him into one of the crags.

Fortunately, his form had Brendan's dexterity, but unfortunately, not his skill at the game. He crashed more often than not.

Laughing, Heidi said, "I hope you navigate better than you fly these ships!"

"Of course, I do. Let's try again."

After that round, which ended just as badly for Dari, she turned to him. "Are you letting me win?"

"No. Not at all. I'm just… out of practice, you see." He thought that sounded like a typical excuse.

Her eyes closed to a slit, looking coy as she tilted her head and smiled shyly. Pure coquettish, he thought. He'd seen that look many times on young girls' faces.

After that, they talked for about two hours, or rather, Heidi did. She'd go on and on about her trip and how she would have been stranded on Andromeda if the Captain hadn't let her come on board. "Why is Grania so reluctant to take a passenger? The ship has plenty of room, near as I can see." Then she remarked on the cabins being pretty nice, so they should be taking passengers since they could command a premium fee for them.

"Is there something secret in the hold?" she said after a brief pause.

Dari stared at her blankly. "What?"

"I asked if you guys have something secret in the hold? I mean, the good-looking guy down there had a fit when he found me there."

"Uh," Dari stammered. "I do not know. But the hold is off-limits to passengers."

"Why?"

Thinking fast, he hoped he came up with a reasonable answer. "Because the shipments are valuable, and we must protect them until they are delivered." It made sense to him and amounted to the truth as he saw it. "The Mo Chroidhe's reputation depends on it."

"Oh." She looked disappointed. "I guess that is a good reason. But how can anyone steal anything when you're on the ship and can't get off?"

"You might be surprised. Let me tell you a story...." And he did, relating a tale of space pirates attacking a ship—although he didn't indicate it was this very one—and having a passenger plan it all. He also omitted the part about a b'ean sidhe and a puca helping the crew.

By the time Dari walked her back to her cabin for the sleep period, she was worn out, barely babbling at all. He hadn't felt so exhausted in many years. While he didn't need sleep, holding Brendan's form this long and listening to the girl had made him weary. He went up one deck and switched to his energy form before settling into a damp cloth he'd set up in a corner of the bridge. No one noticed him there, and he could recover for a bit.

* * * * *

The next few days passed without the Geers girl wandering off to any places she shouldn't, thanks to Dari's Brendan form keeping her busy. When they reached Galaxy Station, they didn't dock but waited at their assigned position for approval to pass through the Longhop Gate. The last one before they reached Outer Rim Station, this gate boasted the longest wormhole jump in the galaxy, covering about one hundred thousand parsecs over seven days. It was a massive fold in space.

Grania chose to bypass the planned stop at Galaxy Station, hoping they wouldn't encounter any delays. When she added the transit time from the gate's end to Outer Rim, they would barely make the deadline to Terminus Station and then on to the other station to deliver the she-bee. Once she contacted the recipient--a man she only had a name and code to reach—she could turn the cargo over to him and be done with it.

"Do ya' ever think it odd that we have these great folds in space for travel?" Brendan asked while they waited.

"I haven't thought about it much," Grania admitted, caught off guard by the question. "What brought that up?" Even Rory tilted his head toward their brother.

"It's only a curious thought. But the majority are natural jumps, not human-created ones. Why would space naturally fold like this unless it was planned? Unless humans and other species were meant to travel through space?"

"Are you suggesting a grand design?" Grania's lips curved in amusement. She'd heard that theory before.

"Maybe. But it seems there must be a reason for the natural space tunnels. I mean, we spend seven days passin' through one and shortcut trillions of miles."

Rory chuckled. "Don't think about it too much, Bren. It'll just distract you, and you won't find an answer."

"Can't help but think about it when we're about to enter the longest one known to us. What if it one dumped us out in Andromeda?"

Grania hadn't considered that possibility. "That could be, but it hasn't been discov—"

"We have clearance, Captain," Kachiri interrupted as soon as the message came through. "We can proceed to the gate, then we will have another thirty mites before we enter."

"Excellent," Grania answered, relaying the information to Sindhu. Once they maneuvered to the gate approach, they detected three other ships in front of them. She was surprised to find that much traffic going their way. For the most part, they'd encountered only one or two other vessels during their journey.

When they moved to the second position, Rory sounded the alert for everyone to check their jump pods. Brendan jumped up, telling Grania that he needed to double-check his to ensure it was fully charged.

This long jump would need every bit of the hibernation drug, oxygen, and nutrients the units held. The ship's life support unit would monitor each pod to ensure they didn't run out. If, at any point during the jump, one of the units failed or ran out of supplies, the system would wake the person and bring the system back up to sustain life.

*****

Dari, still posing as Brendan, was in the galley with Heidi when the alert came. They'd been playing another round of Craters and Bluffs, and Dari was actually winning it so far.

"I'd better check my pod," Heidi said. "When I checked it earlier, it still had about five percent to go to be fully charged."

"Would you like me to go with you?" Dari asked. His voice had that deep, charming tone of Brendan's.

"That would be nice." She paused on the way to the door to wait for him.

He caught up to her, put his arm around her waist, and started down the corridor with her. As they got about halfway, he glimpsed Brendan coming down the stairs. He panicked for a moment, then pretended to stumble into her, pushing her against the wall and drawing her attention to him.

"Sorry, I must have tripped over something on the floor." He looked down, turning his head back toward the direction they'd come from. "Help me look. I don't know what it was, but we don't want anyone else tripping on it."

He figured the diversion would give Brendan time to scoot back up the steps or finish coming down and getting out of sight. When Dari turned to look back that way, he didn't see him anywhere.

"I don't see anything, Bren." Heidi twisted back toward him. "Whatever it was must be pretty small."

"You're right. I can't see it either. I will do a sweep later. For now, we should check your pod."

They proceeded to her room, and as they passed the stairs, he glimpsed a pale face in a shadowed corner behind them. He urged Heidi to her room.

Inside, she went to her pod, checked the readings, then turned back to him. "It's fully charged."

"That is a relief," he said. He meant it sincerely.

For Dari, these past few days had been a strain. Being Brendan was tiring, and he had to be on his best behavior. He'd flirted a little with the girl, but he didn't want to overdo it, so she didn't get any romantic ideas about him.

"We have a little time before we need to go to the pods." Heidi sat on the bunk bed and patted the mattress next to her.

Dari hesitated, seeming to waffle with indecision. "Umm, I think I had best go check me own pod." He had no delusions about what she wanted, but he was not the lad to give it to her.

She pouted, her lips spreading wide and somewhat unattractive. "Just for a little bit, Bren?"

"I need to go now," he said as the alarm sounded, alerting everyone to go to the jump pods. "You should get in the pod now. We'll be goin' through the gate in five mites."

Disappointed, she nodded and watched him as he backed out of her cabin. Once outside, Dari leaned against the wall and let out a sigh. That was getting too friendly for him.

Brendan came down the hall and asked, "Is she in?"

"I think so."

"Check on her, will you, Dari? Nia wants to be sure she doesn't pull any stunts before we jump."

"Stunts?" Dari repeated, not sure what Brendan was saying.

"You know, set up an ambush or contact someone ahead to cause trouble." He slapped Dari on the shoulder. "Just see that she's in the pod." With a nod, he ran on toward his cabin.

At the sound of feet on the stairs, Dari looked that way in time to see Kachiri dashing down the last few steps and running toward her cabin as well. Changing to his energy form, he slipped through the wall. Heidi had changed into pajamas and was sending a message on her mobi. He got close enough to hear that she was dictating the note to her parents.

"...entering Longhop now. I'll see you in a few days." She

sent the unit to charge mode, made a disapproving face at the jump pod, but climbed in and closed the lid. The drugs went to work, and in less than a minute, she was under, eyes closed, and sleeping peacefully.

Dari shot to the bridge to report it to Grania but didn't find her there. Then he realized the ship was now on automatic, and the captain had gone to her cabin. As he darted in there, he found her just getting into the unit. Changing quickly, he startled her, but when she caught her breath again, he reported the girl was in her pod and that she'd messaged her parents.

"Good work, Dari," she replied. "Keep an eye on the ship while we're under. Check on the girl periodically and be there when she wakes. I don't want any surprises." She reached up and pulled the cover down.

The question occurring to him a little late, Dari mumbled, "By 'be there,' did ya mean I should physically be in her cabin or as me energy form?"

Of course, he didn't get an answer. The Captain was already out like a light.

* * * * *

When they arrived at the ending gate, energy speck Dari waited for the girl to wake up. He heard noises from the hallway of the crew coming out of their cabins and heading for either the galley or the bridge. The running footsteps were likely from Rory, heading to the galley to get a snack and coffee before going up the steps. Next, he heard Theos' voice yelling something he couldn't make out after Rory.

A few minutes later, the girl roused from her slumber, sitting up once the lid had fully raised. She stretched and climbed off the padded cushion. Perfectly normal. No problem here.

He started to leave, but the girl picked up her mobi and keyed in a code. Dari waited, feeling a bit anxious about this early call. He didn't hear the voice on the other end, but he heard Heidi's words. "We just exited the jump. I feel fuzzy, but it will clear in a few mites. I'll make my move before the ship gets to the Rim Station. Just be sure you're in place."

That sounded ominous to Dari. Certainly not a call to her parents. As he exited, he heard a static crackle in the room, and Heidi said, "What was that noise?" He vanished, aiming for the bridge.

Chapter Twenty-Seven

Grania woke from their long jump feeling a little stiff but fully rested. Maybe too much. Her head ached as she went through her exiting-the-wormhole routine. Appropriately called Longhop, this one had left them in stasis for just under seven days, about double the time they'd spent traveling the Andromeda jump. Considering how much space the tube folded, it was a relatively short time, although the longest that Grania had experienced.

Satisfied that everything on the ship was normal, she issued the command to wake the crew and headed for the shower, starting the coffee brewer on the way. Alert and dressed with a cup in hand, she headed to the bridge where Rory was already on deck, checking the navigation console.

She almost called Liam before realizing it was Sindhu now to get a status report. "Good day, Sindhu. Is everything normal there?"

When the response was a little slow in coming, Grania wondered if the new guy had come out of the jump pod okay. At last, he reported in. "She all good, Cap'n."

She relaxed, then turned her gaze to the starboard screen where the Andromeda Galaxy appeared much closer than at the previous gate. It loomed out at the edge of the Milky Way, so close now that she could only see a portion of it, the shape almost undetectable in the mass of stars. One day, experts said, that spiral would merge with their own.

Beautiful and inviting though it was, space travelers hadn't yet passed beyond the boundaries of this galaxy to the intervening space between the galaxies. Those who came close reported that the edge was like going into a wild sea with unpredictable currents and unseen objects threatening spaceships. Nonetheless, exploration ships went close to the edge, getting readings and learning more about it. One day, they would make the leap.

Not in my lifetime. For a minute, she considered that a spaceship was like a time machine. The farther you get from the center of the galaxy, the farther back in time you travel. While the distances within the Milky Way amounted to a few billion years, once you got into the next galaxy and the one after, you went back many times beyond the present with each jump.

Returning, you literally moved forward again, adding only a week or so to when you left.

She heard a thud and turned her head to see Dari, in his peasant form, entering the bridge. She rose to her feet at the intrusion, noting the intent look on the puca's face. "What is it?"

Shifting nervously from one foot to the other, Dari repeated precisely what the girl had said.

"Rory. Brendan. Be alert to any vessels near us. We should be a reasonable distance from any others until we get closer to Outer Rim. We might have a threat out there." Turning to Kachiri, she asked, "Have you picked up any signals yet?"

She listened for a moment. "I have the whine from the tracker again and a signal beacon. That's it."

Turning back to Dari, Grania said, "Good job, Dari. Now keep an eye on her. If she does anything out of the ordinary, let me know."

Dari left, his form altering once he passed the bridge doors. As she watched through the transparent walls, Grania marveled at how the puca could transform within a heartbeat. *Magic, pure magic.*

Then she contacted Theos to tell him. From that report, it sounded like he was right about Heidi, and her plea for passage amounted to a ploy to get on board. *Damn. I was a fool to fall for that act of hers. When will I learn? I'm such a softie. First, I take in an old lady who turns out to be a b'ean sidhe, then this girl. But to be fair, at least the first incident worked out in our favor.*

Now, she had to figure out how to protect her crew from whatever might be coming their way. What would the girl's move be? Would she try to take the ship, or was she after the cargo? If she touched that crate, it could blow us all up. If she removed it, then the group monitoring them from Enterprise might do the same.

* * * * *

Still pretending to be Brendan, Dari knocked on Heidi's cabin door. After a few moments, she opened it, and a pleased expression spread across her face.

"Might you be ready for breakfast? I'm feelin' a bit peckish, meself," Dari asked.

"That sounds good, Bren. Let me get my things." She turned, picked up a small black tote, and stepped out of the cabin. He led the way toward the galley, asking her if she had any dreams while she slept.

"Naw, I don't dream in stasis sleep. Nobody does, do they?"

"Not while actually under it, but sometimes as you start to come out, you might. I know a few people who have."

When he reached for the sliding door, he felt a sharp pain in his lower back, just where a human's kidneys might be, and he realized he'd been stabbed. As his knees began to fold, Dari fought to hold his human form, sinking to the floor just outside the galley. He turned his head to see Heidi holding the knife, his simulated blood staining it as a few drops plunged to the deck.

In corporeal form, he duplicated his human shape, but he didn't, by any means, die when the body was damaged. He could switch back to energy in a blink, but with Heidi standing over him, knife raised to attack again, he had to remain Brendan's duplicate. She plunged the dagger down, even as he raised his arms, attempting to reach it before it hit him. He missed and wailed as the blade slid into his chest.

Pain in this form was a new sensation for him, and he gasped, then groaned. Nonetheless, the agony passed quickly as his body healed itself. To all appearances, he had to die so Heidi would go ahead with her plan. He closed his eyes, holding his breath and looking as lifeless as possible. When he heard her footsteps go down the corridor, he opened an eye, watching her pull out her tablet and use it to decipher the lock code on the door to the steps leading to the hold.

As it opened and the girl stepped through, tote still in her hand, he changed to energy again. He couldn't warm Sindhu or Theos in this form, so he returned to Grania, pausing in the corridor just before the Transparisteel windows to change to his country lad form.

He motioned for her to come with him and walked toward her cabin, away from the rest of the crew's view. While Brendan and Rory knew about him, Kachiri didn't, so he wanted to keep it secret for now.

Grania soon caught up with him and asked what had happened. He related the death and resurrection incident, followed by Heidi's successful entry to the cargo hold.

*****

"Damn," Grania muttered. That little liar acted quickly, and she attempted to murder her brother. Thank the fates Dairi had been impersonating him, then she gaped at the puca, hoping the stabbing didn't hurt him. "Are you all right?"

"Of course. I'm eternal." He sounded almost indignant she'd asked.

"Just checking." Yet concern painted her face with a dark look while Grania tapped her mobi, trying to reach Theos. No response. She tried Sindhu. Still nothing.

Turning on her heel, she rushed back to the bridge and ran past the navigation station to the weapons locker at the back. Opening it with her palm print, she reached for her blast pistol on the right-hand wall.

"What's happened, Nia?" Rory asked, stepping into the closet-sized room.

"We may have trouble in the engine room or the hold. Or both. Keep a close watch for anything happening outside the ship. Our passenger appears to be trouble, and she may have brought some friends along."

"Do ya' need help?" Rory asked, reaching for another weapon.

"Not yet. I'd rather you make sure nothing sneaks up on us from here." She glimpsed Dairi standing at the locker entrance and added, "Dairi's goin' down with me."

"I am?" the puca asked. Then added, "Yes. Of course," when Grania shot a hard stare his way.

Together, they ran down the corridor, took the stairs two at a time to the mid-level, then paused at the door to the hold. Grania checked the lock, clicking her tongue in annoyance that Heidi had broken the code so quickly. Easing it open, she motioned to Dari to say silent and stepped lightly on the first step down, listening for any sounds from below. About halfway down the steps, she heard voices, not loud enough to be clear, but it was the girl.

She went down more slowly, then whispered to Dari to change to Brendan's form.

"But she thinks I'm dead," he whispered back.

"It will be a surprise." Her grin looked evil. "Wait here until I call you."

She moved into the aisle to the engineer's office, her weapon ready. Stepping into a narrow opening between crates, she sized up the situation. She saw Heidi standing over Theos' inert body as she pointed a blast pistol at Sindhu. He was pressed back against one of the two computer cabinets with his hands halfway up, fear written on his face.

How did she get that weapon on board? Grania's eyes narrowed, irritated the Geers girl had evaded their detection unit when she boarded. She had to have a blocker on her. *Who is pulling the strings on this? Surely, not a teenager.*

"Open the airlock," Heidi demanded, waving the blast gun in a threatening circle.

Sindhu shook his head, his eyes darting from the weapon to her face. "I do not have authority."

Why does she want the airlock open? Grania thought as she slipped out of hiding to ease her way closer.

Heidi set her feet apart and waved the gun around more as she snapped out her response. "Are you sure about that?"

"No code. I do not have proper code." Sindhu insisted.

"Well, fine. Then we'll all die in here when I blow that big crate to hell. Last chance, open the airlock." Heidi yelled.

Surprised, Grania began to connect the dots. The girl's mission was to locate and liberate the crate, whether she knew what was in it. That meant whoever sent her wanted to retrieve it or blow it up in space. They didn't actually care what the item was, only that it was a weapon to be used against them. Her threat to blow it up was a bluff or a fall-back plan, and she was willing to die for the cause.

Quietly, she stepped back into a space between two rows of creates, tagged Rory, and whispered, "Have you detected any ships near us?"

"Not yet." A soft voice at his end as well.

"I think they're coming. Don't know how many. Prepare to make a run for it. And bring the blast cannon online." She expected trouble, especially if this girl didn't report. The opposition would likely open fire on the Mo Chroidhe to stop them from delivering that crate.

Making her move, Grania stepped out from the cabinet with her weapon aimed at Heidi and ordered. "Put your weapon down and step away from my engineer."

The girl didn't hesitate, swinging her aim from Sindhu to Grania in seconds and firing.

As soon as Grania saw Heidi start to pivot, she squeezed off a blast from her own weapon and stepped to the side, hoping she'd chosen the right direction. The energy bolt struck Grania in her left shoulder, sending a shock of pain that made her gasp down that side, but at least it hadn't landed dead center on her chest.

Grania heard Heidi's pained cry as her blast found its target in the girl's midsection. Through watering eyes, Grania watched the girl double over in pain, wrapping her arms around her middle as the weapon clattered to the floor.

Released from the threat, Sindhu moved like a bug, scrambling to grab the gun. Securing it, he turned to Heidi as Grania gasped, "Tie her up."

Although short of stature, Sindhu easily overpowered the injured teenager, who tried to fight back. Ignoring the pain in her shoulder as best she could, Grania strode to the desk, found a length of unused wire, and handed it to the engineer to bind the girl's hands.

"They'll kill you all." Heidi spat the words at her through

gritted teeth. "You can't take that thing to Desolation."

Well, that might have answered the question of whether Heidi knew what was in the crate. She shoved the young rebel to a chair and motioned for Sindhu to tie her to it. "Make sure she can't get loose."

Pulling out her mobi, she tagged Rory. "See anything yet."

"Sure do," he answered. "A pair of small cruisers, about a third our size. I'm bettin' they're faster and more maneuverable than we are. Pretty sure they aren't a welcome party."

"Is the cannon online?"

"It is. Ready and waiting."

If we have a space battle ahead, we're ready for it. Grania hoped it didn't go as badly as their last fight when the freebooters shot the ship up. "We just got this ride fixed up, Rory. Let's try not to damage her again."

"Will do my best, sis."

"Notify the station we've been attacked and have caught a Desolation rebel on board trying to steal our cargo. Request help."

At his acquiescence, she turned back to Heidi Geers. Thus far, those ships out there had no idea the girl had failed. Grania approached her and knelt to go through Heidi's pockets. The girl squirmed and tried to rock the chair out of the Captain's way, but Sindhu grasped the chair's back, holding it in place.

Reaching into a pocket on Heidi's cargo-style pants, Grania pulled a slim mobi unit out. Turning it on, she thumbed through the messages, looking for any sent after the one Dari witnessed. Only one showed, from about 10 mites earlier, that said simply, "Mission underway." Nothing else, meaning the ships waited for her to signal them or for the cargo to float out into space.

With the threat subdued, if you could call the foul-mouthed teen under control when she cursed and threatened while she struggled against the restraints, Grania turned her attention to Theos. He lay prone on the floor where the girl had attacked him. How had she gotten into a position to manage that? She knelt to check on him and noted he was breathing but unconscious. The girl must have stunned him, then hit him with something. A lump on the back of his head supported her theory, and she did find a laser burn on his clothing mid-torso. She pushed up his tunic top to see if it had burned him. Eyes roaming over the finely-tuned muscles of his chest, she did spot the red-brown burn spot that matched his shirt's damage.

She tapped her mobi, tagging Dairi, and requested "Brendan" bring the Med Kit over. She glanced at Heidi as she said it, seeing her eyes pop wide and her mouth drop as she realized Brendan was alive.

"But I killed him," she blurted. "I stabbed him."

At that point, Dari trotted over, handing her the Med Kit from the wall near the stairs. "See if you can bring him around," Grania pointed to Theos, then turned her attention to Heidi.

"Now, Ms. Geers, what do you know about a certain piece of my cargo?"

"Nothing to concern you. Just open the airlock and toss it out into space if you want to save your ship."

"You want me to dump something representing a large transport fee into space so your friends can do what? Pick it up or destroy it?" She leaned forward, placing her hands on Heidi's forearms tied to the chair.

"If you don't do it, they'll blow this ship up," Heidi insisted.

"How? Did you bring a bomb on board?" A touch of alarm sounded within Grania. She hadn't considered that before.

Heidi clammed up then, and Grania straightened as she heard a gasp from behind her. Theos was conscious. Turning, she saw Dari just standing up, a wad of gauze in his hand and the smell of ammonia wafting from it. Theos had levered onto his elbow, shaking his head, coughing, and wincing at the pain.

She glanced at Dari. "Ammonia?"

"We called it spirit of hartshorn," he replied. "Wakes people up fast."

She rolled her eyes and knelt beside Theos to give him an arm up. "How do you feel?"

"Headache, burned and poisoned. What the hell was that?" he muttered, coughing again. Then he drew in a sharp breath, his eyes narrowing.

Grania glanced at Dari in time to see him putting the burn wound spray back in the med kit. "That should take care of the burning pain. Seems our passenger got past your defenses."

Sitting up, Theos groaned again, glaring at Heidi. The look he gave Grania was pure annoyance. "I told you, didn't I?"

"Let me have that spray," she said to Dari as she reached her open palm out. She ignored the jib, already feeling guilty enough. Dari handed her the antibiotic and anesthetic combination, and she straightened up. "We're expecting an attack any minute now. Are you okay for now?"

"I think so," Theos answered, extending his hand to Dari. "Give me a lift up."

While Dari helped him get upright, Grania went behind the engine room computers, removed her tunic, and sprayed her shoulder wound. Biting on her lip as the cool spray stung the burn, she waited a few moments until the numbing killed the pain. Now, to deal with the girl and those approaching ships.

Chapter Twenty-Eight

With Theos back on his feet, they marched Heidi Geers, still bent over in pain and moaning, up the stairs. "It hurts so much," she whined. "You could at least treat the wound you *shasista* profiteers gave me."

"Not much sympathy here," Theos muttered, ignoring her derogatory swear word.

Having inflicted the wound, Grania did show concern and tried to get a look, motioning for Theos to stop and reaching for the girl's shirt to lift it. Heidi straightened a bit, then her elbow shot into Grania's ribs, knocking her back. Grania staggered back, her hand pressed against her ribs on the right side while she glared daggers at the girl.

The teen twisted in Theos' grip and lunged, legs peddling to catch him in a sensitive spot so she could break free. In less than ten seconds, Theos took the girl to the ground on her stomach. He yanked her arms behind her and pulled her legs forward into a bow shape like hunters tied animals to subdue them. All the while, she screamed, yelling obscenities.

When she recovered from the brief attack, Grania motioned to Dari to hand her the First Aid kit and pulled out a roll of adhesive wrap. She bound Heidi's hands together, then did the same to her ankles. Then she used the tape to connect both the secured appendages together. "That should hold her for now."

Snatching the roll from her, Theos pulled off a few pieces, grabbed the girl's face, and stuck them over her mouth to mute the sound of her curses and screams. He picked her up around her middle to carry her back to her cabin.

"Use this one," Grania said, opening one of the other empty cabins.

He lifted an eyebrow as if to ask why.

"Just a precaution." She stepped aside so he could carry Heidi in. He dumped her on the bed.

The tape over her mouth hadn't held and hung off one side.

"They'll come after you," Heidi screamed. "When they don't hear from me, and that crate doesn't go into space, they'll make sure it doesn't make it to the planet. You'll all die."

"Along with you," Grania answered in an icy voice while Theos improvised another gag.

She took the burn spray, pulled up the girl's shirt, and sprayed it on her wound. She didn't want anyone accusing her of mistreating the teen, but she didn't care if she was in pain or not. Heidi shrieked as the cool spray hit her burned skin.

Grania and Theos left the room, leaving the girl trussed up on the bed. Grania locked it down so Heidi couldn't open it from the inside if she somehow worked her way out of the taped hands and ankles.

"I'm getting a handheld blast cannon and going back down to the hold in case they try to board," Theos said, turning back toward the stairs.

"Lock down the airlocks, and they won't get in unless they blow their way through," she said. Which was a real possibility if they only wanted to destroy the crate.

She scrambled up the steps and down the short way to the bridge, calling, "Status," as she hurried through the sliding door.

"Cannons are online and ready," Rory answered, glancing up from the weapon's station, a small console near the rear starboard area. "The ships are out there but haven't attacked yet."

"Have we gotten anything from the ships or Outer Rim, Kachiri?" She pivoted to face the communications station.

"No, Captain. Nothing at all. I'll tell you if I get anything." Kachiri looked calm, her focus on her job, but Grania noticed a nervous twitch in her cheek as her mouth tightened with tension.

"Stay alert. Once they realize that their spy on board isn't getting the cargo out the bay door or communicating with them, they'll make a move." Grania took her seat at her console, flicking her eyes to the forward monitor. She saw one class five excursion cruiser almost out of view to starboard while the other hovered about three ship widths below it at the far port. It appeared to be about the same size. Both much smaller than the freighter but speedier and more agile, they loomed ready to make a run to either side of the Mo Chroidhe.

Grania tapped her fingers on the arm of her seat as they waited for something to happen. Apart from the muted hum of the ship's engines, the bridge remained silent except for her light drumming. No one spoke or even shifted in their seat. Across the way, Rory kept his hand on the blast cannon's controls, waiting.

Kachiri broke the silence, her soft voice carrying in the stillness. "Copy that, Outer Rim." She twisted toward Grania. "The station has confirmed assistance is dispatched."

"Good. Let's see if they get here before those cruisers make a move." Pleased to have the response, she still kept her eyes on the ships, wondering how long they would wait. Were they trying to contact Heidi before they attacked? She should have brought her mobi with her instead of leaving it in the hold. Her mistake. She hoped it wouldn't cost them now.

As the tension built, the cruisers began to move, picking up speed rapidly as they advanced toward the bridge.

"They're through waiting," Grania said. "Shields up. Be ready, Rory, but don't fire until they fire at us." While the shields were designed for protection from small particles, space dust, or other naturally occurring space objects, they provided some protection from incoming blasts.

"If they're aiming for the hold, they'll be past us before they fire." Rory turned a concerned face toward her, his brow lowered.

"I understand. But we don't want to be the aggressor in this scenario. Not if we want a quick assist from the station. We don't have time to get tied up in legal paperwork." If they fired first, they would need to prove the two rogue ships were threatening them. That could hold them up for days.

First, the freebooters ravaged the Mo Chroidhe in their home system. Now, these rebels wanted to steal and destroy a valuable shipment. She hoped this wouldn't become a pattern to her stint as the ship's captain.

The ship rocked and shuddered as the first blast hit the port side. "Hit on the bay's loading ramp," Theos' voice boomed through the com system. "It's holding. Shook things a little, but nothing broke loose."

"Zeroing cannon on it," Rory said. "Don't think I can get a shot."

Grania knew the top-mounted cannon had limited use to the sides and back of the ship due to the dorsal sail. "Evasive, Brendan." She braced herself for the sharp drop as Brendan took the freighter down hard and to the starboard to bring it around for a front view of their attackers. They were behind them now, both starting to react to the sudden shift.

As soon as the turn was completed, she saw Rory target the vessel on the starboard side. A moment later, he fired the cannon, scoring a direct hit on their starboard engine. The cruiser skipped across space like a stone tossed on water.

The port ship came at them, lining up with the bridge. Grania started to yell to Brendan as the Mo Chroidhe lurched upward at a sharp angle, and the blasts went below them. The crew shifted as the seats turned with the new slope, but they were anchored to the floor, so apart from some awkward body positions while trying to hold onto their chairs, everyone remained in place.

Glancing at the screen, Grania saw the blast Rory had

unleashed from the Mo Chroidhe shoot into the attacking ship and hit its starboard engine dead center. The engine blew up, and a brief burst of fire soon died in the non-oxygen environment.

"Great shot, Rory!" Grania called out.

"The other's coming back," Brendan said, his eyes locked on the screen to the port side. The ship rolled hard to starboard, bringing it around in a wide arc headed straight for the oncoming vessel. "There's your target, Rory," Brendan shouted.

Grania's eyes tracked the two blasts, one chasing the other, as Rory squeezed them out of the cannon. A shot from the other ship came a second later, headed for their lower deck. Before she could even say anything, Brendan had the freighter climbing up again. The blast skimmed the bottom as the Mo Chroidhe lurched upward. Grania clung to the arms of her chair, bracing her feet against the slide of the sharp angle.

She saw Kachiri nearly tumble from her chair, her hands grabbing the station as her feet peddled against the base. She barely avoided being thrown onto the floor where she would have slid onto the lower level.

Grania's eyes stayed with the blasts, gratified to see them both hit their targets, the engines on each side of the small ship's undercarriage. They exploded, disabling that vessel.

"You got it!" Brendan shouted.

Grania turned to give Rory a thumbs up in time to see him straighten up from where he'd been hunched over and clutching the cannon's controls. "Damage?" she asked into the comm link, hoping the ship hadn't sustained much.

Sounding breathless, Theos answered her. "We have a hull breach in the fore section. I've initiated a seal on it. Some cargo is loose in that area. But nothing more serious."

"Did the breach reach the interior wall?" The ship had double walls with space between the exterior and interior walls to maintain integrity. That was to give them time to repair any damage from space debris. Now, it would be to patch a bigger hole.

"Negative. The interior is secure. For now."

She understood. Another hit to the same area would break the inside wall and create a vacuum. Theos and Sindhu would be in severe danger. "That one won't be coming back, but we have one left that's limping."

As she looked up at the port screen, she saw the lame duck ship coming toward them again. Kachiri indicated they had a message coming from the cruiser. "On speakers," Grania ordered.

As the vessel approached them, a man's voice filled the bridge. "Just dump that big crate of yours, Captain. No need for everyone on board to die for that. We can blow it up once it's in space. Or we can blow it up on your ship. Your choice."

Grania made a chopping motion across her throat. Kachiri nodded.

Chapter Twenty-Nine

"Can you target their bridge?" Grania asked, swinging to face Rory.

"Yeah. Not their engines?" His face showed his confusion.

"Use the ion cannon. Do it." She grinned, then turned back to face the oncoming ship. Only it wasn't coming as fast as it had been. In fact, it seemed to be slowing. Why? Her brow tightened as she searched for any possible reason.

Another message came from the ship, and Kachiri put it on the bridge com. The man's voice again. "Don't be foolish, Captain. This is your last chance, or I will blow you all to hell."

"I don't think so," Grania replied. "I don't give up my cargo easily."

She glimpsed the trail of the ion blast heading for the vessel.

Clearly, the man also saw it coming, as he said. "Too late, you're already doom—"

The ion blast hit them as they started to turn, and the transmission was lost. Every electronic thing on the attacking cruiser would be out of commission. No communications, no weapons, no engines, no computers. Not even lights. They would all need to be repaired so that ship was dead in the space lanes.

But his last words sent a chill down Grania's spine. He was saying they were already doomed. How? Panic hit her as she realized a possibility she hadn't considered. She sprang out of her chair, tagging Theos as she ran across the deck. "Meet me on the mid-deck now." To her brother, she shouted, "Rory, I'm going below. Keep watch on those ships."

"The Rim ships will be here in five mites," Kachiri shouted.

"Great. Fill them in on the situation." Grania dashed out, sprinting down the hall, then charged down the stairs. At the end of the corridor, Theos emerged from the lower deck and headed toward her.

"Is there a problem with the girl?" he asked, picking up his pace as he saw Grania hurrying.

"Not directly, but maybe in her cabin. Hurry." She ran toward the original cabin assigned to Heidi and overrode the lock. Going inside, she began going through every item in it, opening the drawers on the vanity and the desk.

Theos stepped in a few moments later. "What's the deal?"

"I think there may be an explosive device in here that's been triggered by that ship out there. Help me look. Heidi Geers must have brought it on board, so it's probably in something of hers." Grania tried to recall everything the girl had on her when she was standing and talking to her. Backpack, belt pack, a loose sweater tied around her waist, and an electronics case. That had been it, so one of those might have a bomb in it. She flung the closet door aside and stared at the open backpack on the floor.

The girl had hung a few things in the narrow space, and a pair of shoes sat on the floor next to the pack, but more stuff remained in it. Picking it up, she dumped it on the bed and shoved the objects around, looking for anything that might be an explosive device. She felt Theos' presence, not to mention the pungent scent of his shaving lotion, as he peered over her shoulder.

Most of the items were readily identifiable and not unexpected for a traveler to carry. She even had an actual book in the bag. Grania shook her head, noting it was a romance novel. Not what she would have expected the young rebel to read. She turned to the make-up bag, examining it more closely. Out of the corner of her eye, she glimpsed Theos reaching for the book and flipping the cover open.

She heard his quick intake of breath, and her hands froze on the bag she held as she looked at him. His face mirrored his alarm, eyes staring intently at the book and his lips a tight line. Her eyes scrolled down to the paperback. In the hollowed-out middle of it, a square black block of explosives nestled amid wires leading to a digital timer. They had a little over four mites, or so the countdown showed.

Mouth dry, Grania choked out, "Do you know how to disarm it?"

"No time," he said, closing the book again. He held it firmly, then ran for the door. "I'm taking it to the airlock."

Grania raced behind him, following as he bounded down the steps to the hold. She paused momentarily when she spotted the number of crates that had broken loose in the earlier blast. Some were still scattered into the aisles.

Handing her the book to hold, Theos went to the environment suits and pulled one that looked his size. It had been Liam's. Yanking it on faster than Grania had ever seen anyone suit up, he grabbed a helmet and clicked it into place. She couldn't resist opening the book again to look at the time. They had forty-seven seconds left. She snapped the book shut as Theos held out his hand. Through the helmet's mic, he said, "I'm going to throw this as hard as I can, but you tell your crew to get us away from this position as fast as possible when you see me toss it. You got that?"

She nodded, worrying that they wouldn't have time. She contacted the bridge and told Brendan to take them to a starboard course away from the area as fast as feasible when she gave the word. Thank goodness, no one questioned her.

Theos entered the airlock and waited fifteen agonizing seconds as it cleared the oxygen, then the door opened to space. Looping his left hand in the airlock hand grip, Theos leaned out the opening and hurled the book away from the ship. While it moved at a decent velocity, they only had seconds before it would explode.

"Brendan, get us out of here." She called. Sidhu already had the engines primed for speed, so it would be quick. The ship lurched to the right as she grabbed one of the railings along the wall. She saw Theos half-fly out the door, and her heart thudded against her ribs. Then, he pulled himself back into the airlock and hit the close button while he braced his legs against the ship's hull to avoid being yanked out again.

The airlock door had barely shut when the explosion rocked the ship, spinning it around like a whirly gig. Grania clung to the railing with both hands, her feet sliding down the floor. She watched Theos trying to hang on to the hand loop but losing it and flying around the airlock with the ease of a stuffed toy in a windstorm. She cringed when he banged into the rear wall where a handrail protruded. He managed to grab it before he went tumbling again.

Miraculously, Brendan and Rory somehow straightened the ship and leveled it. Heaving a sigh of relief, Grania pulled herself to her feet, staggered to the airlock, checked that it was fully cycled, and pressed the open button.

Theos had managed to climb to his knees and was shaking his head when she reached him. "Are you hurt?"

"Ears are ringing… But I think that's all. Bruised, probably."

She offered her arm for support as he pulled himself up, straightening slowly as if testing for any injuries to his legs or spine. Concern in her eyes, she lifted an eyebrow in question.

"I'm okay. I think. Nothing seems broken or strained." He let her guide him into the hold, then she began unclamping the helmet.

"Rim security's here," Kachiri announced over the com. "They are requesting permission to board. A second ship is approaching the ship we just damaged."

"Right," Grania acknowledged. "Tell them we need to reset the airlock. It will be about ten mites. Is everyone okay there?"

"Minor bumps and bangs," Rory answered. "Nia, they have questions about the explosion. What should I tell 'em?"

"That I'll explain when they come aboard. Just tell them we were attacked by the two ships we disabled, and we have an accomplice on board." Grania felt weary as her adrenaline leveled out. She turned her eyes to the oversized cargo box and wondered if it was worth all this. What was the she-bee created to do?

Theos peeled off the envirosuit, down to just a thin tee shirt over his sweaty torso. It did little to hide the planes of his muscles and taut stomach. He was even tighter than Vilnius, and that was saying a lot. She snuffed a breath. Even now, looking at another fine and handsome specimen of a man, she had the station master on her mind. She might have died today without... Without what? She'd broken their relationship.

More to the point, she'd almost lost the ship and her brothers. That would have devastated their family. She turned her gaze back to the ominous box, and anger surged like lava through her body. She hadn't asked for this, and the payment sure wasn't worth what they were going through to deliver it.

Turning back to the airlock, she checked the controls, waiting for the green light to indicate it had recycled and was ready to receive the patrol. Finally, she turned to Sindhu, ashamed she hadn't checked to see if he was okay sooner. "Are you injured?" she asked.

He held up his left hand, which was wrapped in a bandage. "Bad cut from computer box edge when I hit. That is all. I grabbed seat anchor and laid flat." He grinned at her like a kid who'd been on an amusement park ride.

She gave him an okay sign, then straightened her tunic, brushed a hand through her hair, and tried to look presentable when the security team came aboard. She advised Kachiri to let the Rim officers know they were okay to dock.

Muttering to himself, Theos left to shower and change clothes. She could guess why. She felt the bump as the shuttle docked and pressed the connecting gate to allow them to enter the airlock. With a sense of déjà vu, she fidgeted while she waited.

Two officers came on board, dressed in the dark red blousons and black pantaloons of the Outer Rim security patrol. "Welcome aboard the Mo Chroidhe, gentlemen." Grania afforded them a nod and stepped back to sweep her arm in a step-aboard greeting. She was neither military nor governed by them in any way, so she gave them a less formal welcome than they were expecting but still cordial. "I am Captain Grania O'Ceagan."

The first man nodded at her, his deep brown eyes intent as he gazed around the hold. "Sergeant Bronwell." He motioned to the other officer, who barely looked in her direction, he was studying the hold configuration so intently. "Sgt. Finnelle. You requested assistance, so can you tell me what has transpired?"

She relaxed a little. "Certainly. Shall we go up to the mid-deck where we can talk in the galley?"

A dip of Bronwell's head showed his agreement, so she turned to lead them up. She hoped everything wasn't scattered over the floor after their erratic ride, but most things in the galley were stored securely. As they started up, Theos joined them. Bronwell shot a questioning look at him, and Grania introduced him. "Theos is part of my crew at the moment, but he is also here to guard a special shipment. We'll explain more."

For the next forty-five mites, Grania and Theos explained what had happened in as much detail as possible without revealing too much about the cargo that had caused the problem. She told him they had Heidi Geers, the young woman who'd begged passage and turned out to be a spy, secured in a cabin. They wanted her charged with attempting to destroy a part of their cargo and the Mo Chroidhe.

"What is this cargo that caused all the problems?" Bronwell asked. He'd done almost all of the talking while Finnelle made notes and cast wary looks around the ship.

"The manifest says farm equipment," Grania answered, her face schooled to not reveal anything. "I don't have any other information about it. It was shipped by the provisional government on Enterprise. My only connection is to deliver it."

"That's rather general," Bronwell said. "Did they not give you any indication of what kind of farm equipment?"

"They did not."

"And you, Mr. Camber, are assigned to protect this equipment? Is that not unusual?"

"Actually, I'm more of an escort," Theos answered. "I am ensuring it is delivered and fending off any attempts to subvert it."

"I suppose you have no idea what is inside either?"

"That is correct." Theos shrugged as if to say, don't need to know.

"What if I ask you to open it?" Bronwell asked, lifting his eyes wider.

"We can't," Grania cut in. "The whole box is secure-coded. We don't have the combination. I was also warned that tampering with it could cause serious damage to the ship."

"What about scans?" Bronwell asked, his shoulders hunching forward as if that might force a favorable answer.

Grania folded her hands on the table. "You're welcome to give it a try."

A hiss of relief went through the gap in Bronwell's teeth as he shoved the chair back and climbed to his feet. Finnelle made one more note in his mobi and followed. Motioning to Theos, Grania rose and led the way with the others trailing behind like eager suitors.

Back in the hold, Finnelle manned the scanner as Bronwell peered over his shoulder. *These men are supposed to be helping us?* Grania shook her head. They looked like a second-rate comedy team at the pub. Theos nudged her and whispered, "Why didn't you tell them the scanners don't work?"

She tilted her head back to bring her mouth closer to his ear. "It's better if they see for themselves."

After a few mites with the duo shifting their attention and the scanner over half the crate's surface, Bronwell pivoted toward her. "It seems there's a metal box that the scanner can't penetrate covering whatever's inside."

"Is that right?" Grania said innocently.

He nodded as Finnelle returned the scanner to the storage area. "We sure would like to know what's created this situation, but it appears you're not in the wrong for defending your cargo. We'll take your spy with us. Follow us to the station and dock as normal."

"Follow me." Grania turned back to the stairs, motioning for them to come along. She led them to the locked cabin and opened it for them.

Bronwell's eyebrows rose to his hairline as he saw Heidi Geers trussed up and lying on the floor on her side. She rocked back and forth, trying to break loose.

Apparently, the explosion-caused spin had flung her off the cot. Grania didn't have it in her to care. "She bites, kicks, and punches, and she has a foul mouth. You be taking care in transporting her."

Finnelle cast a wary look at her as he followed his partner in to take charge of the girl.

This time, she followed them back down, ensuring the Geers girl was off the ship and didn't escape their clutches. "You can get her things from her cabin after we dock," she told the men as they entered the airlock.

Once they'd gone through, she swung around to face Theos. "Check everything down here to make sure we don't have any stray crates. "By the by, do ya' happen to know which side is receivin' that she-bee?"

A weak smile crossed his face as he turned toward the forward section. "The rebels."

"But those ships out there are from that faction, aren't they?"

"I never said all of them were happy about it." He strolled away to check out the damage while Grania dropped a hand to her hip and shook her head. She didn't understand that at all.

Chapter Thirty

"Any luck?" Grania asked Sindhu via her comlink, hoping the girl had made contact with the recipient of their troublesome cargo.

"Nothing yet, Captain." The com officer sounded as discouraged as Grania felt.

Time was ticking. They'd lost several hours at Outer Rim Station while they made initial repairs to the breach in the ship's exterior hull. This was their fifth attempt since they'd docked at Terminus Station, the last stop for Desolation. From here, the she-bee needed to go down on one of the cargo shuttles. Grania estimated it would take all the available space on the shuttle if they laid the crate flat. She hoped the thing was dormant, or it would end up shaken and probably mad as a… Well, mad as a hornet.

But for the last ninety mites or so, she hadn't connected with Jacob Finestock, the man expecting the crate. She turned to Theos, who'd exited to the station with her while repair workers started replacing the patch job on the Mo Chroidhe. "We're still not getting a response. We've only got another three hours to complete delivery. He's got to sign off on it." Her voice sounded strained as anxiety set in. She couldn't lose the fee for delivering this. She just couldn't.

While they waited, Rory was doing the rounds on the station and learning what he could. Compared to most other stations, this was a little one. They had four docking bays, a crew of six station workers, and an assistant station manager, who reported to Outer Rim. Not many visitors came this far.

Ahead of them, Andromeda Galaxy filled the exterior port window with bright haloed stars on the other side of the hazy mass of the Milky Way's mantle. From the starboard side, the vivid colors of Desolation showed through another panel. Unlike most human-habitable planets, this one looked like its name. Mostly red and yellow land mass with sparse dots of green, blue, black, and streaks of purple.

"Looks hostile," Theos murmured.

"Well, I'm eager to get away from here, but the agreement is I take the crate to the station. I'm going to book a shuttle to take the crate down and hope that Finestock responds soon."

"Right. I'm going down with you, just in case."

As she walked toward the shuttle office, she turned to look at him. "In case of what?"

"Just in case," he repeated as he kept his eyes forward. "You never know what can happen on an outlaw planet."

"What?"

"Well, it's not entirely civilized, you know." He paused to glance at her as they came to the entry. "That's why there's a battle going down there."

Oh, great. We're going into a war zone. Grania sighed, pushed her shoulders back, and marched into the shuttle office.

It took about thirty mites to make the arrangements, and the Captain saw another little chunk of the ship's income going to pay for it. Grania hoped they could contact Finestock in time to get the sign-off before the deadline.

She and Theos watched at the docking bay as the shuttle coasted up next to the Mo Chroidhe, preparing to transfer the she-bee's crate to its cargo compartment. As she expected, the loading crew turned it flat on the floor, and it barely fit. Once loaded, the shuttle backed off before pulling into a shuttle bay on the opposite side of the dock.

As they strolled across to the boarding ramp, Grania made another attempt from her com to reach the recipient, sending a text message advising him they were bringing the crate down. If he wasn't there to connect with them, she didn't have much of a chance to meet the deadline. Just as they started to board, she got an answer, but not exactly what she expected.

"Feck," she muttered as she reread the words on her mobi.

"What?" Theos asked, head swiveling to look at her.

"Finestock wants us to load it on one of the big cargo surface shuttles and bring it to him at a town called Last Outpost North. Where the blazes is that? It sounds remote."

Theos caught her elbow and nudged her onto the shuttle entry. "We'll check the location once we're on board. I'm not familiar with it, but it's sure to be toward the Donquee Desert."

She shot an eyes-wide glance at him. "We're going to a desert?" She'd never been to one and hadn't expected to ever have to do it.

Theos stood aside, offering her the window seat, and she slipped in, settling into it. Through the porthole, she could see the station, and her ship docked across the way. For a moment, she felt an odd sense of loss, as if she might not be coming back. Her deal with the PPG hadn't included going out into a war zone. It was supposed to be a simple delivery.

As Theos settled beside her, he pulled out his mobi and called up an image of Desolation. The stark colors filled the screen, with the predominance of yellow and red leaping out. "All of that is desert," Theos said, pointing to it. Better than seventy-five percent of the planet. Most yellow is laced with prosperitus, so it's very valuable. But it needs to be mined, hence the reason for colonization on this planet."

"What's the red?" Grania stared at the massive streaks of yellow, liking it to the gold rush on Earth several centuries earlier. Fortune hunters rushing to mine the planet's wealth and living in miserable conditions while they worked.

"Red dirt mostly, but it holds decent deposits of ruby crystals and roux-agate, almost as strong and rare as diamonds."

Now, she understood why humans had settled on this planet. It was like any other rush to where a potential fortune might be. Get there, make your credits, then move to a place much nicer. As always, greed drove expansion in the Universe.

As the shuttle turned into a curve down to the landing site, a small port at the bustling city of Wingdang, Grania had a better view of the stark but striking landscape of Desolation. It went from deep gullies to flat deserts to high rocky ridges like someone had carved the dirt from the canyons, spread it across acres, then piled it up high, baked it, and broken off pieces. The predominant reds and yellows varied in shades but looked vibrant in the atmosphere. She'd never seen anything quite like it.

Their pilot advised them to buckle in for the landing, then brought the shuttle toward the long redtop runway that cut across a flat plain in front of a square building made from yellow stone or possibly mud in a simple, ancient style.

Twenty mites later, Grania and Theos stood outside the terminal under a sail-like sunshade. The she-bee's crate sat upright on a lev-dolly while they waited for a response from Finestock. Grania had sent a text as soon as they'd landed, wanting to confirm the address where they were to take the cargo. So far, she hadn't gotten an answer, and she hesitated. Even though Theos had arranged for a van large enough to move the box, she didn't want to start off for Last Outpost North without confirmation from the man.

"Why do you suppose he isn't responding?" she asked Theos as he paced past her for the third time.

Pausing, he shrugged. "I don't have any idea. Maybe he's in the middle of a fight or has poor reception where he is."

"I don't like it." She glanced at her mobi again, saw nothing, and sat on the stone bench alongside a bed of weird-looking plants in the cacti family. "What if we get there and we can't find him?"

Theos squinted at her. "How much time do you have left to deliver?"

"Three hours and fifteen mites." Her mouth turned down, worry and disappointment showing in her expression. "If I don't complete this, I don't get the transport fee or bonus. Then, what do I do?"

"No idea of that either, but I do know that if we have any chance of making that deadline, we need to get going now. It's at least two and a half hours to our destination."

He was right. She couldn't dawdle any longer. "Okay, boy-o. Let's get that loaded and get underway. Are you driving?"

"You don't want to?" His eyes shot to hers as he turned to the lev-dolly.

"I don't know how to drive one of these things. The vehicles for rent on most planets are cars, not this big honking tank of a truck. And they're all pretty much self-driving. This looks like it actually has a gear shift and pedals." She frowned as she looked inside the cab of the transport. "Do you know how to do it?"

She watched as Theos had one of the transport station workers help him load the crate, on its back once again, into the back of the transport. Once the cargo was secured, he shut the doors, then came around to the driver's side to look at the controls.

"Yeah, I can manage this," he answered. "Climb in, and let's get going. It has a nav unit, so program in the destination and coordinates if he gave you any."

While Grania did that, relieved it was similar to the unit on the ship, Theos got the vehicle running and pointed it toward the red-surfaced highway that passed by the terminal. "Which way is north?" he asked.

She looked at the nav unit, noted the marking, then said, "Turn right at the corner. We'll follow this road for about thirty kilometers, then turn to the left and pick up another road heading to our town. It doesn't look like there's much else along the route. Do we have a full tank of fuel?"

"Yep," he answered after a quick glance at the dials before him. "Keep trying to reach Finestock."

Grania sent another message and tried for voice contact. The lack of communication bothered her more than she would admit. Why didn't he respond?

Leaning her head back, she gazed at the houses and buildings they passed. Most were single-story and made of yellow bricks in a basic box shape, much like early villages she'd seen on Earth. Some buildings were two stories with businesses on the lower level and possibly housing above. She'd heard this kind of place referred to as a frontier town. A place where the building was simple, made from the materials at hand, and sufficient for humans to survive.

Beyond the town, a sunflower-yellow desert extended for hundreds of kilometers, or so it seemed. In the distance, a range of red and yellow mountains rose from the flat land like they'd been dropped there. As she contemplated the planet's odd geology, she felt the transport beginning to slow. She turned her gaze to the road ahead to see why Theos was slowing.

Sitting square in the middle of the road, a giant horned lizard-like beast sat eating something that looked like an overgrown beetle. The scaled creature was scarlet, with deep blue speckles and a trio of the same color horns protruding from its head. "Holy fairies, that's bigger and meaner-looking than any lizard I've ever seen," she muttered.

Theos glanced at her, his lips curving in amusement. "Yeah, it's a big one, and I hope we can go around it. Else, we might have to wait until it's done dining and hope it doesn't challenge us."

"Is it likely to attack us?" Alarm raised her voice a little.

"I don't know. I haven't been here before. But we have weapons on this transport."

"We do?" She hadn't thought that they might need a means of defense, but what the hell? If war was raging on the place, it made sense.

Theos edged the transport up to a few meters from the dining lizard and eased it to the far left of the reptile. It paused, turning its head to face them. Grania caught her breath at the fierce look in the creature's deep red eyes. Its nostrils, two pairs of holes alongside a protrusion that could be called a nose, flared at their approach.

"Is it challenging us?" she asked.

"Your guess is as good as mine," Theos answered.

Close up, the lizard looked scarier than it did from a distance. While their transport was bigger than it, the creature stood taller than a car and looked to have huge, bulging muscles in its legs. They would pass it with her side of the van exposed to the monster, so she would take the brunt if it attacked.

"Is the metal on this thing sturdy enough to withstand an attack?" Grania turned her head to see Theos staring at it, his eyes narrowed under a wrinkled brow. Worried?

"I believe it is. Most anything used on the roads here would have to be able to stand up to the local wildlife. But if it charges and hits us right, it might be able to tip the van over."

"I didn't need to hear that." She breathed the words out as she exhaled. "Can you just kill it?"

"I'd rather not unless we have no choice. If it lets us pass, then I have no quarrel with it."

"And if it charges us, do you have time to stop it?"

With the van at a virtual stop, Theos reached behind his seat and pulled out a rifle with a huge muzzle. "You have the open side to it, so point this at it. If it begins to move, shoot it."

"Me? You want me to roll down my window and shoot that thing?"

He nodded. "I'm driving, Grania. You're on target duty."

"Well, if this isn't a fine pot of pickled herring," she grumbled as she took the weapon, checked the firing mechanism, and turned the switch on.

"That's an interesting expression," Theos said with a smirk.

"Old Irish. This job better pay off. We're riskin' our lives here." She rolled the window part way down and propped the barrel on top of it. "Let's go, and don't you take it at a crawl like it's an invitation."

Taking her words to heart, Theos started forward again, gathering speed as they approached the lizard. The garnet-colored eyes watched them come, a golden slit through the middle of them narrowing as they got closer. A loud hiss emitted from it as its mouth dropped open and muscles in its body tensed.

It's goin' to attack. Holy Mother of God, it's going to kill us. Panic hit Grania's throat, but her hands remained steady. It's no different from an attacking ship, she tried to convince herself.

As they drew almost even with it, she saw the back legs tense as it prepared to spring at them. In what seemed like slow motion, the lizard's body began to rise up, starting forward, and her fingers on the targeting and firing buttons depressed one after the other. The weapon bucked back against her shoulder, and a white energy blast hit the creature full-on. It cried out a shriek like she'd never heard before, then dropped flat out to the pavement, landing on top of what remained of the worm and just missing the edge of the transport.

"Oh, feckin' crap," she cried out, shrinking back from the window as the ground beneath them shook for a moment or two, bouncing the van as they hurtled past.

A few meters away in seconds, Theos slowed a bit. "Good shooting, Grania. That'll give that critter a headache."

Her head whipped toward him. "What d'ye mean?"

"That's a stun blaster." He chuckled as he said it. "You just stunned it."

A moment of anger morphed into relief as she absorbed the truth. Only stunned. She hadn't even noticed. She hoped they didn't encounter it on the way back or that it wouldn't remember.

"Are there more beasties like that ahead?" she asked, resting the weapon in her lap.

"Dunno. Could be bigger ones, even."

"That's not reassuring," she mumbled.

Chapter Thirty-One

After clearing the pass, Grania and Theos ventured into a starker landscape. She gazed over the strange-looking desert with twisted vegetation striking out from sparsely rooted centers like spiked streamers tossed by the wind. Across the dunes, tall rock formations resembling unevenly-stacked stone plates rose like silent sentinels. All they needed was a round stone on top to complete the impression.

"What are those pillars? Are they manmade?" Grania asked, admiring the various shades of blue and purple in the objects. Perhaps they'd been painted.

"They're hoodoos," Theos answered. "They're the natural landscape here. Or so I've been told."

"Who told you?" Grania shifted her eyes to him for a few moments before gazing out at the landscape again. The sand, if that's what it was, resembled rusted iron, an orangish tone looking unnatural. She'd never heard of anything called a hoodoo, which sounded like something he'd made up.

"One of my colleagues mentioned it when we were glancing through images of the surface before I accepted the assignment. From what he said, I gathered the word came from Earth, where similar rock formations are found. Most of the fighting is out in the middle of the plain to your right."

She turned to look, squinting into the distance to see it. "I'd call this a desert rather than a plain." She couldn't detect any movement in the stillness, not even a breeze to shift those spindly plants that seemed to grow everywhere. If that's where the fight was, they weren't likely to destroy any property.

Just beyond a large outcropping of hoodoos, a giant reddish-black cliff loomed like a fierce dragon over the land. "That's where we're headed," Theos said, pointing to it.

"The town is there? It looks ominous." She stared at it, seeing the shape and likening it to a mythical beast. A snout seemed to jut out, and a rise behind the lump at the end could be compared to a wing.

"Where's your sense of adventure?" Theos laughed. "We'll be there in about fifteen mites."

"Overstimulated. I could use a break." Grania frowned and peered at the open space ahead, doubting a town could possibly be so close. She couldn't spot anything except those towering rock formations and the bluff in the background. She was beginning to have doubts about Theos and his real purpose for joining this enterprise. If he represented the PPG agency, why was he helping her deliver the she-bee to the opposition?

"What's in this for your people?" she asked.

"What d'ya mean?" Theos glanced at her briefly before returning his eyes to the long straight road ahead.

"Well, if we deliver the package to Finestock, he'll take it to the rebels, who will presumably use it against the local government. So, why would your people want them to have it?"

A thin smile pulled at his lips, and he shrugged. "I'm not exactly sure, to be honest. Maybe they're hoping they'll blow themselves and the creature up when they try to unpack it."

"Hardly a safe bet that would happen. Is there some other twist in the delivery?"

"Honestly, I don't know. My instructions said I was to accompany the ship and ensure the package was delivered. I don't know if the PPG has any idea what's in the crate."

"And you didn't ask any questions about it?" Grania found it hard to believe he wouldn't have wanted details.

"They wouldn't have answered."

"So, you're a poorly informed agent." Her face twisted into a scowl. Did he think she believed that?

"Secret jobs don't always mean you're in on the secret," he answered. "I don't know how you found out what's in the box, but I assure you I had no idea when I took the job. Ah, town's coming up on the right."

She turned her head to look, her forehead wrinkling as she squinted down the road. Where? She only saw one of the stacks, then their vehicle moved far enough ahead for her to glimpse a small sprawl of buildings barely visible in the shadow of the bluff. "That's it? That little town?"

"According to the navigation software."

Within another five mites, they'd come to a turnoff from the highway to the stone and mud buildings comprising Last Outpost North. She pursed her lips. She'd seen bigger outpost stations on an ice planet than this, but it should make finding

Finestock easy.

Like the dirt and the stones around them, the same-colored town buildings looked stacked together and glued with mortar made from the sand. Doors and shutters appeared to be constructed from a woody-looking material. Grania speculated they might be cacti planks. Theos pulled the transport up to a small, deserted-looking building with a faded hand-lettered sign saying depot like a train would come in here. But this was where Finestock had said he'd meet them. Pulling out her com unit, she sent a message and waited, reluctant to leave the van's cab.

Theos climbed out, shut the door, then sauntered over to the building's entrance, a wide-open archway suggesting nothing of value was inside. Grania's nerves twitched, a prickly feeling at the back of her neck making her edgy. Something didn't feel right here. Ten minutes passed while Theos explored inside, and she had no answer from her contact. With her time to complete the contract nearly up, a desperate feeling began to creep up from her stomach. If she didn't get paid for this job, the debt accumulated for the trip would wipe out all they had and then some.

"Come on," she muttered under her breath, and she sent another message to Finestock. Maybe the text message wasn't getting through. She pressed the face contact button, hoping he would respond to it. Another few mites passed with no result.

Theos came back out and sidled up to her window. "No one inside. Looks pretty deserted, doesn't it?" He gazed around the town as he spoke. No one had come out of any of the structures to enquire about their presence, and she'd seen no sign of life so far.

"It's like a ghost town."

"No response, huh?"

"None. Not on video or text. Finestock was expecting us." She looked back toward the road they'd traveled. Possibly he was coming from a different direction.

Theos stepped back. "I'm going to check up the road here. Maybe someone is in one of the other buildings." He turned to walk up the dirt road toward another structure with a sign Grania thought read _o_sta_le, but letters were missing or too faded to fill in the blanks.

Annoyed with the lack of response, she flung the van's door open and climbed down. Now what? If Finestock didn't claim the she-bee, she was stuck with a feckin' giant creature and no money. Could she contact the AUP and see what they wanted her to do? Maybe they had an alternate recipient.

She crossed the road to pound on the door of what looked like a house or shop, hoping to find someone inside.

The door creaked open partway, and a short, scrawny, weathered face peered out. "What d'ya want?" The voice sounded female and scratchy, although Grania couldn't tell by her features; she was so wrinkled and leathery.

"My partner and I are looking for Mr. Finestock. Would you know where we can find him?"

The woman, if she was one, stared at her for several seconds. "What's in it for me?"

Grania pulled a silver twenty-credit piece from her pocket

and held it before the person's nose.

Eyes lighting up, the woman reached for it, but Grania kept it just out of her range. "After you tell me."

The hand dropped, and the face resembled a dried prune scowling at her. "Ain't much to tell. He went off to battle with the rest of the town."

"Where?"

The eyes narrowed, and she peered at Grania like she was some weird insect. "At Hornfeld Flats. Where else?"

Grania's face reflected her lack of recognition, and the person waved her hands around, her face twisting into more wrinkles. She stepped forward enough to lean out and point an arm imperiously toward the long mesa beyond the dragon cliff where those open fields were. The war zone.

"Could you tell me where he lives? Maybe he left a note for me." She could only hope he'd left a clue behind. Or maybe this person was wrong.

She pointed to the house two doors down.

Grania handed her the coin, thanked her, then walked the short distance to Finestock's house, pausing to assess its run-down condition. Peeling paint, broken window frames, and door panels shedding splinters like flowers dropped petals. Clearly, the man didn't bother with little details like his home. She didn't see an envelope or a note on the door, but she walked up and knocked anyway. Maybe someone was still here.

After waiting a few minutes, she tried the knob. No luck. He'd locked it up well. While she could break in, she suspected the old biddy might be watching. Still, it was not like a sheriff, or any other authority seemed to be in town.

She turned away and saw Theos coming back up the street toward her. He gestured with his arms, the wide-open swing suggesting he hadn't found anyone either. Sighing, she crossed the street and strode toward him.

"Finestock's gone to the battle," she announced when she was within hearing distance.

"Looks like everyone has." He jogged the last few steps. "Have you gone inside?"

"It's locked, and the house two over is occupied and might be watching."

He glanced toward it, then strode to the front edge of the house and turned to go to the back. After a mite, Grania followed, finding him fiddling with a window toward the back. In a few more moments, he'd popped it open, raised it up, and climbed inside.

Reluctantly, she followed, certain the old woman would catch them. But then what? For one thing, she needed clues as to who else might accept the delivery and how to open the case without setting off the bomb. If Finestock had the codes, he might have left them behind.

Theos had already started checking the drawers in the desk where an older model computer sat. He flipped it on and waited for it to boot up. "Damn, this requires an optical id. Do you have a video message saved with Finestock's face on it?"

She pulled up the last message on her comm, but the face wasn't easily visible under the brimmed hat Finestock wore. "I don't think it's enough for the machine to detect his eyeball."

"That's out then. Look around for any notes or a journal that might have a clue about the shipment." He shut the computer down and continued his search.

The place was small, just the main room, a kitchen, one bedroom, and a bath. Finestock had only a few furniture pieces—the desk, a sofa, one chair, and the bed. In less than ten minutes, they'd covered everything and found nothing worthwhile.

Theos wiped the perspiration off his face as the day's heat had warmed the house to an uncomfortable level. "Let's find a cooler place to wait."

"Wait for who? Do you think he's coming back?"

He shrugged and led the way out the window. They closed it again, and walked at a diagonal away from it so they returned to the road almost at the next house. Looking around, he pointed to a wooden bench under a shade-offering roof overhang.

She followed him over and sat down, glad to be out of the sun.

"Did you try his mobi again?" Theos spread his arms across the bench's back, stuck his long legs out, and crossed his ankles, looking like he was ready to nap.

"No."

"Then we wait here for a bit. Look, I made a call when I couldn't find anything. Word is, Finestock is dead. Killed in the fighting."

"What? You called someone. Why?"

"Because you have a package to deliver, and we need to get out of this heat."

She swung around to face him, her eyes blazing with anger. "I get paid when I deliver it to Finestock. Not anyone else."

"Well, you can't deliver it to him, can you? So, I found us an alternate buyer."

Her mouth dropped open. *Without talking to me? What the feckin' hell should I do now?* Her voice dropped, and she growled, "Who?"

"Some folks from the pro-government group are on their way. They'll take it to their officers to see if they can use it."

"But it was going to the rebels. That's what my clients intended." Could she contact the AUP and appraise them of the change? She pulled out her mobi, intending to call Rory.

Theos reached over and yanked it out of her hand. "No calls out until this is settled."

She drew a deep breath, muscles tensing when she grabbed for her device. "Give me the communicator."

He held it an arm's length away from her, and she pounded his side with her fist.

His other hand grabbed hers and held it like a vise. "Just cooperate, Grania, and you'll get back to your ship safely. This is the best option we have now."

Her grasping hand dropped to his chest with a thud, and she jerked it away, yanking her other hand free when he loosened his hold. "Was this your plan all along?"

His eyes held hers, and his mouth turned down a bit. "No.

This is a fallback option."

"Will I get my delivery fee?" She needed the credits. This jaunt had cost too much, and the return wouldn't be any cheaper.

"Maybe. If the contents of the crate are worth it." He nodded toward the truck still parked up the street.

She groaned and leaned back against the bench. What a mess.

Time crawled by while Grania fidgeted, paced, and, now and then, glared at Theos. Finally, she planted herself in front of him, arms akimbo. "Let me call my ship. I need to talk to my brothers. They'll be worried."

He shook his head. "Not yet."

"Why not?"

"Because I can't risk it."

Her mouth dropped. "What are you risking?"

He dropped his arms and leaned with his elbows on his knees, hands clasped in front. "This is a delicate operation, and I don't want you to say anything to anyone until we're secure. I don't want any more signals sent that could be intercepted."

Frowning, she dropped onto the bench again. "You think someone is spying on us? Not on my ship. There are only my brothers, Kachiri, and…" She caught her breath. "…the new engineer. Do you think either of them could be involved?"

Theos shrugged. "It's possible."

She looked away, her mind sorting through the trip's events—the stowaway, the new engineer, the attempt to steal the cargo. Even the addition of Theos to the crew engineered by the PPG. Why should she even trust him?

She turned her eyes to Theos, seeing his handsome face with an altered view. Had he told her the truth, or was this all a setup? She glimpsed something in the distance, approaching rapidly and kicking up dust as it came. It appeared their ride was arriving.

Chapter Thirty-Two

Theos jumped to his feet when an oversized, treaded, covered truck pulled up, halting a few yards from the Grania's rented van. A man dressed in camouflage climbed out, stepped onto the road, and marched toward them. Theos motioned to her to follow him, so she fell into line. She didn't have much choice.

The approaching man looked like a bodybuilder with imposing shoulders and a chest with enough definition to show through his sand-colored shirt. His lower half looked equally muscular, and everything about him screamed military. When they'd almost come face to face, Grania saw the insignia on his pocket designating his rank, which she thought was captain. The patch on his right sleeve displayed a logo she didn't recognize, but she presumed identified the Desolation armed forces.

Theos came to attention and raised his right hand in a fisted salute which the officer returned. "Mister Camber. I'm Captain Villalba. I presume the package is in the van?"

Before Theos could speak, Grania stepped forward. "The 'package' is my cargo. I was hired to bring it here, and until I sign a release, it's still mine."

Villalba shifted his steely gaze to her. His dark, almost black eyes challenged her. "And who are you?"

She drew her shoulders up. "I am Grania O'Ceagan, captain of the space freighter Mo Chroidhe."

He blinked. "Well, isn't that a mouthful? So, you were hired to deliver this package here?"

"I was. Payment is due on delivery. Twenty-five thousand credits. You hand that over to me, and it's yours."

He laughed, a roar of amusement. "Is that all? Well, I don't have it with me, and we might have enough to cover the delivery charge at the base. But you'd better come with us to find out."

This isn't going to end well. Grania's lips constricted into a hard line as she blinked and nodded. Again, no choice. She glimpsed Theos' tight-looking face, anger boiling in his eyes. No matter. This was *her* cargo and the only bargaining chip.

She followed the Villalba and Theos back to the newly arrived monster truck where two other men, dressed like the Captain, without the high-rank insignia, waited to transfer the cargo. "It'll be easier for you to back the van up to the rear of the dragon for the transfer," one of the men informed Theos.

"Why don't we just follow you? No need to move the cargo." Grania didn't want them taking it out of her control.

Villalba looked down his nose at her. "Better to take it in the transport capable of handling the road ahead. It's not nicely graded like this one." He motioned to Theos to move the van.

The agent leaned closer to her and muttered, "Don't argue, Grania. He's right, and we can sort this out at the base." Then he ran back to the van to follow Villalba's order.

Within minutes, Theos had the van backed up to the transport's rear, unlocked the back, and climbed into their van, ready to move the heavy crate. Grania stood back, leaning against the nearest building's wall in the slim wedge of shade left. The sun's position would soon bathe the entire town in unrelenting heat.

With a bit of help from the lift equipment the military team had brought, they moved the crate easily. They settled it into the truck's spacious interior, using magnetic clamps to hold it in place.

Theos closed the van's doors and turned to the Villalba. "We'll follow you, sir."

"No. We'll all go in the truck. Leave the van here. I'll have someone bring it to the base."

"It's a rental." Grania stepped in front of Villalba. "We'll drive our van there."

His shoulders rose and his face turned to stone. "I said we will go together. No argument. You will get in the truck's rear seat, or I will have you thrown into the back with the box. No seating there."

She gritted her teeth, wanting, with all her heart, to defy this man's authority, but she stomped to the cab's third door and climbed inside, sliding across the seat in case Theos, the traitor, chose to join her. But he followed the officer to the second door seating, leaving her alone to stew over the situation.

The transport backtracked to the road they'd driven in, then they turned to the right to continue past the ridge. At first, Grania attempted to listen to the sparse conversation Theos started with the Villalba; however, they spoke too low for her to hear anything clearly. After thirty mites, she gave up, leaned back, and closed her eyes, letting the steady sway of the vehicle on the road dull her anger.

Her body ached with the day's activity and the difference in the planet's gravity compared to the ship. *How long is the day here, anyway? We landed early this morning, waited for my contact, then drove at least three hours away from the spaceport to get to Hornfeld Flats. We searched it for well over ninety mites and waited for the truck, which took more time. And it didn't look like the sun had even made its apex yet. Add in the stress of the failed delivery and now this unwanted military connection. No wonder I'm feeling so tired.*

Her brothers must be worried. She'd been out of touch too long. She didn't understand why Theos wouldn't let her contact Rory to assure him she was okay. He might be courting more trouble by not allowing her to check in with them. Then again, if Liam were still on the crew, he'd probably be on his way down to the planet already. She missed him. *And Vilnius would have come down with me.*

The thought surprised her. The station master hadn't been on her mind often since they'd left Zabrowski Station. She'd ended it. He hadn't argued, so it was a mutual breakup. Still, she wished he'd at least tried to convince her they could make it work. So, she'd distracted herself with Theos and likely trusted him more than she should have. Where was her good judgment when she needed it?

She opened an eye when the truck slowed and took in the bleak, forbidding appearance of the desert on this side of the ridge. The colors ranged from dark bronze to almost black, and the soil looked like overbaked cookies with cracks in them. She could see why the planet was called Desolation.

Another right turn took the truck along the ridge's backside, where the rough peaks and deep valleys looked like hard climbing for anyone who might use them for a shortcut to the town on the other side. They bounced along for another ten or so kilometers before they came to a fenced-in military base.

Barracks, trucks, tanks, ion cannons, and other warcraft equipment filled the area. An imposing block building sat close to the rising cliff face. The transport went past the main doors and around to the far end, turning onto a drive leading into the building through hanger doors. When the vehicle approached, the panels opened to allow them entry.

Why did Grania feel like she'd entered the jaws of a *kon-ha* space dragon to be chewed up and her bones spit out like debris? She fidgeted nervously, grateful to be alone on the seat so no one saw her uneasiness. *Buck up, girl. You're a space-faring O'Ceagan, not a weak-willed Nellie.* She heard her grandfather's voice saying it as he had many times when she was growing up. *Damn right! I'm a ship's captain.*

She squared her shoulders, ready to face whatever came. When the truck stopped, Theos opened his door, so she pushed hers open and stepped out into the high-domed building. It looked big enough for a shuttle to park in it, although it was mostly empty now. Villalba took the point, leading them to a regular entry into a command center. Grania glanced back to see the soldiers getting the crate out of the truck and sliding it onto a mag-lift. A bigger warehouse-type door opened farther down the face, which meant they were moving her cargo into it.

Inside, a dozen uniformed men and women worked at computer terminals, either monitoring something or sending messages and updating positions. A giant screen against the side wall showed the battleground.

They hurried through to another set of doors where the Captain used his code to admit them. She followed him through and stopped to take in the emptiness of the facility. Most of it was open space with no windows but a pair of double doors at the back. Where they'd entered, a big room with transparisteel windows across the side faced the room. A row of three offices lined the eastern wall, and an alcove with hygiene facilities led off from the west.

Villalba used a coded card to open the glass room and led them into it. At the back, four vending units provided hot drinks, cold drinks, snacks, and sandwiches. Three tables with six chairs each sat in the middle. A break room, Grania figured. On one side, a cozy-looking sofa offered a comfortable place to stretch out, while the other side had a pair of padded lounge chairs, the kind that could flatten out into a bed if needed.

"Help yourself to food and drink." Villalba pointed to the machines. "We're bringing the package into this secure area.

You will stay in this room, which is impenetrable, while we open the crate."

"You might not want to be doing that." Grania watched Theos amble over to the drink machine, then said, "We were instructed not to open it until it was delivered and the receiving person, Mr. Finestock, entered the code."

"The crate is code-locked?" Villalba frowned.

She nodded.

"Okay. We'll get one of our experts here to get into it." He pulled out his com unit and spoke into it, his voice too low to hear.

Suddenly hungry, Grania strolled to the food machine and ordered a henny-patty sandwich, then turned back to the Villalba while she waited. "They also said the case inside is wired with explosives. If you enter a different code into it, you'll be blowing the whole room and the cargo up. We didn't touch it while we brought it here." Well, that was a lie, but no one would know.

"I see. Did the shipper give you the code?"

She shook her head. "Nope."

"Oo-kay." He turned his head to watch the crate roll into the room. "Make yourselves comfortable. I need to check into a few things."

He pivoted and left, the door locking behind him, turning a red light on the inside handle.

"He's locked us in," Grania said.

Theos picked up a bag of snack chips and shrugged. "Security measure. Nothing to worry about."

"Is this glass cage secure against a big explosion?" She picked up her sandwich, then got a bag of chips and a soda. She sat at the middle table.

"You really think the She-bee is wired to explode without the code?" He sat next to her.

"I do. If she's a weapon, they don't want the wrong hands on her." She gazed out at the now upright box sitting in the middle of the back third of the space. The soldiers took their cart and left. What exactly had she brought across the galaxy? She hadn't wanted to know. Just wanted to get her money and leave, but it didn't look like a viable option now. *They'll blow the bleedin' thing up, and I'll be getting no payment. Fickled fairies, this is a feckin' disaster.*

She turned on Theos, her anger flaring. "And you brought these people into this. Was this your objective all along?"

"No. I'm trying to salvage the situation. The AUP won't pay you; this is your best hope to get your money."

"Not if they blow the she-bee up!" She bit into her sandwich like she was trying to rip him apart with her teeth.

He glared at her. "It doesn't help if you antagonize them. Try to be cooperative." He turned his back and stomped to a lounge chair.

A short time later, Villalba returned with a higher-ranking officer and three specialists. Or so she guessed when they went straight to the box to begin working on it. The officers entered the glass viewing area to speak to Theos and Grania. Well, mostly her. The new one said he was Colonel Mixton, a square-jawed, stern-looking man with about ten kilos of extra weight on his stocky frame.

He looked her up and down. "So, you brought this crate across the galaxy to the Rebels. What's your name, girl?"

She bristled. "I'm *Captain* O'Ceagan. My ship was contracted to deliver the crate to the person the sender requested. I didn't know about the rebellion or anything happening on Desolation when I started. Nonetheless, my contract dictated who would receive it in order for me to get paid. But it seems your forces killed the recipient."

While Theos stood a few feet behind her, ramrod straight, Grania wouldn't give any authority to this man. She stood comfortably with her right hip cocked. She stared back into his icy eyes without flinching. He had no power over her. At least, she told herself as much.

Mixton held her eyes for several seconds before he glanced down. "Who hired you?"

"I am not at liberty to tell you. My clients expect discretion. But you might ask Theos. I believe he has more information than I do." She cast a quick glance at him and just caught the twitch in his jaw while he scowled.

"Did you know these people before they hired you?"

"No."

Mixton rubbed a hand across his chin. "Why did you take the job?"

She shifted her stance, adjusting to a more balanced position, and crossed her arms. "I didn't have any choice. They had the power to interrupt my shipping business. Although they did offer very good payment for a successful delivery,"

Mixton continued to ask questions. How she'd encountered Theos, where she'd gone first, and what route she'd traveled to get to Desolation.

Gazing past him, she watched while the crew he'd brought managed to remove the outer covering to reveal the ornate-looking linsar box covering the she-bee. Dark-colored with an oval shape, the container was about the size of a portable contamination unit. A metal cap covered the entire top, and six venting tubes protruded. Down the front ran a seam where it would open like a closet once the code was entered. Mid-way down, a digital box was attached to the right of it with a number pad below.

Mixton's eyes followed hers, and he turned to face the almost empty space behind him. He studied the object for a mite before he spoke again. "Quite an interesting unit you've brought here. Do you know what it is or what it does?"

Grania shook her head. "No. I have no idea."

"I suppose the digital box is a combination lock. Do you know the code?"

"No, I wasn't given any information about it."

"Who has the code?"

She shrugged. "I suppose Mr. Finestock, the recipient, had it." She added in the warning she'd given to Villalba already about it being connected to an explosive.

"We'll talk more later." He turned on his heel and left the room, Villalba trailing behind him. The door locked behind him, leaving Grania and Theos to watch through the window.

She spun around and stalked toward Theos. "What the

hell is this? Why aren't they questioning you?"

He held his hands up, palms out to her. "Wait a minute. I work for the government, remember? These are allies, and they know who I am. Just keep calm and answer their questions. Everything will be fine."

"Not if they attempt to open the containment unit and blow us all up!" Her eyes blazed with anger and fear. How far would Mixton go?

She yanked out a chair and sat facing the warehouse where the Colonel inspected her cargo. Walking all around it and running a hand across it. Grania cringed when he knelt by the lock, peering closely at it. He flicked a finger at one of the experts he'd brought in. The man looked it over, noting the short antenna on the edge, and shook his head. Grania interpreted the action to mean he didn't know how to defuse it.

Mixton spoke to Villalba loud enough for the mics in the room to pick it up and broadcast it in the glass cell where Grania and Theos observed them. "Send some men to Finestock's home. Look for anything resembling a code. In fact, bring back anything that has numbers on it."

Sighing, she muttered, "He's going to blow us all up."

Chapter Thirty-Three

Rory checked his mobi for the third time in the past sixty mites. Still, no message from Grania. He tried to call her again, but the signal wasn't going through. While he knew a few reasons why it didn't work, like out of range, turned off, or no power to it, he still expected his sister to keep in touch with him.

He perched at the com station, eyes roaming from one signal option to another. Kachiri had retired for the night, leaving only him and Brendan on the bridge. Their engineer was somewhere on the station.

"She's probably fine," his brother said from his position at navigation. "It might be interference from the planet."

"Maybe. I'm not much likin' it. Is there another way to contact her?"

Brendan's brow furrowed while he appeared to consider some possibilities, then he cocked an eyebrow. "There might be one."

Rory waited for him to continue, then prompted. "What?"

"Not what. Who."

"What are you getting at, *deartháir*?" He slipped into the Irish term for brother he used when annoyed.

"I mean, Dari. We can use the puca to reach her."

Rory stared at him for a couple of moments, trying to figure out what Brendan was suggesting. Then his eyes lit up, and his brow lifted. "Ah, maybe." He pressed the ship's com button and ordered the puca to the bridge.

About five mites later, Rory glimpsed Dari trotting down the corridor when he came into view of the Transparisteel windows. He rolled his eyes.

Brendan grinned. "He's a small horse."

The Irish pony passed through the automatic door onto the bridge and stopped before Rory.

"Change to your peasant form," he ordered.

In a blink, the pony disappeared, replaced by Dari's youthful visage. "To be sure, Mister Rory, sir. Or do I call ye captain now?"

"When did you ever concern yourself with formalities?"

"Always with Captain Grania, you know."

That much was true, Rory conceded. The puca always respected his sister. "Right. I have a task for you if you can manage it."

Dari bobbed his head. "At your service."

"Can you travel to wherever Grania is?"

"Where is she?" the puca asked.

"We don't know. She's on the planet's surface, and the last place we heard from her was Last Outpost North. She and Theos had taken the cargo to meet up with the fellow she was to deliver it to, but they couldn't find him. I haven't heard from her since that call, and it's been about five hours. My mobi isn't reaching her."

Dari's face grew still, his expression thoughtful with his eyes narrowing and the vee above his nose pulling his freckles closer together. "There's only one way I think I can do it. Is the Captain carrying her vial of Irish soil?"

Rory nodded. "I think so."

"Well, then, this should work. I trust you both know; I can travel from soil to soil. I can go into your little tube of it and transfer into hers. The only real trick will be getting Captain Grania to realize I'm there, so she opens the lid to let me out."

"If she doesn't?" Brendan asked. He'd moved from his station and stood closer to his brother so he could listen.

"Then I'm either stuck in her vial, or I can return to Rory's."

"Let's try it then," Rory said. They had nothing to lose. "Here's what I want you to tell her and what we need to know."

He proceeded to give the puca instructions and questions to ask if he got through to Grania. Once the message was settled, he opened his vial, assuring Dari he would leave it unopened until he returned.

In a blink, Dari shifted to his base form of dust and darted into the dirt. It glittered briefly with his ethereal form, then returned to Ireland's ordinary, almost black soil.

"Pure magic," Brendan breathed with a sense of wonder in his eyes.

"Yeah. Let's just hope our sister has hers and will recognize Dari is in it." Rory set his own dirt tube in a cup to prevent it from tipping over and dropping the precious soil onto the floor.

But Rory had one more thing he felt he had to do. Grania probably wouldn't thank him for it, but so be it. He went to his communications station and sent a message to Vilnius. He marked it urgent. He needed the stationmaster's advice.

In less than ninety mites, an amazingly short time in Rory's opinion, Vilnius contacted him via voice transmission. While a bit of lag time indicated the call went through a number of relays, it seemed to be a great connection.

Rory quickly filled him in on the events at Desolation. Before he could say Grania was on the surface and out of touch for several hours, Vilnius cut in.

"Is she in trouble?"

"I'm not sure. We haven't heard from her in over six hours now. She was checking in around every two, so we're concerned about her. I just wanted to ask you if there's anything else we can do. I'm thinking about going to the surface, but—"

"No, don't do that. You need to stay on the ship and keep trying to reach her. With Grania down there, you're the acting captain, and Brendan doesn't have enough experience to either take over or go down. I'm on my way there. Should arrive in about sixty-six hours."

"How? It took us almost a week to go through the jumps!" Rory couldn't believe what he had heard. How in the heavens could Vilnius make it there faster than they did?

"Fast ship," he answered. "Is the puca with you?"

"Yes. I sent him to Grania. We're hoping she'll figure out he's in the dirt vial she carries."

"Good thinking. Message me if you learn more, but I can't do anything until I arrive."

After Vilnius ended the call, Rory turned his seat to face his brother. "That's weird, Bren. He says he's 'on his way' like he knew something had happened to Nia."

Brendan frowned. "That is odd. You don't think he's connected with the government stuff, do ya? I mean, he does work for a station, and they're agency controlled, aren't they?"

"Naw. It's not the same agency that's running the space stations." Nonetheless, Rory wondered if there might be a connection.

*****

Grania reclined in the padded chair with the footrest up while she watched Mixton and his men circle the oblong metal object housing the she-bee. Of course, she hadn't told them about the creature inside it. So far, they'd done little more than try to get a scan of the contents, the latching mechanism, and the explosives within the chamber. Just as she and her crew had experienced on the ship, very little could be discerned from scans.

Theos stretched out on the sofa, a headset covering his ears while he listened to whatever was happening in front of their view. Why he was being held with her, she didn't know. Maybe they thought she might confide something about the cargo to him. She tried to get more information from him, but he kept telling her to be patient.

She was bored. Tired of watching the soldiers waltz around the container like the dance would yield a magic opening. Weary of the Colonel pacing back and forth while talking into his com unit in an attempt to get his people to move faster. So long as he didn't order anyone to open the chamber forcibly, they'd be fine.

A deep sigh rolled out of her chest, along with a sensation of warmth at the start of the valley between her breasts. Then, she felt a vibration, like something was shaking... She caught her breath. The vial of dirt she carried around her neck. It rested, hidden under her tunic, just above her bosom, right where the jiggling occurred. Could it be? With certainty, she thought it was either Sheilan or Dari. No other entity she knew could use the soil-to-soil transfer.

She sat up, sprang to her feet, and crossed to the door, where she pounded on it to get the guard's attention. He spoke into the communication box in the door.

"What do you want?"

"I need to use the accommodations. It's kind of urgent." She made sure she sounded stressed. The soldier opened the door partway and looked at Theos. Her companion had sat up when she moved, watching her. Now he gave a sharp nod of approval. She knew he was in on this whole plan, so she didn't understand why he wasn't out with the rest of the group.

The guard opened the door, escorted her to the alcove to the east, and pointed to the door labeled *esquilla*, which also bore a woman symbol. She nodded and pushed inside, finding a room with three semi-private stalls, a pair of washbasins, and a high, narrow window at the end. Small but functional. After checking to see if she was the only occupant, she slipped into the middle stall, locked it, and pulled out the vial.

She carefully removed the cap and whispered, "Dari, are you in there?"

She waited, not sure what to expect. After a few seconds, gold dust rose from the tube and coalesced into a transparent version of Dari's young boy form.

Grania's relief poured into a released breath of air and a small squeak. "Thanks be. I am so glad to see you."

"And I to see you, Captain Grania." Dari finished solidifying so he could speak to her. "Mister Rory is deeply worried about your safety, so he sent me here to help. What can I do?"

"I have an idea, and I need your help. Let me tell you what's happened so you can relay it to Rory. We're in a warehouse about ninety kilometers north of Last Outpost, where we were to deliver the cargo. Our contact had been killed, so..." She continued to give him the details she wanted her brothers to know. "If he can contact the authorities on Desolation, not the military, then perhaps they can take some steps to ensure I'm freed."

"To be sure, I will report all this back to Mister Rory. Word for word, for I have an excellent memory, you know." Dari puffed up with pride.

"But before you go, I need your help with a little deception. Here's my plan..." She went on to describe what she wanted him to do and asked if he could do it.

"Of course, I can." He nodded eagerly.

"Excellent. You can get into my tunic pocket in your energy form, and I'll signal you when the time is right. No one should see you. Now, if you'll excuse me, I really do need to use the services in this room."

Dari winked, changed forms, and darted through the stall's door, leaving Grania alone.

A few mites later, she washed her hands while the puca slipped into her pocket. She stepped into the short hallway, and the guard escorted her back to the glass viewing area. The soldiers sent to find the combination for the door had returned brandishing a folder.

"What's going on?" she asked Theos.

"The searchers found about fifteen possible codes at Finestock's house. But they don't know which, if any, is the code for the door. So, they're going to try them."

"What if there's a failsafe on the lock causing it to detonate it if the wrong code is entered?"

Theos screwed his mouth into a scowl. "Shit. They might not have thought of that." He picked up a headphone and pulled down the microphone. He turned away from her and relayed the question to Villalba.

In the room, a brief conversation between the two officers went back and forth before Mixton pivoted toward the window and shot a glare at her.

Like it's my fault? Grania tapped her annoyance down.

A mite later, the Colonel entered the room with the papers

in hand. "Look at these codes, Captain O'Ceagan. Do any look familiar?"

She took the papers and ran her eyes over the numbers, not recognizing them for any use. Not even a contact code. "No. I told you; I wasn't given any information about the cargo except to not tamper with it. The senders didn't confide in me."

"That's unfortunate," Mixton replied. He motioned Grania and Theos toward the door. "Come with me. Both of you." He led the way, with Villalba following. Two more soldiers fell into line behind the officers.

As he marched them to the container, Grania restated her position. "I don't see why you're holding me. I only transported the thing here. I don't have any information, and I've missed out on a lucrative fee due to the incomplete delivery. I demand to be released."

Mixton stopped before the containment unit and swung around to face her. "While I regret your involvement, you've arrived with a potential weapon in a world engaged in a civil war. We need to know what's inside the very secure box. Now, if you can't provide the code to unlock it, we will force it open and hope it doesn't damage whatever is inside."

Grania noticed a uniformed man holding a laser cutter and waiting for the word to begin. She locked her gaze with the colonel. "I was told the lock is connected to an explosive, and any tampering will trigger it. So, if you're going to force it, I'd like to leave the room."

Mixton held her eyes for a few heartbeats, then asked, "Do you have any other suggestions?"

"Let me take a good look at the unit. Maybe I can spot a weakness in it." She waited for his nod of approval, then stepped closer to the object and slowly walked around it.

When she reached the middle of the back, she tapped her pocket and whispered, "Now, Dari."

An energy flash darted from her pocket into the metal box, then Grania completed her tour around and ambled over to stand by Theos. She braced her left elbow with her right hand and dropped her chin on the knuckles of her hand, giving the image of someone thinking. Theos sidled next to her and whispered, "What the heck are you doing?"

"Trying to figure this out. I'm working on a plan," she answered in a low voice. *How long does Dari need to complete his tasks?*

Eyes shifting to the Colonel, who watched her with a slitted gaze, she asked, "Don't you have a code breaker program?"

"What are you talking about?" Mixton frowned and took a step closer to her.

"You know, one capable of detecting the internal numerical sequence of the lock?" She tried to play it cool. Her whole plan depended on Dari doing what she'd instructed and selling her brother's brilliance to the Colonel.

The colonel turned to look at his experts, and one shook his head. "It appears we don't."

"Oh. That's surprising. Actually, my brother, who is on my ship, is exceptional with numbers and programming. In fact, I would be willing to bet he can send me a program designed to talk to the one in the door and get the sequence." She hoped the colonel wasn't too savvy about programming while she tried to buy time for Dari.

Mixton considered the proposal for a few moments, then nodded. "Go ahead and contact him. But don't tell him anything about where you are or what is happening. We will be listening." He nodded to Villalba, who went to fetch her mobi-com.

Grania clung to the mobi when she heard Rory's voice come through. "Nia! Thanks be. We were worried about you. Are you all right?"

"I'm fine, but I can't talk about where I am or what's happening. Right now, I'm needing to talk to Brendan."

"Ah, all right, then. Hold on."

She heard the click when Rory transferred the connection, then Brendan's voice came across.

"I'm here, Nia. What might you want?"

She quickly explained they needed a program to find the code for a digital lock. "I'll need it to come to this mobi unit and work from it. Can you do this task for me, brother? It is very *cur i gcéill*."

A long silence followed, and Grania hoped he remembered the Irish for hoax and connected it with what she was asking. Her grand-da often used the term for anyone trying to trick him.

"Of course, I am sure I can do it. It may take me about an hour to program it. Will that be okay?"

She glanced at Mixton. "One hour, give or take a few

minutes, to do it. Is it acceptable?"

He nodded.

"Excellent, Brendan. Call me back when it's done."

He started to say something, but she cut him off, not wanting to have to dodge any more questions.

Chapter Thirty-Four

Transformed to a shimmer of golden light, the puca zipped through the metal like it didn't exist. Once inside, Dari got his bearings and darted to the front of the box the long way around, avoiding the occupant and the sticky goo covering it.

When he located the explosives, he hovered and studied them carefully. In his energy form, he saw the setup through his fractal vision. It looked like the bomb material connected via colored wires to a small box, which blinked a short green light every few seconds, but it didn't seem to be attached to the locking mechanism.

While he was no expert with modern electronics or even those dating back several centuries, he did believe breaking the connection between the bomb and the control device would nullify any actions taken on the exterior lock.

He shifted into his wisp form and considered the wires again now that he saw the colors. He'd seen enough human entertainment to know they needed to be broken in a specific order, but which one went first? What was the most common color identification for humans? Red, green, yellow, and blue, but he doesn't see a blue. The last wire was black. He broke it down, thinking yellow meant caution, red was danger, green was safe, but what was blue?

"See if you can disable it," Grania had said, but she didn't give him much more information. Hoping he made the correct choices, he started with green. His wisp form lacked much firepower, but he did have good spark capacity. He tried, hoping for the best, but it wasn't enough. He amped up his power a little more and tried again. The spark almost doubled, sending a flash into the wire, but it still wasn't enough.

Dari puzzled over it, his tiny wisp eyes squinting at the wires. He spun to the side and slipped within the narrow space between the box and the door, where the lock waited for a code on the other side. He gauged he would have enough room to change to his smallest bipedal form and shifted. Now a tiny brownie fae, a smidge larger than a beetle, he clung to the green wire. Pulling himself up, Dari marched to the end of the wire and, using his sharp teeth, bit into the plastic and wire.

Ugh. The puca recoiled at the taste of the wire but forced himself to bite through, tearing at it until it broke apart. He reeled back when he felt a little shock, but it wasn't enough to deter him. One down. He marched to the yellow one next and climbed across the end of the green to reach the point next to the connection.

Dari clamped his miniscule jaws down, feeling the plastic coating filling his mouth and leaving an unpleasant taste. Pushing his sharp teeth into it, he bit into the soft, yet resistant, exterior, and another little jolt hit him. He sat back, wiped a hand across his tiny lips, then tried again. Ignoring any pain in his brownie jaws, he chomped the yellow one apart.

Unfortunately, he had positioned himself on the wrong side of the wire and found himself flying free of the explosive stack, tumbling down with the loose yellow line. He hung on, but it came to a jerk below the electronic box. Determined, he climbed, hand over hand, back up to where the red and black connectors remained intact. His grip slipped on the thick plastic coating a few times, but he finally reached the stack. While he caught his breath, he realized he'd come up on the opposite end. No matter. If he cut them from this side, it would still stop the signal. So, which one next?

Dari stared at the two wires, trying to decide. If the black was the ground wire, he shouldn't have a problem with disabling the red one first. Deciding the red must be the ignition, he chose that one. Biting down, he was prepared for the shock, but it didn't come. Taking another bite, he noticed numbers illuminating on the box, like it searched for the code... or counted down. Since the digits weren't sequential, he hoped he was seeing the code and committed the numbers to his memory. His tiny, sharp teeth broke through the red wire at the same time the last number flashed.

Wide-eyed, Dari froze, staring at the flash. Did he make a mistake?

Chapter Thirty-Five

The time ticked by, and Grania fidgeted; her nerves stretched while she waited for something to happen. Dari had been in the containment chamber for over twenty mites, and she fretted, not knowing if he had been able to disarm the bomb or learn the combination. She stared at the ornate-looking chest with its vents and tubes and wondered what the creature inside looked like. Could it really be alive and what would it do when awakened?

At last, she saw a glimmer of gold streak toward the bathrooms. *It has to be Dari!* She would have missed the shimmer if she hadn't been watching for it. Acting shyly, she stepped beside the colonel and asked to use the facilities. His eyebrows leveled, but he summoned a guard to escort her. Thankfully, not the guard who'd accompanied her earlier.

Turning to go to the alcove, she noticed the colonel walking over to Theos and spoke to him. The man seemed more relaxed and cordial with the PPG agent, and Theos looked at ease with him. *What exactly is his connection with Colonel Mixton? Does it extend to the planetary government?*

Grania pushed open the door to the restroom, and her guard took up his position outside the entrance to wait. Once again, she stepped into a stall, closed the door, and waited for Dari to materialize. In a few moments, he stood before her in his youthful form. She pressed a finger to her lips, then flushed the toilet and motioned to the puca to follow her. She went to a washbasin, turned on the water, and whispered, "What happened? Did you get it done?"

"Faith, I thought I was going to be blowin' us all up," he said in a soft voice, his eyes wide with fear still in them. "I cut all the wires, two from the top where the explosives are located and the red one at the bottom where it feeds into the control box."

"Excellent," Grania said. "So, it's disarmed now. Why did you think it would explode?"

"Well, the wire sparked, and for a bit, I feared I should have cut the black wire, and that one would be sendin' the signal. Then the number showed on it, and I felt certain it was going to blow."

"What numbers?" Grania leaned closer, encouraging him to speak even softer.

"I memorized them, but now I don't recall them all. I knew them for a few minutes, but I think the fear scared 'em out of me."

Grania rolled her eyes. He was a puca. What did she expect? "What do you remember, Dari?"

"The last three numbers were seven, nine, two."

She repeated the numbers. "Grand, Dari. You've done a fine job. Now go back to Rory and tell him everything happening down here, but stress he's to stay on the ship. I don't want him coming down to the planet. Will you do that?"

"I most assuredly will, Captain Grania." The lad straightened his shoulders and saluted her.

Grania opened her vial of dirt, and the puca dissolved into his energy form and dived into it. She twisted the cap on, hoping everything from here on would go well. Although the colonel might still have to force the unit open.

When she returned to the room, she stopped close to Theos, unsure what game he might be playing. The colonel paced around the containment unit for the fourth time in the past thirty mites, talking to the soldier with the laser torch, while he gestured with his hands.

Come on, Brendan, she thought, worried the colonel's patience would give out. When the com signaled the message, she jumped and called out, "My ship's tagging me, colonel." She tapped it on. "Bren, do you have something for me?"

"I do, indeed. Are you ready for the download?"

"You know I am. How does this work?"

"Once you receive it, execute the program, and then connect the com to the lock and tap on the pi. It will do the rest of the job."

"Got it. Download's completed. Hope this works." She ended the call with a quick thank you and none of the words she really wanted to say to him.

She took her com unit to the lock, executing the program as she walked. She located the plug-in on the box, inserted her prong into it, and then tapped the program icon. Numbers flashed on her device while it searched for the code, then they began locking into place. Like magic, the final three digits came up—first the seven, then the nine, and lastly, the two.

The lock flashed a green light, and the door unsealed. How about that? Bren actually managed a working program!

Grania stepped back to allow the colonel and his team access to the doors, although she remained within a few meters of the activity. She wanted to see what this creature looked like.

They pushed the doors open, revealing the nearly three-meter-tall she-bee. Grania gasped, stunned at the first look. Dari's description had nailed it pretty accurately. Half humanoid and half bee, the odd form sported several tendrils shooting off from its head and the abdomen of a bee with thin legs near the back leading to human-like feet with extra-long toes. Armor covered the torso like a metal dress, fashioned to accent the feminine characteristics. The amber liquid covering her had mostly melted or been absorbed during the trip. Dari had described it like almost solid honey covering the she-bee. *Where in the whole universe had anyone found this unusual life specimen? Why ship it here?*

Eyes popping, Colonel Mixton's mouth dropped open in disbelief. "Good God, what is this?" He turned toward Grania. "Did you have any idea what you were transporting?"

She shook her head. "I did not. The United Planetary Government prepared the transport authorization with an official seal, and no one questioned them."

"What does it say was in the crate?"

"Farm equipment and supplies."

"Does that look like a plow or a tractor?" Mixton asked, his voice edged with anger.

Grania shook her head, "No, sir."

He stepped closer, peering at the creature before he motioned a soldier over, voicing a command in a low voice. The soldier saluted, pivoted, and left the room.

Villalba moved in also, studying the creature with interest. "I heard rumors they'd developed a secret weapon. Could this be it?"

Mixton turned his attention to the hardware and some software embedded in the containment case. "We need an expert to take a look at this equipment. I want to know what it's doing. The creature appears to be in hibernation, so let's learn what we can while it's still sleeping."

The two techs he'd brought down scurried to get a closer look. Mixton turned to Grania and pointed a finger at her and Theos. "You two, return to the observation room." He glanced at their guard and nodded.

Without argument, Grania led the way to the glassed room with Theos and the guard following her. If the she-bee was a weapon, she didn't want to be anywhere near when she woke up.

"What kind of weapon could she be?" she asked Theos when they were locked in again.

He strode to the coffee machine and poured a cup, diluting it with milk, then came to stand by her at the window. "Your guess is as good as mine. But I'd say she might have a stinger or two, so maybe she poisons her victims."

Grania shuddered. "A quick death if it's a potent poison. I think I see wings behind her body."

Theos squinted. "I can't make anything out, but it's possible. They didn't give you a clue about it either?"

"Nope. Just told me to make sure it got delivered."

Theos glanced at her, then dropped his head. "They gave me a com number to call in case anything went wrong. I didn't know who would show up. If Finestock had been there instead of off fighting, he would have taken possession. Since he didn't, I called the number."

"I don't understand. The she-bee would have gone to the rebels if we'd delivered to Finestock. Now, she's in the planetary army's hands. Who are they trying to support?"

He shrugged. "I don't know."

Grania's shoulders drooped. This amounted to much more than she'd bargained on when she'd taken... no, been conscripted... to take this job. They hadn't given her an option, but had the government double-crossed someone? She got herself a cup of tea and then sat at the front table to watch the activity. She cleared her throat after the first sip. "Are they going to let me go back to my ship?"

Theos turned and joined her at the table. "I believe they will once they're satisfied with the delivery. To be frank, I'm not sure what Mixton and Villalba are doing or will do. I wasn't expecting any of this. I thought we'd turn the box over to the colonel, and they would pay you for delivery. Then I figured we'd be returned to the spaceport. Something here is not right."

"But you know these people. Am I right?" Grania asked, sipping her tea and trying to figure a way out of this mess.

"I've met Mixton before, but I'm not part of their military if that's what you think. I'm as confused by this as you are."

"I wish I could believe you." Her voice remained soft, but her eyes looked like granite.

*****

After a few more hours, the guard opened the door and told them the colonel requested them in the main hangar. Grania hesitated, not wanting to be there when the she-bee woke up. But she had no choice, and Theos urged her to follow the guard.

Colonel Mixton watched from a dozen meters away while his people buzzed around the creature like servants in her hive. Except they took samples of her blood and tissue, along with her blood pressure, temperature, and everything else the machines attached to her could register in the alien life form.

Grania and Theos stopped a few feet from Mixton and waited for whatever he wanted them present to see. While Grania stared at the containment unit, she noticed a readout screen displaying a countdown. While the number diminished, so did more of the honey-like coating over the she-bee. Now, it had almost gone. The alien's whole form was visible and more imposing than before. The armored body, bee-like torso, and now, her wings began to unfurl, looking larger than Grania had initially thought they were. Several sets of the appendages from her head began to wave, shifting like they detected something in the surroundings.

Grania shivered, all her instincts warning her this wasn't a good sign. She took a nervous step back, wanting to get as far away from the she-bee as possible. Theos shot a glance her way, his eyes seeming to ask why.

"What do you suppose that thing will do when it wakes up?" Villalba asked from behind them.

"I'm sure I have no idea," she answered. "But I'm thinking she's going to be more than a little agitated."

"We've got armed men surrounding the area." Villalba pointed to a trio of soldiers off to their right, bearing laser rifles, ready to aim and fire if needed. Scanning the room, she saw four more units of three equally well-armed men.

She watched one of the technicians use his gloved hand to grab one of the appendages, attempting to get a better look at it. Her inner voice kept saying, *Get away. Get away. Don't agitate the creature.*

Then, Mixton approached her, and he looked like a man on a mission. His eyes drilled into hers. "You appear worried, *Captain*." He said the title like she didn't deserve it, and it wasn't on a level with a military title. "You sure you don't know more about this unusual cargo? Now would be a good time to tell me."

"I don't have any information about it. But common sense is telling me you should be taking more precautions."

"That's all you have?" He snorted a laugh. "We have plenty of firepower in the room. I just hope we don't have to kill it before we learn what it does."

"I think it might be time to tell your technicians to pull

away from—"

At that moment, a trio of stingers shot out of the appendage the tech held and stabbed into him. Shocked, the man fell off the stool he stood on, and the stingers withdrew when he toppled. Once he hit the floor, he started to convulse, arms and legs thrashing around violently until his body arched off the floor. A strangled scream escaped his throat. He smashed back to the floor and lay motionless.

In the middle of the convulsions, Mixton yelled orders to everyone to clear the immediate area and motioned to Grania and Theos to get farther back. She didn't argue, retreating all the way back to the glassed room. Theos stayed a little closer but still several meters farther back than they had been.

The groups of soldiers came to alert, rifles moving to their firing positions, waiting for any orders.

The she-bee's eyes popped open, weird-looking and human-shaped but composed more like a bee. And they looked fierce when she cast them around the room.

.

Chapter Thirty-Six

The remaining technicians in the room scurried away like scared *ostmin*, racing for the exit at the back of the hangar. The soldiers held their ground and waited for a signal from the colonel. He remained planted in the middle of the space with his eyes locked on the she-bee.

Grania tapped Theos' arm. "I'm thinking we'd better get back to safety. Who knows what she's capable of doing?"

With one last look at the creature, Theos spun and followed her into the observation room, pulling the door shut behind them. Their guard nervously stationed himself outside and looked their way, then back to the threat like he wished he could join them.

"I hope these windows are strong enough to hold against her." Grania tapped the glass and gauged the thickness of them.

"I think they're Transparisteel." Theos stood beside her with his eyes centered on the scene before them. The colonel holding his ground, the she-bee taking in her surroundings, soldiers preparing to fire on command, and everyone else backing up against the walls or trying to get to the exit.

Then, she moved. The she-bee stepped out with awkward

movements, lumbering forward as her legs seemed way too frail to support her body weight. When she was several steps out, she flung her wings wide, and in a heartbeat, she took to the air. She buzzed the room from near the ceiling, circling it, looking, Grania presumed, for a way out. She found only the row of narrow windows above the vehicle entrances, which were neither big enough for her to fit through nor easy to break.

Swooping down, she came near a nervous soldier, who twitched back and fired his rifle at her. Unharmed, the she-bee returned fire, spraying him with a fine mist from an appendage on her lower body.

Screaming, the soldier dropped to his knees, hands scrubbing at his face. Within seconds, Grania could see the man's face turn red and then darken as the liquid burned his skin. He shrieked and rolled violently on the floor, agonized cries pouring from his throat until he couldn't make any more sounds. In less than a minute, all his movements ceased.

"Holy mother of God. He's dead!" Grania covered her mouth, fighting the urge to throw up, and turned away from the window. "She's fecking lethal." A shudder rumbled through her body.

Theos stepped back and caught her arm, urging her to come farther away with him. "I've never seen anything like that creature. Not anywhere."

"There *must* be a way to control it!" the Colonel screamed as he ran to the back of the room. In a few moments, he burst through their door, followed by the two soldiers guarding him and the one who'd watched the door.

The she-bee cut loose, attacking the remaining soldiers. Stingers shot from her head appendages while the lethal spray came from the ones on her body. The victims either fell to the floor convulsing or screamed in agony from the liquid. Grania tried to look away, but she couldn't tear her eyes from the horror in the next room. In less than fifteen mites, everyone in the room sprawled across the floor, dead.

While the she-bee circled the hanger a few times, she made no attempts to break through the glass surrounding their secure room. Mixton stood at the window, hands on the glass with shock and horror contorting his face. The soldiers moved to the back of the room, not looking at the carnage. Like their leader, they seemed to be in shock.

Grania understood the horror. She collapsed into a seat and covered her face with her hands while she tried to process the massacre before her eyes. She turned her head and lowered her hands to look at Theos. He stared straight ahead, seeing the horrible scene. Still, his face bore a dumbfounded expression like he couldn't comprehend what had happened.

She rose and stood next to him, her back to the carnage. She tapped his arm, trying to draw his attention. "How could anyone possibly deal with this creature? What was the she-bee sent here to do? Do ya know, Theos? Did your superiors tell you anything?"

She repeated his name several times before he turned to stare at her. "What?"

She repeated her questions, hoping he had some ideas.

He shook his head. "No. I don't have a clue."

"Can you contact the PPG?" Mixton asked, turning his head to look at Theos. "Can you ask them what it takes to neutralize that monster?"

Theos wet his lips with his tongue, tearing his eyes away from the gruesome view. "I can try. I need a com unit with a long range."

Mixton pulled his own from his pocket and handed it to him. "Tell them you're calling on my behalf, and the situation is desperate. We need a plan."

Com in his hand, Theos retreated to the back of the room to make the call. Grania pulled out a chair and sat facing the side so she didn't have to look at the bodies yet could keep an eye on the she-bee.

One of the soldiers wandered over to get a cold drink from a machine at the back, prompting her to look at the food machines. "Well, if we're stuck in here, at least we have food and drink to last for a while. But bug-girl out there will need more food, so maybe she'll get weaker or even go back to her travel case. I wonder if she sleeps?"

"Then what?" a soldier asked. "We try to sneak out and lock it back in? I ain't volunteering for that assignment."

"I won't ask," Mixton said. "I'll order it."

The soldier straightened his shoulders and snapped a salute. "Yes, sir."

"Wha--? What is it doing?" the other soldier asked. His eyes were locked on the she-bee, who had crouched down with its large torso resting on the ground.

The creature leaned over a dead soldier, and a pair of tendrils trailed from her head to the body, where it entered the man's chest.

"Oh, damn," Mixton spat. "She's feeding on him."

Grania looked and couldn't tear her eyes away as the she-bee sucked the blood and internal meat from the corpse. *God help us. She'll be the end of us all.*

But something else drew her attention. At first, she caught a mere glimpse out of the edge of her eye, then she shifted her view to the darker corner where a young woman, dressed in a long skirt and a loose-fitting drawstring blouse, knelt and scrubbed transparent garments in a bucket on the floor. She worked the fabric against the washboard a few times, wringing it in her hands before she flung it out and rose to hang it on a clothesline.

Grania's heart pounded wildly, and she couldn't breathe. She felt like she'd been hit in the chest. *Sheelin. 'Tis the b'ean sidhe. Holy Father, she's comin' for me. 'Tis the first warning.*

She dragged in a breath and nudged Theos. "Do ya see anything in the corner there to the right?"

His face pale from the shock of the feeding she-bee, Theos turned his eyes to peer where she pointed and squinted. "No. What am I supposed to see?"

"Nothin' movin' at all?"

"It's just a corner, Grania." He turned to stare at her. "What are you seeing?"

"A ghost, maybe." Her voice sounded raw while she watched the scene playing out for her.

Done with her task, the b'ean sidhe turned to face Grania and stared her in the eyes, sending cascading chills down her spine. Then Sheelin disappeared. Grania spun away from the glass and retreated to the back of the room. She grabbed a cup, made hot tea, then sat facing the machines. She couldn't watch any longer.

In a few mites, Theos joined her, holding a cup of coffee in his hands. "Terrible business. How can we stop that creature?"

"Isn't that what you're supposed to find out?" Her voice shook a little. She felt betrayed, set up by the government. They *knew* what they were sending. Did they expect this to happen?

"I am trying. I'm waiting for someone to get back to me. Communication from here is difficult. It needs to go through a dozen relays to the galaxy's center. It could take several hours to get to my contact and the same amount of time back."

"In the meantime, the biological weapon in the other room is eating her prey. Is this what the AUP intended? For her to come here and kill everyone?"

Theos stared into his cup like an answer might magically appear. "I don't know. I'm in the same trench with you."

They sat in silence for over an hour, neither wanting to look toward the monster in the other room. Finally, Grania spoke. "Sooner or later, the thing is going to try to break into this room."

"The transparisteel walls will hold," Theos answered. "But how long can we survive on what we have in this room? We need to get help here. I don't know any force capable of taking on the creature to get us out. They'll go straight for destroying it with something that will probably kill us as well."

"Well, now, isn't that just delightful? Thanks for the encouragement." Her voice sounded as bitter as she felt. She'd been manipulated and betrayed.

"Just being straight with you." His com buzzed, and he picked up the call.

Grania hoped the call came from his people, giving him a solution. She stood and walked a dozen feet away to allow Theos privacy. She glanced back toward the corner where she'd seen Sheelin. She didn't know if the b'ean sidhe had appeared a second time since she hadn't been watching the room. Since the spirit had to appear to her, she chose the chance she would appear in her line of sight. She crossed her arms and rubbed her palms against her upper arms like she felt a chill. She turned to look around, but she saw nothing other than Theos near the drink station, where he still talked to the caller.

Just her nerves. She wanted to talk to Rory; see if he had any ideas. She thought Vilnius might have contacts in both government agencies who could help. But she had no way to ask him. Her com unit remained in the room with the she-bee, and she had no chance of getting to it alive.

"They don't have anything yet," Theos said as he strolled over. He'd already appraised Mixton, who now conferred on his com unit with someone. "My colleagues have appraised the council of the situation. They're waiting for answers. Someone should be able to tell us how to control her." He nodded toward the she-bee and looked away again as quickly.

"I don't suppose your com unit would allow me to contact the Mo Chroidhe, would it?" She pointed at the device he held.

"You can try." He pressed it into her hand, trying not to be obvious. "It's designed for long-range communication, but it might reach the ship if there isn't a blocker on it."

"Why would there be a blocker?" She took the unit to the corner behind the vending machines and spoke the call sign for her ship. Hearing a static sound, she pressed send. "Hello, Mo Chroidhe. This is Grania O'Ceagan calling from the planet. Do you read me?"

She waited as more static burst from the unit, but she didn't hear an answering voice. She tried a different channel and repeated the message. Still crackling noises coming through.

She changed to the last channel on the unit and tried for a third time. If this didn't work, she was stuck. She repeated the message and barely got her name out before she heard a crackle and a hiss followed by an urgent-sounding voice she recognized.

"Grania! Where are you?"

"I'm on the bleedin' planet, Vilnius. Trapped here by a hybrid creature that is currently dining on an entire platoon of soldiers. Do you have any contacts with the PPG, AUP, or whoever might be able to help? We need to know if anything can stop this biological weapon the AUP sent to this place."

"I know a few... people... do what I... help... Connection.... fail..." The transmission faltered with static and broken words.

"Losing you," she answered. "Do whatever you can."

"Hold..."

Then, she lost him. *Damn, fickled fecking fairies.* She walked back to Theos. "Got through to Vilnius, but not my ship. Maybe he can get help. Or your people might come up with something." She paused, turned her head to stare at the she-bee, and looked back at Theos. "I do *not* want to be the creature's next meal. So, someone better come up with a plan soon."

As she looked away from him, she caught her breath and froze. The b'ean sidhe had materialized in the southeast corner of the break room.

Chapter Thirty-Seven

The ghostly woman washed the clothes more vigorously than the previous time, her scrubbing bordering on frantic. Scrub, scrub. Hold the shirt up, repeat. Her motions grew more erratic and she tried to pull away from the scenario.

Sheelin was trying to break away from the programmed task. She wanted to talk to her. Grania hurried, pushing chairs out of the way to get to the corner.

"Fight it, Sheelin. Fight it. I need your help." She stood right at the edge of the manifestation, close enough to touch the her if she'd been corporeal.

A shrieking wail burst from the b'ean sidhe and the image shattered. A ghost image of Sheelin remained. She looked right at Grania and her mouth moved, but no sound came out. Grania tried to read her lips, but couldn't make it out. In another ten seconds, the spirit had faded.

A disappointed sob broke out of Grania's throat and she slumped against the wall.

"What was that?" Theos asked as he came closer and peered at the corner.

"Did you see anything?"

Shaking his head, he said, "No. Only you waving your

hands in the corner and yelling at something. But nothing's there."

"You didn't see the spirit." Grania pulled herself straight and stumbled back to the rear of the room. One more warning. She'd only have one more warning, then the she'd die. Given the circumstances, she figured the she-bee would be her murderer.

She collapsed at the back table and dropped her head on her hands. She didn't want to look at anyone or anything right now. In her mind, she pictured Sheelin's face and her mouth, trying to make out the words.

"What spirit?" Theos asked.

She opened her eyes and tilted her head up. He stood in front of her, hands on his hips, and looked down.

"'Tis a family haunt. A b'ean sidhe. She comes to warn someone of their impending death. She's come to me twice now. If something doesn't change soon, the third time will be the last." Her throat felt dry as she choked the words out.

Sheelin had come to her when they were in the Dark Sea and she'd thought her life was over. But she'd helped her then. Just like she seemed to be doing now. The spirt was trying to break out of her assigned task to tell her something. But what?

* * * * *

Time creeped by with only the view of the creature feeding on her victims to catch their eyes. Grania didn't want to watch, but found her vision drawn to the carnage too often.

Exhaustion pulled her toward sleep, her eyes sliding shut when she tried to focus on anything other than what lay beyond the windows.

Across from her, Theos slept on a lounger, a bench seat barely long enough to accommodate his height. She'd volunteered to keep watch while he slept, thinking she couldn't sleep with that monster in the adjacent space.

Her eyes drifted shut again and she let them. Give them a short rest, then she'd be vigilant again.

Thunk! Thunk-thunk!

The thudding sound of something hitting the Transparisteel brought her alert with a jerk and heart pounding in fear. Her eyes darted to the windows and met the multi-faceted ones of the she-bee. She was pressed up against the surface as she stared at Grania. Her mouth went dry and she could barely breathe. Could the creature break through the windows? From the smeared look of the section in front of her, it appeared she had tried.

Earlier, when the she-bee had been rampaging around the hanger, committing mayhem, she'd banged into the windows at high speed, bouncing off them, but this time she appeared to be making a more concentrated effort at breaking through.

Grania raised her hands into the air beside her head to show the insect-woman she wasn't armed. Apart from the eyes and the tendrils coming out of her head, the face looked human. At the moment the bee eyes were watching her hands while the rest of her seemed calm. Was there a thinking intelligence in the creature? Had she gone through a programmed reaction at being attacked when she awakened? Would she have turned into a murdering demon if the soldiers and scientists hadn't immediately threatened her?

Grania continued to watch the she-bee as much as the creature watched her. She slowly lowered her hands and stepped back a few paces so the beast could view her clearly and realize she didn't have any weapons. She even turned in a circle so every view could be seen. When she rotated back to facing her, the creature had retreated from the window and flew back to her compartment, settling into it.

All around the hangar, blood, guts, and half-eaten body parts littered the room. Grania's stomach roiled, and she thought she might vomit. She scurried to the sink in the coffee station and leaned over it, coughing up bile, but not the crackers she'd eaten a couple of hours earlier. She washer her mouth out, then sank into the nearest chair, laid her arms on the tabletop and let her head drop onto to them while she tried to shut out the images reeling through her mind.

How in the cosmos did anyone expect to control this monster they'd created? Had there even been a plan or was the plot to turn the she-bee amok among their enemies and then destroy it?

When Theos woke up, Grania gratefully turned the sentry duty over to him and curled up on the lounge. Her eyes burned, and her head felt fuzzy so she definitely needed sleep, but it eluded her. In spite of the brain fog, she still saw the carnage and a part of her panicked every time. She'd be almost asleep and jerk awake with the images.

"Count sheep or something," Theos said after she'd gasped and bolted upright for the third time.

"Like that really works," she muttered, rolling on her side with her back to him.

"It distracts your mind until you bore yourself to sleep. Just try it."

The lights dimmed in the cafeteria. Grania figured he'd adjusted them down, thinking it would help her sleep. Now she could imagine the creature attacking in the dark. Her eyes fluttered shut and she tried to envision fluffy white sheep bouncing over a fence where she could count them. She made it to one-hundred-forty-two before the sheep turned to giant bees.

Shaking her head, she shifted her body again and turned her thoughts to happier times, like the last evening she and Vilnius had shared at Pelanan Station before he'd returned to Earth's Zabrowski Station. They'd both expected he would be back within months to become the station master. While it still meant they wouldn't be together, it would have afforded them at least three to four times more than they had with Earth's station. Now, they'd split up, her fault, and she might never see him again. Her mouth turned down as she finally fell asleep.

She woke to the sound of Theos' voice and someone else's coming through the comm channel. The transmission crackled and she couldn't make out the words.

"Yes, I got it," Theos answered. "How do I reach the local governor?"

Another crackle of noise. Still drowsy, she gazed around

the room and noticed the colonel and soldiers were no longer with them.

Grania sat up, trying to focus while Theos scribbled something onto a paper. Then he signed off.

"What is it? Did you get some answers?"

"Yes, and no." He turned to face her. "Your boyfriend came though and found someone who had part of the answer. The thing out there,..." he jerked his head toward the she-bee who was wandering the hanger again. "...can be controlled, but you need a coded sequence to communicate with her. And a special device to do it."

"So, who has the device?"

"A very good question. Our contact should have had it, but if it was in his house, I didn't see it. But then, I didn't know what I was looking for either."

Grania pursed her lips, rose, and walked toward the coffee station. She needed a cup of tea or something to face this. "You're saying the only way to control it is a gadget in Finestock's house that we can't get back to because..." Her voice rose as she spun toward him, "... we can't get out of this feckin' stupid building!"

"No, there's more. Get your tea and I'll tell you." Unperturbed, he strolled to the snack machine, found tea biscuits on one of the rows and put in credits to retrieve two packets of them."

Grania sat at the nearest table, back to the windows, and sipped the cup of tepid tea. Not the best brand and the water was barely hot enough to make a decent cup. But it was better than nothing, she reminded herself. Theos deposited the cookies in front of her.

"Breakfast."

"Ta. What happened to Colonel Mixton and the others?"

"They slipped out the back door while the she-bee was sleeping. He said they'd bring help, but for us to stay here where it's relatively safe."

"They left us *here*?" She couldn't believe she'd heard that right. "They feckin' left us while they escaped? And you let them?"

"I didn't have a choice, Grania. They were out the door, slamming it behind them before I could get across the room."

"So, they abandoned us." Fury rose in her. Would they bring help or level the building to kill the she-bee? "Now tell me the rest," she growled.

"If it's any consolation, they didn't make it."

"What?" Confusion twisted her face. What was he talking about?

"Mixton and the others. The creature caught them before they could get out the back door. She dragged their remains out there." He jerked his head toward the bloodied hangar.

"Oh…" She swallowed hard. "Good thing they left us, then."

He sank into the seat across from her and folded his hands on the table. "About the codes. One other person has the same device. The governor of this region was sent a duplicate."

"I didn't know they had more than one region on this planet."

"They have four. It's divided into four quadrants. We're in the southern one, which is the most settled."

She raised an eyebrow. *This is the most settled? Certainly not the most civil? Are the others worse?* "Did you get a way to contact the governor?"

"I did. If our comm will reach him. So far, it's been hit and miss contacting anyone on the planet."

"So, try it."

Theos shrugged and made an attempt to connect with the governor, but he got only static. "Worthless."

"Let me try my ship again," Grania said. She held out her hand for the comm unit.

After a moment's hesitation, he handed it to her. "Good luck."

She set the unit for the channel link to the space station and keyed in the Mo Chroidhe's code. At first, it just sounded dead. Nothing on the line, no indication of any kind to say it was connecting. Grania tried again and got a burst of static, but then a series of clicks and a buzzing sound.

"This is the Erinnua freighter, the Mo Chroidhe. Who is calling?" Kachiri's voice came through the comm loud and clear.

"Ho, Mo Chroidhe, this is your captain. Is Rory nearby?"

"Yes, Captain. Hold a moment." Her voice sounded excited.

Not exactly enthused but grateful, Grania waited and hoped the connection didn't fail.

"Grania? Where are you?" Rory's voice held more than a

tinge of worry.

"I'm still on the bleedin' planet and in big trouble. Theos and I are locked in a breakroom while the farkin' big she-bee dines on the station personnel. Our remaining comm unit is flaky as Granma's pie crust. Can you call the governor at Drinbask?"

"I can. Nothing wrong with our comm except for tryin' to reach you."

"Smashing, little brother. We need you to make a call for us and give the governor a message?"

"All right. Give me the details."

You may or may not be able to call us back on this channel, but give it a shot."

Grania passed the details and exact message to Rory. "Let me know the response. If I don't hear from you in three hours, I'll try to contact you again. I don't know if we'll be able to get a signal out though."

She hated to break the connection with her brother and just before she signed off, she hurriedly said, "Wait, Rory. Send Dari to me again if you can. I'm still wearing my necklace."

"Right, Nia. I'll talk to him." Rory ended the transmission on his end.

"What was that about?" Theos asked when she turned to face him. He held his hand out for the comm.

Reluctantly, she handed it over and sat on the edge of the nearest table. "I may have an idea of how to communicate with that thing out there." She tipped her head toward the hanger." If she was right about what Sheilan had tried to tell her, Dari might be able to help.

"I can't wait to hear it, but I want to try my contacts again to see if they can get word to the governor from there. Not that I think Rory can't handle it, but I'd like another option."

"Sure, then. Knock yourself out."

Chapter Thirty-Eight

How long had they been locked in this room now? Well over a day, but had it become two? Grania had lost track of time. She'd found a plastic bucket they could use for a latrine, but her body had other needs. Not to mention both she and Theos smelled more than a little ripe. The bathrooms weren't far, but might as well be on the other side of the planet with the she-bee in control of the hanger.

She fingered the decorative tube of dirt hanging off the chain around her neck and wondered if Dari would be able to come again. In anticipation, she loosened the lid, sliding it partly open. The puca didn't need much clearance in his energy form.

Outside their safe haven, the she-bee dined again, nibbling away on body parts that, no doubt, were beginning to rot, or perhaps they were her fresher kill. Grania couldn't watch so she turned to face the back of the room.

Theos continued his attempts to contact the governor with no success. She was about to give up on Dari when a sparkly luminosity enveloped the tube and a faintly glowing streak exited from the soil within it. In less than a heartbeat, Dari materialize in the room. Grania gasped at seeing Brendan standing before her.

"Bren--?" She caught her breath at the lifted eyebrow and wide eyes. Not her brother, but Dari. He'd chosen her sibling's form. "Dari, thanks be."

From behind Dari, she saw Theos' jaw drop at the sudden appearance, and she barely restrained a laugh. Nothing she could do except to explain more about her odd crewman.

Before she could speak, Theos came around to face the puca. "Brendan? How did you get here?"

"I'm not Brendan," Dari replied. "I just be borrowin' his form."

Theos looked from Dari to Grania, his eyes even bigger. "How?"

"'Tis a long story. Suffice it to say Dari is a shapeshifter."

Theos's mouth silently formed the words like he was trying to understand what she'd said.

"He's borrowed my brother's form," she explained. Then she waved her arm at the scene beyond the glassy barrier. "This is what we're facing, Dari. Sheelin's come to me twice so far, unable to do anything but her b'ean sidhe act, but she tried to tell me something. I think she wanted me to summon you. Do ya' have any ideas how we can get out of this place without being killed by that monster?"

Dari turned to look at the horrific scene, although he seemed calm enough as he watched the creature feed. "Sure enough, I've seen worse carnage over the years. Ireland wasn't always a peaceful place, ya' know. Still, the soldiers weren't about devouring the dead. But the Morrigan had no qualms." He stepped forward until he could touch the transparisteel wall and peered out at the giant creature. "Mayhap I could distract her long enough for the two of ya' to escape."

"How?" Theos asked.

"My wisp form might draw her attention away from this area and that there door," he nodded toward the locked entry, "giving you the time to get out the exit at the back."

"Is it dangerous for you?" Grania asked, not knowing what might harm an energy form.

"No, Captain. I think I will be safe enough with leading the bee-thingy on a merry chase around the room."

"Let's try it," Theos said. If we can get out, maybe we can contact the governor and turn this creature over to the authorities to deal with."

"Right," Grania agreed. "Do it, Dari."

The puca flashed an uncharacteristic grin, one so unlike Brendan's that it looked weird on his face. In another breath, he'd vanished, and a barely noticeable streak of gold passed through the window into the hanger where a golf ball-sized wisp fluttered toward the she-bee.

Dari's wisp flitted around the creature, keeping a few feet distant from her so she couldn't catch him easily. Her eyes, faceted through they were, appeared pinpointed on the milky-white ball of light. The puca continued his dance, luring her toward the hangar's rear wall where her case rested against it.

When she followed, Grania's hope surged. "Quick!" she told Theos. "Let's go out the back exit while the she-bee's distracted."

Theos tore his eyes from the scene in the hanger and hurried to the locked door. He keyed in the exit code and quietly pushed it open, trying all the while to not make any noise to alert the creature. Grania followed behind him, stepping out of their two-day prison into the hallway, and glancing back to see if Dari still held the she-bee's focus.

The wisp flitted back and forth, even flying into the case in an attempt to persuade the creature to follow. "Hurry," Grania whispered, urging Theos on while the creature remained distracted.

Theos stepped to the coded door and used his keycard to exit the main building. The computer requested his bio-reading, sliding out a reader plate. The slide made an inordinately loud snap, sounding even sharper in the nearly empty space. He pressed his thumb against it as Grania kept watch.

As the reader slid back into the machine, she whipped her head back to the room in time to see the she-bee pivot toward them. Her wings unfolded and she started a rush attack.

"Theos, she's coming," Grania said, turning to look at him.

At the same time, the computer rejected Theos' identification and a red light flashed. He turned, shoved Grania and pushed her back toward the break room. With his card still out, he dashed in front of her to enter it into the lock while she stayed on his heels, trying to not let the over-sized bee woman intimidate her.

Even as they fled to room, Dari's wisp kept darting in front of the she-bee's face, trying to distract her. Grania watched with her heart in her throat as he drew closer and closer. Theos inserted his card in the door, a click followed, and he pushed it open, holding it for Grania to go through first. Then, he jumped in while a long tentacle reached out, almost touching Theos's shoulder. He pulled the heavy metal door shut behind him, clipping about five inches of tentacle off as it slammed into place.

A shrill, buzzing sound filled the hanger, loud enough for the two captives to hear. Pain and frustration, Grania figured. She could sympathize with the creature. Didn't she feel some of that herself?

The she-bee whirled around and targeted the wisp bothering her. She made a leap toward Dari with her tendrils waving wildly around her head. He dodged; the ball of light moving erratically around the room until the creature almost nailed him as a smaller head tube seemed to suck him to her. In an instant, the wisp disappeared.

Grania caught her breath. "Is he gone? Did she catch Dari?" Then, she glimpsed a flash of gold light as his energy form streaked back through the transparisteel glass.

He materialized as his Irish lad form, the small red-haired boy Grania associated with his human form. He panted like an animal trying to catch his breath. "To be sure…that bee-woman… is angry as a hornet and as swift as an arrow in flight with those tentacle thingies. I'm sorry I could not hold her attention long enough." His blue eyes drooped and the color dimmed.

"Ya did all ya could," Grania replied, slipping into the rhythm of his speech. "I thought she might have had ya there at the end. Sure, I'm glad to see ya in one piece."

"Agreed," Theos added. He still gaped at Dari's new form.

"I told ya, he's a puca." Grania waved a hand in front of Theos' face. "He can shapeshift."

"To anything?" Theos turned his face to her, his eyes narrowing as he appeared to be planning something.

"Not anything." Dari sat at the nearest table and took a deep breath. "I can only change to beings I have tasted. Me natural form is a water horse."

"What do mean… tasted?" A touch of alarm sounded in Theos' voice.

"He means a small sample of their DNA. He got Brendan's from a bleeding cut."

"Oh." Theos sat quietly while Grania brewed a cup of tea for Dari.

On the other side of the glass, the she-bee continued to circle the room, displaying her anger, although her furious buzzing settled down somewhat. Drops of ochre-colored liquid oozed in a sporadic stream from her damaged appendage.

Grania set the teacup in front of Dari, then asked, "If you'd been able to lure her back into her carrier, would you have been able to switch forms and get the case closed again?"

He took a swallow before he answered. "I do not think so. Methinks she is too fast. She—"

"What about changing into a creature like her?" Theos asked. While Grania and Dari had talked, he'd gazed thoughtfully at the tendril piece lying near the door. About five inches long, it, too, leaked ochre liquid from the cut end.

Grania shifted her gaze to it, then looked back at Dari, a worried look in her green eyes.

The puca fidgeted, hemmed and hawed for a few seconds before he replied, "While 'tis possible, I think that is an alien form and I've only done me magic with things of Earth and the fae worlds. I don't know how me energy might react with the creature. And to be exceptionally clear, I have no desire to find out." He held up a hand when Theos opened his mouth to speak and continued. "Besides, it takes my specific magic many hours to process and build the new form. Once the pattern is recorded, I can switch quickly, but the more complex the life form, the longer the build."

Theos's mouth popped shut with an audible smack and he slumped in his seat.

Grania was silent a few moments, then ventured a thought. "How have humans in Ireland controlled the bees when they've gone to gather the honey. They must have some trick to get to it without being attacked."

"I believe they do." Dari's eyes brightened along with his smile. "They use smoke pots. Even before that, they built fires and fanned the smoke toward the hives. The bees get confused and drowsy and retreat."

"Would it work on the she-bee, do ya think?" she asked, not expecting a concrete answer.

Silence followed her question as they all thought about the likelihood of this creature being physiologically like an Earth bee. Finally, Theos spoke. "We don't have anything to lose by trying. The issue is what can we burn to create enough smoke?"

"And how do we direct it to her?" Grania dipped her head toward the sulking she-bee, who sat in the middle of the carnage she'd created.

"There's one other thing. How do you keep yourselves safe from being choked by the smoke?" Dari asked.

Theos jerked to his feet, scraping the chair back and strode to the left wall where a building map showed key locations in the building. He studied it for a couple of minutes before turning back to the others. "This is a military bunker. On the other side if this wall are palates of wood, clothing, combustible items, and more we can burn. Behind the wall is the climate maintenance system that feeds air into the vents. Close the ones in here and the smoke bypasses us."

A surge of excitement swelled within Grania then collapsed as quickly. "But we need to get through the door to access it. The problem out there...," she tilted her head to the hangar, "...won't let us get to it."

For a moment, Theos's face crushed as the enthusiasm waned, then he brightened again. "You're right. We can't, but he can!" He pointed his finger at Dari.

Chapter Thirty-Nine

Dari materialized into his Brendan form on the warehouse side. His first instinct called for a check of the area to see if anyone was around. After a quick tour taking him right up to the entrance to the offices, he discovered no one. The place appeared deserted.

He turned to the climate system, noting a plethora of lights and push buttons. The only problem was, Dari couldn't read any of it. What use did a puca have for reading? Even though he'd adopted Brendan's form, his brain skills weren't totally transferred, and this one was missing.

What to do now? Dari stared at the lights as if he might absorb their function simply by looking at them. *Oh, that's truly dumb, boy-o,* he told himself. *The feckin' things don't look any different from moment to moment.*

Perhaps he could dart back to Grania and Theos and report what he'd seen, but how would he tell them when they all looked the same? Maybe he could record an image on the communicator thing. But then, he would be flitting back and forth trying to follow their instructions.

No, this called for some creative thinking on his part. He looked around, seeing the wood, some flares, and stacks of what looked like mattresses stacked on various wooden platforms. A metal cart sat nearby, partially loaded with two cushions. So, an idea presented itself.

*****

Grania paced the room, back and forth like the ducks in a carnival shooting gallery. Her grand-da told her the skill game dated back several centuries and regained its popularity when the colony set up on Erinnua. Somehow, it lost its amusement when she felt like the targeted duck.

She spun around at the end of a pass and turned her eyes to Theos. "There has to be a way to communicate with that creature. How would anyone control it unless the government wants to wreak havoc on both warring factions."

"I'm sure there is," he answered, his voice sounding tired. "But the key's been misplaced or stolen and until we can get word from the PPG, we can't do anything."

"Faith, we're relying on a puca to help us. Do ya' have any idea how scary that is?"

Theos shook his head as his brow tightened, revealing a pair of thin wrinkles.

She sighed. "The puca is a trickster of the ancient world. He was not known as a benign or helpful creature. Neither is the b'ean sidhe. In myth, the puca was known to attack people and lead them to their death. Dari has mellowed over the centuries and is more inclined to help humans. Perhaps he's developed an empathy for us, having witnessed so much violence over our history.

"Be that as 'tis, he's still but a merry fae and apt to follow his own inclinations, whatever they may be."

Theos wet his lip. "Are you telling me he won't help us and might leave us stranded?"

"Maybe. He's been helpful ever since I've known him, but Dari's idea of helping may prove unexpected." In her mind, she recalled the fierce white horse that attacked the pirates' captain while they threatened to blow the Mo Chroidhe apart. Ancient creatures with extraordinary power, but unpredictable. Yet, he was here, helping them.

A signal from the comm drew her attention and Theos picked it up from the table. Perhaps it was Rory or even Dari calling from the other room. Theos answered, then lifted his eyes to hers.

"It's for you." He held the comm out to her.

She took it as she mouthed, who. He shrugged.

"This is Captain O'Ceagan," she stated, not knowing who to expect on the comm.

"Aye, that it is. How are you holding up, Nia?" Vilnius' voice asked. She could hear the concern in it and he used the familiar name with her.

"You're the last person I expected to be hearin' from on this line. Where are you?"

"Heading your way as fast as a government ship can warp. I estimate we'll be landing in about fifteen mites."

"Landing? Here? You're landing on Desolation?"

"I am."

"How? Why?"

"Not exactly the response I expected," he chuckled. "Rory contacted me once you were taken, and I shipped out on a patrol ship within hours."

"It took us weeks to get here," Grania said, not believing he was almost here in two days, or maybe they were into three now. She'd lost count. Still, far faster than they'd traveled.

"Dear heart, there are far faster routes to the Outer Rim if you have the authority and credits to use them. Besides, I wasn't that far away."

"What do you mean? You were on Zabrowski, weren't you?"

"Um, not exactly," he hedged. "Let's just say I was quite a bit closer."

"Vilnius? What is going on?" Why would he be closer to the Rim? He was the Earth's Station Master. Or was he? Had he accepted a different position in this sector?

"I'll tell you when I see you, love. Just hang on, and I'll be there soon with help."

He ended the communication then and with her mouth hanging open, she stared at the comm for several secs before turning her eyes to Theos. "Help's on the—"

A penetrating swoop of excitement interrupted her and drew her eyes to the windows. Dari ran by, shoving a metal cart filled with flames and smoke, obscuring whatever the fire source was into the hangar.

"What in the cosmos--?"

"He's distracting her," Theos shouted. "Let's get out of here while we can." He ran to the door, opened it and stepped into the hall to the exit.

Grania watched the she-bee back away from the flames as Dari wheeled it in a circle around her, trying to force her back to her chamber. He was like a little kid taunting a feral animal while filled with glee. Then, she started to run to the exit. From the hall, she yelled, "Dari, park it to block the hall exit and get out of here as fast as you can."

"No worries, Captain," he called back, his voice carrying a horse-like neighing sound at the end. Was he changing forms?

But she didn't wait to find out. She ran to the now open door and dashed into the warehouse. As she turned to look behind her, she observed Dari shifting to his huge horse form, around two-thousand pounds of muscular animal. He reared up, threatening the she-bee.

"Don't challenge her," she yelled. "Just get out of there." As near as she could see through the smoke, the creature seemed to hang back, not wanting to get close to the flames and recoiling from the smoke.

Dari whinnied, rearing up and striking with his forelegs, then turned and raced toward her. As he approached, she wondered if the horse would fit through the door and backpedaled away to give him space while Theos stood behind the heavy metal plate, ready to swing it shut.

In a horse's snort, Dari transformed back to Brendan's form and sprinted the last few feet through to the room, passing by Grania. Theos slammed the door shut, and they all heaved sighs of relief.

"We did it. You did it," Grania said, offering a grateful grin to Dari. "What did you put to burn on that cart?"

"Just some things I found out here, mind you. A wooden palate, a few uniforms, a box of these..." He held up a red-colored tube to show them. "...and a few more things I could pile on."

"Smoke bombs," Theos said, taking the tube from his hand. "Brilliant." He laughed. "That should drive the beast back into her container."

The roar of a big plane's engine vibrated through the building, cutting his laugh off. "What the hellfire is that?" His eyes narrowed as a frown scrunched his face.

"Sounds like an attack ship's turbos are right above us," Grania said, equally shocked by the proximity of the sound. "Aw, feck! They're going to blast the building. Let's get out of here!" She began running before she finished talking.

In moments, Theos drew up next to her and they darted through the maze of materials stored to the warehouse exit. A wide metal door opened into the front offices, giving them a straight shot to the exterior. Grania glanced behind her, not seeing Dari in any form following her. Had he turned a different way?

"Hurry, Grania!" Theos called from the other side of the open door.

Dashing outside, Grania began waving her arms, hoping to get the attention of the pilot. Theos grabbed her elbow and yanked her away from the building.

Stumbling some on the uneven ground, they raced toward the rocky skirt along the ridge dividing the canyon. They reached it as they heard a whistling sound behind them. Theos yanked Grania into a natural stone shelter just as the explosion rocked the ground and threw debris in every direction, some flying over them.

A piece of shrapnel hit Grania's left upper arm, slicing into it. Burning embers fell on Theos and he slapped at the pieces that clung to his clothing, trying to put them out. An ember settled in his hair, leading Grania to bat it out by pawing at the thick curls.

"I can't believe they did that," she yelled. "They feckin' dropped a bomb on us. If we hadn't gotten out, we'd…" She paused as the enormity of it hit her.

"Be dead," Theos finished for her. "Apparently, the local authorities counted our lives as unimportant compared to killing the monster."

She suddenly felt cold, her body starting to shiver with the shock and her eyes popped wide. "Where's Dari? Did you see him come out?"

Theos jerked his head around, looking toward what was left of the building. "No. I figured he'd be right behind us."

Cautiously, Grania stepped out from their cover, aware of the blood dripping down her arm, but still not feeling the pain from the deep gash. Rivulets of blood dropped to the ground and soaked into the dry soil.

Theos put an arm around her waist as he fumbled with the front of his jumpsuit. "If I can get this open, I can cut a piece of my undershirt to wrap around your arm."

"I don't see him," Grania mumbled, her eyes scanning the destruction and seeing the flames engulf the building. Had Dari gotten out? Was he dead? What about the she-bee?

Her knees felt weak and her head spun. Feeling disoriented, she slipped to the ground, legs folding underneath her as she blacked out.

Chapter Forty

Grania's head seemed to spin as she forced her eyes open. She felt movement, like a vehicle whizzed through the air, then she focused her vision. Curved sides on either side of the uncomfortable surface she laid on indicated a van or a shuttle. The equipment lining the walls, marked with green medical symbols, identified it as a medical shuttle. *Why? Oh, mercy!* She recalled she'd been injured in the fallout from the bomb. She vaguely recalled the uneven whirl of the ground and rock seeming to blend together before she hit the ground.

She blinked, getting used to the dim light in the vehicle and faces became clearer. A man dressed in a gray jumpsuit sat beside her, monitoring her vitals as a machine did all the work of keeping her stable. How much had she bled?

On the other side, a much more worried face watched, his hand gripping hers and gently squeezing. *Vilnius? How is he here? This must be a hallucination. He was on the space station, wasn't he? No, wait, he'd told me he was coming, but he couldn't be here yet.* Nonetheless, she wet her lips with her tongue and croaked out his name.

"Nia," he replied, his eyes shooting to her face. "You're awake."

"How...? How'd you get here?"

"Don't talk right now," the med tech said. "Save your strength. We'll be at the Third Army Infirmary in four mites. We're controlling the bleeding with a pressure cuff, but you'll need the wound sealed."

Now that he mentioned it, Grania realized her left arm was completely enclosed in the aforementioned cuff and she felt the pressure. She opened her mouth to speak, but Vilnius pressed a finger to her lips and said, "Shhh... No talking. But I can answer your question."

He shifted on the bench build alongside the side, moving closer to her. "I told you I would be here when we talked. I landed at the spaceport and commandeered a shuttle to the Third Army Base. We'd just come over the ridge when the pilot dropped the bomb on the building. I can tell you my heart lurched at that sight. I thought I'd lost you."

She shifted her head from side to side a couple of times to indicated no. While she didn't speak, she formed her mouth into the words "she" and "bee."

He got them. "I don't know if she's dead. Initial reports were the travel unit survived the blast. If the creature was inside, she could be alive."

"Dari," she breathed out, barely a whisper. Her eyes misted with concern for the puca. He'd been in his horse form the last time she'd seen him. Did he make it out?

Vilnius shook his head. "I don't know, *Mo grá*. I'll try to find out."

He called her my love in Irish. One of the few expressions he'd learned from her. But they'd broken up. Did that mean he still loved her?

The shuttle docked at the infirmary and the med techs began to transfer her to the surgical center. Vilnius squeezed her hand. "I'll be waiting for you when they patch you up." He paused a moment, waiting as they lifted her travel board onto the gurney, then taking a last moment to lean close and whisper, "I cherish you, Nia."

She was whisked away into the emergency room while the techs directed Vilnius a different direction. Within minutes, she had a cone mask over her face, and she felt herself drifting to sleep.

Grania woke later in a small room with a sink, a separate latrine, and a small closet. A single wide window allowed light into the space. Outside, a tree stood guard, casting a shadow, and blocked some of the afternoon sun. She couldn't see much of the city from her bed.

Gradually, she assessed the damage to her body. She felt sore from the blast and had more scrapes to her arms and legs than she'd realized at the time, but the major injury wasn't troubling her much and a sturdy bandage covered the wound. The healing solution she'd been immersed in had sealed the injury and the healing process was well underway. She'd be as good as new within three days.

A nurse entered the room bearing a tray of food and water. "I saw you were awake and thought you might like some water and a nice broth to give you strength." She smiled at Grania, but her whole appearance suggested military; short hair and light beige clothing cut with a uniform look, including a high-necked collar and a double row of buttons down the front.

"How long will I be here?" Grania asked, concerned about contacting her ship and finding Dari. Maybe he'd gone back to the ship and she needed to let her brothers know she was okay.

Unconsciously, her hand went to her throat to touch the chain with the vial of dirt. It wasn't there. She ran her hand across her skin, seeking the chain. Definitely gone. What happened to it? The dirt connected her to Dari and Sheilan. She frowned.

The nurse set the tray on her drop-down floating table and handed her the water. "I believe the doctor will discuss that with you later today, but I expect it won't be long. Your injuries are minor except for your arm, and that is healing well."

"Could I get a comm device to contact my family?"

"I'll see what I can do. I don't know if we have any available that are non-secure channel ones. Most patients have one with them." She didn't sound encouraging."

"Yes, I understand that most would. Regrettably, mine was destroyed. Anything you could manage would be so appreciated."

With a nod, the woman left, her business done. Grania frowned. Soup and a biscuit along with her water. Was that the best they could do? Nonetheless, she ate it, grimacing at the excess of salt in the broth, but hungry enough to get it all down. Where was Vilnius? Was he really here or did she imagine the whole thing? He said he'd be here.

A different nurse came to remove the tray and Grania asked again about a comm unit. This one knew even less and simply said she'd have to ask someone higher up the chain about it.

She dozed for a short time until she heard the door open. She opened her eyes and acknowledged the man who stood at the end of her bed. Military uniform, four galaxy symbols on the collar. He was a high-ranking officer. A captain, by her reckoning.

"Have you brought me a comm unit?" she asked through a dry mouth. She reached for the water, watching was the officer's eyebrows lifted in an unasked question.

"Mine was destroyed, and I need to contact my ship." Grania pulled herself to a sitting position. "Would you have one I can at least borrow?"

"Ah, no. That's not why I'm here. I'm Captain Hardwick, and I'm here to debrief you. I'd like to hear your side of the story, Captain O'Ceagan." The hesitation in his voice made it clear he didn't equate her status as a cargo freighter's captain to his military rank.

"How about I tell you everything and you lend me your comm unit for a few mites?"

"Um, I can't do that." He pulled up a chair and sat a couple of feet from the bed. "My comm unit is security locked and it would be a violation to let anyone but me use it."

"I see." She wasn't making any progress here. Who would have thought it would be such an issue getting a simple comm unit?

"Tell you what. If you tell me your story, I will get a unit send over. Is that agreeable?"

"Sure enough, I guess it is." Her new Irish accent began to creep into her voice. "I'll be tellin' you everything I can from the time I set foot on this planet with that cursed box. I was to deliver it and collect me fee. That was the whole deal. I wasn't to be involved in any military action and certainly wasn't expectin' to be blown up."

"Of course not," Hardwick replied. He'd pulled out his comm unit and set it to record.

She told him the story, leaving out any details she felt he didn't need to know, like anything about the puca and the b'ean sidhe who came to warn her. But she made it clear it was down to Theos and her holed up in the snack room with the she-bee on the other side.

"The what?" he asked. "Are you referring to the hybrid Zynavian?"

"If that's what you call the killing machine in the golden case, then I am. No one told me anything about that piece of cargo and I never saw it until the techs opened the hibernation unit on the base."

"I see. So, your only interest in this whole affair was simply the delivery of the package. You had no access to the command codes or key to opening the unit."

"Feck no, not a thing. As I said, the man we were to deliver it to wasn't at his home and apparently had been killed in this little war you have going here."

"That should do it, then, Captain. Your story matches that of Theos Camber. He says he joined the crew to help escort the package to the recipient here on Desolation. But like you, he was unaware of the Zynavian. I'll file my report and that should end your involvement with this."

"My involvement?" Grania blinked. "Did ya' think my and my ship were part of this whole mess? I was just doin' a delivery job."

Hardwick's face tightened in a semblance of a smile. "So you were. And once I file this report, you're free to leave the planet with no restrictions."

With that, he rose, put his comm in his pocket, and turned to the door.

"Don't forget to send over a comm unit, Captain." She said his rank with the same nuance he'd used on her. After he left, she fumed. No restrictions. Like she'd done something wrong. Thank the stars that Theos' story matched hers. She was pretty sure he didn't mention the puca and he never saw Sheilan.

She turned her gaze to the window where the sunset poured golden-green rays over the distant mountains. Was the doctor even coming? And would there be another bowl of soup for supper?

A short time later, the door opened again and Vilnius stepped into the room with a pottery vase filled with colorful desert flowers. He set it on the bedside stand that held only a glass of water.

"How are you feeling?" he asked as he leaned over to plant a light kiss on her forehead.

"Am I dreaming again?" she mumbled, not sure she could trust her senses. It looked like Vilnius and the flowers seemed real enough, but how could he be here? Even with faster jump gates, he couldn't have made it here this fast.

He chuckled. "No, love, I'm here. I went to the bomb site to see what I could learn."

"And did ya' find out anything? Any sign of Dari?"

"I found a lot of destruction, but the transport container is unharmed. Whatever it's made of withstood the bombing. And the experts there told me they believe the monster is inside and appears to be alive."

"So, they feckin' bombed us for nothing. If we hadn't gotten out when we did, Theos and I would have died. Dari gave us the opportunity to escape, and I thought he was comin' right behind us when we ran. I am so angry with the government's military right now. Whoever made that ill-advised decision owes me more than a weak apology." She twisted her mouth into an angry line while she felt the blaze in her eyes releasing the fury within her.

Vilnius pulled back a little, hold a hand up. "I cursed them roundly when I heard they were going to bomb the base. Pulling out some good Slovakian curses my great-great-grandmother used. I think my belligerence procured the fast shuttle even though it didn't stop the order."

"But what about Dari? Did you see anything of him?"

He slowly shook his head. "I would have told you that first if I had. But not a sign, not even hoofprints in the sand. But I think he would have switched back to his energy form and transported—"

"To the vial on my necklace," she finished. "But it's missing. I don't have it on." Her voice took on a note of the panic rising within her. She needed that connection and she realized something, softly voicing it. "Sheilan didn't come to me before the warehouse was bombed."

"What?" Vilnius' face reflected his puzzlement.

"Maybe I lost the necklace in the warehouse. My b'ean sidhe didn't appear when I was in danger of being killed. She came twice earlier, warning me of the Zynavian's threat. But not when we were going to be bombed."

"What's a Zynavian?"

She snapped her eyes to him as his question pulled her back. "Oh, that's the she-bee's race according to Hardwick. He visited me earlier. Maybe Sheilan knew I wouldn't die in the bombing. Or… Could she have appeared in the smoky room where I couldn't see her?"

"You're babbling, Grania," Vilnius said, taking her hand and gently stroking the back. "But your necklace is probably with your personal things here in the infirmary."

Of course. She blinked, having forgotten the admitting nurse would take her things to store. Now, she focused on him. "Okay, so tell me how you got here within three or four days. It's impossible."

He laughed. "I did get here quicker than you did; it's true. But I left Earth's station not long after you set out to make the delivery. So I was only a week behind you and I was using a government patrol ship, so we came a faster route with high-level clearances all the way."

"Wait. I'm confused. How could you leave your post at Zabrowski and demand a patrol ship?"

Vilnius smiled sheepishly and met her eyes. "After we fought, I realized I wanted you more than I wanted the station master job and I asked for the Tara transfer, but the position had already been filled. Then I heard some scuttlebutt about this item the Mo Chroidhe was transporting."

"You wanted me more than the job?" Grania repeated, not sure she'd heard that correctly.

"Yes, love. I don't want to be without you. So, I took two weeks leave to pursue this possible transport violation—Not on you," he hastened to add. "That allowed me to contact enforcement and get on a patrol ship headed this way."

Eyes wide, Grania stared at him, amazed by the sheer audacity of this man. And he loved her. "How did you know about the shipment? What tipped you off?"

"Liam. He contacted me before you left Earth's orbit. He was worried about the crate you'd suddenly added to the cargo after a stop at Enterprise that would take the ship to the Outer Rim. He felt something wasn't *ceart*—I think that's the word he used. I had to look it up; it meant legitimate. –with the shipment."

"Oh, Liam… Well, he had reason to worry. Here I am in a hospit… excuse me, military infirmary with no payment on delivery of the cargo and probably a medical bill." Her mouth turned down in an exaggerated pout.

"Well, if the whatever-you-called-her is still alive, then it stands to reason she's your property until someone pays the bill."

"Who would want her? She's a killing machine."

Vilnius lifted an eyebrow. "Exactly. The military wants her and if they can get the command codes, she's controllable."

"They already have her. They took her."

"But we can challenge their possession. I can check around for an attorney to take our case."

"You'd do that for me?" Grania felt all melty inside. "But what about your job? What are you going to do if you're not working on a station?"

"Well, I have an idea about that—"

"Good evening, Captain O'Ceagan," a man's voice interrupted. Grania turned her head toward the door to see a short, portly man dressed in a military medical uniform standing in the doorway.

"I'm Doctor Shibbits. Sorry to interrupt, but if I might have a few minutes, we can talk about your injuries and getting you out of here."

Grania waved him in. "Of course, doctor. This is my good friend, Vilni-"

"Who is just leaving," Vilnius interrupted. He squeezed her arm. "I'll see you a little later, Nia."

He strode from the room, nodding at the doctor on the way, and Grania wondered what prompted his exit.

She turned her attention back to the doctor who peered at his notes on a comm device. "Everything is looking very good with your health. Mostly cuts and scrapes from the explosion and, of course, that deep cut. It could have severed some tendons and damaged muscles badly, but we were able to repair the damage. While it may be sore for a few days, the healing solution has done most of the work and sealed the wound."

"So, I won't have any problem using it?" Grania shifted her bandaged arm to see if it caused pain. Ah, only a little bit.

"I wouldn't suggest you try anything strenuous with it for at least a fortnight, but for simple tasks, you'll be fine. I'll give you a supply of pain relief pills to cover the first few days. So, I feel we can release you first thing in the morning. Checkout is usually at oh-nine—hundred."

"Great. I'll be ready. Oh, what can you tell me about Theos Camber. He's one of my crewmen and was in the explosion with me."

Doctor Shibbits raised an eyebrow and studied his comm again. "Ah, yes. I saw him also. A few second-degree burns, scrapes, and cuts as well. But he is fine, stable, and the burns are healing well. Nothing of concern."

She sighed. At least he was fine. Now, if she could just locate Dari.

"Do you have any other questions?"

"Can I borrow your comm unit to contact my ship?"

Chapter Forty-One

"Sorry, I can't. Military issue, you know."

Grania dipped her head. "Yes, I do. But thanks for everything you did, Doctor."

After he exited, Grania wondered where dinner might be and where Vilnius had gone. She should have borrowed his comm while he was here. But she had so many questions for him. What plan might he have for work where they could see each other often? She had an idea or two, but they might not appeal to him.

She leaned back, her thoughts drifting to the two fae who'd entered her life such a short time ago. A surge of annoyance went through her as she realized she was depending on Sheilan to alert her when she was in danger. A bad practice. The b'ean sidhe's function warned of impending doom but couldn't prevent it. Nor could she stop the inevitable if Grania made a bad choice. No, looking to the fae for help and guidance would dull her survival instincts.

Dinner interrupted her thoughts, arriving without fanfare and as much excitement as her lunch had been. Some kind of stew with greens and something resembling animal protein floated in it. A reddish bread roll accompanied it, along with pudding of some sort. Totally unappealing. Picking up the spoon, she took a sip of the thick broth. Tangy and spiced but not entirely off-putting. She tried the meat, finding it chewy and gamey-tasting. Still, she was hungry.

Her door swung open, and Vilnius waltzed in with a sausage bun in one hand and a comm unit in the other. He grinned, holding up the prized tech. "It's like dissecting a ten-armed Zalgris to get one of these." He handed it to her like it was a trophy from the Halbroc Space Race. Even though she easily imagined her well-fit station master wrestling with the tentacled creature from Albionea for the comm, she grabbed it like the prize he intended.

"Oh, thanks be; I've got to contact Rory."

"I've been in touch with him." Vilnius set the bun on her tray, and she eyed it with saliva building in her mouth.

"You told him I'm okay?" She still held the comm, ready to call.

"Of course. As soon as we got you here, I contacted him. He'll be happy to talk to you directly, but—"

"But I have time to eat that roll first!" She dropped the comm on her bed and grabbed the hot bun. Now this was food.

While she ate, he told her he'd contacted an attorney, and the woman would get them an appointment with the military and planetary government to negotiate for the Zynavian.

"That was fast," she commented between bites. "Does this attorney think we have a chance?"

"She does. Her name is Batalia Stronghorn, and she has a multi-star reputation."

Before they could talk more, a general announcement concluding visiting hours came on the speaker.

"That's it for tonight. I will be here in the morning to get you," Vilnius informed her and leaned forward to kiss her lips before leaving.

Finally getting time alone with the comm unit, Grania contacted the ship, pleased at the transmission quality. Rory came in loud and clear.

"Thanks be, Grania. We were all worried about you, even though Vilnius gave us a call when they'd taken you to the emergency. How are ya feelin'?"

"Not too bad. A little banged up and furious at the local government. I'm aft to suing them for attempted murder."

"D'ya think you'd win?"

She laughed. "Naw, not a bit. Although Vilnius thinks we can get the government to pay for the expenses incurred bringing the creature here. I'm not so sure about that either."

"So, when d'ya think we might be leavin' this place?"

"As soon as possible. I hope in the next couple of days. I'm out of here in the morning. But tell me, has Dari returned to the ship?"

Rory hesitated. "Not that I've seen. I've checked my vial a few times to see if he used a soil transfer, but nothin'. I figured he must still be with you."

Feck, she'd hoped the puca was back on the ship. Maybe he'd gotten back to her vial, or he was a free-roving spirit on the planet.

Changing subjects, she asked if the ship was supplied and

ready to depart soon.

"Aye, Captain," he crisply replied. "And I've lined up a few shipments to help pay the way. Just need to tell them how soon we can load."

"Soon, Rory. It'll be as soon as I can get off this planet. I don't know yet if Theos will be returning with us, but I'm thinkin' we might need a cabin for Vilnius."

"There is one thing," Brendan interjected. "We need a new engineer."

She groaned. Another problem? "Hello, Bren. What happened?"

"Sindhu quit and signed on to another ship. Said he didn't want to hang around this station for long. He didn't share any other reason."

"Well, blast him to the rings of Saturn if that wasn't a rotten thing to do. Have you been looking for a replacement?"

Rory cut back in. "Aye, I have a posting on the board here and have put out the word as best I can. So far, not so much as a nibble."

"This could be a problem. Keep lookin' for someone. Oops, I have to go."

Her brothers signed off, expressing hopes to see her soon, then she turned her attention to the orderly who'd entered the room.

"Just a routine check on your vitals and a blood draw," he told her. He also handed her one of the pain relief pills, which she choked down with bitter-tasting water. One more bad mark against this planet.

* * * * *

Check-out may have been oh-nine-hundred, but it was well after eleven before the medical team did their final checks and released her. She'd dressed in a new city suit and shoes Vilnius had brought her that morning. Her jumpsuit had been trashed from the explosion and her being flung into the rocks. The trendy-looking clothes fit perfectly, a dark green snug-fitting midi-dress with a short cream-colored jacket that came mid-way down her torso. She added the pair of low-heeled pumps, checked her reflection in the mirror, and approved the outfit. Her man had good taste, probably better than hers.

She sat on the edge of the bed and waited for someone to tell her she could leave. About to give up, she stood, ready to walk out, when an orderly arrived with an air-chair.

"I can walk." Grania eyed the air chair suspiciously. Thin-framed with a cushioned seat and back, it looked fragile as it floated on a layer of air generated by the enclosed fan below the seat.

"I'm sure you can," the platinum-haired man agreed with a smile. "Still, the regs require us to see you safely to your transport."

Rolling her eyes, she climbed on board and allowed the orderly to float her from the room. While the chair bobbled like a ripple on water would rock a boat, its comfort surprised her, and she relaxed.

They stopped at the desk where a clerical android asked

her to sign several documents, most having to do with liability, medical statements, and physician's release. One included the medical fees, which appeared to be waived for the most part.

"Am I reading this right? My expenses here are three hundred and fifty credits?"

The accounting clerk turned the tablet toward her and glanced at it before returning it to Grania's view. "Yes, that's correct. It will probably be covered by the Militia Fund since you were injured by their action. If not, you can appeal to the territorial government to cover the damages."

With a nod, Grania signed off on it and handed the tablet back. "Am I free to leave now?"

"Yes, that concludes your release. May your health continue to improve." The clerk plugged the tablet into the bigger mainframe, where Grania presumed it would be transmitted to whatever agencies needed the information.

Then Grania remembered. "Do you have my personal items? I had a necklace when I was brought in."

The clerk processed her request for a few moments before she turned to a locked cabinet against the back wall. "I will check. I didn't see a note on your file." She opened it, hunted through a dozen or so bags in the cabinet, then pulled out one about the size of a sandwich bag. "This must be it. It's identified with your room number." She set it on the counter for Grania to see.

The few things in it looked dusty, from her credit counter to her ship's credential medal and the two-inch tube so dirty she could barely see the gold color. Even though the chain was coated in red dust, the soil vial was there. Her heart lifted. At least she had that, and she hoped Dari would be in it. "Now we can go," she told the orderly, clutching the bag, and they resumed.

When they reached the entrance lobby, she spotted Vilnius a few moments before he saw her and sprang to his feet, striding to her. His broad smile lit up his whole face, illuminating a sparkle in his eyes. She couldn't help responding the same way.

True to his word, her orderly guided the air chair directly to the waiting hover cab, where he offered a hand to help her.

As Vilnius slid the door open, Grania saw Theos in the seat, pressed against the far side. A joyous feeling rushed through her, then she wondered if it would be awkward having her ex-boyfriend—maybe reinstated?—and the handsome Greek in the same space. "You look good," she said and slid beside him. The burns were only tiny reddish blotches on his skin, barely noticeable.

"As do you," he replied. "You didn't bleed to death, although you scared me enough."

Vilnius took the final seat and pressed his thigh against hers. None of them were small people, so she felt rather sandwiched in when they were squashed together. Vilnius verbally commanded the auto-drive vehicle to take them to an address, and it pulled into traffic after verifying it.

"Where are we going?" Grania asked. "The spaceport? Do they have one in the city?" She'd learned they were in Drinbask, the capital city of the legitimate government, not the shuttle port town they'd arrived at when she and Theos had landed.

"We're meeting our attorney for lunch to find out what we can do. Theos can confirm your story, so I thought it would be good to have him along."

Grania nodded, casting a nervous glance at Theos. Had he agreed to this? Did he have anything to gain by helping her out? Aloud, she asked, "You're okay with this?"

He nodded. "Yes, I consented. After all, I need a ride back, or were you planning to leave me here?" He tempered the statement with a hopeful look and a smile.

"Of course not! I figured you'd go back with us." She turned to Vilnius. "What about you? Do you have another ride planned back to Zabrowski or wherever? Or will you be needin' a lift?" She kept it light, not wanting to push or make him think she expected it.

"Actually, I don't have anything planned at the moment except for getting you off this planet safely." His eyebrow lifted, and he slid his hand on top of hers.

She suppressed a smile, took a satisfied breath, and turned her eyes to the city outside the solid window dome. It looked like a modern desert city, mostly rounded or oval buildings built with local clay and granite. While some bore ornate decorations highlighting the curves and the trims, others remained plain, although colorful and inviting. None of the buildings exceeded three levels, save one in the distance, which appeared to be at least seven stories and relatively imposing. A red and black flag flew from the top of the capping dome.

She pointed to it. "What's that?"

"Capitol building," Theos and Vilnius said simultaneously.

"Fancy. Looks like a nice place." She looked from one to the other and almost giggled, turning it into a stifled smile instead. This was awkward.

The hover-cab pulled to the sidewalk in front of a bright blue building embellished with curious swirls and elongated dots, giving it an exotic appearance. "Ah, we've arrived," Vilnius said, pressing a lighted button to open the door. "This is a Brangwold eatery and is reputed to be some of the best food on the planet. Or so our attorney assured me."

Inside, the place reflected the landscape outside; mountainous-looking walls separated it into three dining sections, with the tables resembling the circular plateaus, not quite round, but oddly-shaped ovals. The chairs looked like they'd been carved from red stone. Even the decorative foliage looked like the desert flora Grania and Theos had encountered on their trip to Last Outpost North. So long as a giant lizard didn't bother them, she'd be fine. "I'm starting to get a bit tired of this landscape," she murmured so only Theos and Vilnius could hear her.

Deep golden lighting cast a warm, cozy tone to the room. Grania sniffed, detecting the scent of meat cooking drifting from the kitchen area, or so she surmised.

Vilnius peered around the room, his head turning as he looked toward the far left. Grania looked the same way and saw a red-gloved hand wave. Was that their attorney? Must be, she concluded, as Vilnius led them toward her.

When they got closer, Grania realized the woman wasn't wearing a glove, but her skin glowed with a sunset-red tone. Her wiry-looking hair, pulled into a snug bun, shone with a deep maroon shade. Delicate, spiraled, deep-brown horns protruded from each side of her skull, just above the oval-shaped ears. At least, Grania guessed they were the hearing organs.

"Good day," Vilnius said, bending at his waist in a half bow to her. "I expect you are Barrister Stronghold. I'm Vilnius Majeck. This is Captain Grania O'Ceagan, who is pressing the charges, and Theos Camber, a witness to the events."

Stronghold motioned to the seats, inviting them in. Vilnius sat across from the attorney while Grania took the seat next to him, leaving the one adjacent to the alien woman to Theos. Grania tried not to stare while she contemplated her origin.

"I am pleased to make your acquaintance," Stronghold said. "You may speak in your Earth-based language, and my unit will translate as it does my native words to yours. The food here is excellent, so I have taken the liberty to order some appetizers. Then we will talk."

"Thank you, Barrister," Vilnius replied, settling himself a little closer on the seat.

"You may call me Batalia." She waved her hand toward all of them. Grania counted only three fingers and a thumb-like protrusion.

They replied in kind with their first names, and the conversation started in earnest while the assortment of small bites arrived along with a pitcher of the local ale. Between nibbles of food, Grania began telling her story, highly edited, from when she picked up the Zynavian until the military demolished the base warehouse, nearly killing her and Theos. Stronghold listened, recording the whole thing.

Afterward, she asked a few questions, then turned to Theos. "Can you corroborate all Grania said?"

He nodded. "I can."

"Exactly which government agency employs you?"

Theos opened his mouth, but nothing came out except an "er…" and an uneasy shift of his shoulders.

"Theos, tell her," Grania urged through gritted teeth.

He gulped his ale, grimaced at the taste, then spoke. "When I joined Grania's crew, I said I represented the PPG to help oversee the delivery of the she-bee—that is what we called the Zynavian—to the contracted receiver. I did that until we learned the recipient on the planet had died in the fighting. Unable to contact anyone else, I contacted the planet's official government, which is the organization I represent."

Stronghold blinked, a membrane covering her eyes for a full two seconds before retracting. "So, you are a double agent?"

Theos nodded, keeping his eyes on the table.

Grania felt her stomach flip, and she shifted uncomfortably in her seat. She'd thought it odd Theos had communicated with the official government when the she-bee was intended for the rebels.

"That is something we will not mention in court, but if it

should come up, do not lie about it." She turned her eyes to Grania. "You were unaware of this duplicity, correct?"

"Yes, but I should—"

"No, you were unaware. Say no more," Stronghold ordered. "Now, I believe I have all the information I need to pursue this case, and we have a meeting scheduled at the president's office at three gongs. Let's eat."

As the main course arrived, Grania asked, "What are three gongs?"

"When the tower bell on the presidential palace gongs three times," Stronghold replied. "It's the local time system."

Chapter Forty-Two

As the three gongs rang out, Grania, Vilnius, and Theos walked into the capitol building, where they waited in the reception area for Stronghold to arrive. Grania was impressed the attorney arranged the meeting so quickly. Either Stronghold had some real pull or nothing exciting happened in the city.

While they waited, she studied the grandeur surrounding her. For an outer rim city, the building bore rich and exotic-looking decorations on the supporting pillars that circled the core. Gold and platinum embellishments depicted some of the planet's wildlife in relief panels lining the walls. Like most of the city's architecture, the shapes seemed fluid, possibly resembling the sand dunes more than water waves.

When Stronghold arrived, she offered some quick instructions on what would transpire, which turned into a basic *"don't speak unless the Head Barrister asks a specific question"* advisory. They took a circular elevator to the fourth level, where they exited to a set of heavy steel doors and a pair of guards. Stronghold showed her credentials, and they were admitted into the president's office.

Compared to the rest of the building, this room was more austere and resembled a courtroom. After Grania's team settled in their seats, a military officer and another barrister arrived and sat. Then a magistrate and the president entered, signaling the hearing's start. Batalia Stronghold knew what she was doing and presented the case clearly and with the firm conviction that the government owed both Grania and Theos damages for the attack that injured them and for the transportation fees for the Zynavian warrior.

Grania's eyebrows lifted slightly when Stronghold referred to the she-bee as a warrior. In response, the military was represented by a junior officer called Lt. Padweck. He presented their argument that the warrior was a killing machine and needed to be destroyed at all costs, even with the loss of two civilians trapped in the building. He implied Grania bore responsibility for bringing the killer to the planet and should pay damages to the military for the loss of the building.

Stronghold hopped on that one with a vengeance, pointing out Colonel Mixton seized and brought the Zynavian onto the base without proper investigation into its nature. Furthermore, Captain O'Ceagan and Camber were taken and held without their consent. The barrister also stressed O'Ceagan had no knowledge or other instructions regarding her cargo and, therefore, was not guilty of any crime.

The head barrister stated the Zynavian was not the property of the government or the military and was, indeed, dangerous without the control codes, which were not delivered with the warrior. In his view, the creature did not belong to the military, and the captain was free to dispose of it however she chose, but she needed to remove it from the military's base.

The arguments went back and forth for over an hour, and Grania couldn't tell if they were winning or losing. Finally, a gavel from the magistrate brought both barristers to a halt.

"Whose property is the... He paused to look at his tablet. "...ah, the Zynavian?"

Confidently, Stronghold told them the Zynavian had been shipped to the rebels, specifically to Jacob Finestock, who had been killed in battle. "However, since transport costs have not yet been paid, I submit the captain has a lien against the Zynavian."

"Agreed," the president replied. "If the Desolation Militia doesn't pay the fee, what will she do with it?" He turned his attention directly to Grania.

She pushed to her feet, assuming this was one of those questions she needed to answer. The man, possibly in his thirties with a leather-like tan, locked his piercing eyes on her. "Since I need to get paid for the trip, I would put the warrior up for auction to the highest bidder. While I was unaware of the function of the property I transported, I know it was intended for the rebellion. I imagine they still want the unit."

The president, also the apparent judge, nodded. "I see. In that case, it would appear it's in the militia's best interest to pay your requested transportation fees rather than needing to bid against their opponent. What comment do you have, Lt. Padweck?"

"I need to speak to my commander before I can respond further. A recess of thirty mites, please."

Back in the waiting area, Stronghold seemed pleased. "It is

going well. I think the military will have an offer for you. They will not want that creature to go to the rebels. They can't risk it."

"On the other hand," Theos observed, "if the uncontrolled creature tears the rebel army apart the way it did their militia, they might consider it a risk worth taking."

"But the rebels might have obtained the key codes by now. Someone back on Enterprise has it," Grania added.

"That might be the final nail," Stronghold said. "Let's not mention it until I tell you."

When they returned to the hearing, Padweck spoke first. "I have been in contact with my superiors. The offer is this. If Captain O'Ceagan can provide the codes to control the Zynavian, we will reimburse all expenses incurred, plus pay one-million credits damage fee for nearly killing her in the bombing. Mr. Camber will also receive one million credits for nearly being annihilated."

"Well, that sounds reasonable," the president said, returning his eyes to Grania. "Do you have the code they require?"

"No, I do not. Our contact was supposed to have it, but we never met up with him. Theos… Mr. Camber and I checked his home, but we found nothing. If it was well-hidden, it could still be there."

"No deal unless we have the codes," Padweck stated. "You will get the damage compensation but nothing for the transportation without the codes."

"Would you be willing to give my clients time to acquire

the code?" Stronghold inserted before any more questions could be asked.

"I believe that would be acceptable," Padweck replied. "Not more than two days."

The president appeared satisfied and summarized the hearing. "Very well. The terms of the agreement have been stated. If Captain O'Ceagan can obtain the requested codes, the settlement will be disbursed in full within 24 hours of completion, and the Zynavian will be rightfully transferred to the militia. If she cannot secure the codes, the Zynavian will remain in her possession, and she will receive the damage compensation stated by Padweck. Theos Camber will also receive the same compensation. If all agree with these terms, I will conclude this hearing."

Stronghold spoke for them while the opposing Barrister and Padweck each accepted them.

"That's it?" Grania asked as they exited the Capitol.

"For the moment, yes. You have two days to obtain the codes, if possible. Otherwise, I will contact the militia directly and point out the likelihood of the opposition resending the codes to the rebels, who no doubt will be eager to obtain the Zynavian. To which organization would you prefer to sell the creature?"

Speechless for a few moments at the blunt question, Grania thought about it. She'd contracted, if she could call it that, to deliver the she-bee to the rebel faction. This war didn't involve her; she was the delivery service. Which of the sides was more deserving of a killing machine? "I need to think about it, learn more about the situation."

Stronghold nodded. "Very well. Let me know when you decide what you want to do next."

* * * * *

Over a cup of the local excuse for tea, Grania told Vilnius about the events at Last Outpost and the search for the codes at Finestock's house. "The thing is, the information could still be there. He might have a hidden safe, or it's locked in his computer. We could go back and try to find it."

"Or he might have given it to someone else in the town for safekeeping," Theos added.

"However, having seen the she-bee in action, I don't want her unleashed on either side of this conflict. She's a biological killer. Can she be used as a threat to force both sides to a negotiation to settle their issues?"

Theos shrugged and took a sip of his drink. "It's a noble suggestion, but can the creature be controlled enough to use it that way?"

"One would think the mere knowledge of what it did is enough to bring both sides to the table." Vilnius leaned back in his seat. His eyes seemed to look somewhere in the distance. "Nia, why don't you and I see if we can find that code? Theos, try to contact your people to see if you can get it through them. You should know someone who can get to the right person."

Grania dipped her head in a short agreement, then took a last sip of the tea. Maybe they could discover something they'd missed, and she could find a solution that would leave her conscience clear.

Chapter Forty-Three

Five hours later, the duo climbed out of the speeder Vilnius had hired and approached Finestock's house. The place looked like it had been trashed, damaged inside and out. The militia had nearly torn it apart, looking for the codes.

"I don't think we'll find much of anything here." Grania pushed an overturned chair aside and gazed at the mess. The computer had been compromised, and the militia had removed the hard drive, leaving only the shell.

"I guess Finestock didn't have the codes stored on his computer. Too easy for anyone to hack into it. So, he probably stored it the old-fashioned way…on paper and hidden somewhere no one will look."

"And where might that be? I hope he didn't have it on him when he was killed." Vilnius knelt to peer under the desk. He fiddled with something but came out empty-handed.

She didn't think the searchers missed a single possibility. The desk was torn apart, drawers pulled out, and the bottom knocked out where they'd searched for hidden compartments.

"I don't know…yet." She watched while Vilnius wandered into the kitchen and looked at the open cupboard. Curious at what had caught his attention, she followed, seeing him run his fingers over a square-shaped section lighter in color than the rest.

"What is it?"

"It looks like several notes were stuck on the inside. See, these squares are lighter than the surrounding wood, meaning something had covered it up for a long time. Someone pulled them off."

"I can guess," she mumbled.

He turned and went toward the bedroom. She tagged along behind, still stunned by the absolute mess the militia had left behind. She paused at the door and opened the cap to her dirt vial, hoping Dari would pop out. She'd done it four times since she'd gotten her necklace back, but no indication of any sort hinted at the sidhe's presence. *He's immortal*, she reminded herself. *Maybe he's still at the base site.*

When she entered the bedroom, she found Vilnius standing in the middle of the bed, his arms reaching for the light fixture above it. A combination fan and light, the metal light box had been broken and pulled loose from the ceiling power bracket. "They didn't miss anything, did they?"

"Maybe." Vilnius had pulled a universal screwdriver from his pocket and worked at the power bracket. "It doesn't look like this bracket's been touched in years, but it's possible to slip something thin inside it."

"Huh? You think Finestock might have done that."

"I do. It's an obvious place no one is likely to check. I would do it if I wanted... Ah, there's the screw loose, and I can just crack it open a little." He pressed a button on the tool, activating a thin light. He peered into the opening under the bracket, using the screwdriver to keep the separation. "I need tweezers or needle nose pliers. But I don't have a spare hand. Can you check my right pocket for one?"

"You carry them with you?" Grania climbed on the bed, stepping next to him, then dipped her hand in his right pocket. A giggle threatened as she considered their proximity and what she was doing.

"I never know when I might need to fix something. Can you feel the point on it?"

She rolled her eyes. Her mind had slid to a different protrusion, but her fingers found the plier's handle and pulled them out. Still holding her smirk back, she handed them to him. He grabbed them quickly before the fixture fell. Using his elbow to brace the light, he slipped the small tool into the open space and gingerly pulled out a tiny object.

She narrowed her eyes, trying to see what he'd found. It looked like a chip. "Is that a micro-card?"

"Yep." He replaced the bracket, then screwed the fixture back in, all the while keeping the wafer-thin object in the plier's jaws. Once everything was stable, he took the chip in his fingers and returned the tools to his pants pocket.

He and Grania sat on the bed while he studied the chip. "I think it will fit my comm, but it may be encrypted. And there's no surety this holds the codes."

Vilnius slid the chip into the com slot and instructed the unit to open it. A few secs passed with the unit humming, then it messaged with *Enter Password*. "Protected. I suspected it would be. Let's see if I can break the code." He started another application allowing him to manipulate the programming. While it ran, the app checked the chip for any backdoors or other loopholes in the instructions.

While they waited, Grania ran her fingers along the sides of Vilnius' hair, a smile playing on her lips as she felt the silkiness. His thick, dark hair curled into waves, accenting his Slavic heritage. Unlike her transplanted Irish bloodline, all his family were Earthers, natives for many generations.

"You're really turning down the station master at Zabrowski?" She still couldn't believe he'd done it. With Tara Station no longer an option, no other station slot would be remotely close to her.

"I already have."

"And you don't have another position anywhere?"

"Not yet." His eyes flicked to the comm. "Ah, I think we're in. Give me a few minutes to figure out what I'm looking at."

She slipped her hand to the bed, not wanting to distract him, and gazed at his face, noting the deep burrow across his forehead while he concentrated on the numbers and words displayed on his unit. He frowned, his lips tightening to a thin line.

"It looks like this is a combination command instruction, but only three words are spoken to order the she-bee. The remainder of it seems to be complex coding for the creature. From what I can decipher, this must be inserted into a slot within the casing to feed the codes directly to her brain. Did you notice any kind of slot on the case?"

Grania shook her head. "I never looked at it too closely. I saw tubes and an electronic lock but didn't notice a slot. What are the words?"

He shrugged. "They look alien, possibly Zynavian. It looks like they could be pronounced hou-ye-whena, felk-li-lie-ah, and haah-oh-dilja. I'll run them through the translator to see if they show up."

"Whoa. And some folks think the Gaeltacht is weird."

He lifted an eyebrow and grinned. "It is. Not an easy language at all."

"'Tis a good thing I grew up speakin' it then," she laughed. "So, what should we do now?"

Vilnius' lips tightened to a line, and his eyes focused on her. "What do *you* want to do, Nia?"

Her mood grew somber. "If we take this back to Padweck, I'll cover all my expenses. But it would seem my contract was to deliver it to the rebels. Although it might be forfeited at this point since the original shippers won't pay me because I missed the delivery date. No fault of mine," she quickly added.

Thankfully, her ship was still in one piece, so the AUP hadn't triggered the bomb. She figured they had information relayed from the rebels, and they knew she'd taken the she-bee to the surface. Still, she wanted the explosives off the Mo Chroidhe as soon as possible. Would they retaliate by setting it off if she didn't turn it over to the rebels? Surely not while the vessel was docked at the station.

Vilnius nodded, a slow up and down while she spoke. "I sense an exception coming. What's in your mind?"

"The she-bee is like a small army, hard to stop and extremely deadly. I don't want to see her unleashed on either side. It's a no-win scenario."

"Do you have a plan?"

She pressed her lips together. "I might."

*****

By mid-afternoon, they stood in the bomb blast's rubble at the army camp. Even though several militia buildings partially ringed it a half kilometer away, the site had only a pair of guards to keep strangers away. When Vilnius and Grania identified themselves and the guards checked with their higher ranks, they allowed them to enter.

"Be careful," the young woman warned. "We're not responsible if you're hurt on the site."

"Are there explosives in the rubble?" Grania asked, hesitating to step into it.

"No, just things that can slip or trip you. Then there's the monster in the gold box." The guard's eyes flicked to the she-bee's travel case.

"Okay. Got it." Grania bumped Vilnius' arm. His eyes focused on the case, and she realized he was seeing it for the first time. "Impressive, isn't it?"

"Bigger than I thought it would be. She's huge."

"That she is." She strode forward, picking her way through the debris to retrace her path to what remained of the warehouse.

Off to the right, a few pipes poked out where the crumbled bricks and tile of the restrooms had been. Twisted and flattened metal remained of the break room they'd occupied. Grania shivered when she thought how close she'd come to perishing in this mess when the bomb dropped.

Despite all the destruction surrounding it, the golden sarcophagus remained unblemished. What in Hades was it made of? She closed her eyes for a moment, picturing the last scene when she'd looked back to see Dari's horse charging out of the smoke-filled room and wondering what had happened to him when the bomb dropped. She and Theos hadn't been much ahead of him, but enough that he didn't make it out of the building, at least, not in an equine form.

She paused and unscrewed the cap on her vial, whispering, "Dari, if you're here, come to me. Come to the soil." She waited for a minute while Vilnius stared at her.

"What are you doing?"

"Trying to find Dari. If he's here, he'll come to the home soil. Sheilan told me that. The sidhe need it to refresh."

Vilnius shrugged. "Leave the cap off, then. It may take time for him to sense it."

He moved ahead of her to confront the creature's case. She followed closely but kept back a half-meter while he checked the edges of the case, paying particular attention to the locking mechanism. Dari had opened it the last time; would the chip do it this time?

"What if it doesn't work?" she asked when Vilnius found what looked like a chip-reader slot.

"The chip? Then it won't open."

"I mean, what if the command words don't work, or the one we think means obey actually tells her to kill? Or what if I pronounce them wrong?"

"Stay back about six meters and say the obey command, which I believe is the first one. If it doesn't affect the she-bee, then try another pronunciation and another. I'll be backpaddling as fast as I can once I insert the chip."

Grania swallowed hard and moved back. Suddenly this plan didn't seem like the brilliant solution she thought it would be when they discussed it. She took a deep breath and wet her lips while Vilnius fed the chip into the slot, then he turned and ran.

The unit opened, a flush of cool air turning to vapors as it opened. When the view cleared, the she-bee seemed dormant, then both eyes rotated, and the tendrils twitched.

"Hou-ye-whena," she yelled and peered at the creature. The she-bee paused, flexed her wings, then stepped forward on her bee legs, preparing for flight.

Feck! She'd said it wrong. "How-ye-whinnee."

She waited as the she-bee pulled her torso forward but didn't seem to rush.

"Third try," Vilnius called. He had his stunner in his hand but not threatening the she-bee. It was a last-ditch option if she came at him, and neither knew if it would work.

"Hoouu-yi-winea." She yelled the words, then followed them with, "Hoya-weena." She hoped one of them was right.

Although the creature had raised her wings, she froze on the spot. Grania didn't know which pronunciation did it, but one worked.

"Hey! What are you doing? Are you a loco-manic?" the guard yelled from a distance. "Put that thing back in the box." Clearly, the woman wasn't inclined to help.

Even though Vilnius kept his stunner in his hand, he walked cautiously toward Grania. "Go tell them you need to contact their commanding officer. I'll keep an eye on the she-bee

Chapter Forty-Four

While Grania waited for their invited guests to arrive, she strolled around the wasteland surrounding the docile she-bee. The creature hovered, her wings buzzing like a bee's over a succulent flower. About twenty feet away, six guards stood ready with cannon rifles in case the status changed. Not that the weapons would stop her.

Vilnius sat on what remained of a stone toilet seat, his eyes never leaving the monster in their midst. "With the armor covering the she-bee's body, the only kill shot is into her eyes."

"Let's hope it doesn't come to that. Will the stunner work on the eyes since it's a vulnerable spot?"

"Don't know. But if she suddenly goes lethal, I'll aim for them."

When the first hovercraft arrived, Grania turned back to the main focus of the meeting and stood waiting for the four gentlemen to make their way to her. The second transport, a super-speeder armored tank, kicking up dirt like a trailing cloud, arrived a few mites later. A dozen militia soldiers came to alert, weapons ready, while three men and a woman exited. None wore distinguishing uniforms, but all looked battle ready and marched toward the obvious object. The rebel faction had arrived.

Stepping to the Zynavian's right, Grania started her spiel. "Welcome to the site of the worst destruction I've ever witnessed." She waved her right arm around the area where traces of torn bodies, blood, and military clothing decorated the debris from the bombing. "In this area, two rotations ago, the Zynavian hovering behind me completely destroyed an entire platoon of government soldiers in less than ten mites. Her armor protects her from their weapons, and even the bomb dropped on the building couldn't destroy the travel case where she'd retreated."

The eight people studied the she-bee with interest while Grania continued. "At the time, she was uncontrolled. The codes for communicating with her weren't available, but my partner and I located them. So, with control, she is an extremely valuable weapon. Since I am claimer of the transportation fees and have been granted a lien, I have full authority to auction the Zynavian to the highest bidder."

The military people muttered and shifted. The woman, no rank indicated but clearly a leader, took a step forward. "The Zynavian was shipped to our cause to assist us in our battle against the suppression of the planetary government. She is rightfully ours."

The other side grumbled, and one general said, "The weapon was captured by our units and was in our possession. If we pay the transport fees, we expect the full claim to it."

Grania held up both hands before an argument broke out. "Please hear me out. I have a moral issue with selling this creature to either side. Under control, she is a powerful weapon. Without control, she's a killing machine. Brutal, swift, and she devours her kills. One of my crew and I were the only survivors of her attack, and only because we were behind a Transparisteel wall." She pointed at the twisted metal and pathetically crunched vending machines left after the bombing.

"I don't believe either side should possess a killer of this nature. Instead, I urge you to resolve your issues at the negotiating table, not by fighting each other. But whichever way you choose, this Zynavian will not be part of your war plan. She will not be auctioned. As a unique species, I have a potential buyer who will keep the creature in a controlled environment and out of the hands of either side of the conflict."

"Why did you summon us here if not to bid?" the General gruffly asked.

Her lips parted in a sly smile. "Why, to get both sides to talk to each other. Admittedly, you need your leaders to be the ones negotiating, but I think your ranking fighters should be able to discuss the issues, the great loss to each side of the battle, and the futility of continuing to fight. Take your insights back to your leaders and find a solution. Bear in mind that although this particular Zynavian won't be a part of your battle..."

Grania paused when she felt something thump against her chest. Not anything thrown, but her pendant vial shuddered. Had Dari returned? Pulling her wits back from the distraction, she continued. "This Zynavian won't be part of your battle, but there may be others. The people who experimented with this creature may have more and are trying to manipulate your grievances for their own interests. Trust me, you don't want to go up against more of these giant armored bees. They don't care who you are or what rank you are.

"Now, if you want to start by talking to each other, the base commander has a room where you can begin your discussions. Safety for both sides is guaranteed. Check your weapons at the door." She motioned them toward the security guards waiting to escort them to the base buildings.

Hesitantly, the rebel faction fell into step behind the government militia. Grania could see them chatting back and forth and could imagine the objections already on their lips. The generals weren't less vocal, and one waved a hand to emphasize a point while they tromped out.

"Good job, Nia," Vilnius said, coming to stand by her. "Did Theos confirm his transaction with the Biological Research Center?"

"Almost. He's negotiating the final price since the transportation now will include taking her to Albionea. Now, how do we get the she-bee back in the box and back to the Mo Chroidhe?"

"One of those two remaining commands should instruct her to return to her travel case."

"Uh-huh. But which one, boy-o? The other one tells her to attack, does it not?"

You're right." Vilnius pulled out his comm, called up the phrases, and studied them briefly. He tapped the screen, activating the translator, and slid one into it to see the interpretation. "Try the last one."

She narrowed her eyes at him, not sure if he was guessing. Still, she stepped back another dozen paces from the she-bee before speaking. While the creature didn't attack, she also didn't move. Grania applied a different pronunciation, leading the she-bee to spread her wings wide, lift into the air, and fly forward about two meters. Grania backpaddled while Vilnius brought the stunner up to align with the she-bee's head.

Run! The word echoed in her head. *Why isn't he getting farther away?* She kept moving backward.

Abruptly, the Zynavian flipped around, hovering in front of her unit, then neatly settled into it. The cover automatically snapped shut, once more securing the she-bee inside. Grania's knees felt weak with relief, and she wobbled back to Vilnius, who'd lowered the stunner and bent over, hands braced on his knees.

"You okay?" she asked, coming up to him.

"Yep, just the tension releasing. I didn't know if the thing was going to attack or what. How 'bout you?" He straightened and strolled to the case.

"Fine. Relieved. And hey, I'm thinking Dari's back in my vial. I felt something jiggle it during my speech." She held it up like Vilnius might see something, then pulled the cap from her pocket and twisted it on the top.

He popped the memory card from its slot in the case and handed it to her. "Keep that safe. It should ensure the case won't open without it."

"Or a sidhe who can unlock it from the inside," Grania

quipped.

He laughed and caught her arm. "All right, let's see if we can get a van, load this case up, and return to the spaceport in triumph."

She pressed a hand against the warm metal and muttered, "I never thought I'd be leaving here with this thing back on board."

* * * * *

Eight hours later, Grania stood in the ship's cargo hold, watching while Vilnius and Theos, assisted by two dock workers, secured the still-unboxed travel case to the ship's wall. When they'd left the base, the two sides of the war had still been talking, and she hoped they'd find the start of a solution.

While neither the militia nor the rebels would compensate her for her journey, she and Theos had each received the promised credits for nearly dying in their bombing, so she was well to the good. Now, they had a substantial fee due to them when they delivered the she-bee to the Biological Research Center.

The first task they'd taken before bringing the she-bee onboard was to get an expert to remove the explosives from the ship's engine. Fortunately, she'd negotiated a deal with the militia, and he'd come ahead of the transport with the she-bee. She'd listened to a vehement rant from Rory when she'd told him about that. Her middle brother was exercising his new authority, which apparently included chastising the captain when needed.

"We're going where?" Brendan asked over her shoulder. He'd just come down the stairs from the upper levels.

"Albionea Prime. It's in the Trikleon system. You'll find the coordinates in the computer's memory bank. Plot the shortest, fastest course possible. I won't be happy until we get this thing off the ship." She flashed a brief smile at her youngest brother. She hadn't had time yet to catch up with Bren and Rory since they'd hastened to get the she-bee secured and ready to depart once they were loaded and cleared. "Have you found an engineer replacement yet?"

Brendan's lips frowned, and he gave his head a shake. "Not yet. We don't have many options at this station. Out-of-work spacers don't seem to hang around the Outer Rim."

"Ah, I see that. I think Theos can help us out some. I'm reluctant to ask Vilnius to lend a hand, but I'm sure he will for the ride to wherever he wants to go." Her man, if he was still that, remained closemouthed about his plans. She cast her eyes around the two-thirds full cargo hold. "Looks like we have quite a bit to transport from here."

"Aye, we do. Rory's been booking cargo the entire time you were planetside. I think he's got a few more loads coming over in the next two hours." Brendan's voice reflected his pride in his brother's skills. "He's the best cargo master I've seen."

"You haven't seen many, Bren." Her brother hadn't been on long space jaunts prior to joining the family crew. At his downcast look, she added, "But Rory really is one of the best."

"We're done, Nia," Vilnius called. Hands filled with tools,

he and Theos stepped away from their task.

"Excellent work, men. Theos, can you cover engineering by yourself?"

"What? I don't know enough about it. I can push some buttons, but I'm not much good if anything goes wrong." His eyes had popped when she'd asked.

"I can come down and help—"

"I have a suggestion. Or maybe an offer," Vilnius said as he stepped closer. "I appear to be out of work, and I am an engineer. You know I can run these engines almost as well as Liam did."

Grania's mouth drifted open as she registered what he was saying. "You mean you would be willing to take on engineering on the way back."

He grinned. "I am willing to take on engineering, period."

Her breath left her, and she failed to inhale, coughing as she gasped. "Are you saying as crew?"

"If you'll have me?"

She heard Brendan's whoop, then her brother ran for the steps up to the next level. "I'll tell Rory."

"That settles that," Theos laughed. "I'm going up to the galley for a drink. Catch you later."

Her eyes grew misty, and she reached for him, sliding into his embrace. "Of course, I'll have you, you dolt. I am so gobsmacking lucky."

He pulled her tight, kissing her. With the thrill of contact running through her, she responded, pressing against him when he deepened the kiss. She sighed, snuggling against his neck, but it was all she dared in the presence of the cargo bay cameras. As he withdrew, reluctance in every retreating breath, Vilnius whispered, "Now, do you want to show me to my quarters?"

The End

The adventures of Captain Grania O'Ceagan and her crew will continue.

From the Author:

If you have enjoyed this book, please leave a review wherever you purchased it or send me a note at LillianWolfe.author@gmail.com. For an author, reader comments, praise, and sometimes criticism are the most rewarding aspect of writing. Your feedback is deeply appreciated and reviews help other readers to find my books.

Thank you for reading.

Lily

Glossary

Can't keep all the acronyms straight or confused by the Irish? This will help.

AAPICA is the Alliance of Anti-Political Involvement in Colonial Affairs, which is an organization dedicated to keeping political motives out of the various Earth colonized planets.

AUP is the Amalgamated Union of Planets which is a smaller grouping of representative more closely aligned with the trade and colonization of planets.

B'ean Sheilan is a similar name to the b'ean sidhe, but presumes a race of spirits in a parallel dimension.

B'ean sidhe (banshee) is the Irish term for the white spirit who comes to warn a person or their relatives that are about to die. I have taken liberty with the spirit in my books and made her an energy being.

Chrono – chronometer, a watch

Com, mobi-com, comlink all refer to the communications devices the crew uses on the ship.

Eterian – the sidhe homeland where the puca and the b'ean sidhe originated.

Hóng móguǐ - the red demon star where Chang Station is located.

Iesu Mwar – Welsh for Jesus Christ! or great Jesus.

Lev-dolly is a levitation dolly used to transport goods. It rises above the floor on a cushion of air and moves automatically making it easier for people to move large items.

Mag-lev is a levitation platform dolly used to transport larger items and crates.

Mites is the futuristic term for minutes use by spacers.

PPG is the Planetary Provisional Government, a governing body of representatives from all the planets in the AUP, much like the United Nations.

Puca (pooka) is a mischievous spirit who can change forms to a human, a horse, or a sea creature. Known for luring unsuspecting travelers to their death, my puca has been tamed a little over the centuries.

Ragurans – a sea dragon race on Erinnua that Dari helped to save from a human-caused problem. (In Strange Waters)

Sidhe (shee) is the term for the fae or Irish fairy people, taken from the people of the mounds.

Transparisteel is transparent steel. I am not sure if the term has been used before, but I couldn't find a reference for it.

About the Author

A sometimes musician, sporadic artist, occasional poet, and obsessed writer, Lillian Wolfe has spent most of her life writing something or the other. From fan fiction to short stories, novels, training manuals, newsletters, and other documentation, she has constantly been putting words on paper or a computer screen. She is, in fact, extremely grateful for the invention of the computer because using a manual typewriter is tedious. She loves all types of fiction, but her favorites are fantasy and mystery novels.

Lillian shares her home in northern Nevada with her best friend for the past thirty-odd years, two furry overlords—er—cats, and one feline-dominated toy poodle. She is a member of the High Sierra Writers.

You can contact Lillian through her web site:
http://www.lillianwolfe.online/

or at her Facebook Page:
https://www.facebook.com/LilliansLoft

Other Books by Lillian I. Wolfe

In this series, **the O'Ceagan Saga**:
O'Ceagan's Legacy
In Strange Waters
Outer Rim

Funeral Singer Series:
A Song for Marielle
A Song for Menafee
A Song of Betrayal
A Song of Forgiveness
A Song of Redemption

Time Threads Series
Time Walker
Splintered Time

Short Stories
The Wizard's Gift

Made in the USA
Columbia, SC
18 June 2023